THE LADY HEIRESS

THE LADY HEIRESS

(The Zero Enigma, Book VIII)

CHRISTOPHER G. NUTTALL

The characters and events portrayed in this book are fictitious. Any similarity to real persons, living or dead, is coincidental and not intended by the author.

Text copyright © 2020 Christopher G. Nuttall

All rights reserved.

Printed in the United States of America.

No part of this book may be reproduced, or stored in a retrieval system, or transmitted in any form or by any means, electronic, mechanical, photocopying, recording, or other-wise, without express written permission of the publisher.

ISBN 13: 9798685993045

Independently published.

The Lady Heiress
(The Zero Enigma VIII)
Christopher G. Nuttall

Book One: The Zero Blessing
Book Two: The Zero Curse
Book Three: The Zero Equation
Book Four: The Family Shame
Book Five: The Alchemist's Apprentice
Book Six: The Family Pride
Book Seven: The King's Man
Book Eight: The Lady Heiress

http://www.chrishanger.net
http://chrishanger.wordpress.com/
http://www.facebook.com/ChristopherGNuttall
https://mewe.com/page/5cd32005dc9f631c9973f058

Cover by Brad Fraunfelter
www.BFillustration.com
All Comments and Reviews Welcome!

AUTHOR'S
NOTE

Although I've written *The Lady Heiress* to be largely stand-alone, and the main character has not appeared in any previous book, it draws on characters who were introduced within earlier books, most notably *The Family Pride* and *The King's Man*.
CGN.

HISTORIAN'S
NOTE

The Thousand-Year Empire dominated the twin continents of Maxima and Minima through two advantages, an unmatched command of magic and the development of Objects of Power, magical weapons and tools that made them seemingly invincible. But the Empire fell and the secret of making Objects of Power was lost.

Hundreds of years later, a young girl—Caitlyn Aguirre—was born to a powerful magical family. Caitlyn—Cat—should have been powerful herself, like her two sisters, but she seemed to have no spark of magic at all. She lacked even a sense for magic. In desperation, her parents sent her to Jude's in the hopes that exposure to magical training would bring forth the magic they were *sure* lay buried within her. There, she met Isabella and Akin Rubén, children of her family's greatest enemy. Isabella became her rival, while she formed a tentative friendship with Akin.

Cat developed no magic, but she discovered something else. Uniquely, as far as anyone could tell, she had no magic at all. She eventually discovered that a complete lack of magic was necessary for forging Objects of Power. Far from being useless, her talent made her extremely valuable and utterly irreplaceable. As far as anyone could tell, Cat was the only true 'Zero' known to exist. This led to her—and her friends, Akin and Rose—being kidnapped, then targeted by Crown Prince Henry and Stregheria

Aguirre, Cat's Great Aunt, when they launched a coup against the Great Houses and the King himself. Their subversions—which turned Isabella against her family—nearly led to complete disaster…and perhaps would have done, if Cat and Akin hadn't become friends.

In the aftermath, Cat proposed that she and Akin should be betrothed, creating a marriage bond between their families and making it impossible, at least for the next few years, for the two houses to come to blows. This was—reluctantly—accepted, with the proviso that either Cat or Akin could refute the agreement if they wished, when they came of age. Cat left Jude's to found her own school, where other Zeroes—when they were found—would be taught.

Meanwhile, the Great Houses had to deal with the repercussions of the attempted coup and the sudden shift in the balance of power. Isabella Rubén, condemned as a traitor, was exiled to Kirkhaven Hall, where she discovered a secret her family had sought to bury…and a new secret, one of her own. Others took advantage of the chaos to stake a claim to power themselves, plots that were only foiled through sheer luck and outside intervention. The city remained unstable…

Six years passed, slowly. Akin Rubén went back to school for his final year, to discover—thanks to his father—that he had to compete in the Challenge, a contest to find the 'Wizard Regnant.' Reluctantly, Akin complied, forming a team consisting of his cousin Francis and a handful of misfits, including merchant's daughter Louise Herdsman and Saline Califon, a distant relative who was under a spell cast by her wicked uncle. Despite Francis's betrayal—the result of a shadowy figure from the family's past—Akin managed to realise the true nature of the Challenge and forge a last minute alliance with Alana Aguirre, Cat's sister, that allowed them to share the victory.

This did not please everyone, most notably Adam Mortimer. Disgusted with the Great Houses, and uneasily aware his city was on the brink of exploding into class war, Adam joined the Kingsmen and became instrumental in stopping a plot to use Infernal Devices to trigger the war. However, he was unable to prevent the plotters from damaging the city's harmony…

…And far too many innocents wound up paying the price.

PROLOGUE

I think about my father a lot. Even when I'm trying not to. I still remember the last day I saw him, six years ago. I still remember the day he sent me away.

We'd never really been *close*. He was Lord Lucas, Patriarch of House Lamplighter, and he always had something to do. He'd always been a distant figure. He'd acknowledged me as his child—it wasn't as if I was a natural-born daughter—but he was always too busy to spend time with me. It wasn't uncommon amongst the Great Houses. I was unusual in spending so much time with my mother, rather than being farmed out to a succession of governesses and private tutors. It wasn't until much later that I understood why.

He hadn't sent me to Jude's. I should have gone when I turned twelve, like all the children of the Great Houses, but he'd insisted on keeping me at Lamplighter Hall. I'd argued and pleaded and even resorted to screaming, to no avail. Mother had care of my education, with my aunts and uncles filling in the blanks. It wasn't that they were bad at teaching—I suppose it was easier with only one student to *teach*—but it wasn't the same. Mother kept saying Father would change his mind, yet...I think she knew better. I think she knew he'd never change his mind.

And then she died in the House War.

I don't remember who told me. My memories are a blur. The only clear memory I have from that time is my father saying that he was sending me to school, that he was sending me away. I was too dazed to care. My mother was dead and...it wasn't until I got to Grayling's Academy for Young Ladies that I realised he'd sent me away, that he didn't want to see me again. I was a reject, an outcast like all the other long-term boarders. I was...unwanted.

I don't know why my father did this. He never said. I used to fret endlessly over what I'd done, back before I grew old enough to realise I'd done nothing. I used to wonder if I was—somehow—responsible for mother's death, for my father's constant absences...if, perhaps, my father blamed me for something beyond my control. I wouldn't be the first girl to be sent away because her family could no longer cope, but...why me?

He wasn't a monster. There were fathers who were abusive to their daughters, who shouted at them and beat them and arranged matches to men of good families...my father wasn't like that. And there were fathers who spoilt their daughters rotten or paid no attention to them...as if they were just little people who happened to share the house. My father wasn't like that either. I didn't know why he'd sent me to Grayling's. And I wished—more and more, as I got older—that I could remember his face. My family were little more than shadows. Only a couple bothered to stay in touch with me and *none* of them told me anything useful. None of them told me *why*.

I grew up at Grayling's. I wasn't the only long-term boarder. I wasn't the only one who didn't get to go home over the summer, who grew from thirteen to nineteen without ever seeing her parents. But I was the only one whose family lived nearby, the only one who *could* have gone home...

...Until the day I got the letter that told me my father had died.

And then everything changed.

CHAPTER ONE

I'd always liked secrets.

It wasn't anything bad. Not *really*. Knowledge was power in Grayling's Academy for Young Ladies. Knowing something everyone else didn't know—or knowing something someone else wanted to remain secret—was always advantageous in the endless struggles for social status. I'd grown to adulthood learning to keep my ears open and my mouth closed, learning how to put the puzzle pieces together to work out what was actually going on. I knew more about my fellow students—and the staff—than they could possibly imagine. I knew who had a crush on who, who was sneaking out at night to see her boyfriend, who was plotting against Mistress Grayling…I knew and I kept it to myself. Secrets were currency. They lost their value the moment they became public.

Grayling's had been the making of me, for better or worse. I'd done well in my lessons, both the formal tuition and the other—far more useful—lessons I'd learnt from the other girls. I knew how to evade the locking charms on the dorms, how to hack through the spells on the outer doors and sneak into the gardens…or get over the walls to meet a boy. I knew which prefects could be trusted to turn a blind eye, as long as the relationship was harmless, and which prefects would blow the whistle for the sheer pleasure of watching some hapless romantic be roasted in front of the entire school the following morning. I'd even managed to convince some of the latter to let me go, just by telling them a tiny little secret. They thought I'd snitch on them. Of course they did. It was what *they* would have done.

I smirked as I slipped out of my bedroom and peered down the darkened corridor. It was nearly midnight, but I could see a pair of young miscreants standing at one end of the corridor, hands firmly charmed to their heads. I rolled my eyes at their backs. The sheer illogic of the system had never ceased to amuse me. If a young girl was caught out of bed, but still within the dorms, she was told to *stay* out of her bed…it had never made sense. Or maybe it did. I'd been forced to stand in the corridor, looking like an absolute fool, often enough to learn a few basic heating charms. I supposed it *did* provide a certain encouragement.

And if you get caught once you pass the doors, I reminded myself, *you'll be in real trouble.*

I inched soundlessly down the corridor and around the corner. Kate—my roommate—had stayed outside after Lights Out, planning to meet her boyfriend in the gardens. She'd been confident she could evade discovery long enough to have her fun and sneak back inside, but I wasn't so sure. The Head Girl had been on the prowl over the last few days. Marlene had always had it in for me, and Kate by extension. I'd broken her nose when we were both thirteen years old. Mistress Grayling had been more upset about the punching—young ladies did not resort to physical violence, she'd said—than anything else. She would have been less upset if I'd turned Marlene into a frog.

The charms on the door were complex, but not *too* complex. I'd often wondered if the entire tradition of sneaking out after Lights Out was designed to encourage us to learn skills that would be useful in later life. The staff *could* have kept us locked up, if they'd been willing to put some work into it. I carefully unpicked them, then slipped through the door and into the corridor beyond. My heart started to thump. I was committed. If

I was caught outside the dorms after Lights Out, I'd be called out during Assembly and humiliated in front of the entire school. Not for being out of the dorms, but for being caught.

I donned a pair of charmed spectacles as soon as I was around the corner. I'd often suspected the prefects had ways to track active magic within the school, but they'd find it harder to detect and locate an active Device of Power. The building seemed to come to life, flickers of magic darting through the walls as I hurried to the stairs and headed down. There was something truly *eerie* about the school, after dark. It was easy to believe, suddenly, that the school's ghosts came out and danced in the darkness. I'd heard all the stories. They seemed very real.

The air was silent, too silent. I kept to the side, careful not to put any weight on loose floorboards or squeaky stairs. The prefects might be lurking in the shadows, waiting for me. I hadn't been foolish enough to tell anyone I was sneaking out, let alone where I was going, but it was quite possible someone else *had*. Stealing food from the kitchens for a midnight feast was an old tradition, too. And if someone in the lower dorms had been planning it, they might just have been overheard by one of the prefects. They knew all the tricks. They'd been students too, once upon a time.

Although it's hard to believe, sometimes, I told myself. *I wouldn't have thought Marlene had ever been young if I hadn't grown up with her.*

I smiled at the thought, then put it to one side as I reached the bottom of the stairs. The lobby was empty, although I tensed as I spotted the line of portraits on the wall. Rumour had it the paintings had eyes, charmed to allow Mistress Grayling to see through them. I wasn't sure I believed it, but I did my best to stay out of eyesight anyway. Just in case. The paintings were supposed to show headmistresses from the last three hundred years, but I hadn't been able to help noticing they all looked alike. Rumour *also* claimed Mistress Grayling was a vampire. It was hard to believe she had ever been young.

The thrill of being somewhere I shouldn't was stronger with every passing second. Students weren't allowed in the lobby, unless they'd been ordered to the headmistress's office. It was a silly rule, one of many, but so strictly enforced that I was half-convinced Mistress Grayling really *was* a vampire. Or that she was keeping something from us. Or…I resisted the urge to snort as I crawled under the final painting, then straightened as I stared at the office door. It was far more likely, really, that Mistress Grayling was merely exercising her authority. I'd grown up in a Great House. I knew it was important to use one's authority or risk losing it.

I pressed my fingers against the doorknob, parsing out the charms. They were complex—I'd had a look at them the *last* time I'd been summoned to the office—but not unbreakable. I braced myself, then started to work. The charms hadn't been made *that* tight. Mistress Grayling couldn't keep us out completely without barring the staff as well. Personally, I would have considered that a fair trade. There were some good teachers, but also some I'd pay money never to have to see again.

The door clicked. I froze. The noise sounded very loud in the silent school. If I was caught now, I'd be a laughingstock. Marlene—and everyone else, even Kate—would bray like a donkey if I was caught. The door slid open, allowing me to peer inside. The chamber was as dark and cold as the grave. Mistress Grayling had the largest office in the school—there were *classrooms* that were smaller—but there was no hint of any *personality*. It was as colourless as the woman herself. No paintings, no trophies…nothing. I was almost disappointed as I inched into the chamber, pushing the door closed behind me. There was no other way out. If someone came, I'd have to hide in the shadows and hope for the best. I smiled, allowing my tension to drain away as I walked towards the filing cabinets. I'd often wanted to take a look inside, but I'd never dared. Not until now. The exams were over. Like it or not, I'd be leaving the school forever in a few weeks. It wasn't as if anyone would care if I got expelled.

The cabinet charms were weaker than I'd expected. I frowned, wondering if I'd been tricked. The files—the *real* files—could be elsewhere.

Mistress Grayling's rooms were on the other side of the school. It was quite possible she kept the files there. I felt my heart sink as I unpicked the charms, one by one. Surely, she wouldn't be quite so careless about her files. The *real* charms had to be elsewhere.

Magic crackled around me as I picked apart the last charm and pulled the cabinet open. Rows of files greeted me, each one labelled with a number and nothing else. I muttered a word that would have me going to bed on bread and water if a prefect—or the tutors – had heard. It would be difficult, if not impossible, to figure out whose file was whose. There had to be trick to it…I scanned the numbers, trying to think. I didn't have a student number, did I? It wasn't as if they didn't call me by name. Or…I smiled, suddenly, as my birth date jumped out at me. It had to be my file. I'd have known if someone shared my birthday.

I pulled the file free, unpicked the locking charm and opened the box. My permanent record book sat on top. I put it to one side and inspected the rest of the papers. A letter from my father, pleading for Mistress Grayling to take me as a pupil…it was dated shortly after the House War, barely a day after my mother died. My heart clenched in pain. My father had started planning to send me away at once? And to Grayling's? Tears prickled in my eyes. I blinked them away, harshly. Father had had a good reason. I was sure he'd had a good reason. But the letter merely referred to unspecified reasons…

My eyes narrowed as I skimmed the remainder of the letters and accounts. Mistress Grayling had written to my father twice, demanding payment…payment for what? My head spun as I tried to understand what I was seeing. Payment…for me? If my school fees were unpaid…I'd have been kicked out. I was sure of it. Mistress Grayling wasn't running a charity. She'd told us often enough. But father could have paid easily… right? I skimmed through the rest of the papers, trying to read between the lines. It wasn't easy. My father—and Mistress Grayling—seemed to be committing as little as possible to paper. The only exception was a note from my uncle, asking permission to take me out for a day...I nearly destroyed the letter as I realised it was dated five *months* ago. Mistress Grayling hadn't bothered to ask me if I *wanted* to go. And I would have. It had been too long since I'd so much as left the school.

And Uncle Jalil probably thinks I'm a rude little snob, I thought, angrily. He wouldn't have minded if I'd said no—my exams *had* been coming up—but saying *nothing* was dreadfully rude. *Mistress Grayling's managed to land me in trouble.*

I scowled as I carefully closed up the box, then returned it to the shelf. I'd have to find a way to apologise without admitting what I'd done. And to confront Mistress Grayling. She had every right to bar me from going, if she'd thought I needed to study, but she really *should* have told me. I wasn't sure how. The headmistress would be furious if she knew I'd pried into her private correspondence. The rest of the staff wouldn't be amused either.

My eyes narrowed as I spotted the account books at the bottom of the cabinet. They were covered in charms, charms I'd learnt in class. I picked apart the ones intended to keep unauthorised readers from opening the books, then frowned down at the figures. Mistress Grayling's handwriting was awful. The charms would make it hard to deliberately miscalculate one's sums, but they were still hard to read. It looked as though the school was losing money. I wasn't too surprised. Mistress Grayling had never struck me as a particularly good headmistress.

I tensed as I heard a sound from outside the windows. The grounds outside were dark, but...I remembered, suddenly, how many girls might be sneaking out to see their boyfriends or catch up with their girlfriends. I returned the book to the shelf, hastily repaired the damaged charms and headed for the door. If someone peered in, they might see me. I doubted they'd snitch—it would be instant social death, if we found out who'd done it—but they might take advantage of *knowing*. Who knew *what* they'd demand from me if they knew what I'd done?

My heart started to pound, again, as I heard more sounds outside.

Someone was talking...I winced in sympathy. No one would be talking so loudly if they hadn't already been caught, probably by one of the less amiable prefects. They might manage to talk one of the others into letting them go, if they didn't make it impossible by accidentally waking the whole school. I smiled, even though I knew it wasn't funny. If they got everyone out of bed, they'd have no trouble spotting my absence. And then I'd be in trouble.

I inched into the lobby, closing the door behind me as quietly as I could. The outer door was already opening. I started to move towards the stairs, then caught myself and slipped into the shadows, wrapping the strongest obscurification charm I could around myself. The charms were subtle, so low-power they were very hard to detect...as long as I didn't draw someone's attention. I knew stronger spells, but the mere act of trying to use them might reveal my presence. And if I was caught...

The outer door opened. I knew who it was, who it had to be, before she came into sight. The common or garden students were *never* permitted to use the front door. Even prefects were discouraged from using the door, particularly after Lights Out. It had to be Marlene...my heart sank as the Head Girl came into view, followed by my roommate. Kate had her hands on her head, a clear sign she'd been caught. I felt a stab of sympathy, mingled with fear. If Marlene marched Kate straight back to our room, there was a good chance she'd realise I was missing too. I wasn't scared of being caught, not really, but...I breathed a sigh of relief as Marlene pushed Kate towards the lower door. It looked as if she was going to wake the duty tutor. I thought a string of uncomplimentary things as they vanished into the darkness. Poor Kate would be in real trouble. The duty tutor would not be in a good mood under the circumstances.

And Marlene might be in some trouble too, I told myself. I clung to the thought as I started to inch back up the stairs. *The duty tutor really won't be happy if she's woken.*

I smirked, even though I knew it was unlikely. Marlene was the Head

Girl. She had the authority to wake the tutor if she felt it necessary. And her family was quite well connected. Marlene might get told off, but little more. She certainly wouldn't be stripped of her post. I put the thought out of my head as I hurried back to the dorms, slipping through the doors and into my room. The corridors were completely empty. I was in my bed, pretending to be asleep, when Kate was thrust back into the room. Marlene snapped something at her—I couldn't make it out—and closed the door. I peered out as soon as she was safely gone.

"You okay?"

Kate shook her head. "I'll be seeing the headmistress tomorrow," she said. "And Marlene has me on the detention roster for the rest of the year."

She snickered. "I'm not going to *be* here for the rest of the year."

"How unfortunate for Marlene," I said. "Did you have a good time?"

"Yeah." Kate shrugged. "Better than the bloke my parents wanted me to marry, I can tell you."

I nodded. Kate's parents had tried to arrange a match for her. I'd helped her break it off before it was too late. She'd been lucky. An aristocratic maiden, even one with strong magic, might have found it a great deal harder to stand against parental pressure to marry.

"Better get some sleep," I said. "The morning is not going to be fun."

"No." Kate made a face. "Do you think I'll get expelled?"

"It would be a little pointless now," I reminded her. "You've sat your exams."

I pulled the cover over my head and closed my eyes, muttering a sleep spell. I'd pay for it in the morning with a banging headache, but there was no choice. There were only five hours until I was meant to get out of bed, or there'd be no breakfast. And Marlene would be watching. If she spotted I was tired, she might deduce I'd been out of bed after Lights Out...

...And, five hours later, she tried to break down the door.

CHAPTER

TWO

I jerked awake. "What...?"
The door opened. Marlene burst into the room. I stared at her. She looked...dishevelled, her blonde hair dangling in ringlets rather than being neatly braided. She looked so unlike herself that, for a moment, I wondered if someone was playing games with doppelganger potion. It wouldn't be the first time. A girl had been suspended a year or so ago for impersonating another girl in a bid to steal her boyfriend.

"She wants to see you," Marlene gabbled. "Mistress Grayling. She wants to see you."

I glared at her, mainly to conceal the sudden spike of fear. What did Mistress Grayling know? If she knew I'd been in her office, I was probably in some trouble. No, there was no *probably* about it. Teachers were meant to turn a blind eye to certain things—such as pantry raids—but I had a feeling the list didn't include covert searches of an office.

"You should have knocked," I managed. When in doubt, go on the attack. "I could have been dressing!"

"She wants to see you," Marlene repeated. She sounded as though she'd had a nasty shock. I wondered if she'd been yanked out of bed, just so she could yank *me* out of bed. It was the sort of thing that made sense to tutors, if no one else. "You have to go see her now..."

"Let me get dressed first." I pushed the covers aside and scrambled out of bed. "Do you have orders to escort me? Or are you just admiring my beauty?"

Marlene glowered. "Get down to her office," she snapped. "And hurry."

She turned and stormed out of the room, banging the door closed. I made a hex sign at the door—it would make her life interesting, if she tried to barge in again—and hurried over to the dresser. There was probably no time to shower...I snorted as I donned my uniform, muttering a pair of cleaning spells as I sat in front of the mirror. My skin felt unpleasantly dry as the magic crackled over me, but at least I was *clean*. Behind me, I heard Kate sit up in bed. I doubted she was looking forward to seeing the headmistress either.

"What did she want?" Kate sounded as if she hadn't slept a wink. I didn't blame her. "Or did I just have a nightmare?"

"I have no idea," I said, reaching for the hairbrush. "She probably didn't get much sleep either."

I studied myself in the mirror as I carefully brushed my hair, using the repetitive motion to calm myself. My face looked back at me: light brown skin, dark brown eyes, black hair...the village boys said I was striking, although my features were hardly *that* uncommon in Shallot. I looked more like my mother than my father...I felt a sudden pang as I realised, again, that I didn't really *remember* either of them. I had a pair of pictures in my personal album, but they didn't quite feel *real*. I met my own eyes, schooling my features into calm immobility. Mistress Grayling was probably fishing for information. It wouldn't be the first time she'd done this to me—or another student—when she wasn't sure who'd *really* been the guilty party.

Kate walked up behind me. "Do you want me to come with you?"

"Better not," I said, as I braided my hair. "It might give her ideas."

"I think she already has enough ideas of her own." Kate snorted. "I'll see you at breakfast."

I felt my heart sink—again—as I stood and headed for the door. Breakfast. The mere thought of eating, even something bland, was enough to make my stomach churn. If Mistress Grayling knew I'd been in her office...I told myself, firmly, that the old biddy didn't have any proof of anything. And yet, she'd sent Marlene to wake me...I shook my head. Mistress Grayling would have dragged me out of bed herself if she'd known I'd been in her office.

There was no sign of Marlene as I stepped through the door. I glanced up and down the corridor, then headed to the stairs. It was the quickest way to Mistress Grayling's office, even if we weren't supposed to use them. I composed an argument for any wandering prefects as I hurried down the stairs—Marlene had made it sound urgent, after all—then dismissed the thought. The corridors were quiet. My fellow inmates—students—were probably still trying to sleep. They could catch a few more minutes before the breakfast bell rang.

And the exams are over, I reminded myself as I walked down the stairs and knocked on the headmistress's door. *There's no point in getting up to study now.*

The door opened, revealing Mistress Grayling seated behind her desk. I felt another shiver of nervousness as I entered the room. Mistress Grayling was old—no one knew for sure how old she truly was—but there was no hint of weakness or vulnerability about her. She was tall and stern and very capable of cowing any wayward girl. Her gimlet eyes fixed on me and I cringed, inwardly. And yet...there was something in her eyes I was not used to seeing. Sympathy?

"Take a seat," Mistress Grayling said. She waved a hand towards a handful of chairs, pressed against the far wall. "Please."

I swallowed hard, feeling a growing sense of unreality. Mistress Grayling had never invited me to *sit* in her presence. Young Ladies—you could just *hear* the capital letters thudding into place—were supposed to stand in her presence, hands firmly clasped behind their backs. It was supposed to teach humility. Instead, it taught us how petty and pointless authority figures could be. I reached for the closest chair and carried it back to the desk, almost wishing she *had* made me stand. It would have made it easier to focus.

Mistress Grayling's lips thinned. "I received a letter from Shallot this morning, brought by special courier," she said. "I'm afraid it's bad news."

I blinked, torn between relief and a sudden—crushing—sense of fear. I wasn't in trouble...but while I wasn't in trouble, I was very sure I didn't want to hear her next words. My head spun as I leaned forward, almost wishing I *was* in trouble. It would have made more sense...

"The letter was a formal notification," Mistress Grayling continued. "Lord Lucas, Patriarch of House Lamplighter, has died."

For a moment, my mind refused to comprehend what she'd said. Lord Lucas, Patriarch of House Lamplighter...my father? It was hard to understand that my father might have been my father to me—obviously—but Lord Lucas, Patriarch of House Lamplighter, to everyone else. My breath caught in my throat. My father was dead? My father...I stared at her, the room starting to spin. I would have collapsed, if I'd remained standing. Mistress Grayling had done me a favour.

"I..." I swallowed, hard. "My father?"

"Yes." Mistress Grayling looked...surprisingly sympathetic, for someone who'd once told a twelve-year-old girl to stop blubbering after her pet rat had died. "I'm very much afraid so."

I stared at her, feeling...I wasn't sure how I felt. My father had always been a distant figure. It was hard, somehow, to put a face to him...to realise he was more than just a name. I tried to remember him, but...I couldn't. And...I felt a sudden surge of anger, directed at Mistress Grayling. The headmistress could have softened the blow. She could have...I felt tears prickling at the corner of my eyes. I'd known I'd be going back to Shallot, after graduation. I'd told myself I'd have a chance to meet my father again, to...to take up my place within the family. And...

"There are a number of issues that have to be discussed," Mistress Grayling said. She picked a letter off her desk and eyed it dourly. "Do you wish to go through them now or wait until after Assembly?"

"Now," I said, blinking away tears. I wanted—I needed—something to distract me from the sudden sense of *emptiness* in my chest. My father was gone...it didn't feel real. "Who wrote to you?"

Mistress Grayling ignored the question. "First, you have been named the *de facto* Matriarch of House Lamplighter," she said. There was a hint of displeasure in her voice. "Your father's first will states that you are to be raised to adulthood upon his death, if you have not already been acknowledged so."

I felt as if I'd been hit with a confusion hex. I was an adult? None of the other girls, not even Marlene, were considered adults. They wore their hair in braids...I felt a hot flash of glee at the certain knowledge Mistress Grayling could no longer treat me like a child, mixed with grief and rage that I'd only been raised to adulthood upon my father's death. I'd looked forward to my Season, to being introduced to High Society as an eligible adult...

My fingers moved of their own accord, slowly pulling out the braid until my long hair fell over my shoulders. I'd wear it down from now on, at least until I got married. My thoughts ran in circles. It should have been the proudest day of my life, the day my parents realised I was an adult in my own right, but...the price was too high. My parents were dead. I wondered, suddenly, what had happened to the rest of the family. House Lamplighter was small, but I was hardly *alone*. There were other claimants to the headship. I was a little surprised my father had named me to succeed him before I had a chance to build a power base of my own.

And I haven't been back to the city for six years, I thought, numbly. I'd followed the news as best as I could—Mistress Grayling banned most broadsheets, ensuring there was a lively trade in forbidden newspapers—but it had never felt like something that affected me personally. I lived in a bubble. No, I *had* lived in a bubble. *I have to get back there as soon as possible.*

I straightened and looked at Mistress Grayling, keeping my eyes firmly fixed on her nose. "I have to get back to the city," I said. "Please can you arrange a coach?"

"There are other matters that need to be discussed." Mistress Grayling opened a drawer and produced a file. A very familiar file. "Are you aware your fees are largely unpaid?"

"No," I said, keeping my face under tight control. We'd been taught to be honest, but there were limits. "My fees were never discussed with me."

"You were a child." Mistress Grayling held out the file. "Such matters are rarely discussed with children."

I studied the file, pretending to read it. The school fees were nine hundred crowns a year, a sizable sum even for the aristocracy. Marlene regularly bragged about her family's wealth, but no one could help noticing she was the only member of her family to attend Grayling's instead of Jude's. I liked to think her parents found her as obnoxious as we did, yet...I put the thought out of my mind. It wasn't important. Right now, I had too many other problems.

"You have been here for six years," Mistress Grayling informed me, as if I hadn't already known. "Your father only paid for two of those years."

"I'm sorry to hear that," I mumbled. I read the file again, carefully noting everything I'd missed last night. "Why didn't you expel me?"

Mistress Grayling glowered. "Your father talked a good game," she said. "And I felt sorry for you."

I tried not to snort. Mistress Grayling was not known for being sympathetic to anyone, particularly her students. Their comfort was hardly her top priority. She certainly had no qualms about meting out horrific and humiliating punishment to girls who pushed her a little too far. And she could easily have simply refused to take me if my family didn't pay the fees. I was sure there was something she wasn't telling me.

"Really?" I tried to meet her eyes without *quite* meeting her eyes.

"What did he offer you?"

"Nothing of great importance." Mistress Grayling's expression grew worse. "I'm afraid I'm going to have to ask you to pay."

I snickered. I couldn't help myself. "You're going to drain my tuck shop allowance?"

Mistress Grayling half-rose, then stopped herself. I was an adult now. She couldn't give me a slap—or worse—for cheek. Not now. I felt a sudden thrill, even though I'd been told that adulthood brought its own risks and responsibilities. If she laid a finger on me now, I could drag her through the courts or challenge her to a duel or...

"This is no laughing matter," Mistress Grayling said. Two bright spots coloured her cheeks. "The fees are important and..."

I kept my voice as even as possible. "As Matriarch of House Lamplighter, I will—naturally—honour all debts incurred by the family," I said. "However, I will have to study the records first to determine what, if anything, the family owes you. And, in order to do that, I will have to return to Shallot as quickly as possible."

Mistress Grayling looked irked. "You intend to leave ahead of time?"

"Yes." I stood, holding out the file. "Please have this copied for me, along with a complete statement of what you believe you're owed. I'll collect it before I leave."

"The debt..."

"The debt needs to be confirmed before I can pay," I said, feeling a flicker of guilty glee as I cut her off. I didn't have to listen to the old bat any longer. Adulthood was *fun*. "I'll be in my bedroom. When the coach is ready, send the Head Girl to inform me."

Mistress Grayling looked as if she'd bitten into a lemon. I would have been more alarmed if that hadn't been how she looked most of the time. "As you wish."

"Thank you." I swallowed the urge to tell her *precisely* what I thought of her school—and her teaching style. "I'll need the letters too."

"Yes." Mistress Grayling held them out. "Your formal exam results will be forwarded to you, along with your final records and references from any of your tutors. Should you wish to retake any of the exams, you can apply to the authorities in Shallot."

I nodded, tersely. I had no intention of retaking *any* of the exams. There was no need. I couldn't balance my duties to the family with a career...I frowned, realising—not for the first time—just how little I knew of current affairs. Who would challenge me for the headship? Who would promise to support me overtly and do their level best to undermine me covertly? Family politics were confusing, almost impossible to follow unless you were immersed in them from birth. Sorting out the pecking order, all the little alliances and principalities that made up the whole, was incredibly difficult. It was just like boarding school.

Except worse things can happen than waking up a toad, I thought. A shiver ran down my spine. My father might have named me his heir, but there were limits to how far his writ ran now he was dead. *I might be voted out of the family.*

My heart clenched. I might need those exam results after all.

Mistress Grayling looked down at the file. "I'll have these copied for you," she said. It was a dismissal and I knew it. "And you'll be informed when the coach is ready."

I nodded. "Are there any letters of mine you held back? Letters from my family?"

"It is not school policy to withhold letters, outside exam season," Mistress Grayling said. It was a lie. I'd found the proof yesterday. "If we believe someone...unsuitable...is writing to one of our students, we raise the issue with that student's parents."

You let Christie get letters from her creep of a fiancé, I thought, coldly. *And her family wouldn't object because they're the ones who arranged the match.*

"I'm glad to hear it," I said, artfully. "I'd hate to hear there were letters that went missing in transit."

"Quite." Mistress Grayling's face was a mask, but she changed the subject quickly enough to convince me I'd hit a nerve. "You may take your breakfast in the teacher's lounge, if you like. Or I can have Cook bring you something..."

"I don't feel like eating," I said. I knew I should eat something, but...I couldn't face the thought of food. My stomach was churning. I felt as though I was on the verge of retching. "I...thank you."

I hesitated, then headed for the door. I could feel her eyes burning into my back as I opened the door and hurried out, but she didn't call me back. I was being rude—I should have dropped a curtsy, probably—yet...she'd lied to me. I knew she *had* withheld letters. And I'd make sure to use that information for leverage when she demanded I pay my fees. There were hundreds of students—and former students—who'd be unamused to hear their letters had been held back...

And then it hit me, like a curse between the eyes.

My father was dead.

CHAPTER
THREE

I don't know how I got back to my room.

We'd been taught not to cry in public. Girls who blubbered were mocked relentlessly. It was supposed to toughen us up. And yet...tears welled in my eyes as I stumbled along the corridor and practically crashed into my room. Kate was gone...either to breakfast or to face the music for being caught out of bed last night. I didn't care, not really. Right now, I just wanted to be alone. I sat on the bed, trying not to cry. It was hard, so hard, to remain focused.

I peered down at the letters, trying to deny what I was seeing. My father couldn't be dead, but...he was. A formal death notification, countersigned by two healers...there was no hope, someone had added in pencil, that he'd attempted to fake his death and vanish into the shadows. My eyes narrowed as I read the handwritten note time and time again. Why had they thought, even for a moment, that my father had faked his death?

And they confirmed it was his body, I thought, numbly. *Why did they go so far?*

I tried to reason it out, but drew a blank. It made no sense. My father's death was untimely, but there was no hint of foul play. I read the letters again, noting that his first will had been very short. He'd left everything to me. His *second* will would be read later, if I recalled correctly. *That one would touch on his authority within the family and his successor's* relationship to his clients. I swallowed hard, realising—once again—just how little I really knew. Who were my father's clients? What did he do for them? Would they stay with me?

My eyes started to blur again. I put the letters aside and buried my head in my hands. I was an adult now, not a schoolgirl. I couldn't hide behind the innocence of youth. I had all the rights and responsibilities and freedoms of adulthood, including the freedom to take the consequences. I looked around the bedroom, seeing it with fresh eyes. It had been a nest, a haven from the rest of the school. But I would never sleep in the uncomfortable bed again.

Which is probably for the best, I told myself. *I could lodge a formal complaint about the accommodations now.*

I snickered, then stood and opened my drawers. My clothes—a child's clothes—lay in front of me. We were discouraged from wearing anything too fancy, even outside school hours, but I had a small collection of dresses I'd worn over the summer holidays. My heart clenched. I was hardly the first nor only boarder to stay at the school over the summer, but...I could have gone home. Why hadn't my father let me go home? I wished, suddenly, that I'd sneaked out and walked to the city. It would have been risky, but at least I would have seen my family again. Now...I wasn't even sure who was *in* and who was *out*. I picked up my blazer and stared down at it. I wouldn't be wearing it again. I'd probably wind up donating it to a younger student.

The door rattled, then burst open. Marlene shoved Kate into the room, then stopped and stared at me. I stared back, my mind going blank. What had caught *her* attention? Kate was staring too...it struck me, suddenly, that I looked awful. Tears in my eyes, my hair hanging down...they didn't know what to make of me. I bit my lip. Marlene was no longer a problem. I had bigger fish to fry.

I glared at her. "Get out."

Marlene blinked in surprise, then turned and left. I was surprised she didn't slam the door again. Technically, she should have curtseyed and addressed me by my title or honorific, but...I shook my head. Making her scrape and bow to me would be very satisfactory, I supposed, yet pointless. I was leaving the school. She wouldn't see me again for the rest of term.

Kate glanced at me, one hand playing with her braid. "Lucy...?"

"My father's dead," I said. "My father's dead and...and I'm going home."

"I'm sorry," Kate said. I knew she meant it. "I...when are you going home?"

"Today." I reached for my trunk and snapped it open, then started sorting through my clothes. The uniforms were largely worthless, outside the school. I'd leave them behind for the scholarship girls. The rest would have to be sorted again when I got home. "I'm not staying for graduation."

"Probably a good idea," Kate said. She winced as she sat on the bed. "Marlene was a right"—she chuckled, suddenly—"I can't think of any word rude enough for her."

"Yeah." I grinned, although I felt little real humour. "How badly did she frighten your boyfriend?"

"I think the mere sight of her was enough to make him flee." Kate shook her head. "Can I ride back with you?"

I blinked. "You don't want to stay for graduation?"

"My family can't afford it." Kate looked downcast, just for a second. "I was hoping to cadge a ride with the supply truck, next weekend."

I felt a stab of sympathy. Traditionally, senior students were allowed a little more freedom after they finished their exams. I'd been planning to go wild myself...I groaned, inwardly, as I remembered I was now an adult. I couldn't paper the towers with toilet paper or craft a trap for the prefects, not now. And...I reminded myself, sharply, that Kate's parents weren't aristocrats. They'd had to scrimp and save to get their daughter a place at the school. I hoped it was worth it for them. Personally, I wasn't so sure.

"If you want to come, you're welcome." I picked out a dress and dropped it on the bed, then finished loading the trunk. "I'll be glad of your company."

Kate beamed. "Thanks!"

I smiled back at her, then hastily changed into the dress and bagged up my old school uniforms. They'd be washed, before being dispatched to the thrift shop. I made a careful note to ensure they were handed out for free, rather than being sold to wealthy students and their parents. It was unlikely a *really* wealthy student would wear my cast-offs—aristocrats preferred to have their uniforms carefully tailored and charmed—but I wouldn't put it past the tutors to try to make a quick buck. They charged for everything, jacking the price up as much as possible. I remembered my father's debts and shivered. Why hadn't Mistress Grayling cast me out years ago?

Maybe she did feel sorry for me, I thought. It seemed unlikely, as the headmistress rarely took charity cases. I doubted *my* fees had been paid by one of the scholarship funds. I was a good student, but not *that* good. *Or was she hoping she could claim something more than money from me?*

I puzzled it over as I pocketed the letters and splashed water on my face. It just made no sense. Had she wanted my father in her debt? Or had she been told all fees would be paid when I graduated…I doubted it. I'd studied business in school. It was a lot easier to insist on payment in advance, rather than chasing up debtors after the fact. Maybe she'd thought she could collect the money through the courts. It was possible, but…were they the family's debts or my father's debts? If the latter…I wasn't sure who'd be liable, now he was gone. My lips twitched. I'd been a child, until my father had died. There was no way I could be held liable, no matter what I'd signed. Now…

Kate changed into a simple dress and preened in front of the mirror as she started to braid her hair. "It would be a lot easier if we were allowed to wear trousers."

"You can start a trend," I said, dryly. I agreed with her—trousers were far more practical than dresses—but any girl who wore them could expect a *lot* of sharp and sarcastic remarks from the older generation. I didn't know anyone my age who could start a trend of girls wearing trousers. It would practically *have* to be an aristo, someone who could stand against her own family. "Maybe you could convince everyone to follow you."

"I doubt it." Kate grinned at me. "My father's too busy trying to make money."

"Good for him," I said. "I..."

My heart sank, again. My father was dead. I missed him, suddenly, with an intensity that surprised me. I'd always assumed there'd be time to get to know him, when I finally graduated and returned to the city. And now he was dead. How many others were dead too? How many of my aunts and uncles, the ones who'd tutored me in magic, were still alive? Uncle Jalil had written to me, but what about the others? Why hadn't *they* written to me?

"I'm sorry." Kate rested a hand on my shoulder. "I wish I could make it better."

"Me too." I put my hand on hers, just for a second. "But there's nothing we can do."

Kate hugged me. "The ancients will accept him as one of their own."

I nodded, stiffly. They said no one was ever truly gone until they were forgotten. I'd been taught to recite a family tree that claimed to stretch back all the way to the Thousand Year Empire, although—reading between the lines—our records grew a little imprecise five hundred or so years ago. It wasn't uncommon for the Great Houses to burnish their records and claim ancestors who'd never really existed, although none of them would ever admit to it. I doubted they knew the truth. No one really knew what had happened so long ago.

And not reciting the names of the ancients would have consequences, I thought. I wasn't sure I believed in the ancients, but the thought was comforting. My father and mother were waiting for me on the far side of the grave. *They'll be gone once they're forgotten.*

I felt another chill as I stared down at my hands. It shouldn't take long to organise a coach, surely. The school had a stable full of horses and a team of coachmen to convey us from place to place. Rumour had it the coachman's apprentice was very good at kissing...I snorted, reminding myself how rumours grew and grew until they became completely unrecognisable. It was impossible to say for sure.

There was a knock on the door. "Marlene, I bet," Kate muttered. "Should we pretend we're asleep?"

"She'd just come crashing in," I muttered back, although I wasn't sure that was true. Marlene might be Head Girl, but even *she* had to follow the courtesies. If an adult happened to file a complaint...I dismissed the thought as I raised my voice. "Come!"

Marlene stepped into the room. "The coach will be ready to go in an hour," she said, as she held out a thick envelope. "And Mistress Grayling wanted me to give you these."

"Thanks," I said, shortly. An hour? What was the coachman *doing*? I wasn't sure I wanted to know. "Kate and I will be downstairs in an hour."

"Very good." Marlene hesitated, as if she had something she wanted to say. "I...can I accompany you to Shallot?"

I blinked. "You want to leave the school?"

"I want..." Marlene changed tack, sharply. "I want to go home."

"Really?" I made a show of raising my eyebrows. "You don't want to stay for graduation?"

"I may come back for the ceremony," Marlene said. "But I don't want to stay here any longer."

I frowned. Marlene was Head Girl. Mistress Grayling would hardly object to *Kate* accompanying me—if Kate couldn't pay, she'd be kicked out faster than a thief—but Marlene? She had her duties, didn't she? And she was meant to deliver the address during the graduation ceremony. Mistress Grayling would kick up a fuss if Marlene insisted on leaving the school. If nothing else, she'd have to hastily appoint a new Head Girl.

"As a responsible adult"—I allowed that word to linger on my tongue—"I have to ask if you've checked with the headmistress."

Marlene coloured. "I'm sure Mistress Grayling will raise no objection."

"I'm not." I was tempted to make her crawl a little. I'd never really forgiven her for lording it over me for the last six years. She'd been a heartless so-and-so when I'd first met her and authority had only made her worse. I had the feeling she was in for a nasty shock when she went home. Her family might be powerful, but *she* wasn't *that* important to them. "But if Mistress Grayling feels otherwise, you can accompany us."

"Thank you." Marlene bobbed a curtsy as she headed for the door. "You won't regret this."

"I already do," I muttered, once the door closed behind her. "And I bet you'll make me regret it even more."

Kate shot me an odd look. "Why didn't you just say no?"

I frowned. I wasn't sure of my own motives. I wasn't even sure I was in a *position* to say no. I didn't own the coach, nor did I pay the coachman's wages...if Marlene managed to convince Mistress Grayling to let her go, there was nothing I could do about it. And yet...I shrugged. It was quite possible Mistress Grayling would simply say no. Marlene was Head Girl. She couldn't simply leave the school without a good excuse.

"You'd better tell Mistress Grayling you want to go too," I said, instead. I cast a pair of lightening charms, then picked up the trunk and steered it towards the door. "I'll see you in the hall."

"Sure." Kate waved a hand at the dresser. "What do you want to do with your cosmetics?"

I shrugged. Cosmetics were technically banned, although there weren't many girls who *didn't* bring at least *some* cosmetics to school. The girls who couldn't get them for themselves traded with the girls who could. I'd never really understood the lust for cosmetics when one could simply cast glamours, but I supposed the lure of the forbidden drew students like flies to honey. The handful I owned were reserved for trading with the other girls.

"Leave them," I said, after a moment. "Or take them, if you want them."

"Whoever inherits this room will have a nice surprise," Kate said. "Right?"

I shrugged. We were meant to clean our own rooms—and there were weekly inspections, with the prefects searching for dust—but I was fairly sure Mistress Grayling or one of the housemothers would insist on having the rooms cleaned professionally before someone new moved into the chambers. There were enough horror stories about newcomers finding everything from leftover hexes to downright malicious curses to ensure the tutors would make sure the rooms were safe first.

"I'll see you downstairs," I said. It wasn't that important. Once I was out the door, I'd never be coming back. And I'd be quite happy if I never saw Mistress Grayling again. "Good luck."

I floated the trunk down the stairs—it wasn't as if anyone was going to stop me—and left it in the lobby while I checked out the teacher's lounge. It was certain death—or at least a million detentions—for a student to enter the chamber, with or without permission, but no one stopped me when I peeked inside. I was almost disappointed. The thrill of sneaking into a place I wasn't supposed to go, and the certainty I'd pay a steep price if I were caught, was gone. Instead…I looked around the chamber, rolling my eyes at the stories whispered in the dorms. The teachers looked surprisingly normal. They were drinking coffee like *real* people, not climbing out of coffins or polishing their whips or any of the hundred other disreputable things they were supposed to do in their private chambers. The walls were not lined with gold. I poured myself a mug of coffee, then forced myself to eat a pair of sweet buns for breakfast. They tasted better than the ones served to us, but otherwise…

Marlene was waiting for me when I went back to the lobby. "Mistress Grayling said I could accompany you."

I scowled, kicking myself for not saying *no*. Perhaps I would have been overruled, perhaps not. "Behave yourself," I said, darkly. "I don't want to hear a peep of complaint from you."

"Of course, My Lady," Marlene said. Her voice dripped honey and acid. "It will be my deepest honour, My Lady."

"And you can remove your tongue from my boot," I added. "Please."

Marlene looked as if she wanted to say something cutting, but Kate arrived before she could get the word out. I breathed a sigh of relief as the outer door opened, revealing the coachman's apprentice. I guessed he was taking us to the city. I rather assumed his master had decided the job was beneath him.

Or maybe it's a reward, I thought. *They'd be time for him to go shopping once he drops us off.*

"Goodbye school," Kate said, as our trunks were loaded into the coach. "We won't be seeing *you* again."

"You're still a child," Marlene said. "You might be coming back."

"Never," Kate said.

"Never," I echoed, as we scrambled into the coach. "I have better things to do with my time."

Moments later, the coach rattled into life.

CHAPTER
FOUR

We said nothing as the coach rattled away from the school. I peered out the rear window, watching as Grayling's vanished into the distance. The school was an ugly, blocky building—rumour insisted it had been designed by a madman—that was profoundly unsuited to its role, but it had been my home for the last six years. I'd been allowed to go to the nearest town, from time to time, yet I'd never been allowed to return to Shallot. I had very mixed feelings as we rounded the corner, passing through the gatehouse and driving onto the road. It felt good to be an adult, but...

"It won't be a long drive," Marlene said. "Did anyone think to bring a pack of cards?"

I meant to read my letters, I thought, sourly. *I didn't plan on having you accompany me.*

"Here," Kate said. She produced a pack of cards from her dress. "You want to play Spellbinder or Frogmaker?"

"Frogmaker," Marlene said. "Lucy? You want to play?"

I hid my sour amusement with an effort. Marlene would normally look down her nose at Kate. Kate might be quite a commoner, but Marlene and Kate were not—and never would be—social equals. And yet, trapped in the coach, Marlene was happy to treat Kate as a friend. I wondered if she thought pretending to be nice for an hour would make up for seven years of bossiness, harassment and outright bullying. I doubted she had the self-awareness to even *think* she needed to make up for something. She'd certainly never struck me as intelligent.

"Sure," I said. It would help keep my mind off the coming ordeal. "Deal me in."

"Great," Marlene said. "I'll go first."

I found it hard to care enough to argue. My mind kept wandering. My father's funeral was tomorrow and then…I'd have to face the family conclave. I tried to remember who might be still active, who might have reason to oppose my rise to the headship, but it was hard to draw any real conclusions. Uncle Algernon had been my father's strongest opponent, back in his early days, but he'd been sent into permanent exile for recklessly endangering his children's lives. The others…? I wasn't sure. Auntie Aggie? Uncle Simon? Someone I couldn't even remember? I mentally cursed my father, even as I mourned him. I should have been at his side, learning how to handle the family. I was going to be entering politics blind.

"Lucy?" Kate sounded concerned. "Are you alright?"

"Just tired," I lied. "It's been a long day already."

"You're normally a better player," Marlene agreed. "I just beat you twice."

"Did you?" I hadn't noticed. "Well done."

"Hah." Marlene looked displeased. "Did you also forget about the money you agreed to pay me, if I won?"

I tried not to flinch. That comment had landed too close to home. "I'm still trying to forget," I told her, trying not to sound too angry. "You have to stop reminding me."

The coach rattled—in—as we crested the hill and drove down towards Shallot. I pushed the curtain and peered out the window. Shallot looked…bigger…then remembered, although it *had* been a long time since I'd left the city. I had trouble picking out the three sections of the city, divided by the river as it made its way down to the sea. My eyes moved from ship to ship, from the tramp freighters making their way up and down the coast to the giant clipper ships preparing to sail to Hangchow. I'd heard some men—and women—had made their fortunes in the east. A couple of girls I'd known had talked openly about their dreams of travel. I hoped, just for a second, they made it. I'd have liked to go with them too.

"We'll be stopping in North Shallot," Marlene said. She sneered at Kate, a fitting return to form after an hour of trying to be nice. "Will you be able to get home from there?"

"I'll have no trouble walking across the bridges," Kate said, dryly. "You're the one who tried to cheat on the cross-country dash."

Marlene flushed and glared. I tried not to snicker. Marlene *had* tried to cheat, unaware the games mistress knew all the tricks. Marlene had had to run the dash *again* while the rest of us went for lunch. I would have felt sorrier for her if she hadn't been so awful. As it was, I'd joined in the sniggers. One might win respect by cheating and getting away with it, but there was no sympathy in the school for someone who got caught. It was yet another lesson the school probably hadn't meant to teach us.

I turned away and watched as we passed through the gatehouse and drove into North Shallot. It was the richest part of the city, the roads lined with trees and beautiful mansions surrounded by powerful wards. The men and women on the streets wore fancy clothes, suggesting they were either incredibly rich or doing their level best to pretend they were. I looked down at my dress and frowned. It had been the height of fashion, two years ago. It wasn't any longer. I told myself, firmly, that it didn't matter. Everyone would know me, soon enough. I'd be rich and powerful enough not to have to care what everyone thought.

Marlene tapped on the wood. "Just drop me off after the next mansion."

"Yes, My Lady," the driver called back. "It shall be done."

"After the next mansion?" I rolled my eyes at her. "Don't want to be seen with us, do you?"

"Compared to you two, I look great," Marlene said. "I don't want to outshine you."

I bit down a sarcastic remark as the coach rattled to a halt. Marlene *had* to be really ashamed of us. She'd look odd floating a trunk through the air, instead of being driven to the front door and helped out. But...I shrugged, watching as she scrambled out and collected her trunk from the undercompartment. It was quite possible she wanted to visit a few other places before she went home instead. She might want to visit her friends or...maybe she even had a boyfriend. Marlene was pretty enough, I supposed. She might show a nicer side of herself to a boy she liked. Or a girl. I could see either one *really* upsetting her family if they didn't approve of the partner.

"Where does she live?" Kate looked around with interest as the coach rattled back to life and headed down the road. "Where is she going?"

"I have no idea," I said, with a wink. "She's probably off to meet someone her parents won't like."

I sobered as the coach turned the corner. Marlene might be obnoxious, but she had all the disadvantages of being an aristocrat with few of the advantages. On one hand, her parents and family would do their level best to keep her under control; on the other, she probably wouldn't have much hope of either rising to the top or building a small power base for herself. A crafty person *might* make something of her position, but it wouldn't be easy. The Grande Dames of High Society would do everything in their power to crush a young upstart.

And they're going to have problems coming to grips with me, I thought. *I'm too young for them to take seriously and too powerful for them* not *to*.

"I'll drop Kate off here," the driver called. "It's only a short walk to the bridge."

"Thanks," Kate said. She leaned forward and kissed my cheek. "Take care of yourself, okay? And send me a letter if you need to talk."

"You too," I said. It was a shame I couldn't invite her to stay with me, but I wasn't confirmed yet. Afterwards...I wondered if she'd enjoy visiting Lamplighter Hall. "I'll see you soon."

I felt my heart starting to pound again as soon as the coach rattled to life again. I was going home. I was going home and...I wasn't sure what I'd find. Home had always been where my parents had lived, but my mother had died six years ago and I'd barely known my father before he sent me away. I reached for the letter in my pocket, feeling my heart twinge in pain. It couldn't be all my father had sent, right? I told myself there would be a letter waiting for me at Lamplighter Hall, something my father would have written and charmed so that only I could read.

The driver's voice broke into my thoughts. "The gates aren't opening."

I peered through the window. The gates were closed. The gatehouse was empty. I peered at the sign—LAMPLIGHTER HAL—and swore under my breath. There was a missing letter, an empty space where the letter should have been...I opened the door and jumped out, slipping and sliding on the muddy ground. The road running beside the house was in our care. And yet...I felt my heart sink. Something was very wrong.

"My Lady?"

"Unload my trunk," I ordered, as I touched the gate. The charms woven into the metal recognised me as a family member and unlocked, allowing me to push the gate open. There should have been someone in the guardhouse, but the tiny building was completely empty. I shivered, peering up towards the house. My memories insisted it should glow with light, but instead it looked more than a little faded. "I'll walk from here."

"Aye, My Lady," the driver said. He looked at the house and frowned. "Have we come to the right place?"

I hesitated. I honestly wasn't sure. My memories did not match the scene before me. The drive looked muddy in some places and overgrown in others, the doors looked marred by age and dark magic, the lawn was patchy...the statues of my ancestors looked as if no one had bothered to maintain them. I shivered, again. It was the right place. I was sure of it.

But there was no one hurrying to greet me.

"Yes," I said, with more confidence than I felt. "I'll be fine."

He tipped his hat, then scrambled back into the driver's seat as I levitated my trunk and started up the driveway. A faint smell hung in the air, a faint stench of something I couldn't quite place. I peered towards the distant potions gardens and shivered when I realised the plants had been allowed to grow out of control. They'd have to be trimmed and pruned at the very least, before we could start using them again. It was quite possible the cross-contamination had given birth to something dangerous. There were magical plants that produced deadly gasses when they were burnt. I'd have to arrange for a proper expert to come inspect the garden and do whatever was necessary to clean up the mess. And...

I swallowed hard as I stared at the closed doors. They should have opened for me already. There should have been someone in the hall to greet me...I wondered, suddenly, if I was alone. Or if the hall had been abandoned...I inched forward, directing my trunk ahead of me. What had happened? Why? I touched the door and breathed a sigh of relief as it unlocked and opened. The charms recognised me, even if no one else did. The wards shimmered around me as I stepped into the hall. Someone was coming down the stairs...

"Lucy!"

I stared. "Uncle Jalil?"

My mother's older brother came into the light. He looked older than I remembered, his skin a shade darker, his beard shot through with gray and white streaks. It looked as if he was losing his hair, despite the magic running through his blood. I found it hard to reconcile the man in front of me with the uncle I'd known as a little girl. It had been six years since I'd seen him, but he looked to have aged twenty years in that time. I couldn't believe it.

"Lucy," Uncle Jalil said. His suit looked old too, as if he couldn't afford the latest styles. "Welcome home."

He started to hug me, then stepped back and held out his hand instead. I took it and clasped it lightly, then pulled him into a proper hug. "It's been a long time," I said. "What...what happened?"

Uncle Jalil winced. "I've got a lot to tell you," he said. "And you're not going to like it."

I looked around. The entrance hall was badly lit, but I could see well enough to notice that a dozen paintings—at least—had been removed from the walls. A handful of statuettes I remembered from my childhood, including one that had been damaged when Cousin Oliver threw it at his older brother during a tantrum, were also missing. Dust hung in the air, suggesting no one had bothered to sweep the floors, polish the walls or do *any* of the hundreds of tasks one *had* to do if one wanted to keep a Great House in good condition. I reached out with my senses, studying the wards. They welcomed me. The wards were the only thing within eyeshot that appeared to be in good repair.

"I'm starting to feel that way," I said. I lowered my trunk to the floor, then looked at the stairs. "Where *is* everyone?"

Uncle Jalil winced, again. "The majority of the servants were laid off, or chose to work elsewhere," he said. "Only a handful remained."

I stared at him. "They were laid off?"

"Yes." Uncle Jalil sounded as if he would sooner be talking about something—anything—other than this. "They were let go."

"I see," I said. I didn't, not really. "Uncle...what about the family?"

"Most of them moved out," Uncle Jalil said. "The remainder are largely concentrated in the backhouse. Your father didn't like them hanging around. He didn't trust them. He thought they were plotting against him. I think he only trusted me because I was his brother-in-law, not an actual brother. He knew I couldn't rule the family."

I shook my head slowly. "Uncle...is there something to drink?"

Uncle Jalil laughed, humourlessly. "Come with me."

I followed him down a corridor and into what had once—probably—been a waiting room for the servants. I took a seat and watched as he heated water with a spell, then poured it into two mugs and added tea leaves. It was the sort of simple task most aristocrats would delegate to a servant. I knew girls of aristocratic stock who'd be horrified at the mere thought of brewing their own tea, let alone brushing their own hair or cooking their own food. I supposed boarding school had done *something* for me. I was far better prepared to look after myself than one of those shrinking violets.

"I'm afraid the budget doesn't run to alcohol," Uncle Jalil said, as he passed me a steaming mug. "And besides, as your uncle, I can't serve alcohol to you anyway."

"I have never so much as *touched* a drop," I lied. Actually, one of the girls had smuggled in a bottle of farmhouse whiskey for a midnight feast. It had tasted so vile that I'd sworn off the stuff from that moment on. The banging headache the following morning, when we'd had a charms test, hadn't helped. "Uncle...what happened?"

"It's a long story," Uncle Jalil said. "Where do you want me to start?"

"At the beginning," I said. My patience was beginning to wear thin. "What. Happened?"

Uncle Jalil let out a long breath. "Your father was a very imaginative man," he said, in a tone that suggested it wasn't entirely a compliment. "He'd hoped to repair the family fortunes, which were already flagging when he married your mother, and put them on solid ground. Instead, he had a run of bad luck. Some of his investments flopped, while others failed to make a profit. We were staggering along when the House War broke out. It crippled us."

My eyes narrowed. "Uncle...we didn't take part in the House War."

"Not directly," Uncle Jalil agreed. "It didn't save us. We'd invested heavily on opening new trade routes to Minima and Hangchow. The fighting destroyed our warehouses and wiped out any chance of us recovering our investment, let alone making a profit. Your father did everything he could to conceal it, but the writing was firmly on the wall. He spent the last six years, ever since Razwhana died, trying to save the family."

"He sent me away," I said. I felt another pang. I missed my mother too. "Why?"

"I believe he feared you might be dragged down with him," Uncle Jalil said. "The blunt truth, Lucy, is that the only reason he kept his post was that no one else wanted it. He didn't listen to the conclave—or me, really. They didn't try to vote him out because that would have left them holding the bag."

"And so they all inched away," I said, slowly. I sipped my tea as I tried to think. "I…didn't you try to tell him? I thought you were an accountant!"

"I am," Uncle Jalil said. "Yes, I did try to tell him. He didn't listen. He just went ahead with zany scheme after zany scheme until he finally died and left you holding the bag. As your uncle"—his eyes met mine—"my honest advice is to decline the poisoned chalice he's left you and leave the city for good."

"I can't do that," I said, shocked. "I…"

"I know." Uncle Jalil looked away. "And I am sorry."

CHAPTER FIVE

There was hardly anyone at my father's funeral.

I stood beside Uncle Jalil and pretended to listen as the speaker—Uncle Isfahan, my father's oldest surviving relative—droned on and on about my father's accomplishments to a handful of people who'd probably come to make sure my father was truly dead. Uncle Jalil had suggested hiring professional mourners, but one look at the account books—the ones carefully hidden from everyone else—had been enough to convince me we couldn't afford them. Besides, everyone would know. I couldn't help wondering, as my eyes swept from side to side, if it really mattered. House Lamplighter was collapsing. We had so little, the vultures weren't even bothering to circle.

My heart sank as I surveyed the mourners. Twelve people, just twelve... two of them servants and three more family members who practically *had* to attend. House Lamplighter had once commanded small armies of kin and enough wealth to corrupt a small city, but now...I picked out the names and faces, silently noting who'd been kind enough to attend. I'd make the others pay, I vowed to myself. They should have attended. It was their duty.

The speaker finally droned to a halt and raised his hand, pointing at the pyre. I forced myself to watch as my father's body caught fire, the remnants of magic within his dead flesh sparking brightly as the flames turned him to ash. His soul was long gone; he'd joined the ancients in the world of the honoured dead. I shivered, my legs wobbling uncomfortably as the flames grew hotter. I wanted to believe there was something after death, even though I feared what my ancestors would say. To me, to my father...The world had changed in so many ways since House Lamplighter first rose to power.

I closed my eyes. My father was dead...I felt a gaping emptiness in my chest, a dull awareness that something was missing. I'd been taught that crying was bad, that giving vent to one's emotions was wrong, but...I'd been taught to conceal my pain, yet there was nothing to hide. I felt... numb. I'd seen so little of my father since birth that it was hard for me to feel anything. What had he been like, really? A kind man? A decent man? Or a monster? I just didn't know.

The flames reached their peak, then abated as the remainder of the body crumpled to dust. The ashes would be picked up by the wind and swept over the garden, an offering to the ancestors who'd built the manor so long ago. I wondered, grimly, what they thought of us now. They had to be ashamed. I'd never truly realised how badly my family had gone downhill until I returned home.

No wonder the healers were so determined to ensure it really was father's body, I thought, dully. I'd read the reports carefully, noting just how thoroughly they'd done their work. *They must have wondered if he'd faked his death.*

I swallowed, hard. I'd sneaked into the crypt to view the body, even though tradition insisted that the Heir Primus was supposed to pretend her successor had never really lived. The Head of the Family was dead; long live the Head of the Family. The face had been that of a stranger, a face so unlike mine that it was hard to believe we'd been related, much less father and daughter. I had his colouring—and his eyes, I'd been told—but the rest of my features came from my mother. I supposed that wasn't entirely a bad thing. My mother had been a beauty in her day, everyone insisted. And my father had had a beard.

Uncle Jalil put his hand on my arm. "Do you want to speak to the mourners?"

I shook my head, unable to put my feelings into words. My father was dead...my thoughts ran in circles. I wondered, sourly, just how many of the mourners had come to make sure my father truly *was* dead. I'd heard all the jokes, back when they'd been funny...I supposed it said *something* that so few people had come to make sure of it. My father had lived and died without making many friends, let alone enemies who'd come to gloat. I wasn't sure if I should be relieved or discomfited. House Lamplighter had once been amongst the powerful. Now...how many of us were even *left*?

The wind picked up, scattering the ashes across the overgrown lawn. I lifted my eyes to the mansion, silently calculating everything that needed to be fixed before the building crumbled into ruin. My ancestors really knew how to build, I'd been assured, but even the greatest of the Great Houses needed proper maintenance from time to time. There was no choice. The walls might be solid, and charmed to repel everything from subtle scrying to powerful curses, but the windows and interiors were far less so. We might be left with nothing more than a framework if the rest of the building collapsed. I counted windows that needed to be replaced and shuddered. I'd been taught that putting on a good face was half of making a good impression. My father had clearly forgotten that lesson.

It was relatively cheap to shower, put on makeup and don a fancy dress, I reminded myself, dryly. *Fixing everything wrong with the mansion would be a great deal more expensive.*

My heart sank. I'd donned mourning garb for the funeral—it was tradition, no one would say a peep about it—but I didn't have anything else to wear. I snorted with bitter amusement. There were entire wardrobes of clothes that could be adjusted to fit, but they weren't remotely fashionable. I'd be mocked if I wore a dress from last season, let alone the last hundred years. People would say I couldn't afford anything better. They'd be right. Perhaps I could claim it was a family tradition...the thought lingered in my mind. It was doable. If I made a show of wearing my father's styles...

And then people would be shocked I wore trousers, I thought. *There's no way to win.*

I heard the mourners leaving, Uncle Jalil bidding them a polite farewell, but I didn't look around. We were supposed to host a feast for the mourners, but—as I wasn't technically confirmed as Matriarch—we could skip the requirement without exciting too much comment. I rather suspected no one would care enough to comment. Twelve people, just twelve, had come to the funeral. The servants would be already heading back to their rooms...I wondered, idly, if they'd hold a private wake for their former master. Kate had told me servants and commoners had their own traditions and rituals. I wasn't sure I believed her, but it was nice to think that *someone* would have held a formal ceremony for father...

A tingle ran down my spine. I'd spent the last six years in boarding school. I'd learnt to tell when someone was sneaking up on me, either to slap me on the back or hit me with a particularly nasty hex. I tensed, readying a counterspell as I turned. A young man—a few years older than me, with an artfully bland face—stood behind me. His eyes were firmly fixed on my face. He wore a fashionable suit, the kind of outfit that would be worn by an aristocrat who dabbled in trade, but the way he wore it suggested he hadn't grown up with high fashion. I felt a flicker of envy. There was something to be said for a childhood that didn't include endless etiquette and presentation lessons. Or an environment where the slightest mistake would be remembered and dragged up to be used against you years later.

"Lady Lamplighter?"

I nodded as I studied him. He was handsome, I supposed, but...bland, definitely bland. He had a very forgettable face, neither striking nor ugly enough to linger in my memory. His suit hadn't been professionally tailored either. It fitted him well, but not perfectly. A commoner pretending to be an aristocrat? Or an aristocrat who'd fallen on hard times? I suspected the former. His accent was perfect enough to suggest he was hiding something. A lower-class accent? It was quite likely.

"I am Clive," he said. "I speak for Zadornov."

He spoke the name as though it should mean something to me, but it didn't. I'd never heard of Zadornov, even though I'd been warned to memorise everyone of importance within the city. I was out of touch, but…if Zadornov was important, I'd have heard of him. I'd heard of a great many people who *thought* they were important too.

I met his eyes, feeling my temper start to fray. "And who is Zadornov?"

Clive's eyes widened, just for a second. "A businessman," he said. His voice was polite, but firm. "Your father owes him money."

"My father is dead," I said. I waved a hand at what remained of the ashes. "Dead and gone."

"The fact remains, the debt is now due," Clive said. "My master wishes to discuss repayment."

"Does he?" I groaned, inwardly. "My father's secondary will has yet to be read. If you feel you have a claim on his personal estate…"

"Your father signed agreements, in his persona as Patriarch," Clive said. "Those debts have to be honoured."

I felt a stab of pure anger. I'd just watched my father's cremation. I hadn't even *started* coming to terms with his death, let alone working my way through the account books. I didn't know what my father owned, either personally or professionally, and I didn't much care. I had too many other problems.

"Your father owes my master money," Clive said. I thought I heard a hint of amusement in his voice. "The original sum, combined with interest, is over two thousand crowns."

I blinked. "Two thousand crowns?"

"Yes," Clive agreed. "The original sum was a thousand crowns. Combined with interest…"

"A ruinous rate of interest," Uncle Jalil said, as he came up behind us. "I saw the paperwork, young man. The interest rate was so high because it was a personal loan to Lord Lucas, not a family loan. It cannot be passed to his heir."

Clive shifted, moving uncomfortably. It dawned on me, suddenly, that he was quite young. He couldn't be more than twenty-five, perhaps younger. And yet...I cursed my father under my breath, even though it was technically blasphemy. What had he done?

"If you have a legal claim on any part of my father's estate," I said, "you have to put it in writing before the will is read and approved. That'll be in three days from now."

"I will inform my master." Clive bowed, formally. "A pleasure meeting you, Lady Lamplighter."

He turned and hurried off. I watched him until he'd passed through the gates, then turned to Uncle Jalil. "Who's Zadornov?"

"A loan shark." Uncle Jalil shifted uncomfortably. "That's a person who makes loans at..."

"I know what a loan shark is," I said, crossly. There'd been a couple of girls at school who'd made a tidy profit by loaning money to their fellow students, then collecting it back with interest. "Why did father go to *him*?"

"Because he was short of money and no one was prepared to lend it to him," Uncle Jalil informed me. "You can review the contract if you like."

"I will." I knew more than a little about inheritance law, but I was uncomfortably aware I was out of my depth. Father hadn't *just* been my father. He'd been the Patriarch of House Lamplighter. The contract might be vague on precisely who was liable for the debt, if he died...I scowled. It was going to be a legal headache. How many of father's possessions had really been *his*? "Uncle..."

"We'll talk about it later," Uncle Jalil said. "You have company."

I raised my eyebrows as Ellington, the butler, walked up to us. He was a tall dark man, wearing a simple black suit. I couldn't recall him ever wearing anything else, even when I'd been a child. His family had worked for ours for generations, the older children going into service as soon as they came of age...I wondered, suddenly, if they were really as happy as they claimed. As a child, I'd never questioned it. As an adult...

"My Lady," Ellington said. His voice was formal, as always. "I grieve with thee for thy father, who is now amongst the ancestors."

"I thank you," I said, equally formally. There weren't many people, even amongst the aristos, who used the old terms. "May the Ancients welcome you as well."

Ellington bowed. "It will be my honour to serve you," he said. "And I bid thee welcome to thy home."

I nodded, unsure of the formal response. "I've not been confirmed yet."

"This is your home," Ellington said. "It will always be your home."

He bowed again, then took his leave. I shook my head as he turned away, understanding—finally—what my tutors had meant when they'd lectured me on *noblesse oblige*. Ellington was old enough to be my grandfather—literally—but I was responsible for him. And his family. *And* all of the other servants. My heart sank as I remembered walking the halls, remembering how many servants had once lived and worked in Lamplighter Hall. Now...how many were there? Five. Just five, one of whom was too old to work. They were my responsibility now. I couldn't just kick them out to starve.

Ellington could probably get a job elsewhere, I thought, although I wasn't sure that was true. The Great Houses preferred to hire their kin for the senior household roles, regarding them as more trustworthy than outsiders. *The others...*

"That man is more loyal than your father ever realised," Uncle Jalil said, quietly. "Lucas always took him for granted."

"I know," I said. "What happened to the other servants?"

"They didn't get paid," Uncle Jalil said. There was a hint of waspishness in his voice, as if I'd asked a silly question. "And so they left."

I winced, inwardly. A common or garden servant could get a job anywhere, as long as they had a good character. I'd heard more than enough grumbling about competition for good servants from my mother, back before the House War. The old retainers like Ellington...my heart sank as

I realised I might be wrong. If he left the household, someone would ask pointed questions about precisely *why*. They'd wonder if he'd resigned or been kicked out or...if they thought he'd been disloyal, they'd refuse to hire him. And I was responsible for him. And everyone else.

The wind blew again. I watched the ashes blowing across the grounds, then turned and started to walk back to the hall. The remaining mourners had left without so much as bothering to offer their condolences. I ground my teeth in bitter frustration, even though I was relieved. I didn't want to exchange insincere chitchat with relatives who either wanted the headship for themselves or were silently grateful they'd been spared the poisoned chalice. Idiots. They could have just left. It wasn't as if they *needed* to stay on the sinking ship.

I said nothing until we stepped back into the hall. It should have been warmer inside the building—it was summer, damn it—but it felt cold. I muttered a heating spell as I looked around, my heart sinking as I saw the dust. It felt as if I were walking into an abandoned building, not the heart of a Great House. The wards sparkled around me—they, at least, knew me—but there was little else welcoming. I stared up at the bare spaces on the walls, where the paintings should have been. What had happened to them?

"Your father sold many of them," Uncle Jalil said, as if he'd read my thoughts. "Others were placed into storage..."

"He sold them?" I couldn't believe it. "Why?"

"He was desperate for capital," Uncle Jalil said. "And short of ways to get it."

I felt my heart sink, again. *Again*. "Why didn't he tell me? Why did he send me away?"

"For your own good, I suspect," Uncle Jalil said. "You were the Heir Primus by default, Lucy, but you were isolated from the realities of the role. He kept you in ignorance to ensure you could not be blamed for his failings, let alone forced to pay his debts. You—you *personally*—are not legally responsible for anything he did. If you'd stayed here, if you'd effectively been apprenticed to him, you might have wound up bearing some of the blame."

"Really?" I wasn't sure of *that*. "Do apprentices get blamed when their master makes a mistake?"

"Sometimes," Uncle Jalil said. "If the apprentice is taken on with the intention of eventually inheriting his master's business...yes, he could be blamed. It would be assumed, rightly or wrongly, that he'd played a role in making the decisions. A Heir Primus who was involved throughout his teenage years would certainly *have* played a role..."

"I was at school," I protested.

"Yes," Uncle Jalil agreed. His voice was very calm. "And that's why you have a clean slate."

I nodded, slowly. "I'm going to his rooms," I said. "Meet me there in thirty minutes. I want to know everything."

"I'll be there," Uncle Jalil said. If he took offense at my tone, he didn't show it. "And I'll have Jadish bring us some tea. We're going to need it."

CHAPTER SIX

I felt oddly out of place as I walked up the stairs to the top floor, even though Lamplighter Hall was mine now and the wards parted at my touch. My father's domain had been firmly off limits to everyone, save for his friends and business associates. Mother hadn't been allowed onto the floor, even though…I shook my head as I opened the door and peered into the empty office. My father had lived and worked up here…I thought, just for a moment, that I saw his ghost sitting behind a large wooden desk. The wards crackled around me as I walked towards the desk and sat on his chair. It was mine now, but…it didn't feel right.

The sensation of unreality grew stronger as I looked around the chamber. One wall was covered in bookshelves, crammed to bursting with volumes that looked untouched; another was covered in maps and drawings that didn't seem to be in any reasonable order. A pair of wooden filing cabinets were placed against the third wall, between the windowpanes. My father had been able to stand by the window and stare over North Shallot. I wondered what he'd seen, when he'd had the time. A city of opportunity, or a land of rivals who'd tear him down if he gave them half a chance? Or both?

I tried to open the drawer, but couldn't. The locking charms were designed to keep everyone out, even me. I studied them for a moment, then made a mental note to try to unpick them later. I might need to hire help. My father could easily have woven a lethal curse into the charms, if he'd been sure no one he *liked* would try to break into the drawer. I supposed anyone who actually *tried* would have proven themselves thoroughly untrustworthy. I smiled, although there was little humour in it. He'd gone so far to protect his secrets, whatever they were, that he'd kept them from his heir too.

The smell of old leather rose up around me as I leaned back in the chair. It had clearly been designed for someone bigger than me...bigger than my father too, unless he'd gained weight in the six years since I'd last seen him and his death. I felt silly sitting on the chair, but...it had been my father's. I didn't want to put it aside and bring in something more suitable, not yet. It was all I had to remember him.

I heard a noise at the door and looked up. Jadish stood there, carrying a tray of tea and biscuits. I smiled, feeling oddly conflicted. Jadish—Ellington's granddaughter—had practically grown up with me. We'd been friends, despite the vast gulf between us. And yet...I wondered, suddenly, why she hadn't written to me. She'd shared my lessons. She could read and write better than some of the girls at school.

"My Lady." Jadish dropped a neat curtsy. She wore an old-fashioned maid's outfit that clashed oddly with her dark skin. Her hair was still in braids. "It's good to see you again."

"And you," I said, honestly. She'd be accused of being overfamiliar everywhere else, but...I didn't care. Not here, at least. "I missed you."

Jadish looked down. "The master wouldn't let me write to you. Not one word."

I winced. "It wasn't your fault," I assured her. If father had forbidden her to write, she'd be whipped—or worse—if she went against him. "I... why? Did he say why?"

"No, My Lady." Jadish shook her head. "He just ordered me to mind my own business."

She put the tray on the desk as Uncle Jalil entered, carrying a handful of leather folders under his arm. "We can pour the tea," I said, quickly. "I'll speak to you later."

Jadish dropped another curtsy. "Of course, My Lady."

I watched her go, then tightened the wards as soon as the door closed behind her. "Why did father forbid her to write to me?"

"I believe it would have been improper for you to receive letters from a servant," Uncle Jalil said. "Your father would certainly have believed it to be so."

I scowled. "I would have been happy to receive letters from anyone."

"And those letters would not have remained private," Uncle Jalil pointed out. "Or have things changed since my day?"

"Probably not," I admitted, sourly. We'd had enough hints, over the years, that Mistress Grayling read our letters, even before I'd found proof. I picked up the teapot and started to pour. "Milk? One lump or two?"

"No milk, one lump," Uncle Jalil said. "And you have to remember your father was a very complex man, facing a series of very complex problems."

"Bully for him," I muttered. I passed him a cup, then sank back into the leather chair as he sat facing me. "How bad is it?"

"The tea is very good," Uncle Jalil said. He hadn't touched it. "But I'm afraid our financial situation is very bad."

I took a breath. "Details?"

Uncle Jalil looked back at me, evenly. "Where would you like me to start?"

"The beginning," I said. "I thought we were a wealthy house."

"We were, a few hundred years ago." Uncle Jalil smiled, humourlessly. "Of course, that was before any of us were born."

He indicated the folders on the table. "Like I told you, the family had been in decline for quite some time before your father assumed his position as head. We were finding it hard to concentrate the wealth we needed to invest in everything from farming and mining for forgery and enchantment. We were barely able to meet our obligations to keep things on an even keel. Even when we did"—he shrugged, elaborately—"we were unable to halt our steady decline. Your grandfather tried to cut expenditures as much as possible, but it made no difference. We were being left behind."

I considered it for a moment. "And then?"

"Your father attempted to amass the cash we needed to invest," Uncle Jalil said. "He started well, I admit, but he failed to quit while he was ahead. He made a string of bad calls, investing in unprofitable farmland and mines that proved largely worthless; he invested heavily in international shipping and trade, only to lose most of his investments during the House War. He hadn't bothered to insure most of it, you see, and the insurance on what little he *did* insure was nowhere near enough to repay our losses. He couldn't even get rid of the farmland. People wouldn't even *take* it."

"Ouch," I said.

"Yes." Uncle Jalil stared at his fingers for a long moment. "Your father got desperate. He sent you away, then tried to get more cash. He sold everything he could see, sometimes at rock bottom prices. He took out loans, creating a complex network of deals that even I have been unable to disentangle, throwing money at every halfway solid business opportunity that came his way. And none of them worked. By the time he died, apparently of natural causes, he was deep in debt. *Personal* debt. He had no hope of repaying the loans."

I met his eyes. "*Apparently* of natural causes?"

"It might have been suicide," Uncle Jalil admitted. "Your father was certainly ingenious enough to ensure his suicide looked natural."

"Oh." I wasn't sure I wanted to think about it. "I...how much money do we have now?"

"Almost nothing," Uncle Jalil said, bluntly. "Lucy...what little income we have comes from our lands and we practically *have* to keep reinvesting if we want the money to keep flowing."

I cocked my head. "I thought we grew potions ingredients?"

"Yes, but we're not the *only* ones growing potions ingredients," Uncle

Jalil reminded me. "If we put up our prices, Lucy, we'll lose sales. Customers will go elsewhere."

"And that will be that," I muttered. I'd studied business at school. It had been mandatory for aristos. "What do we have that we can sell?"

"Almost nothing," Uncle Jalil said. "What little we own is entailed. It cannot be sold as long as the family survives. We can't even loan it to someone willing to pay through the nose…if such a person even exists. Your father sold everything he could to raise money. About the only thing he didn't sell was *you*."

I made a face. "He wouldn't have."

"He couldn't have," Uncle Jalil corrected. "As long as you were underage, nothing could be finalised. You could repudiate the betrothal the moment you came of age. And that would have upset a whole string of apple carts."

I shuddered. "Is there nothing we can do to raise cash?"

"Almost nothing," Uncle Jalil said. I was getting sick of hearing that. "We can sell our vote, in Magus Court, but…we only have one seat and no influence. There's no way we can ramp up the price unless the vote is really close."

"I see." I glared at the folders. "What do you advise?"

"Leave." Uncle Jalil met my eyes, evenly. "You're an adult. You can go elsewhere. You don't *have* to stay on the sinking ship. And your father's debts are going to catch up with us sooner rather than later. Whoever becomes head will have to deal with them."

"I…" I shook my head. "I'm Heir Primus."

"By default," Uncle Jalil said. "You didn't come of age until after your father's death. You don't *have* to accept the poisoned chalice. You can go before the conclave and formally refuse to accept it or…or you can just leave. You're an intelligent young woman with a good education. You'll be fine."

I looked at him. "But what about the servants? Ellington and Jadish… what about *you*?"

"I'm an old man," Uncle Jalil said. "What happens to me is not important."

"And the servants?" I pressed as hard as I dared. "What happens to them if the family collapses?"

"Jadish is young and pretty," Uncle Jalil said. "She'll have no trouble…"

"I can't just abandon them," I said. "And I can't abandon the family."

"*What* family?" Uncle Jalil shook his head. "Lucy, the days when there were hundreds of kindred living within this hall are gone. Half the surviving family couldn't be bothered to come to your father's funeral. Walk away. Walk away, now. Leave the ones who haven't already deserted to their fate. You don't have to die with them."

"I can't go," I said. I'd been raised to think of myself as having a duty to the family. "I can't just abandon them. Or the family…"

"Your father spent six years racking up debts as he tried to strike it big," Uncle Jalil snapped. "Lucy…do you think you can do any better?"

"I'm going to have to try," I said. "Will you stay?"

"I don't have anywhere else to go," Uncle Jalil said. He looked resigned. "Lucy…are you sure? Because once you're recognised as Matriarch, you'll be committed."

"I know." I looked around the room. "But I can't just walk away."

"You can," Uncle Jalil said. "Take Jadish with you, if you like. Take Ellington…"

I shook my head. The obligation to the family name was too strong. Yes, I *could* abandon my name and walk away…but I couldn't have lived with myself afterwards. I was Lucilla of House Lamplighter and that was all there was to it. I'd just have to think of a way to raise money that would give us half a chance of saving ourselves. I just wished I knew what that might be.

Start small, I told myself. *And find something you can sell.*

"You're not confirmed yet," Uncle Jalil said. "If you leave before then, you're free and clear."

"I know," I mumbled. A hundred ideas, all wildly impractical, danced through my head. "How many family members are left? I mean…family with voting rights?"

Uncle Jalil grimaced. "Technically, twenty-seven," he said. "A third of them have strong ties to other families, to the point they've effectively cut their ties to us."

I blinked. "They've disowned us?"

"No one's disowned anyone." Uncle Jalil smiled, rather coldly. "They just do their level best to pretend we don't exist."

"Oh." I'd known girls like that at school. They'd been just as irritating as the brats who hurled hexes whenever someone turned their back. "They haven't *formally* given up their vote?"

"No." Uncle Jalil's smile grew colder. "They simply haven't bothered to vote."

"I see," I said. "Can you write them a note as my closest adult relative? Or do I have to do it myself?"

"It depends," Uncle Jalil said. "What do you want to say?"

"I'm going to hold a Family Conclave," I said. "Five days from now…I think that's enough time to clean up the meeting room and go through the accounts. Anyone who doesn't attend will be deemed to have forfeited their voting rights and classed as inactive members of the family. Their children, assuming they have them, will no longer be considered family. The ones who have no interest in salvaging the sinking ship will take themselves out of the picture."

"You'll annoy them," Uncle Jalil pointed out.

"And they'll have to decide if they want to take the role for themselves," I said. I had few illusions—the vast majority of my kin didn't know me and those that did remembered me as a little girl—but I *was* Heir Primus, Matriarch Presumptive until I was voted out of office. It would be hard for anyone to organise opposition without outing themselves as my enemy—there were only twenty-seven voters—and anyone who did would probably find themselves lumbered with the poisoned chalice. "Let them be annoyed, as long as they stay out of my way."

Uncle Jalil raised his eyebrows. "You do *know* your family, right?"

I felt a stab of pain. "I haven't seen any of them in six years," I snapped, a little harsher than I'd meant. "They didn't make any attempt to contact me."

"True," Uncle Jalil agreed.

"And…why didn't they try to stop my father?" I could have kicked myself for not having asked earlier. "Surely, they could have brought him to heel."

"Different reasons for different kindred," Uncle Jalil said. "Some didn't know or care what your father was doing, as long as they received their allowance. Some thought he'd succeed—he could talk the talk, even if he couldn't walk the walk—and stayed out of his way. And others had links outside the family. They were unwilling or unable to say anything, let alone *do* anything."

He made a face. "And Lucy…they don't know just how bad things are."

I shook my head. "They never thought to ask?"

"Your father played games with the books," Uncle Jalil said. "He was quite a creative accountant."

"And you helped him," I said. "Right?"

"I swore an oath, when he married my sister," Uncle Jalil said. "I never married myself. I never had children. At my age, it is certain I never will. Your father—and you—were the only relatives I had left. Now, it's just you."

"I'm sorry," I said. I meant it. "Why didn't you ever…?"

Uncle Jalil said nothing for a long moment. "It never seemed the time," he said. "And now"—he shook his head—"it is too late."

He pushed the folders towards me. "I'll write the letter and bring it to you for approval," he said. "You go through the papers, see how much the family owes…maybe it'll change your mind. You can still leave, Lucy. You don't have to stay."

"I do," I said. "This is my family."

"Make sure you wear armour when you go into the chamber," Uncle Jalil said. "And cover your back. At least *one* of your relatives will try to put a knife in it."

"I'll look the part," I promised. "I'm sure they won't try to kill me."

"Probably not *literally*," Uncle Jalil agreed. "But you know what? They'll do everything in their power to discredit you, if they scent weakness. And you don't have anything like the clout your father or grandfather had…"

"We'll see," I said. I'd already had a couple of ideas. They might just buy me time to come up with something to improve the family fortunes. And if they didn't…I shook my head. I had to be optimistic. "Uncle…can I count on you?"

"You can count on me, as long as you *listen* to me," Uncle Jalil said. "Your father never listened."

"I'll listen," I promised. "But I can't say I'll do as you wish."

Uncle Jalil laughed. "Believe me, I understand," he said. He stood, brushing down his trousers. "Read the papers. Decide what you want to do. Ask me if you have any questions."

"I will," I said. "And thank you."

"Hah." Uncle Jalil didn't look pleased. "I've done you no favours. You really should leave."

I watched him go, then poured myself another cup of tea as I opened the first folder. The accounts were fantastically complex, but…I worked my way through them, doing my best to ignore the growing headache. Uncle Jalil had understated the situation, I realised slowly. My father had mingled his personal accounts with the family's accounts, a major problem if one wanted to sort out what he'd owed personally from what the family owed. It was going to be an utter nightmare. He'd sold stuff to himself at knockdown prices—literally—so he could sell it onwards…

We have nothing to lose, I thought. It was true. I had very little that was truly mine. *So we might as well gamble…*

Slowly, carefully, I started to draw out a plan.

CHAPTER
SEVEN

The meeting room looked...*clean*.

I hid my amusement as my kindred—those who could be bothered to attend the conclave—slowly filed into the room. Ellington had taken their coats, as they entered the hall; Jadish had offered them tea, coffee, juice or water as they passed through the door. They didn't know—they couldn't know—that we'd spent the last three days cleaning the room from top to bottom, brushing the floor, washing the windows and even hanging paintings on the walls to remind the voters that they were family. I wondered what they'd say, if they knew I'd been scrubbing with the servants. They'd probably have a collective heart attack.

My face remained impassive as the room slowly filled. I remembered a couple of voters, vaguely, but most of them were effectively strangers. I wished I knew them better. Uncle Jalil and Jadish had filled me in, as best as possible, but they had no way to know which way the voters would jump when I forced them to make a choice. They might be happy to leave me in control, they might insist on someone older taking the role or...worst of all, they might want me to have the title while exerting real power themselves. I couldn't allow it. I had no intention of allowing them to turn me into a figurehead while they looted what remained of the family's assets and vanished.

I winced, inwardly. If anything, Uncle Jalil—now sitting at the far end of the table—had very definitely understated the case. The accounts were worse than I'd thought. We barely had two bronze ringlets to rub together. What little we earned had to be reinvested immediately, for fear of losing everything. And our debts were terrifyingly high. Even without the money my father had owed, we were in serious trouble. It might take a lifetime to pay them off.

We don't have a lifetime, I thought, as Jadish handed out drinks. Uncle Jalil's figures had been very precise. We were eating our seed corn, what little there was of it. *We have five years at the most.*

Jadish left, closing the door behind her. I walked forward and stood at the head of the table, hands clasped behind my back to keep them from shaking. Mistress Grayling had forced us to give speeches in public, insisting we learnt to speak even to hostile audiences. I silently blessed the old lady, even though she hadn't been able to show us what it was like to speak to a roomful of kindred. The worst threat at school had been public humiliation. Here…I could be kicked out of the family or simply voted off the council. I smiled as best as I could, trying not to show any fear. They'd take it as a sign of weakness.

"I am Lucilla of House Lamplighter, Daughter of Lucas and Razwhana Lamplighter, Heir Primus and Matriarch Presumptive of House Lamplighter," I said. They couldn't dispute my titles without calling the entire family into question. "As such, in line with both family custom and the terms of my father's will, I am declaring myself Matriarch of House Lamplighter. If any of you wish to challenge, or nominate someone else for the role, do so now or forever hold your peace."

My words hung in the air. I looked from face to face, wondering if anyone would take up the challenge. They'd certainly had ample time to do it over the last six years. Instead, they'd practically rubberstamped my position. I suspected that meant they didn't realise how bad things had become. They'd have thought twice about my father nominating his successor if they'd understood just how much damage he'd done.

I gave them nearly two minutes to formulate a response, then pressed on. They'd had plenty of time to plan a counter-nomination, if they'd wished. Only twelve kindred had bothered to attend. I snorted, inwardly. One didn't have to be as cunning as Jagi Lamplighter, founder of our house, to realise someone could easily have packed the seats to ensure their candidate was selected. It would only have taken a handful of votes to unseat me, making it difficult for me to rule the family even if I regained my place. They knew it as well as I did. I knew better than to think it was a vote of confidence.

"Very good," I said. "And now, as Matriarch of House Lamplighter, I want my year. If any of you wish to oppose me, do so now or wait for a year. Anyone who attempts to oppose me before then will be regarded as a traitor and summarily disowned."

A rustle ran around the table. I waited, feeling my heart thudding in my chest. If they refused to oppose me now, I'd have a year without any opposition from within the family. It was tradition, but House Lamplighter was in trouble. I wanted—I needed—to make it clear I was going to have my year. They couldn't object if I hammered someone for opposing me before the year was out.

"You are young," Auntie Dorcas said. She was old enough to be my grandmother, although—as far as I could tell—she'd done nothing for the family. "You will require advice."

"I will happily *listen* to advice," I told her. It was true, even though I doubted the elderly woman would have anything useful to say. "I will not brook open opposition."

I pushed on before someone else could throw the outcome into doubt. "This is your chance to oppose me," I said. "After that, you have to give me my year."

Auntie Dorcas looked thoroughly displeased. The remainder of the kindred didn't look any happier. I'd backed them into a corner. They could oppose me now, which would mean trying to find an alternate candidate, or let me have my head. They'd be disgraced if they tried to challenge me before the year was through. No one would ever trust them again. I suspected it didn't matter as much as they thought, but my successor—whoever was unlucky enough to get the nomination and win the vote—would assume they'd put a knife in his back at the earliest opportunity. Either they stood against me now or they gave me a chance to prove myself.

"I will take your silence for consent," I informed them. "And now, I have something important to say."

I gathered myself. "The family is in serious trouble. We are practically *bleeding* money. We are the laughingstock of the city. Our industries are barely bringing in enough to repay their costs, our clients have largely deserted us and we have very little of value left to sell. Our goal, from this moment forth, will be to save ourselves from complete destruction and start the long climb back to the top. Do any of you have any objection to this goal?"

There was no answer. I smiled, inwardly. Of *course* there was no objection. They weren't fools, no matter what my father had thought. They knew the family's position was steadily weakening, even though they hadn't bothered to unseat my father before it was too late. I doubted it would have made much difference, although...who knew? I had only a handful of ideas and practically *all* of them were risky as hell.

"I expect you to put the family first," I said. "*All* of you. Whatever we say or do in private, I want us to be one big happy family in public. No public arguments. No public disgraces. No secret off-the-record whining to the newspaper muckrakers. No scandals that make us look stupid or greedy or evil. Those of you who have married into other families"—I allowed my eyes to linger on two aunties who'd married out years ago—"will still be obliged to put our family first. If you want to leave now, then go. There will be no hard feelings. If you try to walk a line between the two families, or serve the other family solely, it will be regarded as betrayal and treated accordingly."

I braced myself, half-expecting half the table to stand and go. Auntie Gladys and Auntie Emma stood and headed for the door. Auntie Erica shifted, as if she was unsure if she should stay or go. I felt a flicker of sympathy, even though I knew it could be dangerous. Auntie Erica had married out, years before I was born, but her husband had died shortly afterwards. She was not wholly part of either family. It was easy to feel sorry for her, but I had no time for divided loyalties. I needed the council behind me. Anyone who refused to commit themselves had to go.

"This is a mistake, child," Auntie Erica said. "I can remain part of both families."

"Choose," I said, remorselessly. I felt a pang of guilt, which I swiftly and ruthlessly suppressed. "One family or the other."

Auntie Erica opened her mouth, as if she intended to continue the argument, then closed it again without moving. I made a mental note to keep an eye on her, if she wanted to stay. No one would trust her again, if she betrayed me after a very clear warning, but that might not keep her from doing something stupid. I hoped I could rely on her...I turned away, deliberately giving her the chance to leave. I doubted she'd go. Her other family had little time for her. She'd failed to get pregnant before her husband died.

We're cruel, sometimes, I reminded myself. I knew the reason. I knew all the justifications. But I couldn't shed the feeling I'd done something wrong. Auntie Erica had done nothing to me. She certainly hadn't been one of the older women who'd tried to make a lady out of me. *I'll do what I can for her, afterwards.*

"Very good." I sat, indicating the discussion was now closed. I didn't think they'd be loyal—and I doubted it would be a year before they started plotting against me—but I'd won some breathing space. "I assume you've all had a chance to read my father's will. Do you have any comments?"

"Just one," Uncle Stefano said. "Does he have any *right* to leave so much to you?"

Uncle Jalil cleared his throat. "Lord Lucas stated that his entire estate, save for a handful of individual bequests, was to be passed down to his sole child. There is no question he had every right to dispose of his property however he pleased. The only real question lies in what was his personally, as opposed to what was in his custody in his role as Patriarch, but as his heir in both roles is the same person I think we can afford to overlook it."

"It is never a good idea to overlook anything," Uncle Stefano said. He was a lawyer, although he'd been out of practice for years. "We do not wish *more* of our property to be sold off."

"I have no intention of selling anything off," I said. It wasn't entirely true. I did have *one* thing that could be sold. "And we do have time to go through the collection and sort out his personal possessions. There's no great hurry."

"Perhaps the matter could be put to a committee," Auntie Dorcas said.

It would certainly keep you out of trouble, I thought. *But I want to go through my father's papers first.*

I sighed, inwardly, as the argument roared around the table. It was pointless. The councillors wouldn't be able to claim or use *any* of my father's possessions, personal or not. They were wasting their time. I wondered, sourly, if they knew it. They might not have realised how bad things truly were.

"There's no great hurry," I repeated. "Either way, the possessions will come to me."

"Perhaps you should draw up a will of your own," Uncle Stefano said. "And make provision for your children."

"I have none," I said, dryly. "Right now, providing for my children is hardly important."

"You do need to think about the future," Auntie Dorcas said. "And you have to designate a Heir Primus."

"I'll give the matter some thought," I assured her. There weren't any real candidates, not if I wanted to stick with tradition. The Heir Primus should come from the next generation, a generation that didn't even exist.

I had a pair of distant cousins who might qualify, but their parents hadn't bothered to attend the conclave and they weren't even in their teens...I made a mental note to look into it. The wretched elder was right. I did need a named heir, at least until I had a child myself. "Perhaps you could form a committee to look into that as well."

"It might be better to look for a prospective husband for you," Uncle Randolph said. "A child of your body would be..."

"The question of who I marry is none of your concern," I said, cutting him off sharply. His point had hit too close to home. "My father did not see fit to arrange anything for me, Uncle, and he was the only one with the authority to do so. I can handle such affairs myself."

"The council is required to approve," Auntie Dorcas said. "I believe we have *that* right."

"Not entirely," I said. "By custom, the Family Head is required to approve. He—*she*—has the right to veto, or place conditions on a match. The council has the right to overrule the judgement, if the happy couple wish to challenge."

I allowed myself a smile. It was a rather convoluted piece of reasoning, but it should stand up to scrutiny. I'd be in the odd position of approving my own match...my smile grew wider. Technically, I'd also be passing judgement on myself. I'd hardly appeal against my own decision. And I had a year to do whatever I pleased before they could turn on me.

"I intend to take this family back to the heights of power," I said. "Rest assured, I will do nothing to harm it."

The words hung in the air for a long moment. "We'll meet again in a week," I added, keeping my voice calm. "Before then, I want you to prepare lists of your skills—magical, social, whatever—and those of your servants, clients and friends. We have a lot of work to do and I intend to hit the ground running. Our ancestors are looking down on us. I do not intend to disappoint them."

I smiled, then stood. "Thank you for coming. I'll see you next week."

The councillors stood as I turned and headed out the room, signalling the meeting was over. They'd stay and chat, I suspected, although they wouldn't say anything useful. I was the wardmaster. They'd have to assume I'd be listening to them. The hell of it was that I hadn't had *time* to rig the wards, or do more than take control and add a handful of minor flourishes. They could sit and talk about the weather in perfect privacy.

Jadish stood outside. "My Lady? Should I serve food?"

I was thrown, very briefly. "If they want it, then do," I ordered. It was hard to keep things straight in my head. Jadish was a friend and a servant and a friend...she'd seen me on my hands and knees, scrubbing the floor like a common laundry maid. "If they want shown out instead, please escort them to the door."

Uncle Jalil caught up with me as I walked back to my father's office... to *my* office. I frowned inwardly, then remembered he probably wouldn't have been welcome once I'd left. He wouldn't have been welcome at all, not really, but they would have been politer while I was in the room. He wasn't *real* family, they'd say. He'd married into the family. It didn't make him trustworthy...

I have to trust someone, I thought. I couldn't do everything alone. *And I trust Jalil far more than any of the aunts and uncles back there.*

"You did well," Uncle Jalil said, once the wards were firmly in place. I had no doubt my relatives would try to spy on me if they could. "Although you did back them into a corner."

I nodded. "I don't want them to have any room for...creative misinterpretations," I said, flatly. I'd spent half my time at school coming up with loopholes in the rules, but the stakes were a little higher now...and the consequences for failure far worse. "I need them behind me, Uncle, or at least not trying to stab me in the back."

"You bought yourself a year," Uncle Jalil said. He strode over to the window and peered at the overgrown garden. "What are you going to do with it?"

I said nothing for a long moment. I'd gone through the accounts as carefully as I could, highlighting various points for later consideration. I'd studied the reports from the farms, contemplating the prospects for investment...I'd even read the newspapers, looking for ways to make money. I was starting to understand, almost despite myself, my father's desperation. We needed to spend money in order to make money and we couldn't make money because we didn't have the money to spend...

No wonder they didn't oppose me very effectively, I thought. It would have been amusing, if I hadn't been the one in charge. *Even a token show of resistance might have left them holding the bag.*

I turned to face him. "Desperate times call for desperate measures," I said. I did have one thing that was solely within my power to sell. Myself. "I'm going to get married."

CHAPTER EIGHT

"What?" Uncle Jalil caught himself as he turned to face me. "You're going to get married? To whom?"

"Good question," I agreed. "You can help me find a prospective husband."

I tried not to smile at his expression. He looked as if I'd punched him in the stomach or gone out in public wearing trousers. It really shouldn't have surprised him *that* badly. I was nineteen, easily old enough to marry. My father would have been looking for a husband for me from the moment he formally acknowledged me as an adult. I'd known girls who'd been engaged and married before they left school. Now…

Uncle Jalil found his voice. "Lucy…what are you thinking?"

"Desperate times call for desperate measures," I said. I looked him in the eye. "What are my chances of marrying another aristocrat?"

I watched his mouth move silently as he tried to compose an argument that wasn't completely wrong-headed. "You do have a famous name," he said, finally. "And there are families who might value you…"

"No." I shook my head. "We'd be the junior parties in any aristocratic match. The only thing we have of any value is our seat on Magus Court and they'll insist on gaining control as part of the marriage agreement. We'd continue to exist as a name, but little else. House Lamplighter will effectively vanish from the books. And that's the *best*-case outcome."

I went on, trying to hide my own doubts. "And even if that wasn't true, who'd marry me? I don't have wealth or land or anything, really. The most eligible bachelors won't be interested in me. The ones who have power—or will inherit power—will be discouraged by their parents and families. It would have to be someone on the edge of their family and...they wouldn't have any real influence, with or without me. There's no way we can ally ourselves with another Great House."

Uncle Jalil didn't look reassured, but he couldn't dispute my logic. "What do you have in mind?"

"There are commoners, wealthy commoners, who want to move up in the world," I said. "And we have something *they'll* want."

"I..." Uncle Jalil broke off and started again. "You want to marry yourself to a commoner?"

I nodded, trying to ignore the memories of schoolgirls sneering at aristos who married beneath themselves. A commoner might be wealthy enough to stand amongst the aristocrats, perhaps even outshine them, but he wouldn't be able to claim a title dating all the way back to the Thousand Year Empire. The most impoverished Great House was socially superior to a merchant family who could buy and sell everything the aristocracy owned out of pocket cash. I'd heard enough rumours, at school, to know there were merchants who wanted to buy their way into the aristocracy through marriage. They'd had few takers.

"We have something they want," I said. "A name, a title, and a voice in government."

"And everyone else will look down on them," Uncle Jalil said. "They won't be *real* aristocrats."

"Their children will be counted amongst the aristocracy," I said. The Great Houses had no qualms about convincing powerful common-born magicians to marry into their ranks. "My husband might not be counted as their equal, but my children will be aristocrats in their own right."

Uncle Jalil shook his head, slowly. "And that's your plan?"

"Not quite." I tried not to show my own qualms. "I have some ideas for making money, but a terminal shortage of cash. We need money and quickly before we can do anything. So...we find a wealthy commoner who wants to marry into the aristocracy and come to terms with him. A year-long engagement, backed by cash. If I decide, at the end of the year, not to go through with the marriage, we repay the cash. It's simple."

"Really." Uncle Jalil didn't sound pleased. "You're basically selling yourself for money."

"We take the money they give us and use it to make *more* money," I said. "And then we repay them and break the engagement at the end of the year."

Uncle Jalil snorted. "And what if you can't repay them?"

He turned and paced over to the windows. "Lucy, you'd be putting your name to a contract stipulating that you'll be marrying him, or his son, in a year. What happens if you *can't* repay him? You'll be sued. You might wind up having to marry him anyway."

I smiled at his back. "What's the worst that could happen?"

"You might wind up having to marry him anyway," Uncle Jalil repeated, with icy patience. "Or you might wind up being kicked out of the family... which will make life interesting because there's no one who can take your place in the marriage agreement. Or...the best you could hope for, I think, is becoming a laughingstock. No one would ever take you seriously again."

"I don't think they take me seriously now," I said, as I reached for the newspaper. There'd been a time when changes in House Lamplighter would have been reported in breathless tones. Now...I'd read the newspapers religiously since I'd returned to the city. We hadn't been mentioned, not once. My name hadn't even been included in the list of debutantes who'd be starting their season in a few weeks. "Has *anyone* made an offer for my hand?"

Uncle Jalil swung around to face me. "Lucy, this isn't funny," he said. "You're agreeing to marry a stranger, to bear his children..."

"I know." I shook my head. "Do you have a better idea?"

"No," Uncle Jalil said. "But as your uncle I have to warn you…"

"We have very little we can leverage to obtain money," I said. I understood his concern, but we were short on options. "My hand in marriage is the only thing we can offer, as far as I can tell; it's the only thing that will give us the leverage to get what we want on favourable terms. And even if it goes wrong…it won't be the end of the world."

"You may feel differently, after you're married," Uncle Jalil warned.

"Good point," I agreed. "You'd better make sure you find someone young and handsome as well as someone wealthy."

Uncle Jalil emitted a strangled sound. "Lucy…are you sure?"

I met his eyes. "Yes."

"I hope you're right," he said. "You want me to handle the search?"

"Yes." I couldn't trust anyone else to handle it. I couldn't handle the search myself either, not when I was the one who'd make the final decision. Uncle Jalil could always tell an unsatisfactory partner he'd have to check with me, giving him a chance to break off the negotiations without insulting the other party. "Someone wealthy, someone with resources we can use"—I allowed my voice to harden—"and someone desperate enough to pay in advance."

"I hope they gave you the talk when you were at school," Uncle Jalil said, darkly. "You don't know what you're getting into."

I snorted. I'd grown up in the aristocracy. I'd known my parents would have a say in who I married, unless I wanted to elope. The concept of being married to a stranger was hardly unknown. The aristocracy tried hard to ensure the couple had a chance to get to know one another before they signed the contract, but they could never be left alone together. I remembered some of the stories from the dorms and shuddered. There was no shortage of tales about girls who only discovered the terrible truth about their husband on their wedding night. I hoped most of those tales were exaggerated.

"I know," I said. "Once you have a list of prospective candidates, let me know. I'll go through them before we make any final offers."

Uncle Jalil nodded, curtly. "I'll see what I can dig up," he said. "But it won't be easy."

"Just don't tell any of the others," I said. "We don't want them insisting on having their say."

"They'll insist anyway, when they find out what you're planning," Uncle Jalil said. "I doubt they'll be happy if—when—you marry a commoner."

"No," I agreed. "But they'll just have to cope."

I looked down at my hands as he left the room. Uncle Jalil was right. It was a gamble. It was a terrible risk. No one would say anything if we repaid the money before the deadline—marriage contracts were rewritten or broken all the time as the balance of power shifted from side to side—but if we failed to repay the money, we'd find ourselves in hot water. We *would* be sued. Or worse. I could easily see my prospective husband using the disaster as evidence we shouldn't be trusted with his money. *That* would be awkward.

Particularly if he has to take on our debts, I thought. I'd seen the figures. We were in deep trouble. *He might balk at letting us have anything*.

I tried to put the thought out of my mind as I opened the newspaper and started to skim the society pages. As always, the news was a mixture of gossip, rumours and statements put out by paid shills...I shook my head as the reporter detailed the deeds of a notorious rake old enough to be my father. The rake should have shown a little decorum, the reporter insisted; I had the feeling, reading between the lines, that the reporter was a little envious. I rolled my eyes and read the next story. The wedding of Akin Rubén and Caitlyn Aguirre would be formally announced later in the summer—I was sure I'd read the story somewhere before—but no date had been set. I frowned, feeling a twinge of envy. Akin Rubén and Caitlyn Aguirre would be one hell of a power couple. No one would ask *them* to repay their debts.

"If they even have debts," I muttered. I flicked through the pages as a thought crossed my mind. "If she's producing Objects of Power, she can practically set her own prices."

I cursed under my breath. Some people had all the luck. There'd been a flurry of interest in girls who had little or limited magic, the year after the story broke. Grayling's had tested each and every girl in hopes of finding a Zero, to no avail. Everyone had magic, even the ones who could barely cast a spell to save their lives. I'd never been *good* at forging—it wasn't a reputable career for a young lady—but if I'd been a Zero…

There's no point in fretting over what could have been, I told myself. *I'll just have to make do with what I have.*

I found the page I was looking for and read it again. And again. House Rubén and House Aguirre were planning to hold their first joint ball in two weeks, but they didn't have a venue. Or so the reporter claimed. It sounded silly on paper—both families had multiple properties within the city—and the reporter clearly thought they were being stupid, but I could see the problem. Neither of the Great Houses would want to give the impression that they were submitting to the other. If one Great House hosted the ball, the other would be offended. And there wasn't anywhere neutral…

"Everyone's taking sides," I muttered to myself. I'd heard the rumours. House Rubén and House Aguirre were just too powerful. The remaining Great Houses were starting to unite against them. "But no one thought to ask us."

I felt a twinge of irritation at being ignored, even though I knew I should be relieved. We had no armsmen, no army of powerful sorcerers and forgers to take the war to the enemy…the last House War had broken us and we hadn't even been involved in the fighting! We'd been collateral damage. A handful of the more alarmist rumours even suggested we were staring down the barrels of another House War. House Lamplighter might be obliterated in passing or snatched by whoever came out ahead. And that would be the end.

The thought I'd had earlier resurfaced. "We don't owe anything to either side," I muttered, as I put the paper to one side. "*We* could host the ball."

I stood and headed for the door. Dust hung in the air as I walked along the corridor and down the stairs, trying not to notice all the missing portraits. There'd been a painting of me as a baby hanging at the bottom of the stairs, if I recalled correctly. Where was it? I couldn't believe father had managed to *sell* it. Who'd want to buy? I told myself I'd check the basement as I walked into the ballroom. It was dark and cold. Dust lay on the floor like sand on a beach.

Tears welled up in my eyes as I looked around. I'd been a child, the last time we'd held a ball, but I still remembered the lights and sounds and fancy dresses as aristocrats moved around the room. I thought I could hear the band playing a dance tune as I ploughed through the dust, peering into alcoves and small hidden rooms where the *real* business had been transacted...once upon a time. The rooms were shabby, the privacy wards frayed and old. I was surprised my father hadn't maintained them. Surely, he'd hoped to give me a Season...

He didn't have the money, I thought. My heart twisted. I'd been promised a Season...I tried to tell myself I was being silly, or selfish, but it still hurt. I'd heard the stories of fancy gowns and glittering lights and adoring hordes and endless dances while one's parents hammered out the marriage contract. *Father couldn't have afforded a Season for me.*

I gritted my teeth. Kate had pointed out, rather sarcastically, that the debutantes were treated like prize animals, put on display for potential buyers. There was no difference between a debutante ball and a shop window...I'd been mad at her at the time, but I was starting to think she had a point. Maybe *she* was the lucky one. *She* wouldn't be put on display... she might even have the freedom to say *no*, after both sets of parents had hammered out the contract. Akin Rubén and Caitlyn Aguirre might have the power to say no and stand against their families. There weren't many others, boys as well as girls, who could defy their elders without getting kicked out and disowned.

The sinking feeling in my heart grew worse as I walked up the stairs. I remembered the marble shining under the lights, but now it was gray and dull. The dust had made the stairs slippery. I held the banister as I reached the top of the stairs, trying not to curse as the dust—somehow—grew thicker. The spells that should have kept me safe were long gone. I made a mental note to replace them. Nothing could be left to chance. The railings on the balcony didn't look very safe either. I'd have to have them checked too.

Ellington stepped out of a servants' entrance and looked at me. "My Lady, the remaining councillors have left the hall."

"Good," I said. I waved a hand at the floor below. "How long would it take to clean up and fix everything?"

"If we had the staff, a week," Ellington said. "Right now, we don't."

I nodded. He was right. "I want you to think about how to handle it," I said. "If we hire the staff…how much do we need to do to make the hall presentable…things like that."

"My Lady, it would require time and money," Ellington said. He looked around the giant chamber, then back at me. "There are literally *hundreds* of things we'd need to do."

"And what we'd have to do to host a ball," I said. "How long would *that* take?"

Ellington said nothing for a long moment. "Assuming we had the staff, and assuming money wasn't a problem, we could clean the first and second floors in a week or two. We'd have to clean the kitchens and replace some of the equipment before we could cook enough food…we'd probably have to hire more kitchen staff too. It would be tricky."

I nodded. "Start putting together a list of what we need to do, so we can host a ball," I ordered. "Let me worry about getting the cash."

"Yes, My Lady," Ellington said. His expression was bland, but I could hear the doubt in his words. There were aristocrats who'd give him the boot for that. "It will be *quite* expensive."

"I've spotted a gap in the market," I told him. It was true. There *were* advantages to being weak and irrelevant. No one would take advantage of us, or attack us, if there was nothing to gain. "And we have to move fast if we want to take advantage of it."

"Yes, My Lady," Ellington said. He raised a single, polite eyebrow. "Would you like me to put together a more balanced budget as well?"

"No," I said. We'd only get one chance to make a splash. "We have to make this place look perfect. Dust the floors, wipe the windows, polish the brass and gold, refresh the spells, hang up the paintings…everything. We have to move fast."

"Yes, My Lady," Ellington said. I knew him well enough to know he still had his doubts. "I'll see to it at once."

"Please." I smiled at him to conceal *my* doubts. "It's time to bring the hall back to life."

CHAPTER
NINE

"Shit!"

I swore as my father's spells snapped at me, blue sparks burning my skin. His drawers were locked solid, sealed against anyone...even me. He'd been a better sorcerer than I'd realised, I reflected sourly as I rubbed my hand. I supposed I was lucky he hadn't used a stronger or nastier curse. He could have turned a would-be thief into a frog, or frozen him in time, or simply killed him outright. What had my father been trying to hide? I'd spent two days trying to hack the spells and gotten precisely nowhere.

"Language," Uncle Jalil said. He stood in the doorway, his face grim. He held a leather folder under one arm. "You're not old enough to swear like a trooper."

I swallowed the response that came to mind as I straightened up. "Right now, I feel old enough to be a grandmother," I said. My hand hurt too much for me to be polite. "What was he trying to hide?"

"I don't know," Uncle Jalil said. "You might want to call an expert."

"Maybe later," I said. I didn't know who I could trust. "Did you get my note?"

"Yes," Uncle Jalil said. "It's a good idea, if you can get the money."

I sat down, resting my elbows on the table. "And *can* we get the money?"

"If you're determined to go through with your mad plan..." Uncle Jalil nodded as he sat down, resting the folder on his lap. "I have a handful of prospective candidates."

"Good," I said.

"I was very careful," Uncle Jalil said, "but you really didn't give me enough time to do a proper write-up on all of them. Basically, I looked for candidates who wanted to buy their way into the aristocracy, who could afford it and, most importantly of all, didn't have the ability to simply dominate us. Anyone who had strong connections to another Great House was dismissed out of hand. I also decided against a couple of men old enough to be your father and one who could easily have been your grandfather."

"Good thinking," I agreed. An older man would be harder to control. He'd want to control me. "What do we have?"

"I went through the list to confirm they really *were* wealthy, then narrowed it down to nine possibilities," Uncle Jalil explained. "Two of them are rich in their own right, the remainder are sons of wealthy men. Their fathers would be happy, I suspect, to meet our terms. They really *do* want to buy their way into the aristocracy."

"And they'd jump through hoops to get in," I mused. "What's the best choice?"

Uncle Jalil looked displeased. "You're the one who's going to get married, if your scheme fails," he said. He passed me the folder. "I think you should decide for yourself."

I opened the folder and skimmed the contents. Uncle Jalil had done a good job, although—as he'd warned—two days was hardly long enough to carry out a proper background check. It was quite possible to put on a show of wealth that would keep people from asking questions...I had the feeling, looking at the account books, that my father had spent most of his time pretending to be rich. And yet...I shook my head. There was no point in worrying about that now. I had to look to the future.

The first file was a middle-aged man, twenty years older than me. I dismissed him instantly and moved to the next. He was younger, but there were question marks over the precise origin of his wealth. I frowned, putting him aside for later consideration. I had few scruples, but there were limits. I couldn't take the risk of running afoul of a con artist. It would destroy my chances of rebuilding the family fortunes. The third was a young man, a year or so older than me, whose father's money rested in land. I studied the folder for a long minute, thinking hard. The father was definitely wealthy enough to buy House Lamplighter out of pocket change.

"This son should be married already," I said, holding up the file. "What's *wrong* with him?"

"I believe he's completing a charms apprenticeship," Uncle Jalil informed me. "His sister appears to be the one who'll be taking over the family firm. She's got a reputation as a shrewd businesswoman."

"I see," I said. I read the rest of the file. "They're very determined, aren't they?"

"Yes," Uncle Jalil said. "And desperate to be recognised as aristocrats."

I nodded, slowly. The family patriarch had made his money by purchasing land and houses in Water Shallot, then renovating them to sell to families from South Shallot. He been in the right place at the right time to take advantage of the gentrification of the riverside, I noted; he'd reinvested his first fortune, purchased *more* houses and started to rent them out. There was no doubt he was a wealthy man. Uncle Jalil had collected copies of the title deeds. He could easily raise millions of crowns by selling half his properties.

"He doesn't have any land in North Shallot," I mused. Land in North Shallot was expensive, but not *that* expensive. "Why not?"

"I believe he was frozen out, when he tried to buy," Uncle Jalil said. "The landowners were pressured not to sell."

"That makes sense." I winced in sympathy. The aristocrats wouldn't hesitate to slap down a commoner they felt was getting too big for his trousers. They could bring one hell of a lot of pressure to bear against anyone they felt was likely to sell. "I'm surprised my father didn't sell to him."

"The only property we have in North Shallot is Lamplighter Hall," Uncle Jalil said, "and that's entailed. It cannot be sold."

"Yes." I put the file to one side and scanned the others. Two more looked possible, although I didn't care for the way they did business; the remainder had too many warning signs for me to be entirely keen on making them an offer. "They do seem the best candidates."

I turned back to the file and scanned the notes. "Gary Prestwick, charmsmith," I read. "I see he got good marks at Jude's."

"And a good character," Uncle Jalil reminded me. "He wouldn't have gotten his apprenticeship if his tutors hadn't vouched for him."

"I know." I continued to read, wondering if I would have known and liked him if I'd gone to Jude's myself. It was unlikely. He was a commoner. I might not even have so much as known he existed. The year between us would have been an unbridgeable gulf. "He did well, didn't he?"

"Yes," Uncle Jalil said. "Does he take your fancy?"

I gave him a sidelong look. "Does it matter?"

"It does, if you wind up spending the rest of your life with him." Uncle Jalil looked as if he wanted to say something else, but thought better of it. "Lucy...this could go horribly wrong."

"How so?" I could *tell* there was something he wasn't sure he should say. "Uncle...what aren't you telling me?"

"Lucy..." Uncle Jalil let out a breath. "Your parents saw their marriage"—he stopped and started again—"your parents were *mature*. They had come to an agreement about how they should share their lives, after their marriage was arranged, and they stuck to it. They...your parents both knew how things worked. And that's true of their peers too. There are families that exist in name only, with both partners seeing other people. It works because everyone involved knows the score. As long as the families remain united, as long as there's an heir or two, people don't care.

"But your parents both grew up in the same environment. The young men I picked out for you grew up in a very different environment. They might expect something more from you. They might expect…" He shook his head. "I understand your logic, and I do appreciate what you're doing, but you have to be careful. There's only so far you can push someone before they break."

I stared down at my hands. "Uncle…I know the risks."

"We shall see." Uncle Jalil collected his files. "Do you want me to open formal talks with the Prestwick family?"

"Yes," I said. "And we have to hurry."

"That'll give them an advantage," Uncle Jalil warned. "They'll know we're short of cash."

"I know." I wouldn't be surprised if they *already* knew that. If they were that desperate to join the aristocracy, why hadn't they made my father an offer already? I shivered, wondering if they *had*. My father could have declared me an adult years ago, if he'd wished. "We need the money."

"Yes," Uncle Jalil said. "If you want to refurbish the hall in a week, you'll need a *lot* of money."

"And try to pressgang the rest of the family into picking up brushes and helping," I said, dryly. "Do you want to help?"

"Not really." Uncle Jalil shrugged. "I'll open negotiations with them, see what they say."

"Please." I stood. "This is our only hope of overcoming our debts and making something of ourselves."

"I think there are limits on how much we can make by offering the hall as neutral ground," Uncle Jalil said. "They're not going to pay for *everything*."

I shrugged. "We'll see," I said. "They might pay for refurbishing if they see the advantages of having neutral ground."

Uncle Jalil stood and headed for the door. "I'll be back as soon as possible," he said. "And you'd better read the contract carefully."

He left, closing the door behind him. I scowled, unwilling to admit his warnings had resonated with me. I'd heard all the stories about how marriage *really* worked, but I hadn't believed them until now. The dreams of romantic love had always been a chimera for me and my peers. I wondered, suddenly, which families truly existed in name only. As long as they put a happy face on in public, no one would give much of a damn.

But it's different for the commoners, I told myself. *Isn't it?*

I stood, pushed the chair back and knelt beside the charmed drawers. They remained firmly closed—the scars on my hand bore mute testament to their defences—even as I muttered a pair of countercharms. The locking spells held firm. I briefly considered getting a spellbreaker or wardcracker and putting it against the drawers, but I had a feeling that would trigger an explosion. There *was* a fairly simple spell designed to disintegrate everything inside the container if the wards started to fail. My father wouldn't have needed help to cast it. He'd been a skilled sorcerer.

Blue sparks snapped at me. I yanked my hand back, muttering words I wasn't supposed to know. Now…I snorted as I studied the keyhole. I was an adult. I could swear blue murder if I liked, although—as a young aristocratic debutante—I probably shouldn't swear too loudly. The Grande Dames of High Society, who'd be on the prowl for any excuse to tear down someone younger and prettier than themselves, would take advantage of my lapse to crush me. The men wouldn't care, but…they'd be made to care. Or at least to pretend to care.

My eyes lingered on the keyhole for a long moment. It was nothing more than a formality…or was it? I knew a hundred charms that could open and close simple locks. I'd used them time and time again, at school, until I could cast them without leaving a trace. No sorcerer worthy of the name would rely on a simple physical lock. It could be picked easily…

I drew a hairpin from my hair and poked the lock gingerly. Nothing happened for a long moment, then blue sparks lashed out at me. I threw myself back just in time. The charms still held good. I glared at the keyhole, wondering why it was even there. I'd seen trunks and drawers and even cabinets that had no visible keyholes. They'd just drawn attention…I stood, brushing down my dress. Father hadn't been stupid. If he'd left the keyhole in place, there must have been a reason.

My eyes drifted around the room. The bookshelves looked untouched. The cabinets were open, but useless. I'd gone through the paperwork and found nothing beyond account books carefully sorted into two piles. Father had clearly kept a *lot* of secrets from the rest of the family. I wondered, as I inched towards the bookshelves, why no one had thought to question him. Had they been afraid of what they might find?

Up close, the books definitely looked untouched, as if they'd been purchased in bulk and then simply placed on the shelves and abandoned. I scanned the titles, wondering why my father had even *wanted* them. Books on every magical subject under the sun contrasted oddly with titles on distant lands, empires that had died so long ago no one remembered their names, and tomes on theories most people considered absurd. Why…I remembered my schooling and smiled. A bookshelf was a great place to hide something you didn't want found. I started removing the books on the topmost shelf and feeling behind them. It wasn't long before my fingers touched something metallic. I picked it up and carried it into view. It was a tiny gold—and charmed—key.

"Clever," I said, as I carried it back to the desk. "The charms can't be undone without the key."

I knelt beside the drawers and pushed the key into the lock. Magic sparkled over me, then faded as I turned the key. The drawer snapped open. I pulled it out and peered inside. A handful of account books, a pair of notebooks and a spellcaster that felt…*wrong*. My skin crawled when I touched it. I had no idea what my father had been doing with it, but it had clearly left a mark. I tried not to disturb it as I removed the account books. There was a small pile of letters underneath. I took them too, then closed the drawer. I'd have to go through them all.

The letters were charmed, but I had no trouble opening them. Mistress Grayling's handwriting, all too familiar from my years at school, leapt off the page. She'd written to my father to remind him of the deal he'd made, the deal that allowed me to stay at the school...I frowned, wishing she'd been a little more direct. The letter was suspicious, but hardly incriminating. I suspected that meant they were trying to hide something. If they'd come to an agreement to defer payment for a few years, they'd hardly have been reluctant to write it down.

I frowned as I read through the remaining papers. Father had written to everyone for money, it seemed, and they'd all turned him down. I spotted a handful of very familiar names amongst the letters, names I knew from school gossip. And, at the bottom, there was a letter signed by Zadornov. It told my father, in no uncertain terms, that he had two weeks to repay his debts. There was no 'or else' but it was clearly implied. The letter was dated ten days before my father's death.

A shiver ran down my spine as I reread the letter. Uncle Jalil hadn't said much, hardly anything, about Zadornov. Who was he? Why had he loaned my father money? Why had he made a *personal* loan? I opened the account books and frowned as I ran my eye down the figures. The interest rate *had* been impossibly high. My father must have been mad. Or desperate...

And yet, he didn't try to marry me off, I thought numbly. *That speaks well of him, doesn't it?*

There was a knock at the door. I hastily put the letters and notebooks back in the drawer, then concealed the key in my pocket. "Come!"

Uncle Jalil stepped into the room. "I spoke to Danny Prestwick, Gary's father."

I blinked. How long had I been lost in my thoughts?

"Good," I said, absently. I was still reeling from the letters. "What did he say?"

"He's prepared to advance us the money," Uncle Jalil said. He reached into his pocket and produced a slip of charmed parchment. "He wants a very solid agreement in exchange, Lucy, and he wants you to get to know his son too."

I took the parchment and read it carefully, line by line. Mistress Grayling had told us, more than once, that we had to pay close attention to *anything* we signed. It was quite easy to accidentally sign away *everything*, if we weren't careful. Danny Prestwick's lawyer was surprisingly blunt. If we failed to repay the advance one year after the contract was signed, I would have to go through with the marriage or lose everything.

"It might not hold up in court," Uncle Jalil said. "But we can't afford decent lawyers."

"We do have Uncle Stefano," I reminded him.

"Stefano hasn't argued in front of a court for years," Uncle Jalil snapped. "I wouldn't trust him to argue that water is wet or that two plus two equals four. And even if I did…there's very little room for creative misunderstandings. Lucy…he thinks he has us over a barrel. That's why the negotiations were so short. If we don't repay him, you *will* have to go through with it."

"So you keep saying." I reread the parchment carefully. "Do we have a choice?"

Uncle Jalil said nothing.

"No," I said. "What happens if *he* refuses to go through with it?"

"I imagine his father will deal with him," Uncle Jalil said. "That will be…unpleasant."

I stared down at the contract. If something went wrong…I was going to marry someone I didn't know, someone I hadn't even *met*. And too many things could go wrong. I wished, suddenly, that I'd turned my back and walked away. But I couldn't. It would have meant abandoning the family.

"I'll meet him at the ball," I said, as I signed. "And, as soon as I get the money, we'll start work."

CHAPTER TEN

"You'll be pleased to know that House Rubén and House Aguirre have accepted your offer to hold the ball," Uncle Jalil said, five days later. "They've even agreed to pay for your services."

I nodded, feeling stiff and sore. Ellington had gone to the Hiring Hall and hired a hundred maids, cleaners and part-time sorcerers to prepare for the ball, but it was still a staggeringly huge task. I'd watched maids working in droves to dust the floors, polish the brass and everything else we needed to do, then walked down to the kitchens to check on the hired staff as they cleaned the stoves, replaced the preservation spells on the cellars and stockpiled enough food and drink to accommodate an army. I had the nasty feeling an army might be preferable. We'd told everyone who'd listen that the hall was neutral ground, that we had no interest in the feuds and infighting that dominated High Society, but the only thing keeping the Great Houses from trying to drag us into the fray was the simple fact we had nothing to offer. That might change, if my plans worked.

Unless they're happy to let us stay in the middle, I thought, as I brushed sweat from my brow. I'd hoped and prayed to my ancestors, but there'd been no guarantee House Rubén and House Aguirre would accept my proposal. It was all too easy, as I tossed and turned in my uncomfortable bed, to fear the worst. *We want them to think of us as harmless middlemen.*

I scowled as we walked through the hall, keeping a respectful distance from the hired men. Jadish stood in a crowd of maids, directing them to clean the bedrooms, change the bedding and scrub the bathrooms before the first guests arrived. I doubted we'd have many, at least the first time, but we couldn't keep the hired servants forever. They'd go back to the Hiring Hall when the money ran out. I nodded to her, then led Uncle Jalil up the stairs to the uppermost floor. It had been carefully sealed off before the hired hands had been allowed to enter the hall. Anyone caught there would be sacked without reference.

"They're working wonders," Uncle Jalil said. "I didn't think they could get the dust out of those carpets."

"Me neither," I said. The drapes had once been colourful, if my memories didn't lie. They'd been so laden with dust they'd been on the verge of collapse before they'd been cleaned. "Did they have a chance to clean your room?"

"I can handle that myself," Uncle Jalil said. "Right now, you have to worry about the hall."

"Tell me about it," I said, as we entered the office. "What about the other Great Houses?"

"I've had sniffs of interest from several others," Uncle Jalil said. "I think they're waiting to see how the first ball goes before they commit themselves. They'll definitely see advantage in holding some of the other mixed balls here, particularly given the rumoured troubles between Bolingbroke and McDonald, but it all depends on how we do."

"Then we'd better do very well," I said. "I put Ellington in charge. He's doing a good job."

"Your aunts won't like it," Uncle Jalil said. "Have you told them you're engaged?"

I winced. Auntie Dorcas had thrown a fit when I'd told her. The others had either screamed or fainted. Apparently, I was marrying beneath myself. No one short of an Heir Primus would suffice for me. They didn't seem to know, or care, that no Heir Primus would marry me and, if one *did*, the family's independence would vanish like morning dew. I'd heard more nonsense in half an hour from my relatives than I'd heard over the last six years at school, where one couldn't reasonably expect the snooty girls to know better. To hear them talk, you'd think I was defiled forever. I might as well be marrying the lad who ate the dung.

"Yes," I said. Uncle Jalil hadn't been there, for which I was grateful. He already had enough enemies on the council. "They weren't pleased."

"As I expected," Uncle Jalil said. "The next year will be very interesting."

"Hah." I made a rude sound as I sat behind the desk. "Either we earn enough money to repay the loan and break the agreement, or I get married."

"And they try to strip you of your post," Uncle Jalil said.

"We'll see," I said. If my plans failed, I probably would lose my post. I wondered how *that* would affect the marriage contract. It was quite possible they'd sue us for breaking the agreement…. I shrugged. It wouldn't be my fault. "Uncle, I need to ask you something. Again. Who's Zadornov?"

Uncle Jalil let out a heavy sigh. "I'd hoped the matter would remain forgotten."

"I don't think this is something that'll go away," I said, as I opened the drawer and removed the secret accounts. "Uncle…who is Zadornov?"

"Officially, he's a businessman with a somewhat shady reputation," Uncle Jalil said, with another sigh. "Unofficially, he's a loan shark, a smuggler and quite possibly a few other things as well. Rumour insists he's been connected with everything from arson and theft to kidnapping, rape and assassination. There's never been any evidence of anything beyond making dubious loans."

"Like the one he made to my father?" I passed him the account books. "What was he thinking?"

"Your father? I imagine he was desperate." Uncle Jalil skimmed the books with practiced ease. "And Zadornov? I dare say he thought he could get something out of the deal."

I let out a breath. "What do we *do* about it?"

"Legally speaking, the debt died with your father," Uncle Jalil said. "There are no grounds for him to demand the money back from you, or the family as a whole."

"And practically speaking?" I ran my hand through my hair. "If he demands the money back, what then?"

"I don't know," Uncle Jalil said. "We got a nice lump sum, but..."

I met his eyes. "It's not enough to cover the debt, is it?"

"No." Uncle Jalil shook his head. "I'm afraid not."

"We'll just have to wait and see if he comes calling," I said. "And then decide what to do about it."

"I think he'll wait until you become successful," Uncle Jalil said. "There's nothing to be gained by trying to force you to give him money you don't have."

"Yeah," I agreed. I cleared my throat, changing the subject. "Will Gary be at the ball?"

"Yes." Uncle Jalil paused, meaningfully. "We *are* obliged to provide a chaperone."

I made a face. Traditionally, the chaperone should be an older woman, but there weren't many candidates. Auntie Dorcas would be unbearable, no matter who I married. The others were even worse. I could ask a girlfriend, but most of my old friends were either still at school or disqualified. Kate would be terribly out of place. Marlene...I shook my head. I needed it examined for thinking of her, even for a second. She'd embarrass me in front of the Great Houses.

"Jadish can chaperone us, when we're not in public," I said. It wasn't perfect, but I could rely on Jadish to cover for me. "It should please everyone."

"It'll please no one," Uncle Jalil predicted. "They'll insist you ordered Jadish to lie."

"We'll just have to live with it," I said. "There aren't any other candidates."

"If you say so." Uncle Jalil returned the account books. "I'd say your father was insane, but...I know he was desperate. And the way all his endeavours kept failing...I'd almost say he was cursed."

"I didn't think that was possible," I said. "Is it?"

"He had a habit of taking risks," Uncle Jalil said. "And eventually they caught up with him."

There was a knock on the door. I looked up. "Come!"

Jadish stepped into the room and dropped a curtsy. "My Lady, the dressmaker is here."

I groaned inwardly as I stood. "Show her to the fitting room," I said. "I'll be down in a moment."

"Yes, My Lady," Jadish said.

"I'll talk to you later," I told Uncle Jalil as Jadish withdrew. "And we can decide what to do about the secret debts after the ball."

I felt cold as I walked down to the fitting room, feeling—again—a grim awareness of just how poor we truly were. I'd hired one of the most exclusive dressmakers in the city, but she normally catered to the upper middle classes. The Great Houses had dressmakers of their own, dressmakers and tailors who'd grown up in the families.... I gritted my teeth in frustration. It would be decades, at least, before House Lamplighter reached the heights again. I doubted my children would want to train as dressmakers.

"You must be Lucilla," the dressmaker said, as I stepped into the fitting room. She was a short woman with a bright smile and white hair. I had the feeling she was plump, but her long dress made it hard to be sure. "I'm Garland. Just Garland."

"Just Lucy," I said. Lucilla might be my formal name, but I'd always preferred Lucy. "Thank you for coming."

"It's quite alright, my dear." Garland patted me on the shoulder, then pulled me into the centre of the room. "You want a formal dress, right? Just one?"

"For the moment," I said. Dresses were expensive. Marlene and her peers might be able to buy dresses by the cartload, but I'd bankrupt myself if I tried. "And I need it fast."

"So I hear." Garland pulled a spellcaster out of her pocket and waved it around me. "Your measurements are pretty simple. I can tailor another dress to fit you, if you like. It'll be cheaper and quicker than making something new."

"That would be good," I said. "What do you have in mind?"

"Depends on you, my dear," Garland said. "You're the host, if I understand correctly, but not the centre of attention. You want to look masterful, to make it clear you're in charge, yet you don't want to dominate the room. That's quite a challenge."

"Men have it easy," I said, as she wrapped a measuring tape around my thighs. "They don't have to wear fancy dresses."

Garland winked at me. "It takes more effort to hide their bellies, my dear."

I had to smile. "I'll take your word for it."

"You should." Garland winked, again. "You don't want to compete, so I suggest you keep it simple. A long evening gown, perhaps. Your family crest will go on the breast, but nothing else. Keep your neckline clean, without even a necklace. I'd suggest tightening the garment around the breasts, but not actually revealing any bare flesh. You don't want them thinking of you as a young woman, or indeed a woman at all."

"I don't think that's possible," I pointed out. "I've got breasts."

"And you can dress to draw attention away from them, my dear," Garland explained, as she kept poking at me. "Dress is half the battle."

She leaned back and looked me up and down. "White, green or blue would go well with your skin, but they're striking. I'd suggest a dull red. I should be able to alter a couple of dresses to fit you, if you like those colours. Or you could wear black, in memory of your father. I think you could carry it off nicely."

I held up a hand. "I'll stick with red," I said. "What else do you advise?"

"Red should suffice," Garland said. "I'll have to make you something else, if you go to another ball. You won't be running the show there."

"No," I agreed. "Green, for the second dress. I don't want to look too striking."

Garland nodded as she finished taking measurements. "I'll be back tomorrow with the refitted dresses," she said. "I normally charm them against everything from rain to ill-use, and I can weave a handful of cooling charms into the garment if you wish, but I'm not sure how well the refitted dresses will take the charms. You may have to renew them. I can also add a deflation charm, but…"

I shook my head. "I think I can manage without," I said. "How quickly can you finish the work?"

"It shouldn't be more than a day or so," Garland assured me. "I'll do much of the work when I get back to the shop, then I can either finish the job here tomorrow or bring them back to you the following day. You'll have them in time for the ball."

And hope they don't look second-hand, I thought. The Grande Dames would be watching me like…Grande Dames. Even *hawks* weren't as perceptive as Grande Dames looking for something to complain about. *That might get embarrassing.*

I sighed inwardly as I rang the bell for Jadish. Garland was right, in at least one sense. It wasn't really *my* ball, even though I was the hostess. I wasn't going to be the centre of attention…and yet, by hosting the ball, I was going to *attract* attention. It was going to be an interesting balancing act. Hopefully, the old ladies would think I'd have a Season next year…or that I'd been denied the chance to have one through no fault of my own. *Father* could have given me a Season. Holding one for myself would have seemed a little…egotistical.

And pointless, given that I'm not going to marry a fellow aristocrat, I told myself, as Jadish escorted the older woman off the premises. *Why would anyone come to my Season if they know I'm not going to marry them?*

Jadish returned, looking grim. "My Lady," she said. "Lord Jalil said you wished to see me."

"I need a chaperone," I said. "Will you do the honours?"

"I…" Jadish caught herself. "My Lady?"

It was hard to put my thoughts into words. "The man I might marry is coming to the ball," I said. "I need to speak to him. Alone. But not alone. I need you to be with us, your ears jammed firmly shut."

"Yes, My Lady," Jadish said. "Do you want me to look away too?"

"Perhaps." I felt myself blush. Thankfully, my colouring hid it. "It depends."

"Yes, My Lady." Jadish dropped a curtsy. "I'll do as you wish."

I smiled, then sobered. "How are things? I mean...how are things really?"

Jadish hesitated. "We're going to need more staff...more *permanent* staff," she said, carefully. "We just can't keep the hall going without more people. There's no way we can keep the place clean, let alone do anything else..."

"I understand," I said. "And I'll work on it. My father..."

I looked at her. "How *was* my father?"

"I really couldn't say, My Lady." Jadish looked down. "It isn't my place..."

"Yes, it is," I said. "I won't be angry, whatever you say."

Jadish didn't look convinced. "He was never able to focus," she said, finally. "And he was never concerned with running the house."

"Thanks," I said, rather sourly. I'd guessed that much for myself. "I'll try and do better."

I dismissed her with a nod, wondering if she wanted the post of housemistress. Jadish was young, but there wasn't anyone more familiar with the house. We'd explored every last inch of the building, save for the uppermost floor, as children. Ellington would probably be pleased if his granddaughter was promoted. The old man was getting on in years, no matter how he tried to hide it. Perhaps that was why he'd allowed the hall to decay. He'd simply been too tired to do his job.

Time to go back to work, I told myself as I headed back to the office. I had to take the long way around. The painters were hastily slapping paint on faded wallpapers, muttering spells to ensure the paper was thoroughly hidden under the paint. *There's too much to do.*

The days seemed to blur together as the ball came closer. I worked from dawn 'til dusk, checking and rechecking everything to ensure nothing went wrong. I barely had time to get my dress fitted, even though I knew my aunties would make a fuss if I looked anything less than perfect. They were largely useless...I wanted to disown them, simply because they refused to do anything to help prepare the hall. There was no reason Auntie Dorcas couldn't have helped host the ball, damn it. I didn't *think* she was public enemy number one, although I wasn't sure of it. It was certainly odd for her—and the others—to refuse to help when they could have taken advantage of the work to make new contacts. I was more than a little worried about it.

And we're spending money we might not be able to repay, I reminded myself. Ice congealed in my heart every time I thought about it. The money—my dowry—had been a sizable sum, only a few short days ago. I'd done everything I could to cut costs, but we were still spending money like a teenage aristocrat...the irony wasn't lost on me. *What happens if we can't pay it back?*

The question mocked me. I knew the answer. I'd get married and then...

I shook my head. It wasn't going to happen. I was going to take what I had and parlay it into money and rebuild my family and repay the loan and...

And I'll have to come up with something else, I told myself, feeling a twinge of desperation. I had a year, but I already felt trapped. *Merely hosting balls isn't going to be enough.*

CHAPTER
ELEVEN

"Why aren't the debutantes walking down the stairs?" Auntie Dorcas whispered, as we stood by the doors and welcomed the guests to the hall. "They're entering like commoners!"

I resisted the urge to say or do something thoroughly unpleasant. Auntie Dorcas had finally—*finally*—agreed to help host, but she'd spent most of the afternoon either criticising or complaining. Nothing was good enough for her, from the piles of food and drink to the dresses I'd had cleaned for the rest of the family. If there had been any other choice, any at all, I'd have banned her from the entrance and probably from the entire hall. It wasn't as if she hadn't had *days* to offer her comments.

"This is an informal ball," I muttered. It was really more of a formal informal ball, but the nasty part of my mind insisted she wouldn't understand. "It isn't a formal coming-out."

I pasted a smile on my face as the Aguirre triplets stepped into the hall and curtsied to me. Alana was tall, a sharp smile on her dark face; I felt a stab of envy, knowing *Alana* and her sisters would never have to worry about money. House Aguirre was rich and powerful beyond words. Bella looked bored, despite the opportunities for networking; Caitlyn looked as if she would rather be somewhere—anywhere—else. The three girls still had their hair in braids, even though they were passing eighteen. I was pretty sure that burned, even though it had its uses. They'd be spared the worst consequences of their mistakes.

"Thank you for inviting us," Alana said, in a tone that suggested I should be grateful she'd darkened my door. "And congratulations on assuming the Matriarchy."

"I thank you," I said. It would be a long time before *Alana* became Matriarch of House Aguirre. I was pretty sure, from what I'd read in the newspapers, that she was already undergoing a long apprenticeship. Her father probably already bounced ideas off her...I kept my face under tight control, trying to hide the sudden spurt of grief. I'd have sold my soul for a proper relationship with *my* father. "I trust you'll enjoy the day."

They curtseyed again. I tried not to stare at the Object of Power dangling from Caitlyn's neck. It was hard to tell what it *did*—I guessed it was a protection charm of some kind—but it was a sign she could not be taken lightly. I'd heard the rumours about her, back when I'd been a child. She'd had no magic, they'd said. I had a feeling all the people who'd mocked her—and her family—were kicking themselves. Caitlyn's talent was all the more important for being so *rare*. If there were any other Zeros around, they were keeping their talents to themselves.

I watched them go into the hall, then turned to meet the next set of guests. They started to blur together as the evening wore on, from older men and women who seemed disinclined to take me seriously to younger aristocrats who almost seemed...*envious*. I supposed they didn't *know* how desperate we were. They probably thought I had wealth and power and the freedom to do whatever I wanted. They didn't realise I was trying to find a way to keep the family afloat.

A low gong echoed through the hall as the servants brought out the first trays of food. The band started to play. I turned to stare, feeling oddly out of place in my own home. Ellington and the staff had done a wonderful job. I barely recognised the hall. The dust was gone, the marble and brass had been cleaned, banners hung from the walls...I shook my head, trying to pretend—just for a moment—that it wasn't borrowed glory. Jadish had been right. We simply didn't have the staff to keep up appearances. And yet, appearances were all we had.

"Go circle the room," Auntie Dorcas advised. "Press the flesh. And be *seen* to press the flesh."

I nodded, not trusting myself to speak. I was the hostess. Everything rested on me. And I had to look as calm and composed as a duck drifting on the water. I smiled, remembering how my etiquette tutors had explained that ducks always looked calm on the surface, while paddling desperately underwater. My staff knew what to do, I reassured myself. I could afford to relax, just a little bit, and enjoy myself.

The dancers moved onto the floor and started to dance in time with the music. I watched, trying not to feel too envious of the other girls. They wore fancy dresses, each unique…I hoped. I'd heard the rumours of what had happened when two aristocratic women had attended the same ball, wearing the same dress from a supposedly exclusive designer. Their frank exchange of views had turned into a full-scale brawl, with hexes and curses flying everywhere. I prayed that wouldn't happen in Lamplighter Hall. I'd done what I could with the wards, but they were nowhere near as strong and capable as I wished.

I walked from group to group, feeling ever more out of place. I didn't fit in with the girls my age, the ones who had their own little cliques from Jude's. They seemed unsure what to make of me. I was their age, yet I was the host. And the older aristocrats had no place for me either. They seemed to think I was too young to be taken seriously…or, perhaps, they knew I had little to offer. I drifted around the room, acknowledging the handful of bows and curtsies I got from the other aristocrats. And…

"You wouldn't believe just how much money I made in the last week," a voice said. I turned, trying not to prick up my ears *too* obviously. If there was one thing I'd learnt at school, it was how to listen without making it obvious. "I found out what Tailstock wanted, and by golly I gave it to him."

I felt a sudden flicker of interest. The speaker—Robin Bolingbroke, if I recalled correctly—was an unpleasantly corpulent man, one arm wrapped around a woman several years his junior. He was holding forth to a cluster of other men, all of whom were listening to his drunken rambles with rapt attention. I felt a flicker of distaste, mingled with interest. Robin Bolingbroke was something in finance, if I recalled correctly. He had to be rich, with his own money as well as his family allowance. The woman next to him, wearing a dress so low it was on the verge of slipping off, wouldn't have given him the time of day if he didn't have money.

Robin Bolingbroke went on and on, babbling about dealings I could barely follow. He'd figured out what someone wanted, I thought from what little I could understand, and found a way to give it to them...creaming off a hefty profit in the bargain. I silently replayed what he'd said in my head, trying to sort out what he'd done. He couldn't have done it without money...could he? A thought started to nag at the back of my mind as Robin turned away, guiding his mistress towards the private rooms. I felt a stab of sympathy for the poor woman. Who was she? And why was she desperate enough to ally herself with...him?

I put the thought out of my mind as I continued to circle the room, listening to private conversations. Robin's plan had worked, I suspected, because Robin had had the money to gamble. He could lose his personal fortune, if things went wrong, but simply fall back on his allowance. And he was hardly the Patriarch. Simon Bolingbroke had no obligations to pay Robin's debts. The wretched man couldn't lose.

"It's not easy to get the parts these days," another man said. I recognised him as a distant relation of Lord Carioca Rubén, although I couldn't place the name. "The artificers are doubling their prices and refusing to experiment."

"Then you should invest in more artificers, Albrecht," his partner said. "Or maybe work to convince them to experiment."

I frowned as I walked around them, mentally picking apart the conversation. It was hard to believe House Rubén, of all the Great Houses, was short of artificers and forgers. It wasn't as if they didn't have the money to invest in experimentation either. And yet...I listened as covertly as I could, then moved on before they noticed. I had a feeling there was an *in* there, if I could find it. I promised myself I'd consider it later, when the ball was over. Right now, I had too much else on my mind.

The evening slowly turned to night as I kept moving, my eyes crisscrossing the ballroom. Caitlyn Aguirre talked to Akin Rubén, her betrothed; a pair of older women stood nearby, close enough to keep a sharp eye on them without actually listening. I wondered, idly, if I could arrange a private meeting between them...it would be good to have one or both of them owing me a favour. Ayesha and Zeya McDonald were flirting outrageously with a pair of boys I didn't recognise, both countrified by their accents; I had a feeling the flirtation was going to end in heartbreak. Saline Califon strode across the room, her face grim and cold. And, behind her, I saw Marlene. She looked, in her own way, as isolated as myself.

My eyes narrowed. *That* was odd. Marlene had always bragged about her friends back home...

A hand touched my arm. I tried not to jump as I turned to see Auntie Dorcas. I mentally kicked myself for allowing myself to get lost in my own thoughts. I'd exposed my back...I told myself, sharply, that I was no longer at school. High Society had its dangers, but being hexed in the back was not one of them. Probably. It would be the height of rudeness to throw a hex at the hostess in her own domain.

"Lucilla." Auntie Dorcas said. "Your young man"—her lips thinned with distaste—"is waiting in the green room."

"Thank you," I said, feeling my heart skip a beat. It was a business transaction, nothing more...yet I couldn't help feeling nervous. The meeting could end badly. "I'll be there in a moment."

"I shall accompany you," Auntie Dorcas said. "Your reputation must not be tarnished..."

It was all I could do not to scream, even though we were in public. "I need you on the floor," I said, pitching my voice as low as I could. "Jadish will chaperone us."

Auntie Dorcas looked irked. I gave her a warning stare, then turned and walked through the throng. She'd probably hoped I'd put up with her peering over my shoulder, rather than make a public fuss. It would have made me look weak, whatever happened. Auntie Dorcas might pretend she cared about my reputation, but I knew better. She thought she could limit my authority. I took a breath, calming myself as best as I could. She'd had her chance. I wouldn't hesitate to banish her if she challenged me too openly.

I passed Auntie Ainslie, who was cheerfully assuring a group of old biddies that House Lamplighter was honouring its ancestors by wearing their clothes. It was hard not to smile at her blatant lies—we would have bought new clothes for everyone, if we could have afforded them—even though I had to admit it was a pretty good story. I made a mental note to work on it. The Great Houses were *big* on tradition. We might start a whole new fashion by going back to a very old one.

Jadish waited outside the door, wearing an outdated maid's uniform. It was far too frilly for my tastes, but she made it look good. She curtsied as soon as she saw me, then stepped back. I felt oddly nervous, unsure of myself. I'd spoken to boys before—I'd even had a couple of local boyfriends, when I'd been at school—but this was different. It was a business transaction and yet it wasn't...I winced, inwardly. It didn't matter. I was committed. I'd been committed from the moment I signed the contract and taken the money.

I pushed open the door, telling myself—again and again—that I could cope, that I could handle whatever happened...that, as a mature woman, I could deal with anything. And yet, I didn't *feel* mature. I wished, suddenly, that my mother was still alive, or that I had a female relative I could trust. I'd hate to take advice from Auntie Dorcas. She'd always keep one eye on how she could make a situation work for her.

"Lady Lamplighter." The boy inside the room stood and bowed. "I'm Gary Prestwick."

I studied him, all too aware he was studying me too. He didn't *look* any older than me...indeed, his curly hair and babyish face made him look slightly younger. His skin was strikingly pale, his rounded head topped with blond hair that reminded me—however faintly—of Akin Rubén. I wondered if there might be a family connection, then snorted at myself for the thought. Blond hair proved nothing. Uncle Jalil's background check hadn't turned up any links to the aristocracy.

My eyes roamed over his body, reading the clues. His black suit was simple, yet perfectly tailored. He looked slim, although he lacked the sporty appearance that was so fashionable amongst the aristocracy. His hands were faintly scarred, suggesting a background in forgery as well as charms. There were strong ties between the two disciplines, if I recalled correctly; a charmsmith could easily become a forger, without needing to start again.

Jadish closed the door behind us, a little louder than necessary. I was almost grateful for the reminder she was there. Auntie Dorcas would have been obnoxious, at the least...and she was the *best* of my female relatives. I wondered, not for the first time, why my father hadn't offered my hand in marriage well before I'd left school. Sure, I could have said no...but why hadn't he even tried to talk me into it?

"Gary," I said. My throat was suddenly dry. I was all too aware of the wards pressing down on us. The family might be *spying* on us...I didn't *think* Auntie Dorcas could hack the wards, but it was possible. She'd lived in the hall long enough to fiddle with the spellforms before she moved out. "I'm Lucy."

Gary sat down, looking just as awkward as I felt. "It's good to meet you," he mumbled, glancing nervously at Jadish. "I've heard a lot about you."

"Oh dear." I managed a smile at the weak joke. "Don't believe everything you read in all the major newspapers."

"I never read them," Gary said. He grinned. I was surprised by how much it lit up his face. "They told me you were good at charms."

I wondered, idly, who'd told him that—and why. I'd done well in charms—and I'd learnt how to hack them, thanks to school—but I wasn't an expert. Perhaps Uncle Jalil had been trying to convince Gary I'd make a good match. That was odd, but my uncle was perhaps the only one who'd understand Gary's point of view. He was minor aristocracy, only a step or two up from a commoner. Auntie Dorcas would be completely unsympathetic to him. She'd assume he'd be grateful to marry into the family.

"I like to study them," I said. It was true, sort of. "Perhaps we can talk about them in a less…formal…setting."

"I think I'm supposed to clear my throat here," Jadish said. She made a sound that was more like a lion preparing to roar. "Right?"

I had to smile as Gary flushed. "Maybe not," I said. "Tell me about yourself."

It had been, I decided as our meeting finally came to an end, a pleasant hour. Gary didn't disgrace himself. I hoped I hadn't disgraced myself either. It would be embarrassing if Gary's father demanded the money back ahead of time, or forced his son to stay with me even though he disliked me…I'd seen unhappy marriages amongst the aristocracy. I'd heard the stories and rumours too. They never ended.

"I'll see you again," I promised. Jadish would show him out, ensuring the guests didn't have a chance to see him and gossip. "Somewhere better, I think."

Gary smiled as he stood and bowed. "Be seeing you."

I nodded, then walked back to the ballroom. It had grown later than I'd realised. The guests were starting to drift outside, summoning their carriages and heading home. A gust of wind blew across the lawn, bringing with it the promise of a better future. I saw Robin Bolingbroke clambering into his carriage, accompanied by his mistress. He was too drunk to get inside until she helped him with a quick spell. I hoped he forgot how talkative he'd been. He'd given me an idea…

Marlene walked up to me. "You threw a good party, Lucy."

"Thanks," I said, sardonically. It had been a ball, not a party. I doubted she cared. "Did you have a good time?"

"I met my friends," Marlene said. "So, yeah…"

I watched her walk down to the gate and frowned. She didn't have a carriage? She shouldn't be in any danger if she walked home—she had strong magic, as well as a family name—but it was odd for an aristocrat to walk. People would talk. I shook my head—it wasn't my problem—and turned to head back inside. I was tired, desperately tired…

…And an idea, a very interesting idea, was starting to take shape in my mind.

CHAPTER TWELVE

"Have you seen the papers?"

I scowled at Uncle Jalil as I stepped into the kitchenette. My uncle looked disgustingly fresh and alert for someone who was not only old enough to be my father, but couldn't have gone to bed last night any earlier than I had. A small pile of letters and newspapers rested on the table beside my chair, half of them probably nothing more than brief notes of thanks—written and signed by the secretary's secretary—for hosting the ball. I poured myself a mug of coffee, silently grateful I hadn't joined my peers in drinking. I'd managed to get drunk once, just once. The hangover had been bad enough to convince me to swear off drinking for life.

"No," I said. The coffee tasted vile, but it woke me up. "What do they say?"

Uncle Jalil picked up the society pages and made a show of reading aloud. "A fantastic debut…a glimpse of a brighter future…a stunning new face on the scene…marvellous food…wonderful drink and plenty of it…"

I snorted. "How much did we pay the reporters?"

"We didn't." Uncle Jalil grinned, although there was little real humour on his face. "How many invitations do you think the reporters will get if they badmouth the hosts?"

"None." I sat down and picked up the closest newspaper. "Do they get paid by the superlative?"

"Probably." Uncle Jalil shrugged. "Oh, by some standards the ball was boring. Boring and...well, boring."

I smirked, despite myself. "How *boring*."

"Point is, you don't want the ball to be *too* exciting," Uncle Jalil said. "You hosted two rival families—and a bunch of others—and no one got embarrassed, or cursed, or killed, or anything. A good time was had by all. You'll be able to host more balls in the future."

"How lucky for us," I said, sourly. The ball might have gone well, but I'd been too stressed to enjoy it. "Are they going to pay us to host more balls?"

"Probably," Uncle Jalil said. "As word gets around, we'll have more offers."

"As long as they pay for it," I muttered. I *really* didn't want to look at the account books, not today. I was all too aware we'd paid too much for the ball, even though House Rubén and House Aguirre had met some of our expenses. They hadn't been interested in paying for the cleaning. "We're going to need more money, uncle."

"I know." Uncle Jalil sobered. "But we should start earning money shortly."

I scowled, then turned my attention to the newspapers. Uncle Jalil had been right. The ball *had* gone well, as far as the reporters were concerned. I had to smile as I read one reporter's description of a dance that made very little sense. It felt like padding. He was probably paid by the word. Another reporter lingered on Alana Aguirre's dress, talking about her outfit in ways that made me feel dirty. I suspected the reporter was going to find himself in hot water very quickly, even though he—technically—hadn't broken any laws. His editor would put a knife in his back in a desperate bid to avoid trouble for himself.

"They do seem to think we did well," I said. "Have you heard anything from anyone else?"

"You have a stack of letters," Uncle Jalil reminded me. "I think you'll find that half of them are invitations."

I glanced at him, then started to open the letters one by one. He was right. I had invitations to a dozen balls, dances and parties, ranging from

House Bolingbroke to House Rubén and House Aguirre. I felt a thrill, dampened only by the certain knowledge I didn't have friends in *any* of those houses. My father had made a serious mistake by not sending me to Jude's. I didn't know anyone in the city, not personally. My peers would have no interest in welcoming me into their group...why should they? I winced, remembering how hard it had been to enter Grayling's a year ahead of everyone else. It had taken far too long for me to make even *one* friend.

"I can't take Gary, can I?" I knew the answer already. I might be as poor as a...well, as an heiress whose father had spent her inheritance before she came of age, but I was still an aristocrat. Gary was a commoner. "Who *should* I take?"

"Not me," Uncle Jalil said, quickly. "And I'd suggest, if you happened to ask, that you didn't take Uncle Hove either."

I nodded. Uncle Hove was old and long-winded and convinced he was an expert at wheeling and dealing. He was just like Robin Bolingbroke, except older, uglier and broke. My father had marginalised him a long time ago, even though—I tried not to groan—they had an awful lot in common. I couldn't take Uncle Hove anywhere. People would assume he spoke for me, then try to *sue* me when he promised them something he couldn't deliver. It probably wouldn't get that far—the people he wanted to engage knew very well his family was poor—but I couldn't take the chance. It would be a headache I didn't need.

"Maybe I'll ask Auntie Dorcas," I said. She'd be a millstone around my neck, but she had enough sense not to start high-level discussions without my permission. Except...it would make me look weak too. "Or maybe a friend from school."

I felt an odd little pang as I opened the rest of the letters. Marlene, Kate and I had left school...but the rest of our class would be graduating in a day or two. They'd be filtering back to their homes, heads filled with knowledge and skills...not all of which, I was all too aware, their parents would like. There was no way I could go back long enough to attend the ceremony...I wondered, not for the first time, if *Marlene* would go back. She was—or at least she'd been—the Head Girl. She'd been meant to give a speech.

And she also knows some of us were plotting a humiliating revenge, I reminded myself, dryly. There were few secrets at Grayling's. Marlene had been unpleasant enough, even before she'd been given authority, that quite a few girls had been plotting something nasty. Making Marlene's clothes fall off in front of the parents might be a step too far...no, I knew girls who wouldn't hesitate to plot such an atrocity. *Maybe she was just looking for a way to escape before it was too late.*

I put the thought out of my head. Marlene didn't matter any longer. Kate...I felt a pang of guilt that I hadn't been to visit my friend. I should have, damn it. Commoner or not, Kate had been a better friend than most. I made a mental note to write her a letter, asking if we could meet. She might be busy...I wondered, suddenly, if she knew Gary. Her father was an artificer, if I recalled correctly. It was quite possible they *knew* of each other.

Uncle Jalil returned to his paper as I made myself breakfast and forced myself to eat. I knew girls who'd have a heart attack at the mere thought of cooking their own food, let alone cleaning the dishes afterwards, but Grayling's had taught me how to take care of myself. We'd had fun heating soup in the dorms...we'd nearly been caught, a few times, yet that had been part of the thrill. What was the point of cooking and eating after Lights Out if there wasn't a chance we'd get in real trouble?

"You met Gary," Uncle Jalil said, from behind the newspaper. "What did you think?"

I glowered. "Did the muckrakers have anything to say about it?"

"No," Uncle Jalil said. "As far as I can tell, no one apart from us knows he came."

"Good," I said, curtly.

I felt...unsettled. I'd liked Gary, but...I knew marrying him would be seen as something tawdry, even though everyone knew everyone did it. I was pretty sure Caitlyn Aguirre and Akin Rubén weren't marrying for *love*. They were both so important and powerful that their families would do everything in their power to ensure they got married as soon as they came of age. Aristocrats got married for money and power all the time, but...there was normally a fig leaf of respectability around it. I wouldn't have that, once I married Gary. There'd be no cover. Or...was that true? Gary was an apprentice charmsmith. He'd be a good match...

But not good enough for the Heir Primus, I thought, sourly. I tried to imagine the reaction if Akin Rubén decided he wanted to marry a common-born girl, even if she was the most powerful sorceress in the world. If Caitlyn had been a commoner, heads would explode the moment they heard about the match. *It isn't going to be easy.*

I bit my lip, feeling a flicker of guilt. It was a business transaction. It was a business transaction. The thought went through my head time and time again, mocking me. It would have been easier, I supposed, if Gary had been as coldly pragmatic as myself. We could have worked out a simple agreement, made arrangements for one or both of us to have relationships on the side and kept our disagreements private. But I liked Gary. And I knew he was far too open for a simple business arrangement.

Unless he's playing you, my thoughts mocked. *You've met quite a few slippery people who looked and acted like total fools.*

Uncle Jalil cleared his throat. "Lucy?"

I blinked, realising I'd lost track of the conversation. "I'm sorry. You were saying?"

"I was asking what you made of him," Uncle Jalil said. "And if you'll be *happy* with him?"

"I don't think we get to be happy," I said, dodging the question. "I am required to choose my husband for the good of the family. Being *happy* doesn't come into it."

I met his eyes. "Were my parents happy?"

"I believe so," Uncle Jalil said. "Your mother certainly never complained to me."

"Right..." I wasn't sure what to make of it. I'd heard schoolgirls complaining about overbearing or bratty brothers. I didn't have any siblings, but...if I had, I wasn't sure if I'd take my complaints to them or not. Siblings were meant to love each other, yet if the stories I'd heard were true...I shook my head. "Why did they only have one child?"

"I don't know," Uncle Jalil said. "I never pried into their personal lives."

I finished my breakfast and put the plates in the sink for later cleaning, still feeling unsure of myself. My parents *should* have had more children. Everyone knew that twins and triplets had greater magical power than singletons. But they hadn't...did they think they couldn't provide for them? They'd certainly have had problems providing a dowry for me...I shook my head as we walked up to the office. It didn't matter. They'd both died before they had to make some hard decisions about my marriage.

And this way, you'll be making the choices yourself, I thought. *You won't be able to blame a bad match on your parents.*

Uncle Jalil took his seat as I walked to the window and peered over the city. "I've been going through the accounts," he said. "I'm afraid it's bad news."

Ice gripped my heart. "We've spent everything already?"

"No, but we don't have *that* much money left," Uncle Jalil said. "And there's no point in trying to reinvigorate the mines. Or the farmlands."

I turned to look at him. "Is there no hope of"—my imagination failed me—"of digging up more ore?"

"Right now, if I understand the reports correctly, we cannot produce metallic ore cheaply enough to compete with the other families," Uncle Jalil said. "Our extraction costs are higher, forcing us to either raise our prices or sell at a loss. Either way, we lose."

"Then..." I felt a twinge of desperation. "Are there no other uses for abandoned mines?"

"Not that I'm aware of," Uncle Jalil said. "It's possible a speculator might buy the mine, but..."

He paused. "There are some mushrooms and fungi that have alchemical uses," he added. "We might be able to grow them underground, but we'd still be competing against long-established producers."

"We could undersell them," I said. "Right?"

"I doubt it," Uncle Jalil said. "They'd know what we had in mind. They'd either lower their own prices for a while or simply ignore us, on the grounds we couldn't produce enough to compete with them. They might even be right."

I cursed under my breath as I turned back to the window. There were a dozen mansions within view, each one owned by a family that had money to burn. Literally, perhaps. They had so much money that all they had to do was leave it in the bank and it would make *more* money. I ground my teeth in resentment. The other Great Houses didn't have money troubles. Some of them had so many advantages that it was hard to see how they could ever be unseated.

Not like us, I thought, sourly. Desperation clawed at my heart. We'd put on a good show, but that was all it was. There was no way we could translate the ball—or a series of balls—into real wealth and power. *We can't win for losing.*

"Look into it," I ordered, as I walked back to the desk. "We'll have to be very careful with the rest of the money."

"Yes," Uncle Jalil said. His voice was very blunt. "We have debts to service."

I understood, suddenly, why my father had turned to a loan shark. He could talk a good game, as long as he kept up the appearance of wealth and power. No one would demand immediate repayment, until word started to spread that he might not be *able* to repay his debts. And once word *did* get out...I shuddered. Everyone would demand repayment at once, even if it meant giving up some of the interest. My father had to have been desperate, if he'd gone to a loan shark. He had to have been unable to think of any other way to save himself.

Keep running, I told myself. A shiver ran down my spine. I had a sudden vision of my father running like the wind, chased by a horde of faceless enemies. Like it or not, I was in the same boat. I'd bought time, but nothing else. And now I was running too. *If you stop, they'll catch up.*

"I'll talk to you later," I said. I sat down and picked up a charmed notebook. "I need to think."

Uncle Jalil stood and left the room. I opened the notebook and started to write. I'd always had a good memory, something I'd been encouraged to develop at school. We'd been meant to keep diaries, but we all knew that everything we wrote down would be used in evidence against us at some later date. I'd read a few of the diaries. They'd been so boring I thought they could have made an effective substitute for sleep potions. I smirked at the thought—it was a shame I couldn't turn the effect into a charm—then wrote down everything I'd overheard at the party. Most of it was useless, and some—I suspected—was actively misleading—but there were some gems amongst the manure. Robin Bolingbroke had given me an idea.

It will be risky, I thought, as the idea took shape in my head. *And if I get caught...*

I shook my head. I was desperate. I wanted—needed—to save my family. That was worth any risk...I stood and walked to the cabinets, digging into my father's private files. He'd collected a lot of information over the years, ranging from facts and figures to floor plans and spell charts. I wasn't sure what to make of it. Information was power—I'd learnt *that* at school—but there seemed to be no rhyme or reason to his files. Perhaps he'd never intended me to inherit them. Perhaps he'd planned to reorder or destroy them before I returned from school. Or perhaps...I shook my head as I started to work through the files. There was an entire section on House Bolingbroke, including a collection of rumours that veered between plausible and utter nonsense, often in the same story. Father—and whoever he'd hired to dig up dirt—must have been going out of his mind with frustration. The stories were so absurd it was hard to believe there was even a grain of truth to them.

Shaking my head, I collected the files and carried them to the desk. I'd have to go through them one by one, to study and swot as intensely as if I were still in school. I couldn't afford a mistake…I scowled, remembering how many times my tutors had given us false or misleading information to catch cheaters. They'd been easy to spot, if one had the slightest background knowledge or even a hint of common sense…

If this works, it will be brilliant, I thought. My stomach threatened to curdle. I felt sick, a tension I hadn't felt since the first time I'd slipped into someone's room to hex their bed sheets. There would have been no excuse, none at all, if I'd been caught. *And if it fails, the entire family will fall with me.*

CHAPTER THIRTEEN

Bolingbroke Hall was big enough, I decided as I hopped out of the carriage, to make Lamplighter Hall feel tiny. The building itself was ugly as hell—there was no elegance to its simple, blocky form—but it glowed with light and power. A small army of servants waited by the entrance, taking our coats and cloaks as Auntie Dorcas and I walked into the building and down the stairs to the ballroom. It was bigger—far bigger—than mine. I thought it was large enough to encompass the entire floor.

"Remember to pay your respects to the young lady," Auntie Dorcas shouted, once we were inside. The band was loud, making it hard for me to hear. "And then you can dance with the young gentlemen."

I shot her a sharp look as the ballroom continued to fill with guests. House Bolingbroke had so many friends, clients and enemies that the hall was absolutely packed...I felt a twinge of envy as I made my way around the room, noting who was in and who was out. The Grande Dames were cutting some younger women dead, probably for an imagined slight or two. Or simple jealously. The younger women were prettier, at the start of their lives...and, I realised suddenly, soon to be in a position to wield *real* power. I felt an odd flicker of sympathy as I started to eavesdrop again, hoping to hear something useful. The Grande Dames were utterly dependent on their families, yet powerless to influence policy. They dominated the social scene because it was all they had.

The thought depressed me as I circled the room, turning down a couple of invitations to the dance floor. I liked dancing, normally, but that wasn't why I was here. The young men didn't seem to care. I allowed myself a droll smile as I noted where the exits were, carefully matching them to the floor plans my father had obtained. Bolingbroke Hall was a business centre, as well as a home. And I knew where Robin Bolingbroke lived and worked.

I took a drink and sipped, pretending to be sociable as I picked the man himself out from the crowd. He was dancing with his mistress, defying social convention with a zest I couldn't help admiring even as I felt sorry for the poor woman. The Grande Dames didn't try to hide their disgust. They'd have done something a great deal worse if they weren't dependent on their family. Robin had enough influence to smack down anyone who tried to impede his life.

The music died away. I tensed as the crowd pushed me forward, lining up by the stairs. A whisper of anticipation ran through the air, all eyes turning to the upper levels. Clarian Bolingbroke stood at the top, wearing a virgin-white dress. Her hair fell to her shoulders, no longer in braids. She walked down the stairs with a grace I could only admire, presenting herself—for the first time—as an adult in her own right. My eyes picked out Alana, standing at the other side of the hall. Her face was unreadable, suggesting she was far from happy. It couldn't be easy for her to watch her peers become adults. *Her* hair was still firmly in braids. I wanted to tell her not to be silly. She'd become an adult soon enough.

When it's politically convenient, I mused. *And who knows when that will be?*

Clarian Bolingbroke reached the bottom of the stairs. A young man came forward, took her arm and led her onto the dance floor. I guessed, from the way he held her, that House Bolingbroke had chosen him for political reasons. There was no hint they'd known each other before the ceremony. Other dancers moved onto the floor as the band struck up a merry tune. Clarian would dance with dozens of young men. She couldn't show favour to anyone unless she was already betrothed or engaged.

I slipped away, making my way towards the side doors as more and more dancers hurried onto the floor. No one spared me a glance as I slipped into the corridors, then headed up the stairs. House Bolingbroke provided private rooms for the guests—although how private they *were* was anyone's guess—on an upper floor. I felt my heart pound as I reached the second floor, then headed up another level. The wards didn't seem inclined to notice me—there was something weird about them, as if they'd been put together by someone who didn't quite know what they were doing—but I was sure that'd change before too long. They'd almost certainly be privacy wards on the bedroom doors.

Sweat prickled on my back as I reached Robin Bolingbroke's office. I'd prepared a cover story, but I knew it would raise suspicions if I was caught. I wouldn't be looking at a year's detentions or a simple caning *this* time. There was a charm on the doorknob, a simple alarm spell combined with a lock…I studied the spellform as quickly as I could, then started to push it aside. It would have been easy to simply take the spell apart, but that would be far too revealing when Robin Bolingbroke returned. Instead, I weakened it enough to allow me entry without setting off any alarms.

I braced myself as I stepped inside. I really *was* crossing a line. If I was caught…I put the thought out of my head as I closed the door behind me, glancing around with interest. The room was crammed with filing cabinets, the walls practically covered in them…I wanted to stay and search, but there was no time. Instead, I hurried to the desk and peered down at the paperwork. Bills of lading, private notes…a handful charmed so heavily that their mere existence was more than a little revealing too. No one would go to so much trouble unless they had something to hide. I felt another stab of envy as I studied the paperwork. Robin Bolingbroke handled more money, with each transaction, than I'd handled in my entire life. I wasn't sure how he got away with it.

Because he's good at what he does, I thought. I'd seen the man drunk out of his mind, but...I'd seen him at his worst. He was probably much better behaved during the day. *And because he has the contacts to make things go smoothly.*

I forced myself to go through the papers, one by one. Individually, they told me little of use. Together...I frowned as I realised Robin Bolingbroke was hoarding Silverdale ore. It was odd. Silverdale was used to make a handful of Devices of Power, from what little I recalled of my forging classes. It was important, but not *that* important. Why would anyone want to hoard it, particularly in such vast quantities? What was he planning to do?

It's the only thing he's keeping for himself, I thought, as I finished searching the visible papers. *Everything else...he's the middleman.*

I straightened up, glancing around the room. It was bare and barren, save for the filing cabinets and the handful of trading newspapers pinned to the noticeboard. I hurried over and peered at the snippets. Raw ore prices, combined with production costs...? I smiled as the truth struck me. House Bolingbroke's mines were running dry. There were other seams, from what I recalled, but they'd take time to develop. The price was about to go up...

Time to leave, I told myself. The dancing wouldn't last forever. I was morbidly sure Robin Bolingbroke wouldn't stay downstairs forever. He'd have to make a show of supporting his...niece? Great-niece? I didn't know, but I doubted it mattered. He wouldn't stay any longer than strictly necessary. *He'll be up here soon enough.*

I walked back to the door, paused long enough to make sure there was no one on the other side, then sneaked outside, returning the charm to its normal level. The wards seemed undisturbed. A chill ran down my spine as I realised I'd pushed my luck as far as it would go. I turned and hurried down the corridor, hoping and praying I'd reach the stairs before someone came along. I might be able to talk my way out of trouble, I might not. I'd been able to sneak into student bedrooms and read their papers—or do worse—without being detected, but a Great House was a far harder nut to crack. Next time, it might be a lot harder. Robin Bolingbroke needed to keep his office fairly close to the doors. The Patriarch had no such requirement.

It was hard not to break into a run as I slipped down the stairs and headed back to the hall. There was nothing more suspicious than someone on the run, save perhaps for someone whistling tunelessly while pretending they were doing nothing. I breathed a sigh of relief as I returned to the ballroom, hoping no one had noticed my brief excursion. I didn't think anyone would care if I sought a private room…I shook my head. It was over. Over and done with. And I had a piece of very useful information indeed.

A young man popped up in front of me. "Would you like to dance?"

"Why not?" I allowed him to lead me onto the dance floor. "It's been too long since I danced."

He grinned. "Just don't step on my foot too often," he said. "Please."

I allowed myself a smile, remembering the handful of carefully-chaperoned dances at Grayling's. They'd been the only time men—boys, at least—had been allowed onto the grounds. We'd had to practice by dancing with other girls, leading to endless arguments over who was the man and who was the woman. I felt my smile grow wider as we swayed around the dance floor. Robin Bolingbroke was still dancing with his mistress, pawing at her as they moved in time to the music. I wondered if I could hit him with a tripping hex, then put the thought out of my head before I could act on it. My family didn't need more enemies. I'd be in enough trouble if they realised what I'd done.

My partner winked. "Do you want to sneak off?"

I felt myself blush. "My auntie would have something to say, if I did," I said. I was surprised he'd made the offer so…publicly. I'd certainly overhead a *lot* of very useful titbits of information on the dance floor. Did he know who I was? I didn't think so. His offer had too many political implications for me to take it seriously. "I don't even know your name."

"Brantley. Brantley of House Braddock." He smiled at me. "I'm sure you've heard of us."

"I might have heard a whisper or two," I lied, mischievously. House Braddock was a younger house, with a surprising amount of power and influence for such a relative newcomer. They even had a seat on Magus Court. "Lucy. Lucy of House Lamplighter."

His expression froze, just for a second. "I look forward to meeting you at *our* ball," he said, so smoothly it would have been hard to tell he'd been surprised if I hadn't seen his face. "I hope you'll do us the honour of attending."

"I'll certainly do my best," I said. Another young man waved at me. "But I can't dance with you all night."

I thought fast, allowing my body to move on instinct as I glided from partner to partner. He'd definitely heard my name…I told myself I was being stupid. My name had been in all the papers, only a week ago. It was quite possible Brantley would have backed off, if I'd so much as *hinted* I might be interested. I didn't think he was the Heir Primus—I thought that was his older sister—but I could be wrong. If something—or someone—happened to the older girl, he'd be first in line to inherit…

And you're thinking like a silly little girl, I told myself, sharply. I'd become an adult, the moment I allowed my hair to hang down. *You cannot let yourself pretend there will be no consequences any longer.*

I nodded to my latest partner as the music came to an end, then headed for the buffet. There was no sign of Auntie Dorcas, somewhat to my surprise. She was old enough to be a Grand Dame, but…would they accept her? She didn't have a major family allowance or any real influence…perhaps she'd tell them I did whatever she said. *That* would blow up in her face, if House Bolingbroke realised what I'd done. I was almost tempted to hint at it…I shook my head. If someone was to take the blame, it would have to be me.

"Hey." I looked up to see Clarian Bolingbroke's pale face. "I've been hoping to meet you."

I tried not to show my surprise. Clarian Bolingbroke was a year younger than me…and a stranger. I didn't think I'd ever spent time with her when

I'd been a child. It was possible, but unlikely. I straightened, studying her with interest. She was tall, yet almost disturbingly thin. Raven-black hair hung down to the small of her back. Her face looked almost like a china doll. I was suddenly afraid to touch her for fear she'd break. It was an odd look, striking yet slightly disconcerting. I wondered what she was trying to achieve.

"Fantastic," I said. I knew how to make nice with people I neither liked nor trusted, but...there was something about Clarian that made it hard to know how to handle her. "What can I do for you?"

Clarian looked down. "What's it like, running a family?"

"Very hard," I said, slowly. Clarian would never have to worry about money—or anything, really. She could sit back and let her parents run her life. I told myself that wasn't a good thing. "But at least I get to tell the old folks to shut up every so often."

She smiled. It made her look even *more* like a doll. "That must be fun."

"It is my solemn duty to tell them to shut their mouths every once in a while," I said, my best deadpan look on my face. I didn't want to *like* Clarian, did I? "It's a dirty job, but someone has to do it."

Clarian's smile grew brighter. "We were planning to hold a party," she said. "Can we hire your hall?"

My eyebrows crawled up. *We?* "I certainly think so," I said. "Who's running the party?"

"Me." Clarian hesitated, noticeably. "Me and a few friends."

"All young, I take it." I felt a flicker of envy. Clarian and her friends were too young to be taken entirely seriously, even if they no longer wore their hair in braids. "Drop me a letter and we'll make the arrangements."

I winced as I saw Auntie Dorcas emerge from the throng and start waving at me. "And I have to go," I added. "I'll speak to you later?"

Clarian nodded and headed off. I watched her go, then turned and joined Auntie Dorcas as she set course towards the exit. I was tempted to point out she should have *asked* before she headed outside, but I was ready to go too. If someone realised what I'd done...I shook my head. They wouldn't make a scene in public. Not here, not where it would highlight weaknesses in their defences. They'd do something later, where it wouldn't be seen.

"I made some useful contacts," Auntie Dorcas said. "We'll have to invite them to our next ball."

"Oh goody," I said. My mind was elsewhere. "Do you think they'll be beneficial?"

Auntie Dorcas sniffed as we clambered into the carriage and rattled back home. I did my best to ignore her. I could have walked, easily...I doubted anyone would have really noticed or cared. I wasn't that important. Remaining unimportant—or at least neutral—was the key to our survival.

"I'll see you later," I said, when the carriage reached Lamplighter Hall. Thankfully, Auntie Dorcas had declined to move into the hall. "Have a good evening."

I jumped out of the carriage and walked up the driveway. The lawn looked freshly mown, even though I knew it was an illusion. The potions gardens had been carefully sealed off...we were going to have to deal with them, somehow. I'd have to hire a gardener, if I couldn't find a master who'd be interested in taking care of it. I knew a little something about potions, but not enough to handle it myself.

Uncle Jalil met me as I stepped into the hall. "Did you have a good time?"

"Yeah." I met his eyes. "And I want you to do something for me."

His eyes narrowed as I headed for the stairs. I didn't want him asking questions, not now.

"I want you to take the rest of the money and purchase as much Silverdale ore as you can," I said. "Do it covertly. Try to make sure no one actually *knows* what we're doing. But try to build up a hoard as quickly as possible."

"What?" Uncle Jalil sounded disconcerted to be firing questions at my back. "Lucy...what do you mean?"

"I mean I want you to purchase the ore for me," I said, crossly. I was too tired to think about anything else, not right now. "And I don't want anyone to know what we're doing."

There was a long pause. "Lucy...is that what you want?"

"Yes." I stopped and turned to face him. "We have to gamble. So, we're going to gamble."

Uncle Jalil looked displeased. "Yes, My Lady."

CHAPTER FOURTEEN

"I don't really feel bad about missing graduation," Kate said, as we sat down for dinner in a cafe. "Did you hear the news?"

I raised my eyebrows. "No. What happened?"

Kate smiled. "Apparently, Capua got covered in paint," she said. "Someone who shall remain nameless, even though everyone knows who did it, rigged a charm to drop paint on her when she was midway through her speech."

I giggled. Capua had been one of Marlene's cronies. "And what happened then?"

"Well, according to the letter, everyone laughed like loons," Kate said. "How terrible."

"How terrible," I echoed. "I don't know how she ever made prefect."

"I think someone bribed Mistress Grayling to promote her," Kate said. "Her parents must have made the best offer."

"Probably." I studied the menu for a long moment. "Or maybe someone *else* bribed her."

Kate grinned. "How so?"

"Capua was pretty lazy," I reminded her. "She wasn't a very effective prefect."

"True." Kate considered it for a moment. "She never caught anyone, did she?"

The waiter approached and bowed. "Are you ready to order?"

"I'll have the cheese and ham," I said. The cafe wasn't normally patronised by aristocrats—the food was strikingly plebeian—but I could eat anything. Boarding school had taught me how to force even inedible gruel down my throat. "Kate?"

"I'll have the same," Kate said. "And a mug of tea."

She smiled as the waiter bowed and retreated. "I saw your name in the papers," she said, once he was out of earshot. "You're doing well for yourself."

"I wish it felt that way," I said. Uncle Jalil had bought the ore, as I'd ordered, but the price had yet to rise. "I never realised just how easily a mansion could become a millstone around my neck."

Kate lifted her eyebrows. "Really? How come?"

I shrugged. "Long story," I said. I didn't want to moan too much. "Let me just say that maintaining everything I've inherited is expensive."

"Dad says the same," Kate said. "He can pay for basic maintenance now, at low cost, or replace his tools later at a much greater cost."

"But when you don't have the money to pay for maintenance, you find yourself deferring it until it's too late," I said, sourly. "My father did that, I think. I had to shell out a *lot* of money just to arrest the decline."

Kate shot me a sharp look. She was far from stupid. Her family wasn't wealthy enough to send her to Grayling's without a scholarship. I was fairly sure she was smarter than pretty much everyone else in my year, perhaps even me. She'd certainly be clever enough to guess I had money problems. I wouldn't be grumbling about the expense—it was a point of honour among the aristocracy never to look at the price tag—unless I really *didn't* have the money to spare.

"That's basic economics," Kate said, finally. "What *did* they teach you in school?"

I stuck out my tongue, very maturely. "How to walk with a bucket on my head," I said. It was true. "And how to sneak around without getting caught."

"I don't think they'll put *that* on your certificate," Kate teased. "What about the rest of the lessons?"

I blinked. "Lessons? There were lessons?"

Kate started to say something, then stopped herself as the waiter returned and placed our food on the table. It looked simple, but better than anything I'd eaten at Grayling's. I took a sniff, nodded in appreciation and tipped the waiter. His eyes lingered on me for a long moment before he turned away and vanished into the backroom. I grinned. He really had *no* idea who I was.

"Welcome to adulthood," Kate said. Her hair was hanging loose too. "How does it feel?"

"Strange," I admitted. "When did you become an adult?"

"Dad said it was high time I earned my keep," Kate said. "He removed my hairclip and that was that."

I frowned. "Nothing more?"

"Dad wouldn't have thrown a party for me," Kate said. "Even if he'd had the money, he would have refused to do it."

"Yeah." I flushed. Of *course* Kate wouldn't have a Season. She was a commoner. And yet, I couldn't help feeling her father had been a little neglectful. "I didn't have time to have a Season."

"Which might be for the best," Kate pointed out. "Right?"

"Probably," I agreed. High Society didn't know I was—technically—engaged. "My father died before he could introduce me to society."

Kate took a bite of her food. "Is that good or bad?"

I shrugged. "I don't know," I said. "It depends."

Kate looked down at her hands. "Dad's been having problems at work," she said. "He's got several ideas for new Devices of Power, but...he's been unable to attract any interest from outside investors. He just doesn't have the money to develop his ideas."

I frowned as a thought struck me. "He's an artificer, isn't he?"

"Yeah." Kate frowned. "But it's very hard to convince anyone to take an interest."

Someone with money and contacts, I translated, mentally. There was a good chance Kate wanted *me* to take an interest. She thought I was wealthy...maybe. She might have guessed, from what I'd told her, that money was in short supply. I wondered why she hadn't come out and asked me. *And what does he actually need?*

My mind raced. The Great Houses had entire *armies* of artificers, charmsmiths and forgers. They didn't need outsiders, particularly outsiders who couldn't or wouldn't marry into the family. Kate's father would be unable to attract any real interest unless he came up with something *really* new. Or old, if he found a way to produce Objects of Power. There were artificers who devised workarounds, tricks to produce Devices of Power that mimicked Objects of Power, but they rarely lasted long. The Great Houses certainly didn't need an upstart artificer to produce them. They had more than enough artificers of their own.

But was that actually true? I recalled Albrecht Rubén, complaining he couldn't get the components he needed. It was odd to think House Rubén might be having problems...their Heir Primus was on the verge of marrying the one and only Zero. Their marriage was practically a licence to coin money. If Albrecht Rubén was having problems...I leaned forward, an idea slowly forming. I might just be able to turn the situation to my advantage.

"We need to talk bluntly," I said, casting a privacy ward. "Can we?"

"You're the one who got me out of a bad match," Kate said. "What can you say to me now that's worse than what you said then?"

I smiled, even though I knew it wasn't funny. "I can't afford to invest in your father's workshop," I said. The words hung in the air for a long, chilling moment. "Not now. But I do know someone who *might* be interested, depending on what you're offering. There's no guarantee of anything, but I could try."

Kate met my eyes. "And what would you want in return?"

I tried not to feel a pang of guilt. Favour-trading was common amongst the aristocracy. The entire patron-client system was nothing more than favour-trading on a colossal scale. And we'd traded favours at school, learning the ropes as we swapped positions and punishments until everyone was reasonably happy. And yet...Kate was my friend. I felt guilty even treating her like a potential client. She wasn't someone who'd do an essay for me in exchange for me taking the watch after Lights Out.

"A share in the profits," I said. "I'll make the introductions. I'll ensure the contracts are drawn up by aristocratic lawyers, who understand how to manipulate the system to best advantage. And, in exchange, you give me twenty percent of the profits."

"Five percent," Kate said. Her voice was light, but I knew her well enough to hear the discomfort under her words. She was an adult now, just like me. She could land herself in hot water very easily. "And you actually have to *work*. You're not allowed to just perform introductions and vanish."

"Introductions are work," I said, although I knew she wouldn't believe me. My name *might* convince Albrecht Rubén to give us a hearing, or it might not. "And you'll have to make a case. I don't know what'll convince him."

Kate frowned. "Are you sure he—whoever *he* is—will listen?"

"No." I shook my head. There was something about the whole affair I didn't understand. Why did Albrecht Rubén need more artificers in the first place? I was missing something, but what? "You'll have to make a *good* case."

"Which isn't going to be easy, seeing we know so little about the affair," Kate said. She took a sip of her drink. "We might be wasting our time."

"I'll be wasting mine too," I said. "Tell me about your father. What does he do?"

"He runs a workshop," Kate explained. I listened carefully as she outlined how her father's business actually worked. It was a very simple model, I had to admit. He'd hired a handful of artificers and set them to work crafting components that could be assembled, with an infusion of magic, into Devices of Power. There was little room for expansion, without outside investment, but it should bring in a solid profit. "What do you think?"

"I think your father needs some investment," I said. The workshop lacked the finesse of a forgery, and there was something crude about her description that irritated me, but it hardly needed to look good as long as it turned a profit. "How far is he prepared to go?"

"I'll have to ask him," Kate said. "He's got me working in the shop as an alchemist."

I grinned. "Try not to blow up the cauldron again."

Kate coloured. "That was because Marlene threw tree-of-life into my brew," she said. "And she got away with it."

Only because no one ratted her out, I thought. It was the schoolgirl code. Better to get in trouble than to tattle, even if the person being tattled on thoroughly deserved it. In hindsight, it sounded rather stupid. There was a difference between tattling out of spite and tattling because someone was deliberately putting lives in danger. *She would have been in real trouble if the tutor had known who to blame.*

"You don't have to worry about her any longer," I said. "How are the other apprentices?"

"A couple are quite handsome," Kate said. "And they even asked me out."

I grinned. "What did your father say?"

"Nothing, yet," Kate said. "I haven't decided if I want to walk out with them."

"I suppose it could be awkward," I said. Relationships between apprentices and masters were strongly discouraged, but what about relationships between apprentices and the master's daughter? "Don't get yourself in trouble."

"I'll try." Kate grinned. "And what about yourself?"

"I..." I hesitated, unsure how much to say. "Have you ever heard of Gary Prestwick?"

"No." Kate sounded bemused, as if the sudden change in subject had caught her by surprise. "Related to Danny Prestwick?"

"He's Danny's son," I said. "Have you heard of him?"

"No." Kate snorted. "*Danny* Prestwick is a landlord. His reputation is...somewhat mixed."

I frowned, feeling a flicker of alarm. "How so?"

Kate stroked her chin. She knew I had a reason for asking beyond simple curiosity, even if she didn't know what it was. There was no logical reason for *me* to have heard of Danny or Gary Prestwick. The only reason I knew *Kate* was that we'd gone to school together. There might be male aristocrats who bragged of roguish dealings in Water Shallot, in hopes of making the ladies blush, but I was fairly sure most of them were talking nonsense. Aristos didn't go to Water Shallot for diversion unless they were desperate or stupid or had tastes forbidden even to them.

"He buys up old buildings and renovates them," she said, finally. She sounded as if she was choosing her words with great care. "He does good work. He takes crappy tenements on the verge of falling down and turns them into upper-class properties, then he sells or rents as the fancy suits him. But he's also driving prices up. Five years ago, riverside property was relatively cheap. Now, whole neighbourhoods are becoming too expensive and the poor are being priced out. They're having to move, because they can't afford to live there any longer."

She grimaced. "Even if they own their property, Lucy, they still have to buy food and everything else they need. Those prices are going up too."

"I see," I said. "Thank you."

"I'm surprised you asked," Kate said. "Why?"

I wasn't sure how to answer. She was my friend. I wanted to tell her the truth. And she already knew—or suspected—I had money problems. There was certainly no other reason an aristocrat would consider Gary Prestwick a suitable husband. I liked him—he was a decent person, from what I'd gathered—but romance couldn't be allowed to play any role in my decision. I had to marry for the good of the family.

"I might be marrying Gary Prestwick," I said, finally. "And I wanted to know if you'd met him."

Kate frowned. "I can't imagine your family being happy with that," she said, finally. Her commoner roots had caused her enough problems when she'd been a schoolgirl. It would be a great deal harder for a commoner who married into the aristocracy. "Are they desperate?"

"I'm desperate," I admitted. "We don't have much else to use."

"Which is why you're offering to perform introductions," Kate said. "And why you want a share of the profits."

"Yes," I said. There was no point in trying to deny it. I just had to hope she wouldn't take advantage of me. I trusted Kate—and I was fairly sure she wouldn't try to cheat me—but I barely knew her father. He'd only visited the school once. "Like I said, we don't have much else right now."

"I see," Kate said. "Lucy…if you can get us some investment, we'll happily share the profits."

I met her eyes. "Will your father agree?"

"I think so," Lucy said. "But I can't make any binding promises."

The waiter returned, carrying the bill. I paid, trying not to wince at the price. It was very low, compared to restaurants in North Shallot, but I simply didn't have much free cash. The waiter's eyes followed us as we stood and headed outside, breathing in the warm summer air. I guessed he hadn't been able to work up the nerve to ask either or both of us out.

"There's been some unrest here recently," Kate said, as we walked along the riverside. The waters looked muddy brown as they carried silt from upstream down to the sea. "And all the gentrification doesn't help."

I glanced at her. "Because people are having to move out?"

"Yeah." Kate ran her hand through her hair. "And because the price of everything is going up."

I said nothing as we walked past a row of shops. They looked dark and dingy compared to the shops on the other side of the river, and I couldn't help noticing the layers of protective spells woven into the storefronts, but they looked to be doing a roaring trade. I rolled my eyes as we passed a fishmonger, trying not to gag at the smell. Prices were lower here, I noted. And yet, it was the same fish…perhaps I should encourage the cooks to shop on *this* side of the river. Or would it simply drive prices up for everyone?

"I'll do what I can," I promised, as we reached the bridge. "And I'll get in touch."

"Please." Kate smiled, rather wanly. "And good luck with the marriage."

"If it ever happens," I said. I knew how High Society would react. They'd accept my children—they'd *have* to—but they wouldn't be very welcoming to my new in-laws. "I don't know how things are going to go."

Kate gave me a hug. "Me neither," she said. "Hey, maybe you could tell Marlene. I'm sure she'd have a heart attack."

I shrugged. "Marlene's been acting oddly," I said. "Perhaps some dark secret is preying on her mind."

"Or perhaps she just has a hangover after drinking too much of her own potions," Kate countered. "It could be something as simple as that, you know."

"I know." I grinned, then sobered. Marlene had been thoroughly unpleasant to me, my friends and everyone else she didn't consider her social equal. Her problems were not *my* problems. I had quite enough of my own. "I'll try not to think about her."

"Good idea," Kate agreed. "Good luck!"

She raised a hand in salute, then turned and left. I waved at her back before walking over the bridge and into North Shallot. There were a handful of armsmen from a dozen different families manning the guard post at the far side. They eyed me curiously, but said nothing before waving me on. I frowned, inwardly. It looked as though they were preparing for war.

I shrugged as I continued walking, enjoying the fresh summer air. I'd have to start researching, as soon as I got back to the hall. I'd have to figure out what Albrecht Rubén really wanted and how to give it to him, in a manner that ensured I'd get some profit. Kate didn't understand, not really, how weak my hand truly was. I didn't have anything like enough influence to balance House Rubén, if things went badly. They could simply twist arms until they got what they wanted...

I'd better make sure nothing goes wrong, I told myself. *I can't even afford one* mistake.

CHAPTER
FIFTEEN

I couldn't help feeling a flicker of envy, pure unadulterated envy, as the open-topped carriage passed through the gatehouse and drove towards Rubén Hall. The mansion was colossal, easily large enough to swallow Lamplighter Hall in a single gulp. I sensed powerful wards crackling through the air as the driver brought us to a halt outside the main entrance, a perfectly turned out butler already waiting. House Rubén had money to burn and it showed. I felt sick as the butler assisted Kate to scramble down, then stepped back to allow her father to descend. If my family had been as rich...

"Welcome to Rubén Hall," the butler said. "Lord Rubén awaits you in his office."

I took a breath as he escorted us through a pair of massive doors and into a giant entrance hall. A maid took our coats and cloaks as we looked around, Kate and her father trying not to gape openly. I found it hard not to stare as well. A portrait of Akin Rubén and Caitlyn Aguirre stared down at me, their features so idealised I wouldn't have been sure it was them if Caitlyn hadn't been wearing an Object of Power. Another portrait, black-edged, showed a young man a year or two younger than me. I guessed the family was still in mourning, in line with the old traditions. House Rubén honoured traditions everyone else had forgotten long ago. Akin had a twin—Isabella—but there were no visible portraits of *her* anywhere. Isabella had been banished from the city years ago. I doubted she'd ever be allowed to return.

And she would have been executed, if she'd been an adult, I thought. I was mildly surprised she hadn't turned up at Grayling's. *She was lucky*.

Kate inched up to me as we were escorted down a long corridor, pitching her voice low so we wouldn't be overheard. "Why isn't he coming to greet us?"

"We're supplicants," I replied, bluntly. My pride rebelled against the suggestion. I told it to shut up. I had no time for pride, nor reason to be prideful. "He won't come to us. We have to go to him."

I felt nervous as we passed through an antechamber and into a comfortable meeting room, outfitted for informal discussions. There were comfortable chairs and sofas, instead of wooden tables and hard chairs; a notice board hung on one wall, covered with pieces of paperwork and snippets from newspapers. Albrecht Rubén sat in an armchair, his hands resting comfortably on his lap. Akin stood behind him, his hands clasped behind his back. I guessed Akin was supposed to observe the discussions, then report to his father. I felt another stab of envy as Albrecht Rubén stood. Instead of shaking my hand, he brought it to his lips and kissed the air above my skin. I guessed he was having some problems deciding how best to treat me. I was a supplicant, but supposedly I was also a powerful aristocrat...

Not that powerful, I reminded myself. *There's no way House Lamplighter can stand against any of the other Great Houses*.

"You must be Jackson Farthing," Albrecht said, to Kate's father. "I've heard a lot about you."

"All of it good, I trust." Kate's father was a tall, powerfully-built man with a nasty scar on his face. No one would hold the mark—or his burnt hands—against him. Indeed, they'd see the scars as a badge of honour. "It's a pleasure to meet you."

"Please, be seated." Albrecht waved us to the sofa. The maids brought us glasses of fancy wine, then withdrew as silently as they'd come. "I understand you have a proposition for me."

I leaned back in my sofa, doing my level best to appear calm and unconcerned as Kate's father started to outline his business, his future plans and his need for investment. I'd heard the speech before—I'd insisted on rehearsing it, time and time again—but I had no way to know what Albrecht would make of it. Or what he'd ask. I'd thrown every awkward question I could at Jackson, just to prepare him for the interrogation to come, but…I was all too aware my imagination might not have been enough. If Albrecht asked the wrong question, we might not have a good answer.

My heart sank as Albrecht showed no visible reaction to the speech and paperwork. I still didn't understand why he *wanted* artificers, even though he'd accepted my proposal quickly enough to convince me he *did*. I'd researched Albrecht and his family as thoroughly as I could, only to draw a complete blank. They could satisfy their needs easily, without doing deals with commoners like Jackson and Kate. I just didn't understand.

"A decent suggestion," Albrecht said, finally. At least he hadn't told us to get lost. Behind him, Akin studied the designs. "What are you prepared to offer, in exchange for investment?"

Jackson showed no hint of weakness. "One-third of our component production, My Lord," he said. "And a share of the profits if our long-term project works out."

"Interesting." Albrecht stroked his chin. "You do not, of course, offer a guarantee."

"No, My Lord," Jackson said. "We believe we can adapt a handful of Objects of Power, as I described, but there's no guarantee the concept will work. Makeshift Objects of Power simply do not last for long, if they work at all."

I saw Akin shift behind his uncle. That wasn't entirely true. Caitlyn could make *real* Objects of Power…but she was unique. Jackson's two concepts were more of a way to get around the problem than overcome it. And...I felt cold. If only I'd had the money to invest in the concept myself. There was a better than even chance that Albrecht would try to steal the idea.

"Your designs for Devices of Power seem crude," Akin said. "Do they work?"

"Yes," Jackson said. "By mass-producing components for Devices of Power, we can cut down assembly time by an order of magnitude. Furthermore, by making the components interchangeable, they can simply be swapped out and replaced when they fail. There is a certain crudity to the designs, as you say, but that is born of simplicity. We can cut the price by fifty percent."

And once the concept is proven, I thought, *everyone will start copying it.*

"You'll also be putting the work in the hands of unskilled craftsmen," Akin added. I reminded myself that rumour insisted Akin was a skilled forger in his own right. It was an odd choice of major, for an Heir Primus, but very few people would tell him no. "How do you know they'll do a good job?"

Jackson tensed, very slightly. He *was* a skilled craftsman. His reputation depended on hiring men—and women—who could handle the work. It was a reasonable question, I supposed, but also a very insulting one. Craftsmen who couldn't do the job—and didn't have a powerful family backing them up—tended to be reassigned, or simply fired, very quickly. I prayed he wouldn't lose his temper. If he raised his voice, Albrecht would be perfectly within his rights to have him—and us—evicted.

"First, my craftsmen are required to pass a basic training course before being allowed to take a position within the workshop," Jackson said. "Second, we have prepared spells to check each component before forwarding it onwards. Those that are not perfect will be melted down and recycled. Third, the Devices of Power will simply be unable to maintain a spellform if they are not perfect. There *is* a certain degree of variance, I will admit, but very little. We'll know of any failures long before they reach the public."

"Thank you," Akin said.

Albrecht studied the paperwork, then looked up. "We have artificers of our own," he said, finally. "And"—he nodded to Akin—"soon to acquire the world's foremost forger. Why should we come to terms with you?"

I saw a flicker of discontent pass over Akin's face. Caitlyn *was* the world's foremost forger by default, but...she was more than *just* a forger. I felt a sudden flicker of sympathy for the boy, caught between calling his elder out for being obnoxious in front of outsiders and simply letting it pass. I hoped he'd give Albrecht a lecture when they were alone, after the meeting was gone. I'd only met Caitlyn once, but she deserved better. She'd have enough problems fitting into her new family without being treated like a piece of balky spellware.

"There are limits to how many Devices of Power—or Objects of Power—that can be produced." Jackson's voice was very calm. "There will still be a demand for Devices of Power, even if you find a way to produce *Objects* of Power without a Zero. And that demand will only rise. My workshop would not have been so successful if there wasn't a steadily growing demand. One forger, no matter how skilled, cannot hope to meet it."

Particularly as everyone wants her to work on flying machines and teleport gates and other things that'll change the world, I added, silently. *You won't want her to waste her talents.*

"I see." Albrecht returned his eyes to the paperwork. "Will you excuse us a moment? The maids will refresh your drinks."

He stood and left the room, followed by Akin. I tapped my lips, warning them to say nothing as the maids entered. They'd be loyal to their family. They'd report anything they overheard to their masters. And even if they didn't...the wards buzzed and crackled around the chamber. I was fairly sure they were designed to relay our conversation to listening ears. It was an old trick...I stood, brushing down my dress as I walked around the room. The notice board was covered with clippings promising a grand future for Albrecht's house. I wondered, rather sourly, if the board was genuine or if someone had set it up to waste my time. It would be foolish to leave something incriminating visible where just *anyone* could see it.

It doesn't have to be incriminating, I thought, as I turned back to the sofa. *It just has to suggest things are not as rosy as they'd like us to believe.*

I sat and waited, reminding myself I could be patient. I'd spent hours in detention, standing in the hall with my hands on my head...it sounded like nothing, until one actually *did* it. I had a comfortable seat here, as well as something to read...I reread the proposal, trying to think of ways to present it to another house. House Rubén was a good choice because they were too wealthy and powerful to cheat us—they wouldn't feel the *need* to cheat us—but there were others. We might have to rewrite the proposal...

The door opened. "We have considered the matter," Albrecht said, as he closed the door behind him and sat down. "We are prepared to provisionally accept your offer, assuming we can come to suitable terms. For example, we require half of your output for the next five years."

My eyes narrowed. *That* was odd. Albrecht would be paying for it, by investing in the workshop, but...why did they need the components? Were they planning to flood the market with Devices of Power? It was possible, but they hadn't known about Jackson's plan before I'd brought it to their attention. They'd clearly been planning something before I'd contacted them. I made a mental note to look into it again. Whatever it was, I wanted to know.

"Once we are set up for mass production, that shouldn't be a problem," Jackson said. "Prior to that, My Lord, we will have to plough most of our production back into the business..."

"I quite understand." Albrecht cut him off. "Your funding plan looks acceptable. We'll invest what you said, plus ten percent. You may require extra cash."

I sensed, more than heard, Kate gasp. I felt the same way too. Albrecht had casually pledged enough money to keep a mid-sized family comfortable for decades. House Rubén was rich, but...I shook my head. They were rich enough to consider the entire sum a trifle. They could even afford to write it off, if something went wrong. I seethed with envy as Jackson and Albrecht discussed terms, the former sounding a little shaken. I didn't blame him. He'd been given everything he wanted on a silver platter.

"My people will be in touch with your people," Albrecht said. He stood and held out a hand. Jackson shook it firmly. "The final issues should be settled quickly."

Too quickly, I thought. Uncle Stefano had warned me that it might be weeks before the contracts were signed…and months before we saw any profits. *What do you really want?*

"Thank you for your time," I said. Beside me, Kate curtsied. "It was our pleasure."

"I look forward to doing business with you," Albrecht said. "The butler will show you out."

I said nothing as the butler entered and escorted us back towards the entrance hall. There was no time to sneak away, not even to use the washroom. The wards were just too powerful. House Rubén felt as if it were preparing for war. Perhaps it was. They—and their partners—would have a serious advantage, when Akin and Caitlyn married. The others were probably already plotting their countermoves.

"They agreed," Jackson said, once we were back in the carriage. He sounded a little dazed as he looked at me. "Thank you!"

"You're welcome," I said, feeling torn between relief and a grim sense I'd taken advantage of my friend. "I hope you earn as much as you think."

"You'll get your share of the profits," Jackson said. We'd settled on ten percent. "And I hope we'll see you at the workshop soon enough."

"If you know anyone else who might need an introduction, feel free to give them my name," I said, as we headed for the bridges. "I might be able to do something."

"We will." Kate gave me a mischievous smile. "There's quite a few clever people on the other side of the river, you know?"

"I know," I said. "I look forward to hearing from them."

We dropped Kate and her father off at the bridges, then drove back to Lamplighter Hall. I wasn't sure how to feel about the whole affair. I'd done well, yet...I'd really done very little. And yet, without me—and Uncle Stefano—Jackson Farthing would have gotten nowhere. He certainly could not have hoped to maintain some of his independence, if he'd gotten into bed with Albrecht Rubén. We'd ensured he'd have a degree of freedom even as he took their money.

I jumped out of the carriage as soon as we reached the hall and walked up to my office. Preparations for the next ball were well underway, even though we were running short of money again. I silently thanked the ancients that they'd paid in advance. It was going to be tight, but we'd already done most of the work when we'd hosted the first ball. I told myself, rather curtly, that I shouldn't be complaining. I was doing better than I'd had any right to expect.

And I have to go to another ball this weekend, I thought, as I cancelled the wards and stepped into the office. *My* office. The tables were covered in price sheets, maps and mining output projections. *And I have to see what else I can dig up.*

I sobered as I sat down and studied the charts. It was starting to look as through the price for Silverdale ore was finally starting to rise. I might have made it worse, by purchasing every last gram I could find. I'd done my best to calculate how high the price would rise, but there was no way to be sure. There were other mines, other seams. The Great Houses would probably be already trying to source new supplies. And if I got the timing wrong, I'd be lumbered with a vast quantity of ore I could neither sell nor use.

Which would mean disaster, I reminded myself. I counted the days in my head, trying to work out how long it would be until new supplies could be imported. *I'd never be able to repay the money.*

I felt a thrill at gambling, even though I knew I couldn't afford to lose. I'd learnt that was part of the fun, back at school...I shook my head.

Agreeing to do someone's homework or perform an embarrassing forfeit or *something* was hardly the end of the world. It just felt that way. But now...I could lose, and lose badly. I could lose everything. And it was part of the thrill. What was the fun in gambling if you could afford to lose?

Perhaps I should have joined the tables instead, I thought. Aristocrats won and lost fortunes at the gaming tables every day. I knew a dozen ways to cheat, most of which didn't involve magic. No one, even the most notorious rakes, could cheat like a schoolgirl intent on making her social superiors look like buffoons. *But I wouldn't have been able to raise enough money.*

I sighed, then placed my bet. I'd sell in a week, unless the price started to fall dramatically. If my projections were accurate, the sales would bring me a tidy profit. Not enough to repay Danny Prestwick, but enough to allow me to gamble again. And again. And again.

"And if it fails, I'll just have to try again," I told myself. "I still have cards to play."

CHAPTER
SIXTEEN

"A very good day's work," I said, as I ate breakfast. "We made a tidy profit."

"Yes. We did."

I glanced at Uncle Jalil. He looked grim, as if he needed to ask a question he didn't really *want* to ask. I'd thought he would be pleased. The price had risen faster than I'd anticipated, to the point where I'd seriously considered holding onto our stockpile of ore for a few more days. We'd made enough money to service at least *some* of our debts. There was nothing in the paper about it, of course, but that didn't worry me. Better they talked about the parties I hosted than the money I'd made.

And the last party was very helpful, I thought. I'd overheard a few more conversations, enough to let me place another set of bets. *Who knows how much money I can make in a year?*

I allowed myself a tight smile. Kate had been as good as her word, forwarding my name to a dozen businessmen who wanted me to act as their agent. I was still going through their proposals, but it was starting to look as if I could match at least *two* of them to aristocrats with more money than sense. My share of the profits would be low, but...it would all add up. Given time, I could start investing on my own and build up a real empire. I might not come to enjoy the wealth and power of Lord Joaquin Aguirre or Lord Carioca Rubén, but my children would be able to look their children in the eye as equals. Or so I hoped. It wasn't going to be easy—I knew I'd gotten lucky—but I had more room to manoeuvre now.

"We'll have to plan our next investment carefully," I said. I was due to attend the Braddock Ball the following day. Brantley had already written me a note, asking if he could take me to the ball. Who knew what I'd discover, if I had a chance to roam the halls? "We need to get our money's worth."

"Yes." Uncle Jalil still didn't sound happy. "We do."

I frowned inwardly as I finished my coffee, then piled my plates in the sink. We'd reopened the old kitchens and fancy dining rooms, but there was no point in using them until we had more servants. Besides, I didn't see the point. There was nothing to gain by dressing for dinner, let alone eating expensive food, unless we had guests. Why bother donning an outfit no one would see?

I'll have to wear something new tomorrow, I reminded myself. The dressmaker had already been contacted. Thankfully, she already knew my measurements. *But I don't want to attract too much attention.*

I headed up to my office. Uncle Jalil followed, walking so loudly he was practically stomping. It was silly, the kind of immature behaviour I expected from toddlers and aristocrats too useless to trust and too high-ranked to be discarded. My father had once joked a particularly useless family member should be given as a gift to a family we disliked...I smiled, then sobered. It hadn't been much of a joke, yet it was one of the few memories I had of him. I'd thought better of Uncle Jalil. He had a working brain.

I turned as soon as I entered the office. "What's the matter?"

Uncle Jalil shut the door, his eyes never leaving my face. I held his gaze evenly, feeling like a schoolgirl who knew she was in trouble even if she didn't know why. I reminded myself, sharply, that I was no longer a schoolgirl. I was the Matriarch, Head of House Lamplighter, and I was in charge. He might be my uncle, my mother's older brother, but I was in charge. It didn't make me feel any better. I needed him. I didn't have many other relatives I could trust.

"Lucy." Uncle Jalil stopped, as if he didn't want to continue. He sounded like someone who'd had a particularly disturbing revelation from the ancients. "Lucy, Lucky Lucy, how exactly did you know what to buy?"

I kept my face under tight control. "I got lucky."

"Too lucky." Uncle Jalil snorted, rudely. "*How* did you get lucky?"

It was all I could do to hold his gaze. I was a practiced liar, but I'd never had to lie to someone I liked and respected before. "I deduced the price would go up and…"

"I am an accountant," Uncle Jalil said. "Do you think I can't recognise the signs of insider trading? You made a call that just *happened* to be right, that just *happened* to be perfect, and you did it with precisely *zero* experience in investment. Or mining. How did you know the price would go up?"

I felt my legs wobble. I held myself straight, somehow. I'd coped with disapproval before, but this…this was worse. I didn't much care, at base, what Mistress Grayling had to say. I didn't care about Marlene's opinion. I was quite happy to nod my head at the right places and carry on doing my own thing as soon as they stopped babbling. But Uncle Jalil was my *uncle*. I liked him and respected him and…I'd never even considered he might catch on to what I'd done. It had never crossed my mind.

"I saw some papers suggesting the price would go up, and that certain parties were hoarding stockpiles for themselves," I said. It was technically true. "And I thought we could try it for ourselves."

"Lucy." Uncle Jalil closed his eyes for a long moment, as if he *really* didn't want to ask the next question. "Where did you see the papers?"

"Robin Bolingbroke's office," I said. There was no point in trying to hide anything else. "I sneaked inside when I attended the ball."

Uncle Jalil swayed, his face going pale. "Are you out of your mind?"

He walked past me and sat down, without waiting for an invitation. It was technically rude—the office was mine, in all senses of the word—but he was too far gone to care. I composed myself quickly, before he looked at me again. What was done was done. It could not be changed, not now. And I'd done it for the family. My lips twitched, humourlessly. Uncle Jalil was the only person in the hall who wouldn't consider that a valid defence.

"Lucy." Uncle Jalil looked up. "Do you have any idea how much trouble you could have gotten into?"

"Yes," I said, flatly.

"Really," he said. His lips flattened into a humourless line. "I very much doubt it."

"I know," I insisted. "And I didn't get caught."

"I saw the papers," Uncle Jalil said. "Anyone who studies them with a cynical eye will have good reason to suspect insider trading. Either you were allied with Robin Bolingbroke or you somehow obtained the information from him. Sure, it isn't *proof* of anything, but you know how quickly rumours spread."

"There are always rumours," I said, tartly. "How many of them are true?"

"The *evidence*," Uncle Jalil said harshly, "suggests that you had inside information. The *real* insiders will know they didn't give it to you. They'll start to wonder where you got it. And then..."

"Maybe I did get lucky," I said. I'd gone through the facts and figures very carefully, looking for proof the mines really *were* running dry. There'd been a handful of hints...I grimaced as I realised someone without inside information might not have drawn the right conclusions. Prices rose and fell all the time. It was quite possible someone would believe it was just a random flux that would be corrected soon enough. "The figures..."

"The odds against you making the right call, in a manner that earned you a massive profit, are staggeringly low," Uncle Jalil said. "Sure, you can make a lot of money by predicting the future successfully. People have made reputations by doing just that. But I'd expect to see more people— many more people—lose money by predicting the future *unsuccessfully*.

You simply cannot come out ahead on your first try, unless you're either very lucky or you're cheating somehow."

He looked, for a moment, as if he were blinded with rage. "Didn't they teach you anything at school?"

"Yes." I glared at him, unwilling to let him cow me. "They taught me how to play the game, how to remain stoic and not make a sound even when someone twists my ear. They taught me how to sneak around, how to collect information I could use for later advantage. They taught me I had to support my family, come what may. And they taught me that anything went, as long as I didn't get caught."

"As long as you didn't get caught," Uncle Jalil echoed. His voice turned mocking. "What do you think will happen to you—here and now—if you get caught?"

"And what do you think will happen," I snapped, "if we don't pay our debts?"

I went on before he could even *try* to answer. "There's nothing to sell. Everything we have is entailed. But the courts will seize it, if they are pushed. We'll lose everything, even the clothes on our backs. You watched my father drive us deeper and deeper into debt. How long can we keep papering over the cracks before the centre can no longer hold?"

"You had some good ideas," Uncle Jalil said. "Hosting parties, making introductions…"

I cut him off, savagely. "We could host every ball for the next ten years," I snapped. "We could introduce every last businessman in Water Shallot to aristocrats with lots of money and little common sense, taking half of each loan as payment. We could jack up the prices of everything we sell tenfold and…

"Uncle, we still couldn't even *begin* to service our debts. We need money. And fast!"

"I told you not to take up the post," Uncle Jalil thundered. His face darkened alarmingly. "Why didn't you listen to me?"

"Because it was my duty," I said. "I had to…"

"No, you didn't." Uncle Jalil stood and paced over to the window. "There's no obligation to serve. Heir Primus or not, you didn't have to succeed your father. You could have simply left. You could have built a career of your own, instead of being encumbered with debts you can't hope to repay."

He turned to face me. "And what do you think will happen if you get caught?"

"I won't get caught," I said.

"Fine words," Uncle Jalil said. He waved a hand at the window. "On a very clear day, you can see Skullbreaker Island. I'm pretty damn sure, *Lucy*, that every last criminal dumped on that island and left to rot told himself he wouldn't be caught either. You know why they're there? *They got caught!*

"You could have left. You could still leave."

My heart twisted. "I can't," I said. I didn't want to believe that was true. "Not now."

"Change your name, get some false papers," Uncle Jalil said, shortly. "It's easier than you might think. The family will collapse, of course, but you don't have to be here for it."

"And that will be the end," I said. "What'll happen to House Lamplighter then?"

Uncle Jalil shrugged. "Does it matter?"

"It matters to me," I told him. House Lamplighter had made me. I owed it. "I *need* to rebuild the family."

"For what?" Uncle Jalil laughed, humourlessly. "What does it gain you?"

I hesitated. Cold logic suggested he was right. There was nothing to be gained by trying to rebuild the family. Our debts were so great that it was unlikely we could ever rid ourselves of them. I could leave…and yet, the family was *mine*. Uncle Jalil had married into it…no, his *sister* had married into it. How could he understand what it was like to grow up as Heir Primus? I'd known I would inherit the family one day. I just hadn't expected it to be so soon.

"The family," I said, finally. The family was *mine*. "I can't just walk away."

Uncle Jalil glared. "And do you think you can just walk away, if you get caught?"

I turned away, unwilling to let him see my face. He was right. There might be no formal punishment if I was caught, but word would go around High Society and doors would start slamming in my face. High Society would normally expect the Matriarch or Patriarch to punish me, to cleanse the family's reputation by disowning or exiling me, yet...I *was* the Matriarch. They'd expect me to punish myself. I snorted at the thought. Maybe I could give myself a stern talking to...

"You are facing an uphill challenge," Uncle Jalil said. His voice was a little gentler. "You cannot afford to destroy your reputation, not now."

I snorted. He was right. If I'd just wanted money, I could have engaged myself to *all* the possible candidates, taken the dowries and run. There were a dozen money-making schemes I could have tried, if I didn't care about staying in the city afterwards. I'd considered them, but...I'd have had to run or face the music. And that really *would* be the end.

The people who sell fake Objects of Power always run before they can be caught out, I reminded myself. I'd met my share of peddlers at school. Nothing they sold lasted longer than a few days. *I have to stay in the city.*

He rested a hand on my shoulder. "Lucy, you're the closest thing I have to a daughter," he said. His voice turned reflective. "I think you're actually my only living blood relative. And I don't want to see you destroyed, not for this. Not for *anything*. Quit while you're ahead."

"I know what to watch for," I said. I relied on Uncle Jalil to handle the buying and selling. I could master the art, given time, but as long as I didn't handle it personally I could put the brakes on at any moment. There was something to be said for negotiating through intermediaries. "I will be making other trades."

"Lucy..." Uncle Jalil let out a breath. I had the feeling he'd had a similar argument with my father. "Listen to me. Quit while you're ahead. Please."

He strode through the door, closing it firmly behind him. I sagged into the nearest chair, feeling as if I'd just been put through the wringer. It was worse, somehow, to be lectured by someone you respected. I'd never liked or trusted any of my tutors—and I'd barely seen my father even before he'd sent me away—but Uncle Jalil was different. He had a point. I *was* pushing the limits as far as they would go. Sure, anything went as long as you didn't get caught...as long as you didn't get caught. I knew the rule. And yet...

I need the money, I told myself. *And I need inside information to get it.*

But it was more than that, I acknowledged privately. It wasn't *just* the money. It wasn't just the desperate need to boost the family fortunes. It was...it was the thrill of doing something dangerous, something that could easily get me in real trouble, and getting away with it. I hadn't *had* to sneak into Marlene's room, or bolster my reputation as a fourth-year troublemaker by raiding a prefect's room...I'd done it for the thrill, for the joy of knowing I'd outwitted an older student, and for the admiration of my peers. And they *had* admired my pluck.

They didn't know everything I did, I reminded myself. There were secrets I'd kept firmly to myself, tricks and pranks no one had ever pinned on me. *But I knew.*

Uncle Jalil had a point, I told myself again. I *should* quit while I was ahead. But I couldn't. I needed the money and the thrill and...I remembered, suddenly, the day I really *had* been caught. The prefect should have been a little more careful. I'd hexed her and run and...the unwritten rules were clear. If someone got away, they got away. They couldn't be punished later. And the way she'd glowered at me until she'd left the school the following year had merely been the icing on the cake.

I stood and walked to the desk. The latest figures waited for me. We'd definitely made a sizable profit. I was starting to build a reputation as a canny investor. I even had a good excuse, if anyone came asking why I wasn't investing more often. And...I smiled as I started to sift through the information on House Braddock. They'd done very well for themselves.

I knew there had to be *something* of value within the house. I just had to find it.

Uncle Jalil would not approve. I knew I wasn't going to tell him.

There's no choice, I told myself. We needed the money. And I needed the thrill. I couldn't stop, not now. I wanted to keep going until…until when? Never, perhaps. Uncle Jalil *really* wouldn't approve. And yet, it was easy to convince myself it didn't matter. *He'll do as he's told.*

It was an unworthy thought. I admitted it, to myself if no one else. But it was true. Shaking my head, I reached for the papers. It was time to start laying my plans.

CHAPTER
SEVENTEEN

"I'm surprised you came alone," Brantley whispered, as he swung me around the dance floor. "Don't you have a maiden aunt to watch over you?"

I allowed myself a tight smile. "She had something else to do with her time," I said, with a wink that would have given Mistress Grayling a heart attack. "I think I've got too many relatives. It's time for a cull."

Brantley snickered at my joke. We'd been dancing for hours, slowly growing closer and closer. I was mildly surprised he hadn't made a move already as evening turned into night and dancers spilled onto the lawn to mingle with their peers. There was an edge in the air that bothered me, whispered conversations that grew quiet whenever one of the younger generation approached. I had a feeling the elders had more important problems, right now, than paying attention to us. It would have been insulting, if it hadn't been so useful. I didn't want people watching us as we finally left the dance hall.

He tugged on my arm as we swung near to the door, pulling me into the side corridor. I could have broken his grip easily, but chose to let him take me out of the hall. Charms hung in the air, making it harder to see clearly as we walked down the corridor. There had to be a *lot* of backroom dealing going on, between parties that would normally prefer to die than to be seen together in public. I felt a twinge of envy—the parties I'd hosted hadn't been anything like so influential—but told myself not to be silly. There were limits to what I could learn by eavesdropping on powerful people.

"In here," Brantley said, pushing open a door to reveal a small room. "The wards are..."

"Not here," I said, quickly. "Upstairs. Take me to your room."

I saw the struggle on his face. Taking me upstairs would get him in real trouble if he were caught. The Great Houses had always had double standards—I'd never understood them—and there was nothing we could do about it, but he wanted me. I could tell, from the way his hands had wandered during the dance. I did my best to look beguiling as he made up his mind and tugged me towards a statue. The stairwell behind it was neatly hidden behind a pair of cunningly-designed wards. I'd never have been able to get up the stairs without him.

"I can't take you to the uppermost floors," Brantley whispered, as we reached the second floor. The corridor felt cold and empty. The house servants would have gone downstairs to help with the party. "But I can take you to my office."

I smiled at him, feeling a twinge of relief. Brantley had spent hours bragging about his political and financial acumen. I thought he was making a play for my hand, unaware I was already engaged...I tried not to feel guilty as he pulled me into his office, closing and locking the door behind me. The chamber was so ornate—and in such terrible taste—I was almost disappointed. A man of true wealth and power wouldn't feel the need to advertise it so blatantly. Everything was handmade, from the chairs and sofa to the giant desk. The desk was edged with gold. I scowled, inwardly. Brantley had wasted more money on his office than I'd spent on renovating the hall.

Brantley pulled me to him and kissed me, hard. It took everything I had not to recoil as he mashed his lips against mine. He was *not* a good kisser. I'd kissed boys who were bold and boys who were nervous, but

Brantley...he acted as if I was nothing more than a slattern. I felt a hot flash of anger as he tugged me towards the sofa, his hands already fiddling with my dress. Any qualms I might have had about taking advantage of him vanished like dew on a sunny morning. How dare he?

You could have said no at any moment, I reminded myself, dryly. *And instead you chose to let him think you were interested.*

I braced myself as he sat on the sofa and pulled me onto his lap, then cast the charm as our lips met again. Brantley was hardly defenceless—he'd woven a handful of protective spells around himself—but I could bypass most of them simply by touching his bare skin. And the charm itself was very subtle, hard to fight off and harder still to break once it took effect. I smirked, remembering late night sessions in the dorms where the prefects had taught the younger girls charms to protect themselves when young men went a little too far. I could have turned him into a frog, or given him a very nasty shock, or simply stopped him in his tracks...and it would have been perfectly legal. It was supposed to be hard, we'd been told, to cast the spells unless there was a serious threat to our lives or our virtues. Brantley fell back, a dazed expression crossing his face. I smirked. The charm would let him think he'd had his way with me. His imagination would fill the gaps in his memory.

And make it harder for him to suspect anything bad happened, I thought, as I stood and brushed down my dress. My lips felt as if they were covered in slime. *He won't want to think anything else.*

I put the thought aside as I carefully reached out with my mind, assessing the charms surrounding the room. There was a simple privacy ward, nestled within the house wards, and a locking spell on the door that promised to keep the rest of the world out for hours. I smiled and walked over to the desk, keeping my senses open. There were a handful of locking charms on each of the drawers, so many of them layered together that they were actually interfering with each other. I allowed myself a smile—it was clear Brantley hadn't gone to Grayling's—as I started to work. Brantley had bragged of his skill in magic, but the charms on his desk had been put together by rote. It was surprisingly easy to weaken them to the point I could pull the first drawer open.

My heart sank as I surveyed the paperwork. The papers were scattered so badly that there was no obvious order, if indeed there was an order at all. My eyes narrowed as I caught sight of a marriage contract between Brantley and Lady Saline...he had a marriage contract and he'd risked making love to me? I rolled my eyes. The match had probably been arranged, but that didn't excuse humiliating one's fiancée in public. I told myself, firmly, it was none of my business as I worked my way through the rest of the drawers. It was hard to escape the impression I'd risked everything, for nothing. Brantley didn't seem to have any *real* power or influence, beyond the little that came with being an adult aristocrat. I cursed under my breath as I glared at his slumbering form. I wanted to give him a *real* curse. The prefects had taught me those too.

I opened the next drawer and peered at the letters. They were surprisingly alike, even though they came from different people. My eyes narrowed as I read a dozen polite rejections...rejections of what? It looked as if Brantley had tried to recruit his fellow students...for what? Reading between the lines, it sounded as if his fellow students had had enough of Brantley while they'd been at school. I knew how they felt. There'd been girls at school I never wanted to see again. I memorised the names, intending to look them up as soon as I had a moment. Brantley would have gone to Jude's. His classmates would be listed in the school yearbooks.

One letter references potion brewing, I mused, as I put the letters back in the drawer. *Was he trying to recruit potioneers?*

I shrugged, then opened the final drawer. It was something I'd have to consider later. The last drawer held a collection of title deeds, all issued and charmed by Magus Court. I blinked in surprise, feeling—for the first time since I'd charmed Brantley into quiescence—as if I'd hit paydirt. The title deeds *had* to belong to Brantley. He wouldn't have kept them in his desk if they weren't *his*. I scanned them quickly, laying them on the gilt-edged desk. Brantley was steadily buying up a whole string of properties in Water Shallot...a whole *block* of properties. It wasn't obvious until I looked at them as a group. Brantley had laid claim to an entire city block. No, not an *entire* city block. A couple of properties were still out of his grasp. And that meant...

He was bragging about making a killing in property, I reminded myself. I'd dismissed it as worthless nonsense when we'd been dancing, but maybe he'd been telling the truth...I allowed myself a smirk. Wonders would never cease. *What is he doing?*

I sat on his sinfully-comfortable chair—it felt like a throne—and went through the documents for the second time. The properties were definitely all connected. If one person held the title deeds to them *all*, he could practically set whatever price he liked. The demand was much higher than the supply, particularly as the title deeds included the land as well as the buildings. I made a careful note of the address, intending to look the remaining properties up as soon as possible. If I got my hands on them, Brantley would have to pay through the nose if *he* wanted them. And I had a feeling he'd be reluctant to pressure Magus Court to seize the land. Even if compensation was paid, it would open a whole new can of worms.

Brantley moaned. I glanced at him as I hastily returned the documents to the drawer and rebuilt the charms. I'd done it before at school, although I hadn't always been successful. A couple of older girls had detected me, I was sure, and sought revenge rather than ratting me out to the teachers. I was fairly sure *that* was where some of the nastier hexes had come from...I shook my head. As far as Brantley knew, we'd spent the last half-hour making out. He wouldn't want to think otherwise. I felt a moment of sympathy for Lady Saline. She didn't deserve to be wedded to him. I didn't know anyone who *did*.

Except possibly Marlene, I thought. *But Marlene has enough magic to keep him in line.*

I finished rebuilding the charms, then stood and looked around the room. There were no filing cabinets, no hidden safes...the only object of interest was a giant drinks cabinet. I opened it and peered inside, snorting as I saw the small collection of expensive wines and potions. He'd spent more money on alcohol than I could afford to spend on just about everything. I shrugged and closed the cabinet, then headed back to Brantley. It was time to bring him out of the trance. I tried not to look disgusted as I sat on his lap and carefully undid the spell. I couldn't risk his memory being jarred. It might lead him to question everything he thought to be true.

Brantley shifted against me. "You're good. You're very good."

"Thanks." I tried to sound as if I'd had a good time. "You're very good too."

There was a sharp knock on the door. I jumped back, nearly falling on my rump. Brantley caught my arm as the knock came again, his eyes flickering from side to side as he tried to find a place to hide me. Whoever was on the far side wasn't going to go away in a hurry. The knocking was too authoritative to be anyone but a senior aristocrat. A servant would never have knocked so hard. Brantley's eyes widened in near-panic. There was no washroom, no wardrobe, nowhere he could hide me...I nearly smiled. In hindsight, the lack of any such facilities was a fairly clear sign he was nowhere near as important as he claimed.

Brantley jabbed a finger at me, casting a spell. I had to bite my lip to keep from crying out—or trying to fight the spell—as the world shrunk around me. It was hardly the first time I'd been turned into something, but...I felt my vision shift and blur as the magic took hold. I could neither move nor speak. He'd turned me into...I wasn't sure what. An object, obviously...I forced myself to wait, even as he picked me up and put me in his pocket. It was good thinking on his part, I supposed. He couldn't leave me in the room alone.

"Brantley," a voice said. Female, old enough to issue orders and expect them to be obeyed...his mother? Or auntie? "Why aren't you downstairs?"

"I got bored of dancing," Brantley said. "And I came upstairs to do some work."

I was morbidly impressed. His tone was languid, without even a hint of resentment he'd been interrupted. I guessed he'd learnt to dissemble young, just like me. There was nothing like boarding school to teach you how to pretend it didn't hurt, even if it did. Weakness was…well, weakness. A weakling had no friends, for fear it might rub off.

"Work," the voice repeated. "And what *work* is so important you neglect your duty to the family?"

I felt Brantley shifting angrily as he spoke. "I want to make something of myself…"

"Which you will, by serving the family," the voice said. "These are trying times. We've given you tasks to do and you haven't done them. House Aguirre already has too big an advantage. We needed the contacts you bragged you had."

My mind raced. Contacts? Contacts for what? Potions? House Aguirre was famed for its potions. And Brantley had been trying to hire potioneers? I would have grinned, if I still had lips. I was fairly sure I understood why he'd been unsuccessful. I'd sooner become a lady of the evening than go to work for Brantley and his cronies.

"I did my best," Brantley whined. "If you'd given me the power to offer patronage at school, I could have…"

The voice cut him off. "You had the power," she said. "Now, go back to the party and try and act like a decent man. I'm not shelling out thousands of crowns—again—to save you from the consequences of your own stupidity. Go."

"Yes, Auntie," Brantley said.

I felt him walking through the door and down the stairs. I hoped he'd have the sense to stop somewhere and drop me off, either undoing the spell or letting me break it from the inside. It would be dangerous to cancel the spell while I was in his pocket, although…I shuddered as I silently replayed everything I'd heard. If Brantley's aunt had paid thousands of crowns to cover something up...what had he done? There weren't many possibilities. But I could guess.

"I'm sorry," Brantley said. I felt him pull me out of his pocket and put me on the floor. "I had to hide you."

The spell broke. I snapped back to normal. We were in one of the small meeting rooms. I brushed down my dress, then took a compact from my pocket and examined myself in the mirror. I looked a little flushed, but otherwise decent. Brantley smiled at me, shifting from side to side. We'd come very close to being caught. I wondered, idly, what his aunt would have said if she'd caught us. It would have been a major scandal if it had become public. But that was part of the fun.

"I understand," I said. It had worked out in my favour, I supposed. "But we can't see each other again for a while."

Brantley's expression darkened, looking alarmingly mulish. I winced inwardly, wondering if I'd have to do something desperate. I didn't need him trying to cling to me, even though he thought we'd been intimate. I guessed he felt the thrill of doing something he shouldn't too...I cursed under my breath. What *had* Brantley done? I was sure it had involved a girl, one well-bred enough to make a fuss and yet too low-born to *guarantee* it. And probably not one who knew how to defend herself.

"We can meet elsewhere," Brantley said, stubbornly. "I'm sure you enjoyed it too."

"I did," I lied. "But we cannot be caught."

I waved at the door. "You go now and mingle," I said. "I'll go the other way in a couple of minutes."

Brantley bowed. "Come back soon, please."

"I don't want to risk being caught again," I lied. No, it wasn't *entirely* a lie. Getting caught poking through someone's drawers was entirely different to being caught with an entirely unsuitable boy. "It would be... unpleasant."

"Really?" Brantley sniggered. "I thought *you* were the Matriarch. What are you going to do? Flog yourself?"

It would have been funny, I supposed, if so much hadn't been at stake. I pointed at the door. "Out."

He left, leaving me alone. I took a deep breath, calming myself as much as possible. I'd learnt something useful, even if I wasn't sure what to do with it. And I had an excuse for avoiding him in the future. And...

Poor Lady Saline, I thought, as I cast a glamour and headed for the door. *She doesn't know what she's getting into.*

CHAPTER
EIGHTEEN

"Father was very pleased with the tip," Gary said, two days after I'd visited Braddock Hall. "He's upped the price for the last two shops considerably."

I nodded. We sat together in my sitting room, drinking tea. Jadish had chaperoned for a few minutes, to satisfy propriety, then gone off to do something else with her time. I wasn't sure if she thought she was doing me a favour or not. I liked Gary, but…I wanted to make enough money to repay the dowry and break the engagement before it became public. And yet…I liked him. There was something about his manner that appealed to me. I wasn't sure what it was. He wasn't as entitled or obnoxious as most of my male peers. Instead, he had an air of calm competence that suggested he knew precisely what he was doing.

"Just make sure you don't let them know who tipped you off," I said. "Ideally, don't let them know it's *you* who purchased the shops."

"Dad knows what he's doing," Gary said. "He already owned one of the shops."

I smiled. I had no intention of *stopping* Brantley from purchasing the entire block and selling it to a developer, or perhaps even developing it himself, but I intended to make sure he paid a steep price for it. I'd get enough of a cut to…I wasn't sure what I'd do with it, not yet, but I would do something. Perhaps I could invest in more clients. If I'd learnt one thing in the last few weeks, it was that I could build up a retinue of commoners by investing in their careers.

"That's a stroke of luck," I said. "Did he know what'd happened to the others?"

"He knew someone was buying them up," Gary said. "The new owner didn't know to hide his tracks."

"So I gathered," I said, trying not to wince. Uncle Jalil's words haunted me. He'd made it clear that *someone* might guess what I was doing and why. I'd done my best to start working out excuses, to come up with explanations that might conceal the truth, but I knew they might not be believed. Mud stuck, particularly when people *wanted* it to. "I'm sure he'll pay well above the odds for the remaining buildings."

Gary grinned. "So I'm told," he said. "What tipped you off?"

"I heard some chatter," I said. "And then I put the pieces together."

"Good." Gary sipped his tea for a long moment, clearly casting around for another topic of conversation. "Did you get your exam results?"

"Not yet," I said. "They're probably still laughing their heads off."

"I doubt it," Gary said. "You're far from stupid."

He smiled, suddenly. "Are all the stories about Grayling's true?"

"Well..." I drew the word out as much as possible. "It rather depends on which stories you've heard."

I studied my tea for a long moment. "It...I never had the impression the school was *that* interested in teaching, if you know what I mean. I got good marks, but the quality of the tutors was very limited...some of them did a very good job and others were clearly doing nothing more than going through the motions. A lot of the students weren't welcome in their family homes, for one reason or another..."

Gary coughed. "They weren't welcome?"

"They were embarrassments." I felt cold, as if my heart had turned to ice. "Or they simply weren't welcome back home."

I pushed on before he could ask any awkward questions. "Life in the dorms could be good or bad. If you played the game, if you learnt to stand up for yourself and your friends, you had a really good time of it. If you didn't...an outcast's life is simply not worth living. We had gangs and groups and all sorts of clubs and we spent an awful lot of time fighting each other and sneaking around...I always had the impression the teachers didn't care what we did, as long as we didn't do it openly."

"It sounds just like Jude's," Gary said. "Weren't there any boys there?"

"No." I shook my head. "Some of the girls dated boys from the nearest village. Others developed pashes—crushes—on their girlfriends. There were rumours about a boy's school on the other side of the mirrors, but... it was just a silly story. Someone cast a spell on a mirror so anyone who looked at their reflection would see a boy and the story just got out of hand."

"There are lots of silly stories at Jude's too," Gary said. "Believe me."

"I do," I said. "I..."—I found myself looking for another topic too—"tell me about your apprenticeship."

"I've been studying charms," Gary said. His face lit up as he started to talk. "There are layers upon layers of charms most people don't know exist."

I listened, occasionally asking questions as he talked. I was pretty good at charms, both the ones I'd been taught and the ones I'd picked up on my own, but Gary was head and shoulders above me. He knew how to alter charms to respond to different people, how to set up wards that were far more discriminating than even standard house wards and...I made a mental list of questions to ask him, of spells he could teach me. I didn't have to tell him what I wanted them for, I told myself. He could give me lessons without ever knowing what I intended to *do* with the knowledge.

"There are some trunks that belonged to my father I haven't been able to open," I told him, when he'd finished talking. I didn't want him to think I wasn't interested. "Would you take a look at them?"

"I can," Gary said. "But I can't promise anything."

I stood. Auntie Dorcas would have a minor heart attack, if she knew

I'd taken Gary to the uppermost floor. I was almost tempted to tell her. It wasn't as if she could badmouth me to the matriarch. I put the thought firmly to one side as I stood and led Gary up the stairs, silently grateful there were so few people living in the hall. Auntie Dorcas hadn't even *hinted* she'd like to move back home. I wondered if she thought I was going to crash and burn or…if she just hated the idea of making her case to a woman she probably remembered as a little girl. It would have to sting.

"And all of this is yours?" Gary looked around, his eyes wide with wonder. "Yours and yours alone?"

"It belongs to the family," I said. I didn't have the heart to tell him that House Lamplighter was more than a little shabby. We'd done a little cleaning and renovation on the uppermost floor, but it had been a low priority. No one was meant to see it, not yet. "It's mine as long as I serve as matriarch, but it isn't mine personally."

"The perks of the job," Gary said.

"In a way…" I felt a twinge of guilt as I led him into one of the smaller offices. We weren't married *yet*. We might *never* be married. "The job comes with a price."

I scowled to myself. Gary and his father *knew* we were short of money. We wouldn't have humbled ourselves in front of them if we didn't *need* them. I wondered just how much they knew—or cared—about our situation. They wouldn't have loaned us the money if they hadn't known we were desperate, if they hadn't thought there was a reasonable chance we wouldn't be able to repay. I felt another twinge of guilt. Gary was nice. He didn't deserve to find himself in a loveless match.

"This was your father's office?" Gary's voice was incredulous. "Or his bedroom?"

"No." I laughed. "His bedroom is on the fifth floor."

I understood, all too well. The office was empty, save for a handful of trunks and charmed boxes. The walls were grey, stained with dust. I wasn't sure why my father had kept his schoolboy trunk, let alone turned it into a repository for...for *something*. He'd done a good job, I admitted sourly. I knew how to break into someone's trunk—I'd done it enough at school—but father's trunk was beyond me.

"Where do you want me to start?" Gary looked around the room. "Do you have anything in mind?"

"That one," I said. My father's old leather trunk should have gone to me. He'd purchased a new one for me when I'd been sent away. I hadn't thought anything of it at the time—I'd been too young to understand the tradition—but it bothered me now. Why had he paid so much money when he could have given me one of his? "And be careful."

Gary knelt beside the trunk. "I've seen a couple like this," he said, more to himself than to me. "They went out of fashion ten years or so ago. The leather simply didn't hold charms for very long."

I watched, fascinated, as he went to work. Some of the charms he used to probe the trunk were familiar; others were new. His magic drifted over the trunk without ever quite touching it, parsing out the defences without triggering them. I felt growing admiration as he worked out the spells, figuring out how to break them. Gary knew what he was doing. I hadn't met anyone so focused in years. It was impressive.

He's got strong magic, I thought. It wasn't uncommon to have powerful magicians marry into the aristocracy. I was the matriarch, admittedly, but there was a shortage of other candidates. *Perhaps being married to him won't be so bad.*

Gary looked up. "There's two layers of spells on the trunk," he said. "I think your father must have been a skilled charmsmith, as he's actually woven them into the leather and metal and made them stick. I think"—he frowned—"I think he worked blood into the material as a base. I can't think of anything else that would remain so powerful for so long."

I winced. "Did he use dark magic?"

"That's debatable," Gary said. "If it was his own blood...no, technically."

"I see," I said. I'd been given the same warnings as everyone else.

Anything that called for blood was to be regarded with extreme suspicion. The spells weren't automatically dark—blood-based potions often made the difference between life and death—but they could be very dangerous. "Can you open it?"

"Perhaps." Gary met my eyes. "I'd need to use some of your blood."

"And it might not work anyway," I mused. If my father had keyed the trunk specifically to himself, *my* blood might trigger an explosion. His parents were long dead and he'd never had any siblings. Uncle Stefano was the closest except for me, and he was a second cousin. "I think"—I swallowed, hard—"show me what to do."

Gary looked nervous, which didn't make me feel any better as he started to talk me through the procedure. I'd spent enough time around men and boys to know they loved explaining things, particularly to women they were trying to impress. Gary wasn't like that—I thought—but he'd still like to show off, just a little. If he was reluctant to show me how to perform the spells...they had to be dangerous, more dangerous than he'd claimed. I knew enough about blood magic to know how easily it could go wrong.

And all of the nonsense people say about it doesn't help, I thought, as I tried to focus on the charms. Gary was a good teacher, but there were gaps in my knowledge. *There's too much we don't understand about how it works.*

I cut my finger, just slightly, and pressed the blood against the trunk. Magic crackled around me, the spellform seemingly unable to decide if it wanted to let me in or throw me out. I cursed my father under my breath, realising—too late—that my blood would be unmistakeably female. I was very definitely not my father, whoever I was. The magic flickered—for a moment, I was sure it was going to try to kill me—and snapped out of existence. The trunk clicked open. I opened the lid enough to confirm I could open and close it at will, then put it to one side. I'd have to study the contents later.

"Well done," Gary said. "Do you want to do the others?"

"I'll let you do the next one," I said. It would mean giving him a little of my blood, but it would be very educational. "Please."

Gary nodded and went to work. I watched, studying precisely how he charmed my blood to fool the wards. It was a cunning trick, one that wouldn't last for long, but...it worked. I watched him open two more, planning to find a way to practice as soon as possible. Gary wouldn't be happy, I was sure, if I told him what I wanted to do with the knowledge. There was no way I could ask him directly.

"There are a few other wards I can't change," I said, carefully. "Would you like to take a look at them?"

"Sure," Gary said. "It should be fun."

It was, although perhaps not for the reason he had in mind. I watched and learnt as he cast spells and manipulated the wards, keeping up a running commentary that both educated and suggested lines of enquiry for later experimentation. I didn't have a big library—my father had apparently sold most of the books to raise funds—but I was fairly sure I could get access to Magus Court's library if I wanted. I was an aristocrat with a family seat, after all. Gary seemed to grow more and more enthused as the hours wore on, dragging me along as he studied the older wards. Who'd have thought there were so many chinks in our defences?

"It's an old problem," he said, when we were both tired and happy. We headed down to the kitchenette. "The more complex the wards, the smaller the space they can cover."

I nodded in agreement as I heated the water and brewed tea for both of us. Brantley, damn the man, would have been flabbergasted if I'd made tea for him. He honestly wouldn't have known what to make of it. I could have taken off my clothes in front of him and he would have been less shocked. A member of the aristocracy, a girl born with her nose in the air, making tea? It would have been astonishing. Gary, of course, didn't know there was anything unusual about it. He had no way to know most Grande Dames would sooner have died than admit they couldn't afford a servant to make tea.

"Thank you," he said, when I placed the mug in front of him. He didn't know or care it wasn't served in the finest china, perhaps with a hint of fancy cream. "I...next time, maybe you can come to my house."

"That would be nice," I said. I wasn't sure that was true. "I...thank you for your help."

"You're more than welcome," Gary said. "Do you want to do some more?"

"I think so, later," I said. I'd have to do some research, perhaps figure out what questions I needed to ask. And what questions I *could* ask. "I enjoyed it."

Gary blinked. "Really?"

I had to smile. "Yes, really."

"You're the first person who's ever said that," Gary told me. "My father and sister thought I was mad to go into charms."

"They have their uses," I said. I'd bet the family fortune—which wasn't very much, come to think of it—that Gary's house was practically invulnerable. "Why didn't your sister study magic?"

"She knows some," Gary said. "But she had to help Dad with the business."

"I see." I sipped my tea, thoughtfully. I needed a shower and then... and then I needed to go through the opened boxes very carefully. "Gary... can you think of a good reason for hiring a bunch of potioneers?"

"To make potions?" Gary made a face. "Why else?"

"I don't know," I said. In hindsight, I was fairly sure House Braddock had been trying to hire potioneers without making it obvious. It wouldn't have been *hard* to hire potioneers, particularly if they just wanted someone to follow the recipe and not make any improvements along the way. "It just bugs me."

"Well, whoever is hiring them might want to mass-produce something," Gary said. "Healing potions, perhaps. Or something used to make Devices of Power."

Or Objects of Power, I thought. *Brantley's Aunt mentioned House Aguirre, didn't she?*

"Perhaps." I finished my tea and stood. "Thank you very much for a lovely afternoon."

Gary smiled. "It was a very interesting afternoon," he agreed. He stood, looking as if he wanted to take me in his arms. I recognised the signs of a boy who wanted to be forward, but didn't quite dare. "And I hope to see you again soon."

I hesitated, torn between the urge to kiss him and the grim awareness it would only hurt him. He was no aristocrat who'd expect a political marriage...I felt another twinge of guilt as I rang the bell for Jadish. She could take Gary downstairs and show him out while I showered, then went back to the office to read my father's notes and work on the puzzle. Why *did* House Braddock want so many potioneers?

And how, I asked myself, *can I turn it to my advantage?*

CHAPTER
NINETEEN

"Welcome to House Aguirre," Alana Aguirre said, as she led us into her father's study. "I've heard a great deal about you."

"All of it true, apart from the lies," I said. Alana sounded almost... envious. I found it hard to hide my irritation. Alana had more wealth and power now, as Heir Primus, than I had as Matriarch of House Lamplighter. And yet, her hair was still in braids. "It's a pleasure to meet you and your father formally."

I curtsied as Lord Joaquin Aguirre, High Magus of Magus Court, stood and walked around his desk. He was a tall man with very dark skin and darker eyes. His hair was woven into a fancy design that might, or might not, be a wig. His suit was finely-tailored to show off his form without either displaying his muscles or hiding a paunch. I felt a glimmer of respect, mingled with envy. House Aguirre was so wealthy that this man—and his children and grandchildren—could spend madly, without ever bankrupting themselves.

"Lord Aguirre," I said. I indicated my companions. "Please allow me to introduce Stefano Lamplighter and Jayne Parkinson, Master Brewer."

Lord Aguirre bowed in greeting. "Please, be seated," he said. "I was very interested to read your note."

I nodded as I took my seat, studying Lord Aguirre and his daughter thoughtfully. Alana was striking rather than pretty, her face a little too hard-edged for my tastes. I'd met enough girls like her over the years, far from stupid and yet very entitled and demanding. I wondered, idly, if her father had started to consider possible husbands. Alana would need to marry well, just like me. It didn't help that her sister was already betrothed to an Heir Primus. There was no way Alana could marry *that* well.

"My clients and I have a proposal," I began, trying not to show my concern. I'd done a *lot* of research over the last few days, but it was hard to be *sure* I was right. Brantley and his family might have been up to something completely different. "And I think it may be of interest to you."

I spoke rapidly, explaining that I'd agreed to serve as representative for a small association of potioneers. They weren't *precisely* my clients, but I'd been the one who'd called them together and promised them gainful employment. House Aguirre could outbid House Braddock even if Brantley hadn't been such a pain in the neck. I'd made sure to approach most of the potioneers he'd asked, the ones who might be interested if someone else had made the offer. If House Aguirre really did want the potioneers, they'd have to go through me.

Unless they want to undercut me, I thought. They could, if they wanted, but it would cost them in the long run. Besides, I didn't really care. The real objective was to take a look inside Aguirre Hall. *Let them think they have the advantage if they want.*

"Interesting," Lord Aguirre said, when I had finished. "Alana?"

I smiled, inwardly, as I looked at the other girl. Alana was only a year or so younger than me, give or take a month or two, yet she wore a dress that looked surprisingly like her father's suit. She would spend most of her life training for a job she could only inherit, if she inherited it at all, after her father died. And yet…he seemed intent on giving her a voice. I wondered if she was getting more training or if she'd been primed to ask the right questions or…there was no way to know. Lord Aguirre had been in power longer than I'd been alive. He was too experienced to take lightly. He certainly wouldn't reveal his hand so easily.

"We are famous for our potions," Alana said, citing the family line. "Why would we need to hire more potioneers?"

"Because there's a limit to how much you can produce in a given space of time," I said, calmly. She had to know it. I was sure of it. "And your Potion Masters need time to experiment if they want to devise new potions."

Alana smiled. "True enough, I suppose."

Lord Aguirre turned to Jayne and bombarded her with questions. Jayne replied, calmly and thoughtfully. I was impressed, even though I'd made sure to sit her down and force her to practice answering questions from a hostile questioner. Lord Aguirre had thought of a few questions I'd never considered, but—thankfully—Jayne was able to answer them. I suspected he knew he could cheat me out of my share of the profits, if he wished...I dismissed the thought with a shrug. Better to be thought a fool than something worse.

"We will be interested in hiring you as a group," Lord Aguirre said, finally. "I believe we can discuss terms..."

"My lawyer will handle the negotiations," I said, indicating Uncle Stefano. I'd given him careful orders to prolong the discussion as long as possible. "Mistress Jayne and I should not be involved."

Lord Aguirre smiled, very briefly. "Alana, perhaps you could escort Mistress Jayne and Lady Lamplighter to a waiting room," he said. He didn't sound surprised by my stance. It was better to have a go-between when it came to handling negotiations. "I'll talk to you later."

"Of course, father," Alana said. She sounded more pleased than I'd expected. "If you'll come with me..."

I stood and allowed Alana to lead us down the corridor and into a finely appointed waiting room. A maid stood by one wall, ready to serve tea or coffee. Alana sat on a comfortable sofa and motioned for us to sit beside her. I hesitated, then explained I needed to visit the bathroom. Alana pointed me down the hall as she started to talk to Jayne. I was fairly sure *she* was planning to undercut me, whatever her father said. I hid my amusement with an effort. Brantley was probably planning to undercut his family too.

The corridor felt strange as I headed down it, trying to look as if I were lost as I kept my eye out for anything interesting. My father's notes had suggested there were at least four offices on the floor, although the papers were outdated and it was hard to tell how much of the information remained useful. Sweat trickled down my spine as I passed the bathroom—it wasn't obvious, I told myself—and kept going. The first office door was closed and locked. I knocked, planning to ask for directions if someone answered. There was no answer. I breathed a sigh of relief, then opened my senses to feel for the charm on the door. There wasn't one. I blinked in surprise, casting a lock-picking spell. The door clicked open. A trap? Very few people would risk using a merely *physical* lock to keep a door closed, particularly in a school—or a Great House—full of magicians. I nudged the door open and peered inside. The office was larger than mine, but surprisingly modest. A small portrait of the Aguirre Triplets hung on one wall, a slightly larger painting of Akin Rubén on the other. I stared at it for a moment, then hurried forward. Time was not on my side.

My eyes narrowed as I surveyed the desk. There were no protective charms, nothing that might slow me for even a second or two. The desk itself was bare, save for a single notebook that appeared to be blank. I stared at the chair, oddly bemused. There was nothing there, no hint it was anything more than a stage...a shiver ran down my spine as I turned away. The drawers wouldn't be left unprotected unless there was nothing to protect. I muttered a curse as I headed for the door, then froze. I heard footsteps coming down the hall.

And the door is open, I thought. I'd nudged it closed, but I hadn't relocked it. *Crap.*

I hastily wrapped an invisibility spell around myself. It might not last long—I had my doubts, particularly if whoever was coming was already suspicious—but it might just last long enough to let me get out. If they thought to use the wards to look for me...I braced myself as the door was pushed open and Caitlyn Aguirre stepped into the room. I froze, hardly daring to breathe. I'd hidden from older students before, but Caitlyn was a girl with a very unusual talent. The rumours were so wild that it was hard to know what to take seriously and what to dismiss as obvious nonsense. She'd been popularly supposed to have *no* magic, as a child. I hadn't known her—we hadn't moved in the same circles—but I doubted the rumour would have been so persistent if there hadn't been some truth to it. And there had.

My eyes bored into her back as she walked across the room. She wore a short-sleeved white dress covered in burn marks and stains that suggested she'd been hard at work. Her muscles stood out, suggesting she was a *lot* stronger than most girls her age. Forgers generally were, but aristocratic parents usually tried to keep girls from becoming forgers out of fear they'd injure or kill themselves. I caught a glimpse of a scar on her hand, one nasty enough to make me wince. She'd probably hurt herself long ago. She was prettier than Alana, the catty part of my mind noted, but...different. There was something *odd* about her, something *wrong*. I could feel it.

I glanced back at the door. It was still open. Caitlyn rustled through the drawers, looking for...something. I guessed it was her office. Who else would have a painting of Akin on their wall? I braced myself, then started to inch towards the door. Caitlyn had gone to school too, but she'd only lasted one year. She'd gone elsewhere, when her talents had become apparent. I wasn't sure why she'd left—she could have built an entire web of contacts over the last six years—but it didn't matter. The odds were good she didn't know what to listen for, the subtle signs that someone was creeping around under an invisibility spell. I felt sweat trickling down my back as I slipped out the door, hoping and praying she didn't hear anything. If she came after me...

A thought crossed my mind. *If she doesn't have any magic, and she doesn't have any way to see me when I'm invisible, she must be terrifyingly vulnerable.*

I hesitated as I reached the bathroom and stepped inside. My hands were starting to shake. I dispelled the invisibility charm as quickly as possible, taking deep breaths until I was sure I had everything under control. I sagged against the wall. That had been too close. If Alana had been there, or Bella, it would have been the end. Caitlyn was the only one who might not be able to see me, not without help. I stared at my reflection, trying not to remember what had happened the last time I'd been caught. That had been bad. Getting caught here would be worse. I splashed water on my face, then headed for the door. I'd already been away far too long.

Alana glanced up as I entered the library. "You took your time."

"It's a very bad time," I said, shortly. I was fairly sure she'd draw the right conclusion, without me having to spell anything out. "I'm sorry."

"No worries." Alana nodded to Jayne. "We were just talking about practical potions."

"Good." I forced myself to sit and relax, drinking my tea. The day hadn't *quite* been wasted—I'd still get something from the visit—but I'd come far too close to total disaster. "I enjoy working with potions. Sometimes."

Alana looked as if she thought she'd managed to get an edge over me. I found it hard to care. Much. I'd never cared for girls like her...I shook my head. It didn't matter. A dozen nasty comments ran through my head, a dozen topics that would put her firmly in her place...no, it would be pointless. Alana should enjoy what remained of her childhood as long as possible. She'd be an adult soon enough, perhaps within a couple of months. Her family could hardly refuse to recognise Caitlyn as a legal adult for much longer. Their enemies would call foul.

"I know a couple of boys who are looking for wives," Alana said. "Are you interested?"

"I'm always interested in opening discussions," I lied, smoothly. Alana wouldn't have raised the subject out of the goodness of her heart. There had to be something in it for her somewhere. "But I can't promise anything."

"I suppose not," Alana said. "Perhaps you can meet them at the ball."

"Perhaps I can," I said. I supposed it must look easy, to her. I could propose someone as a match to myself, then ask myself for my approval. "What about yourself? Has anyone sought your hand in marriage?"

"Too many." Alana's hand played with her braids. "I'm still looking for the right one."

Someone wealthy and powerful, I mused. It wasn't going to be easy. There weren't *many* boys who came close to her in wealth and power. Akin was the only one who came to mind—at least, the only one of the same age—and he was already betrothed to Alana's sister. *She might have to look for someone outside the city.*

Alana looked up. "They're calling us back," she said. "Shall we go?"

I tried not to show my concern as she led us back to her father's office. If someone had spotted me, or sensed my presence, they could use the wards to track me. I wasn't fool enough to think I could fight my way out. And even if I could...I shook my head, putting my fears out of my mind. If I fled the hall, I'd have to flee the city too. That would be the end too.

"We've haggled over terms," Lord Aguirre said. He held out a legal scroll. "And we believe we have reached something suitable."

I took the scroll and opened it so both Jayne and I could read. The terms were very simple, surprisingly so. The potioneers would brew potions, following a recipe—or a set of recipes—laid out by House Aguirre. They'd be paid a reasonable rate and supplied with most of the ingredients free of charge. And I'd get a tiny percentage of the profits. It wasn't much, by House Aguirre's standards, but it was a steady income I desperately needed. I'd find a use for the money. I already had a couple of ideas.

"I think this would be acceptable," I said. I could have demanded a bigger share, if the potioneers had been my clients, but I doubted it would work here. "Mistress Jayne?"

"It looks good," Jayne said. "I notice it can be cancelled by either or both parties."

THE LADY HEIRESS

"We may decide we don't need your brews," Lord Aguirre said. "And you may decide you don't like working for us."

I frowned, wondering—not for the first time—why they needed so many brewers. It wasn't something I could ask. I had a feeling he wouldn't tell me. And...I shook my head. It didn't matter. I wasn't competing with House Aguirre. I'd be squashed flat in seconds, and that would be that. I would just have to keep manipulating things until I earned enough money to start climbing back to the top.

And throwing cash at vague ideas, I mused. There were a dozen Great Houses that had started their climb to power through patenting something that had proved impossible to duplicate. *If we got sole control of a really big breakthrough...*

We shook hands and exchanged polite and largely insincere compliments before we were shown to the door. I felt sweat on my back as we walked down the stairs and clambered into the carriage, feeling as if someone was pointing a spellcaster at my back. If I'd been wrong, if Caitlyn had sensed me...nothing happened as the carriage rattled into life, heading down the drive and out onto the street. I told myself I'd been lucky, and...

I felt a thrill as I leaned back in my seat. I hadn't tried to sneak into the very highest levels of the mansion—I doubted I could do that, not without help—but still...I'd sneaked in and out of one of the most heavily-defended buildings in the city. I felt my smile grow wider as I realised I'd gotten away with it. I was safe. And I could do it again.

Quit while you're ahead, my thoughts said. They sounded like Uncle Jalil. *You don't need to keep taking these risks...*

But it's fun, I answered. The thrill hadn't faded, not yet. *I can't stop now.*

"Thank you for this," Jayne said. She shook my hand, firmly. "We'll make sure you get your share of the profits."

I nodded, feeling a twinge of...disquiet. The contracts were boring. Honest business work was tedious. I needed to do it, but...it was mind-numbing.

I wanted to plan my next move, not spend hours wrestling with contracts or paying bills or any one of a thousand duties that had fallen to me. I understood, now, why my father had kept rolling the dice. Gambling was addictive, even if one was losing. And neither of us could stop.

Like father, like daughter, I thought. The thrill was just too great. *I can't stop now.*

CHAPTER TWENTY

The chaos that gripped the city over the following month—the infernal devices, the socialist marches—had surprisingly little impact on me or my house. There were some advantages to being *small*. House Lamplighter had no assets to target, no stake in the fight...I listened to arguments from both sides in Magus Court, then sold my vote to the highest bidder. I spent the time hosting parties for the aristocracy, learning and practicing all kinds of magic and doing everything in my power to gather more information I could use. I wasn't always successful—I made the mistake of taking one braggart seriously, when I should have just dismissed him—but I made enough money to start planning for the future. It was just a shame there were so many limits on my resources.

"We could replace the farm managers with new staff," I said, one afternoon. I'd read a story in the newspaper about a farmer who'd turned a dying farm into a money-making machine and started undercutting his competitors. "The demand for cheap food is soaring."

"The family council would revolt," Uncle Jalil pointed out. "They made commitments to the managers and their families a long time before your father took up his post."

I scowled. I'd gone through my father's private notes, but found almost nothing of importance. He'd collected books and scraps of information and very little of it was particularly helpful. I was gloomily aware I was barely keeping the family afloat, despite the money I was earning through insider trading. Six weeks of running the family had convinced me I might have made a mistake when I'd accepted the post. It might have been smarter to turn the family over to one of my elderly relatives—tradition be damned—and try to find a place somewhere else before the inevitable collapse.

"Perhaps we could find a way to dislodge them," I said, although it was little more than wishful thinking. What sort of idiot made farm management hereditary? Reading between the lines, I had a feeling family politics had gotten poisonous seventy years ago. I was fairly sure someone had pulled a fast one. I just wasn't sure who. "Is there nothing we can offer them?"

"No," Uncle Jalil said. "You can't offer them anything that'll make up for losing their position as big fish in a small pond."

"Fine." I glared down at the account books. "We'll just have to find another way to deal with them."

Uncle Jalil shot me a warning look. He hadn't said anything since he'd chewed me out for insider trading, but I was fairly sure he knew what I was doing. I let out a heavy sigh. I couldn't think of any other way to make money, not in the time I had. The family council was probably already on the brink of revolt, silently counting down the days until I could be removed on some trumped-up charge and replaced by someone who'd... who'd do what? I snorted at the thought. If one of the old fogies had a way to save us, surely they would have suggested it? I had few qualms about stealing an idea simply because it came from an elderly relative. It might even have worked.

"You have to get ready for the ball tonight," Uncle Jalil reminded me, instead. Perhaps he thought it would distract me from something dubious. "You'll have people coming from all over the city."

I nodded, stiffly. The younger aristos were throwing party after party. I'd worked hard to make sure most of them were held at Lamplighter Hall.

The younger aristos appreciated the limited chaperonage, while the older generation understood things wouldn't be allowed to get *too* far out of hand. It wasn't ideal—I had a feeling my ancestors were sharpening their knives, just *waiting* for me to join them—but it was better than nothing. Besides, I'd taken advantage of the opportunity to listen to the guests. I'd picked up quite a few tips just by overhearing their conversations. I was even starting to build a public reputation as a shrewd investor.

"I'll see to it," I said. I'd hired more servants for the balls, but I couldn't afford to permanently put them on the payroll. The party season would dry up when the summer came to an end. "You concentrate on the accounts."

Uncle Jalil bowed stiffly, then left the office. I felt a pang of regret. We'd never been quite as close since he'd figured out what I'd done, even though he hadn't been able to suggest anything better. He *was* an accountant, after all. He knew the risks...he'd pointed them out, in great and tedious detail. I stood, brushing down my dress. We simply weren't bringing in enough money to meet our expenses, no matter how much we scrimped and saved. The farm managers weren't the only people standing in my way.

And we can be outbid by almost everyone else, I mused, as I turned my attention to the stack of letters and invitations. I'd been invited to a dozen new balls, including Ayesha and Zeya McDonald's coming out party. Their family was wealthy, wealthy and powerful enough to claim a place at the very heart of the city. *There has to be something I can learn there.*

I smirked at the thought. It had been a long time since I'd laid eyes on Ayesha and Zeya McDonald, but I knew their family by reputation. They had a history of feuding with nearly everyone else, even though there was a great deal more to be gained by cooperation. Now...they had to work with the other Great Houses if they wanted to forestall House Rubén and House Aguirre from dominating the city. I had a feeling that wasn't going to go well. A Great House with a reputation for vindictiveness would have problems coming to terms with its neighbours. If I wasn't so desperate, I would have thought twice about trying to search their hall.

But we are desperate, I reminded myself. *We simply don't have any other options.*

I spent the afternoon reading files, practicing spells and—finally—changing into my hostess outfit as the first guests arrived. The only real advantage to being host, I decided, was that I didn't have to compete with the other girls. I didn't *have* to wear an exclusive dress, I didn't *have* to flirt with all the boys, I didn't have...I shook my head as I made my way downstairs. I wasn't content to be a brainless beauty, parading around the dance floor and leaving everything to my elders and betters. I wanted to do something more with my life.

"Lady Lamplighter," Akin Rubén said, as he was shown into the hall. "Thank you for hosting us."

"It's my pleasure," I assured him. Akin had planned the party, at least partly—I was sure—to give him a chance to spend time with Caitlyn away from home. They'd be closely watched when they were together, I was sure. Too much rested on their match for their families to take any risks. "I hope you have a pleasant evening."

Akin grinned. "We'll see," he said. "It depends on the guests."

I nodded as the hall started to fill up. It said a great deal about Akin's importance, I reflected rather sourly, that his guests weren't *that* fashionably late. The majority came within ten minutes of the opening time, rather than delaying long enough to make it clear they were honouring him with their presence. I doubted I could have convinced half the guests to come, let alone arrive within half an hour of the announced start time. They just didn't care about me.

The band—the Howling Gales—struck up a dance tune. I tried not to wince. Modern music had never appealed to me. I had a feeling the only reason the younger generation liked it was because it annoyed their parents. The dance steps seemed to be completely random, rather than the ritualised formality I'd been taught in school. I saw a young man dance up to a woman, bumping her into the next man. It looked like a chain of dominos, but if there was any pattern, I couldn't see it. I silently thanked my ancestors that I didn't have to dance. I couldn't follow the steps.

But at least the racket provides a distraction, I thought. The band's magic was casting all sorts of weird images across the hall. It felt small and cramped even though it was the largest chamber in the hall. I watched a couple of aristos I vaguely recognised popping in and out of view, half-hidden within the smoke and flickering lights. *No one could be sure who's going in and out of the room.*

Akin bowed, then hurried off as Caitlyn and her sisters entered. I was mildly surprised they hadn't brought a chaperone. Alana had never struck me as the kind of person who'd worry about protecting her sister's reputation, while Bella was popularly supposed to be lazy. She certainly *looked* a little soft…I reminded myself, sharply, that it could be an act. Bella could make almost anything of herself, perhaps literally. She had the wealth and power and connections to make herself very important indeed.

I put the thought out of my head as I walked around the room. The guests were chatting loudly, but their words were drowned out by the music. I muttered a pair of spells to sharpen my ears, blocking out the racket as the singer started to mangle a popular song. *His* version seemed to include a lot of swearing and other unpleasantness. Mistress Grayling would have had a heart attack if she'd heard the din. She'd hired bands to play at school dances, but they'd all been very traditional.

"Lucy! So good to see you again!"

I turned to see Ayesha and Zeya McDonald. The twins grinned at me, their hair and clothes practically identical in every way. I felt a twinge of envy. They were tall girls, with long brown hair and willowy bodies that suggested they spent a lot of time taking care of themselves. They wore their dresses low, exposing a hint of cleavage without showing off too much. I rather suspected their parents didn't know what they were wearing. They'd be in deep trouble if they were caught.

"It's been a long time," I said. I wasn't sure which of them was which. "I missed you."

The twins smirked, suggesting they knew perfectly well I was lying. We might have had a playdate or two, back when we'd been children, but we wouldn't have been close. The year between us might as well have been a decade, or a century, when we went to school. And I'd gone to Grayling's...I told myself, sharply, that there was no point in fretting about it as they hinted they wanted to talk to me alone. What was done was done. I'd just have to catch up the hard way.

There are some advantages to being isolated from everyone else, I told myself, although I knew it wasn't entirely true. *Everyone knows I'm not involved in their petty little power games.*

But I wanted to be, I reflected as we walked into the side corridor. Half the private rooms were already closed and locked, occupied by couples who wanted some time together without the omnipresent chaperonage. The wards crackled around us, ensuring that names and faces would be concealed as long as the observer didn't look too closely. I had a feeling the guests would keep each other's secrets, just as my classmates and I had done when we'd been students. There was a difference between exploiting a secret for oneself and tattling. The guests wouldn't tattle for fear they'd be tattled on themselves.

I could still hear the music, despite the wards, as I led them into the final room and closed the door behind us. There was nothing *in* the room, beyond a handful of rickety chairs and a small table. I motioned for them to sit, then sat myself. It was hard not to envy them as they brushed down their dresses. They had the insane self-confidence that came with being incredibly wealthy and well-connected. Who cared if people talked? They were the next generation of the aristocracy and they knew it.

"You'll be coming to our ball, of course," Ayesha—or Zeya—said. It wasn't a question. She *knew* I'd be at the ball. "I hope you'll enjoy it."

"I'm sure I will," I lied. I didn't want to watch another pair of girls enter society as adults, not when it was another reminder I'd never be one of them. The only advantage to attending was the chance to search their hall for useful information. "Do you have matches already lined up?"

"We do," Ayesha—or Zeya—said. I studied their faces, trying to determine how to tell them apart. They were so close that even their *magic* felt identical. "And we'd like to get to know them here."

I allowed my eyes to sharpen. "After your ball, I assume?"

"Of course," Ayesha—or Zeya—said. The innocence in her voice would have grated even if I hadn't *known* it was an act. "We can't meet them before we come out. People will talk."

"They do," I agreed. My mind raced. I could use this…somehow. I'd have to think about it. "Why can't you meet elsewhere?"

"Because someone would be looking over our shoulders," Ayesha—or Zeya—said, in a tone that suggested I'd asked a stupid question. "And it would be hard to get to know the boys if they know they're being watched."

"I dare say I can arrange a private room, for later considerations," I said, slowly. I grinned, suddenly. "You'd better not dress the same or the boys won't know which of you they're meant to be courting."

The girls laughed. "That's part of the fun," Ayesha—or Zeya—said. "We can maintain deniability."

"It sounds like a bad romance novel," I said. I'd read a handful when they'd been passed around the school. I might have been innocent, for a given value of innocent, but even I'd known the stories were—at best—completely exaggerated. The books had been confiscated when they'd been discovered and we'd all been given detention. "You'd better be careful."

"But you'll let us come?" Ayesha—or Zeya—smiled. "You'll invite them too?"

"If you want," I said. It would let all four of them maintain plausible deniability. "But I will demand something in return, later."

"Anything," Ayesha—or Zeya—said.

"Within reason," her sister added. She looked very firm. "We're not going to give you *everything*."

I grinned. "Not a chance," I said. "My demands are very reasonable. I just want a million billion trillion crowns."

They laughed. "There *isn't* that much," Ayesha—or Zeya—said. She was probably right. I had no idea how wealthy the greatest of the Great Houses truly were, but I was fairly sure they weren't *that* rich. "Maybe you should ask for just *ten* crowns instead."

"I'll want a favour instead," I said. I had no idea what, not yet. I didn't have to use it at once. I could keep it for years. "One from each of you."

The twins glanced at each other, then nodded in unison. I wished, suddenly, that I had a sister. It would have been nice, I thought. I'd often wondered why my parents hadn't had more children. Had I really been that expensive? Or had my parents simply decided they didn't want to bring more children into the world? They hadn't been able to provide a dowry for *me*, let alone a second child.

"It will be our pleasure," Ayesha—or Zeya—said. She stood and held out her arms for a hug. I hugged her tightly. "We'll be in touch."

"After the ball," I said, as I hugged her sister. My fingers pulled a loose hair from her dress and concealed it within my palm. "We don't want anyone to notice before then."

"Of course not," Ayesha—or Zeya—said. She hadn't felt a thing. "And we look forward to seeing you at the ball."

I concealed the hair within my pocket, wrapping a pair of protective spells around it as they left the chamber. It wouldn't last long, but—if I was lucky—it would last long enough. I smiled to myself and followed them out, turning a blind eye as Akin and Caitlyn emerged from another room. Caitlyn looked slightly mussed. I resisted the urge to wink as I returned to the ballroom, hoping her sisters weren't keeping an eye on her. They might not be willing to lie, if their parents asked.

And I got a hair, I thought. It had been sheer luck, but I was quite happy to take advantage of it. *I can use it.*

Akin caught up with me. "Thank you for hosting," he said, again. His lips looked slightly puffy. "It's been a wonderful evening."

"It was my pleasure," I said. The music was starting to die away as the party came to an end. I'd have to hurry to the door, just so I could bid farewell to the junior aristocrats before they left. "I'll see you again soon."

I leaned forward. "And you need to cast a glamour on your lips," I added. He'd owe me a favour for pointing it out, before someone else noticed. His parents would probably inspect him when he returned home. "Quickly."

Akin blushed.

CHAPTER
TWENTY-ONE

"Welcome to McDonald Hall," Lady McDonald said, as I entered the hall. "It is our pleasure to welcome you."

I nodded as I dropped a curtsy. The container in my pocket felt heavy, too heavy. I'd wrapped every concealment spell I knew around it, but there was a very good chance it would be detected by the household wards. It wasn't uncommon for guests to bring concealed items with them—I'd taken the precaution of purchasing a small present for Ayesha and Zeya McDonald to conceal the hair—but it was still a risk. I'd been tempted, very tempted, to simply leave the hair behind or destroy it. Only the grim awareness I needed it—and the thrill of using it—had convinced me to keep it.

"I thank you." I straightened up. "It is my pleasure to attend."

I kept my thoughts—my real thoughts—to myself as I entered the hall. Powerful wards and charms hung in the air, their mere presence a grim reminder that the family had enemies. I saw little groups of aristocrats scattered all over, each reflecting divisions within the wider society. None welcomed me. The air was thick with tension, as if the slightest cough would be enough to start something violent. I told myself I should be grateful as I got myself a drink and started to wander around the room. They wouldn't notice when I left. They had too many problems of their own.

My eyes flickered from group to group, silently assessing who was *in* and who was *out*. I recognised some faces, but others were strangers. They might be kindred who'd been brought to the hall to show support for Ayesha and Zeya McDonald or...they might be strangers from the other side of North Shallot. A small army of servants glided from group to group, proffering food and drink and then scarpering away before they could be given orders. It looked as if every servant and armsman within the building was in the hall, as well as a handful of others hired on short notice. I spotted a pair of armsmen keeping watch and smiled. The hosts were too worried about their guests hurling curses at each other to keep an eye on me.

The room filled slowly as the more important guests arrived...fashionably late, of course. I spotted Akin keeping company with Alana, rather than Caitlyn...I wondered, idly, if someone had noticed he'd been a little *too* close to his betrothed last week. Or...they were both first in line to inherit their families, when their fathers died. I suspected they had strict orders to pretend to be friends, even if they hated each other. It wasn't the first time they'd had to work together. They'd been Head Boy and Head Girl of Jude's, if I recalled correctly. And they'd survived the year without trying to kill each other.

I felt a twinge of envy—again—as the herald called for our attention. Ayesha and Zeya McDonald descended the stairs, wrapped in white dresses that sparkled with gold and diamond jewels. They shone so brightly they were the centre of attention, even when two young men came forward to ask them to dance. It was so strictly formal I understood perfectly why they wanted to meet their prospective partners somewhere away from the hall. Everyone was following a script. There was no hint of reality about it. And who knew what the young men were *really* like?

The music—very traditional music—started to play. I danced a single dance, then hurried to the washroom. The ball was scheduled to last for hours, with at least ten formal dances before Lord McDonald left the chamber, his absence indicating his guests could leave without giving offense. I plucked the hair out of the container as I walked past the washroom, muttering a pre-prepared spell as I brushed my fingers against the hair. The wards were already configured to realise that Ayesha and Zeya McDonald might be in two places at once, I thought. They might not notice if there suddenly appeared to be *three* girls, particularly if two of them were very close together. The sheer number of blood relatives on the dance floor would make it harder to determine that one of the girls was a fake. Or so I thought...

The hair felt warm in my palm as I pushed my way into the corridor, then walked up the stairs as if I owned the place. The wards should have turned me back—or worse—if they thought I didn't belong there. I was fairly sure that Ayesha and Zeya McDonald knew how to find and use the servant passages—it was common among aristocratic children, even if it was officially forbidden—but *I* didn't know where they were. My heart beat like a drum as I kept moving upstairs, wrapping an obscurification charm around me. I might pass unnoticed—the combination of the borrowed glamour and the obscurification should hide me—but I didn't know for sure. It was a gamble, yet...what was the point of gambling if one could afford to lose?

I put the thought out of my mind as I reached the top of the stairs and looked around. The walls were lined with portraits of the family's ancestors, all of whom seemed to be glowering at me disapprovingly. I smirked as I walked past a line of red-haired men and women—I had no idea why Ayesha and Zeya McDonald had brown hair—and headed to Lord McDonald's office. My father's plans had been quite complete. The inner chamber might be beyond me, hair or no hair, but the outer chamber should be accessible. I'd heard Ayesha and Zeya McDonald were both being raised to take their father's place. I wasn't sure that was a good idea, but...the twins actually seemed to *like* each other. That was less common than one might think. Both Akin and Caitlyn had real problems with their siblings.

They got better, if rumour is to be believed, I thought, as I touched the lock gingerly. The charm was solid, but—thanks to Gary—not solid enough. The glamour—and my unlocking spell—was enough to open the door. *But there's still some bitterness there.*

I stepped inside and surveyed the office. It was surprisingly small for the nerve centre of an entire family. There were four desks, one significantly bigger than the others. Lord McDonald's, I guessed. The others would belong to his daughters and his secretary. I walked over to the biggest desk, then stopped dead. There were a pair of warning hexes hanging over the desk, the hair tingling unpleasantly against my palm. His daughters weren't allowed to use the desk. I smiled—I understood the feeling—and checked the second desk, using the hair to feel out the charms. The secretary wasn't allowed to keep his superiors—including Ayesha and Zeya McDonald—out. The drawers clicked open at my touch. I poked through the papers as fast as I could, cursing under my breath. It looked as though the secretary was sending orders to the mines to double their production.

Good luck with that, I thought. My family had learnt the hard way that there were limits to how much one could pull from a mine. *Why are you...?*

I frowned as I read the next set of documents. The McDonalds were purchasing *more* mines, all of which produced ore for Objects and Devices of Power. Come to think of it, I considered, they wanted ore that was mainly used for Objects of Power and their spin-offs. My old forgery teacher—we'd all considered *him* a bit of a forgery—had insisted that some of the ores and metals simply didn't work very well these days, as if we'd forgotten how to refine them after the Thousand Year Empire died. I'd thought he was mad, but he might have had a point. Most *Devices* of Power were forged with more modern ores.

Unless they're trying to snap them up to keep Caitlyn from producing more Objects of Power, I mused. It was possible, I thought, but...it made no sense. *She's not going to run out of ore in a hurry, is she?*

I doubted it. House Aguirre owned mines too, lots of them. They'd even put a bid in for one of *my* mines, which had puzzled and alarmed me when I'd read the note. Either they thought the mine wasn't worked or... or what? Did they know there was something there, something useful? I had no idea. I had no way to find out, either. It wasn't as if I could ask...

I can use this, I thought, although I wasn't sure how. *I...*

A shiver ran down my spine. I hadn't heard anything, but instincts I'd honed to a fine point at boarding school insisted I was no longer alone. I readied a spell, preparing to fight and run as I turned slowly. I'd been caught before, when I'd been younger...there was no one there. The door was open, but the corridor was empty. I inched forward, peering around for a hint someone was hidden behind magic. Maybe I wasn't the only one intent on raiding Lord McDonald's office. I glanced back at the desk, then headed for the door. I'd pushed my luck too far. The wards weren't paying any particular attention to me, as far as I could tell, but there was no point in taking any more chances. If someone was suspicious, better to pull out while I was ahead.

The sense I was being watched grew stronger as I made my way back to the stairs. The portraits hadn't changed...I found myself staring at their eyes, wondering if they were charmed into surveillance spells. It was a common trick, although my charms should have kept me hidden. I reached the stairs and inched down, hearing the dancing master call for the next dance. I checked my watch as I reached the bottom of the stairs and headed into the washroom. The hair would have to go. I couldn't afford to have it discovered, not now. I disentangled the spells, dispelled what remained of the magic and flushed the hair down the toilet. It was unlikely it would be discovered. Even if it was, no one would think anything of it.

Sweat trickled down my back as I washed my face, then turned and walked back to the ballroom. The private rooms were all closed and locked... it looked as if there were dozens, perhaps hundreds, of meetings taking place. I frowned as I spotted two mid-ranking noblemen heading along the corridor, murmuring. They fell silent as soon as they spotted me, keeping their mouths firmly shut until I was past. I was tempted to stay and listen, but they looked alert. Besides, I had already pushed my luck too far.

And you know something now, I told myself. I might not be able to sell one of *my* mines to the McDonalds—they'd want to be sure the mine wasn't worthless first—but...there were other options. *I could buy broken Objects of Power and start melting them down.*

I pasted a polite expression on my face as I stepped back into the ballroom. The music was louder than before, but the air still roiled with tension. I felt a flicker of sympathy for Ayesha and Zeya McDonald as they whirled around the dance floor. The younger generation was dancing, but the older aristocrats seemed more interested in talking amongst themselves than honouring their children. A girl's coming-out was the most important event in her life, at least until she got married or had kids. It was their day. Ayesha and Zeya McDonald should have been feted by their parents and envied by their peers. Instead...

My skin prickled as I sensed someone behind me. "Lucy?"

I turned. Marlene stood there, looking tired. She...I frowned, inwardly, as I studied her. She looked...*wrong*. The girl I remembered was gone. She wore a long dress that looked a little too big for her, her hair hanging in braids that looked almost...*defiant*. For a moment, I honestly wondered if it *was* Marlene. She could have been someone else...no, it was Marlene. It couldn't be anyone else. But...

"Marlene?" It was hard not to feel sorry for her, even though she'd abused her authority shamelessly. "What are you doing here?"

Marlene flinched. I blinked in surprise. I'd never seen her *scared* before. "I was invited," she said, as if she expected me to dispute it. "And yourself?"

"I was invited too," I said. "Ayesha and Zeya McDonald invited me personally."

The puzzle nagged at me. Marlene had always claimed she was rich and powerful—or, rather, her *family* was rich and powerful. And yet she was standing here, alone and isolated, wearing a dress that was almost certainly second-hand...it made no sense. Unless...was her family poor too? It was possible. I'd never realised how little money my family had until I'd taken up my post.

"I hear you've been hosting parties," Marlene said. I had the feeling she was torn between the need to talk to someone—anyone—and the urge to turn her back and flee. We'd never been *friends*. The only times she'd been civil to me had been when the tutors were watching…and, I supposed, when we'd been on field trips to other schools. "Why are you doing it?"

"It's a dirty job, but someone has to do it," I said. It was a joke, but she flinched again. "It's something to do."

Marlene said nothing for a long moment. "Are you looking for a co-host?"

"Not at the moment," I said. What was going on? "Why do you ask?"

"I need something to do," Marlene said. "Please…"

I stared at her, bemused. Marlene was hardly *stupid*. I hated to admit it, but she'd got the better of me a few times. And her grades were generally good. I wasn't sure how Grayling's compared to Jude's—I had the feeling that Grayling's was more concerned with keeping girls out of sight and out of mind than actually improving our minds—but Marlene should have had no problems getting an apprenticeship. Her family could have arranged it. I honestly didn't understand why she was asking me for anything. The summer would be over soon and…and I'd have to find some other way to make money.

"I can't," I said, finally. Kate would never speak to me again if I took *Marlene* into my hall, let alone into my confidence. I'd shrugged off most of Marlene's pranks, then gotten even. Kate hadn't had the luxury of being able to strike back. "It's just me."

Marlene looked as if she wanted to beg. Instead, she turned and hurried off. I watched her retreating back, feeling as if the world had stopped making sense. The girl I'd known at school and the girl I'd just met appeared to be two completely different people. I shook my head slowly, then turned to go back to the dancing. The last dance was being called now. I'd have a turn on the floor, then depart as soon as I decently could.

"Lucy," a voice called. I looked up to see Brantley, holding out a hand. "Would you like the pleasure of this dance?"

I winced, inwardly. I hadn't seen him since...since I'd enchanted him and searched his office. I'd heard rumours that there were problems between him and his family, although...I shrugged. They weren't *my* concern. I looked around, hoping to spot someone who'd be happy to play along and pretend he'd marked my dance card. But there was no one. The only boy in sight I knew was Akin, and Caitlyn was already leading him onto the dance floor.

"Sure," I said, without enthusiasm. I took his arm and allowed him to pull me forward. "It's been a while."

"I didn't get an invite to the last ball," Brantley said, as the music started to play. "Should I be offended?"

"I have no idea," I said. Brantley was behaving himself. "I didn't write the guest list."

"I think we should host a party of our own," Brantley said. "And I'll write my own guest list."

"I'll have my secretary send you a note of terms," I promised. If I was lucky, I'd never hear anything from him again. "The cost is quite reasonable..."

"Cost?" Brantley sounded shocked at the mere idea of someone actually asking him to *pay*. "You mean...money?"

"I have to pay for the food and drink somehow," I said. "And if you're hosting, *you* have to pay."

"We'll discuss it later," Brantley said. The music came to an end. "Do you want to go into the garden?"

"No," I said. I spotted Lord McDonald heading for the stairs and smiled in relief. "I want to go home and sleep. I have important meetings tomorrow."

Brantley shrugged. "So do I," he said. "Be seeing you."

I nodded, then left the hall, collected my cloak from the servants and headed back to Lamplighter Hall. I'd buy up all the old and broken Objects of Power I could, in hopes of turning a profit. I wasn't sure if it was workable, but…it sounded promising. And…I'd proven I could sneak through stronger wards. I could do it again and again and…

And if you play your cards right, I told myself, *you might even build up enough money to reinvigorate the family.*

CHAPTER

TWENTY-TWO

"My Lady?"

I looked up from my desk. I'd intended to spend the morning in bed—I'd gotten home rather later than I'd intended, after the McDonald Ball—but the experience of six years in boarding school had driven me out of bed before nine. The pile of letters on my desk had somehow managed to grow overnight—I was sure they bred when I wasn't looking—and I'd found myself going through them one by one. The vast majority were useless, but they had to be filed anyway. High Society would never forgive me if I forgot to acknowledge a thank-you note or failed to RSVP a party invitation.

Ellington stood by the door, looking dapper in his new uniform. "You have a visitor, My Lady," he said, holding out a card. "He wishes to speak to you."

I blinked in surprise as I took the card and read the single name. MALACHI RUBÉN. The forename meant nothing to me—I'd never heard of Malachi Rubén—but the surname was quite indicative. He'd be one of Akin's relatives, although probably not a very close one or I would have heard of him. I turned the card over and over in my hand, pretending to study it closely. There was no title, no address, no contact point, just a name. It was…odd. It was a cheap design, but printed on expensive cardboard.

"Please, show him into the visitor's room and offer tea." I stood, hastily checking my appearance in the mirror. I'd showered and changed into a simple morning dress, but I hadn't bothered to do anything with my hair or face. I hadn't expected visitors. "I'll be along in a moment."

Ellington bowed and retreated. I put the card on the desk, then hurried into the washroom, splashed water on my face and brushed my hair. There was no time to change into something less comfortable. I looked decent, but hardly *aristocratic*. My lips twisted into a frown as I headed for the door. It was rare for someone to just drop in for a visit without calling ahead, unless they were close friends. Malachi Rubén was a stranger. I opened my father's filing cabinets and went through the records, but found nothing. My father hadn't considered Malachi Rubén to be important either.

I pasted a smile on my face as I walked down the corridor and into the visitor's room. Jadish and I had cleaned it from top to bottom, then installed comfortable chairs, a sofa and a simple wooden table. Malachi Rubén sat on the sofa, his eyes flickering over me as I entered. I felt something nasty crawl down my spine. He didn't look anything like Akin. He looked…like a creep.

Malachi stood and held out a hand. "Thank you for seeing me."

"You're welcome," I lied. His hand felt unpleasant to the touch. "Please, be seated."

"Of course." Malachi sat, resting his hands in his lap as Ellington poured two mugs of tea and retreated. "I must say you've done wonders for your family."

I kept my face expressionless as I studied him. He might have been a genial man, if he'd smiled more. Instead, there was something sour in his expression. He looked unhealthily overweight, despite the best efforts of his tailor. His eyes looked beady as they peered at me from a jowled face. It was hard to believe that Akin and Malachi were related. Malachi wasn't even blond. He had to be a relative through marriage, if indeed he was a relative at all. I was starting to doubt it. He looked more like a commoner putting on airs than an aristocrat who'd fallen on hard times.

"Thank you," I said. I had the oddest feeling the ground was shifting under my feet, as if I were being made the butt of a joke I didn't understand. "I must say I was surprised to receive your card."

"Quite." Malachi smiled. It made him look cruel. "I didn't want you to turn me away. Not yet."

"I'm not in the habit of turning anyone away," I said, slowly. Who *was* he? And what did he want? "I'm quite a busy person and…"

"And so you have little time for me," Malachi finished. "Or so you think. You actually have quite a *lot* of time for me."

I stared at him, honestly surprised. If Malachi had wanted a long meeting, he should have written first and *asked*. I had nothing against him, or his family. Even if I had, it would have been rude to turn him away. And yet…it was equally rude to call on me without warning and demand my time. He couldn't expect more than a few minutes of my time before I returned to my planned schedule.

"Indeed?" I found it hard to meet his eyes. "If I had time…"

Malachi reached into his pocket and produced a small glass ball, only slightly larger than a marble. I blinked as he held it out. It couldn't be anything overtly dangerous, or the wards would have sounded the alert…I frowned inwardly, hastily readying a shielding spell. I knew, all too well, that it *was* possible to smuggle something that wasn't necessarily dangerous through the wards. Malachi could have brought a weapon in pieces and assembled it while he was waiting. Or…whatever the orb was, it wasn't something the wards *recognised* as a weapon. I knew how easy it could be to outsmart them too.

"Here." Malachi held out the orb. "Take it."

I hesitated, then took the orb and stared at it. The glass was enchanted… I frowned, but was somehow captivated. It pulled at me…for a horrible moment, I thought it was literally trying to pull me *inside*. My magic sensed nothing, but…the world seemed to twist, as if a scene inside a snow globe was bursting into the light. I blinked…

…And found myself watching someone walking down a corridor. Ice ran through my veins as I recognised the scene. It was the corridor I'd walked down myself, yesterday…I froze in horror as I recognised myself. It was me! I walked down the corridor, opened the door and slipped into Lord McDonald's office. The scene seemed to bobble as it rounded the corner and peered through the door. I was rifling through the secretary's desk, bringing up papers and looking through them. I'd been seen…

…I looked up, suddenly suspicious that I was being watched. The scene shifted again as it backed away, then blanked…

I found myself back in my body, staring at the orb. I'd never seen anything like it. I'd never even *heard* of anything like it. One could use crystal balls or viewing pools to spy, if one wished, but they couldn't work against even the slightest resistance. A sorcerer didn't have to be the greatest of the great to keep prying eyes out of his lair. I'd heard tales of how the Great Houses spied on one another, but…I swallowed hard as I looked up. Malachi looked like a predator who'd just spotted its prey.

"Impressive, isn't it?" His voice made my skin crawl. "The magic records a person's memory in every detail. There's so much detail that even the most cynical viewer will have to claim the memory is real. And quite beyond fakery."

I said nothing as I stared at the orb. It was…I probed it with my magic, figuring out how it worked. The magic was both surprisingly simple yet strikingly complex. I triggered the spell and watched the memory again, noting how it bobbed with the unseen watcher. A man, I thought; it had to be a man. He'd spent too long studying my rear as I walked down the corridor. And I hadn't sensed his presence until it was far too late. Who'd recorded the orb? Malachi himself? I doubted it. It had to have been someone who'd had a legitimate reason to be there.

"Well?" Malachi's voice grew more demanding. "What do you think?"

"Very impressive," I managed. "But you could have faked it."

Malachi snorted. "I had a look at your record," he said. "You've been *very* good at guessing which way the market will go. *Very* good. *Suspiciously* good. Oh, you made a couple of weak calls, but no real *bad* calls. And every one of the calls you made came *after* you attended a party. I dare say you've been sneaking around like that"—he waved a hand at the orb—"for a very long time."

I felt cold. "Do you think you can prove it?"

"I think it doesn't matter," Malachi said. "There's nowhere near enough proof to land you in jail, *My Lady*, but it will mean certain social death. No one will invite you to their balls if they think you'll search their halls. No one will attend your parties if they think you'll take advantage of them. And what will it mean, I ask you, when you're cut out of *everything*?"

My heart seemed to freeze in my chest. Disaster. Total disaster. House Lamplighter would crash so completely there'd be no hope of ever resurrecting the house. We'd probably face a coalition of outraged aristocrats, pushing for us to be stripped of our seat in Magus Court and…we'd vanish without trace, even if they did nothing else. And…and…and…my thoughts ran in circles. Uncle Jalil had been right. I should have quit while I was ahead.

"They'd know about you," I said, desperately. "And whoever gave you the memory."

Malachi smiled. "I think you have more to lose."

I looked at the floor. He was right. Malachi himself…whatever he was doing, he clearly didn't fear the consequences. And the servant who'd watched me, who'd peered through my charms as I'd sneaked into McDonald Hall…I doubted Malachi cared about him either. He was just a servant. For all I knew, he'd taken Malachi's money and vanished as soon as he'd handed over the memory. No one would know what he'd done, unless the truth came out and…I'd be ruined. The family would be ruined. Our names would be stricken from the books.

Ancestors, I thought, numbly. *What have I done?*

Malachi leaned forward. "I think you should go on your knees."

I stared at him. I wanted to refuse. I wanted...I felt sick as I realised he had me over a barrel. If he released the memory, if he sent orbs to Lord McDonald or one of the others, I was dead. They'd ruin my family and send assassins after me and...I wobbled to my feet, then knelt like a servant. Malachi's eyes gleamed as he studied me. He was enjoying himself. He was...I thought I understood, just for a second. He was getting more pleasure from forcing me to jump through his hoops than anything else. The blackmail—and it *was* blackmail—was secondary. He hated me just for existing.

"Very good." Malachi smiled, savouring the moment. "Keep your eyes down."

I hated him, hated him so much I wanted to summon my magic and blow him into little pieces. I could have killed him. The hall was my place of power. He was right in front of me. And yet...I knew, as I stared at his feet, that he wouldn't have come to me unless he knew he could keep me from killing him. There'd be copies of the memory elsewhere...if it was possible to copy a memory. I didn't know. I'd never seen anything like the memory orb. Whoever had designed it would have had to combine at least three different disciplines, and then...

My knees started to ache. My cheeks burned with humiliation. I'd never knelt to anyone, not in my entire life. I tried to think, tried to calculate what he might want. If he knew anything about House Lamplighter, he had to know we didn't have much. I wouldn't have risked everything if I hadn't been desperate...I wanted to laugh at myself. I'd only thought I was desperate. I was desperate *now*.

He's enjoying himself, I thought, numbly. I'd met prefects who enjoyed pushing the younger girls around, who'd looked for any excuse to increase punishments and savoured the helpless rage they caused. Malachi was just like them. He was old enough to be my father—he looked old enough to be my *grandfather*—but he had the same attitude. *He wants me to resist so he can punish me.*

I shuddered, inwardly. He had me...he *knew* he had me. He could demand *anything* from me. I could run, but...could I hide? Lord McDonald was known to be vindictive. He'd send assassins after me, even though I hadn't *done* anything with the knowledge yet. What did he want? My imagination provided a hundred horrific possibilities, each worse than the last. I'd heard whispered stories of girls who compromised themselves...I tried not to think about them. I wanted to ask, but I didn't dare. He'd see it as a sign of weakness.

Malachi sat up and patted my head, as one might pet a favoured dog. I shuddered at his touch.

"What do you think I want?" He shifted until we were uncomfortably close. "What do you think I want?"

My mouth was dry. I swallowed, hard. "Money?"

Malachi reached out, placed his fingers under my chin and lifted my head until he was gazing into my eyes. "And do you have enough money to make it worthwhile?"

I shook my head, not daring to speak. His touch felt repulsive. I wanted to lash out with my magic, but...it would be the end of me. I was dead...my thoughts ran in circles. Dead or alive, I was dead. I was dead. I was dead...

"No." Malachi's hand cupped my face. "What do you think I want?"

I tried to look down. I had too many ideas, none of which were good. And...

"I need an assistant," Malachi said. "You can work for me. Or else."

What? I stared at him, half-convinced I'd misheard. An assistant? Me? What did he want from me? He had me over a barrel! He could demand *anything* from me! And he wanted an assistant? *It makes no sense.*

I found my voice, somehow. "What do you want me to do?"

"I'll give you tasks," Malachi said, calmly. He stood and started to pace the room. It was rude, but at least he was no longer touching me. My skin felt unclean. "There are places you can go I can't. People you can talk to I can't. You'll go and you'll speak with my voice."

"I..." I swallowed and started again. "Can I have some time to think about it?"

Malachi laughed, nastily. "Do you think you have time?"

I tried not to flinch as he stalked around the room. I *didn't* have time. I had to agree or start running or...I couldn't think of a third option. The family would pay the price for my sins, even if I...I tried to think. There had to be a way out. But what? I had no illusions about Malachi. He would never let me off the hook. No matter what I did, it would never be enough.

"...No," I said, finally. I'd play along and then...and then what? I needed time to think and plan and...and I wasn't going to get it. "What do you want me to do?"

"Right now, nothing," Malachi said. I could tell he wanted me to dangle on his chain for little bit, just long enough for my helplessness to settle in. "I'll give you your instructions later."

He walked around until he was standing in front of me. "No, I tell a lie. There's something I *do* want you to do for me."

My blood froze, again, as he lowered his voice. "Kiss my feet."

I couldn't move. My stomach churned. Never, never in my entire life, had anyone demanded *that* of me. I couldn't do it. Never...

"Kiss my feet," Malachi repeated. His voice was suddenly hard. "Press your lips against my boots and hold them there."

My heart twisted. I was suddenly sure my ancestors were looking away as I forced myself to bend my head. No one, not even King Rufus himself, could demand my prostration. I didn't think servants and slaves prostrated themselves. And yet...I wanted to rebel, to hurt him even at the cost of destroying myself and my entire family...shame burned in my gut as I lowered my lips to his boot and kissed it. I heard him snigger—the bastard was enjoying the show—as I held myself still. Bile boiled in my stomach. It was all I could do not to throw up.

"Stay like that," Malachi said, as he pulled his boot free. My lips hit the floor and stayed there. "Don't even think about moving for ten minutes."

I sensed him opening the door, leaving the door open as he headed for the stairs. It was no consolation to know there were only a handful of servants in the hall, that there was a good chance that no one would come along and see me in helpless submission, it was…I cursed myself as savagely as I knew how, all too aware that I'd doomed myself. It was my fault. Malachi had me over a barrel. If I didn't do whatever he wanted, the entire family would be destroyed…

…And it was all my fault.

CHAPTER
TWENTY-THREE

I don't know how long I stayed there.

It was longer than ten minutes. Every minute felt like an hour. The thought of someone—Ellington, Jadish, Uncle Jalil—seeing me like that was horrifying, yet I couldn't move. I felt as if I were gripped by a spell, a spell I couldn't evade or fight. Malachi Rubén had beaten me, beaten me so completely I could barely consider any form of resistance. And I'd practically done it to myself. I'd compromised myself and...

My thoughts ran in circles. I'd compromised myself. High Society would shun me. And they'd shun my family too. I was the Matriarch; I was the one who set the tone for the entire family. There was no one who could punish me or disown me in hopes of appeasing the mob. I'd destroyed the entire family. I'd...

I forced myself to stand, slowly. My body ached. I rubbed at my muscles, trying to think as I staggered to the nearest chair. There had to be a way out. There had to be...but nothing came to mind. I slumped in the chair, my thoughts twisting in on themselves. There'd been no time to try to capture or kill Malachi before he'd left and...I was morbidly sure he'd taken precautions to ensure his safety. Whatever he'd learnt about me—and everyone else—would be released if he didn't return home. Fear gnawed at me, burning through my thoughts. It would have been better if he'd simply revealed the truth, if he'd let me face the consequences for what I'd done. Instead, I was dangling on the edge of disaster. I had no choice. I had to jump through his hoops, or face destruction.

My hands shook. I stared at my fingers, willing them to be still. They refused to obey. I hadn't felt so scared, so defeated, since...since ever. I'd been frog-marched to the headmistress's office more than once, but... Mistress Grayling hadn't threatened to *destroy* me. The worst she could do was expel me. Malachi, on the other hand, could take out the entire family. I tried to tell myself that it wouldn't be *that* bad, but I knew it to be a lie. It would be worse. No one would ever trust us.

And why would they? My thoughts mocked me. *They'd know what I did.*

I'd been a fool. I knew it now, even though...I glared around the room. I'd told myself I had no choice, that I had to do everything in my power to staunch the bleeding and rebuild the family. I'd told myself...I'd *lied* to myself. Better I married Gary and absorbed his family, better I let his father take the reins, than risk total destruction. Better...I swallowed hard as I realised I might have doomed Gary and his family too. They didn't deserve to be caught up in my scandal, but...they were going to be dragged down with us. It just wasn't fair.

A hundred schemes ran through my head, all too risky to contemplate. I could run, but I couldn't hide. There was no way I could evade the hunters who'd be put on my trail. There was no one who would hide me, no one who would help...there was nothing I could offer to convince someone to take the risk. The only things I had of value belonged to the family, not to me. I couldn't take them with me. And there was nothing I could do to Malachi either. What would it profit me to take him down if it meant my certain destruction too?

And I might not be the only one caught up in his web, I thought. I knew nothing about Malachi. I hadn't even *heard* of him until he'd walked into my life. *He might have enough dirt on wealthy and powerful people to save himself from jail.*

I rubbed tears from my eyes. I'd made a terrible mistake. I'd treated High Society like...like school, where you took your lumps if you were caught and then everything went back to normal. People thought it was *funny* if someone was caught at school, as if there was nothing wrong with doing wrong as long as you weren't caught. I'd internalised that attitude and it had bitten me, hard. The people I'd offended wouldn't treat me like a naughty schoolgirl. They'd consider me a thief who'd betrayed their welcome. My life wouldn't be worth living, even if they didn't kill me. I'd die a thousand deaths before someone put me out of my misery.

My thoughts mocked me, again and again. I had no choice. I had to bow the knee to Malachi or face total destruction. And yet...what did he want? The sheer uncertainty of *not knowing* was worse than being told. He could make me do whatever he wanted...as long as it was something I *could* give. I swallowed hard, my aching muscles reminding me of how he'd forced me to kneel and kiss his boot. I knew the type. He'd enjoyed watching me humiliate myself. He'd make me do it again, for the sheer sadistic pleasure of forcing me to do as he said. I swallowed again, tasting bile. He wanted me to crawl. And he could *make* me.

I looked up as I heard footsteps, hastily blinking away tears. Jadish looked in, her eyes going wide as she saw me. I cursed under my breath. It was too late to cast a glamour, too late to hide...Jadish knew something was wrong. She'd never seen me cry since...big girls *didn't* cry. It was a lesson I'd had hammered into me, the first night in the dorms. If you cried, you got picked on. And yet...

"My Lady?" Jadish sounded unsure of herself. "Should I...?"

"Go away," I ordered. I was ashamed of myself for snapping at her, but...I couldn't help myself. "Just...go away."

Jadish hesitated. A surge of anger rose up within me, threatening to overwhelm me. I hated myself for wanting to shout and scream, for wanting to do unto her as had been done to me...I understood, suddenly, why so many of my peers had been so horrible to the younger girls. I guessed there were Grande Dames who were worse to their servants. If one was being tormented, and one had no way to strike back at the tormentor, one had to get rid of the anger somehow. And servants were the easiest targets. What could *they* do to their mistress?

Betray her, I thought, numbly. Someone in Lord McDonald's hall had watched me and, instead of contacting his master, passed the memory to Malachi. *How many other servants has he subverted?*

I shuddered as the full implications struck me. Servants were *everywhere*. Marlene and her ilk had bragged, time and time again, of small armies of servants at their beck and call. I'd known girls who couldn't even brush their *hair*, let alone dress themselves, without help. A servant would see his master or her mistress at their worst, be it plotting a business coup or committing adultery or…or anything. Malachi might have subverted enough servants to collect hundreds, perhaps thousands, of memory orbs. And who knew what he might know?

"My Lady?" Jadish sounded as if she was no longer sure of herself. "Would you like me to bring you tea?"

I almost laughed. Tea? It was absurd. It wouldn't make me feel any better. And yet…I looked into her dark face, wondering if she was truly loyal. She could have gone elsewhere—it wasn't as if she was tied to the house—and yet…she'd been my friend, once upon a time, but things changed. What if she betrayed me? What if…?

"Please." My voice sounded weak, even to me. "And then leave me alone."

Jadish curtsied and retreated. I watched her go, feeling lost, helpless and alone. I'd messed up and…what if she couldn't be trusted? What if *no one* could be trusted? What if…I tried to think of everything I'd done, everything Jadish might have seen. What if…I shook my head, cursing myself for being paranoid. But even *paranoids* had enemies. Jadish—or her father—might have reason to betray *my* father. Or me.

She returned, carrying a tray with a steaming pot and two mugs. I stared at it dully, my dazed mind unable to comprehend *two* mugs. My heart sank as Uncle Jalil followed Jadish into the room. I wanted to curse Jadish. She had to have told him *something* was wrong. I...I wondered, suddenly, if Uncle Jalil could be trusted. Could *anyone* be trusted? I didn't know anything any longer.

I said nothing as Jadish poured the tea, then withdrew. Uncle Jalil cast a handful of privacy spells into the air, isolating the room from the rest of the hall. I stared at the floor, all too aware he was studying me. It felt as if I'd been called on the carpet, even though I was the one in charge. I wanted to laugh, despite everything. Malachi had taught me I was not in charge any longer, if indeed I'd *ever* been in charge...

"Lucy." Uncle Jalil's voice was calm and reassuring. It made me want to scream. There was no reason to be either calm or reassured. "What happened?"

I shook my head, not daring to speak. My mind raced. I'd clearly had a terrible shock. He knew it. I would never have presented myself to him—or anyone—in such a state if I hadn't. And...I wondered, sourly, just what *his* imagination was suggesting. Uncle Jalil had never been known for imagination, but he was far from stupid. He might have guessed the truth.

"What happened?" Uncle Jalil leaned forward and put a hand on my shoulder. It wouldn't have bothered me, normally, but now...I flinched. "Lucy?"

"I've screwed up," I admitted. Maybe something *could* be done. The family conclave could strip me of my post, then kick me out of the hall. And yet...I'd foreclosed that option when I'd demanded a year's grace before they started to challenge me. Even if I went along with everything, they'd still be seen as backstabbers. I was doomed whatever way I turned. "I've *really* screwed up."

"So I gather," Uncle Jalil said. I had the nasty feeling he'd already guessed part of the truth. He'd been the one to warn me I was riding for a fall. I wished I'd listened. I could have saved myself before it'd been too late. "Lucy, what happened?"

I forced myself to concentrate as I outlined everything, from the moment I'd sneaked into Lord McDonald's office to Malachi's visit. Uncle Jalil started to say something, then stopped as the words kept tumbling out. I hadn't wanted to tell him about being forced to kneel, but...somehow, I couldn't stop myself. It was all I could do not to start crying. If he turned and left...it might be the smartest thing to do. I couldn't even fault him. He'd warned me. And I hadn't listened.

Uncle Jalil said nothing until I'd finished. "If I was a cruel man," he said finally, "I'd say I told you so."

"I know." I choked back a sob. "You did. And I wish I'd listened."

"You're just like your father," he said. There was no anger in his voice, just a bitter resignation that felt a thousand times worse. "You think you can keep rolling the dice until you come up trumps, but instead you lose everything. I told him, time and time again, that he was gambling with money he didn't have! And he didn't listen."

"I..." It was all I could do to force myself to look at him. I couldn't meet his eyes. "I'm sorry..."

Uncle Jalil let out a heavy sigh. "You're sorry? Do you think that saying *sorry* will fix everything?"

"No." I shook my head. There was no one who could help me, no one I could appeal to...I didn't even know much of anything about Malachi and his allies. His card—I'd put it on the table—read MALACHI RUBÉN. Was he *really* a Rubén? It was odd for someone who bore a family name *not* to be linked to the family, although...I supposed it could happen. A natural-born son? Or someone who'd adopted the name? "I don't know what to do?"

Uncle Jalil picked up the memory orb and stared into it. "Interesting," he said. I realised he must have seen the same memory. "I don't think this can be faked."

I felt my heart sink still further, as impossible as that seemed. Malachi had said as much, but...I'd hoped, deep inside, that he'd been lying. The memory might have been nothing more than an illusion, put together with magic in a manner that would allow the viewer's imagination to fill in the gaps...no, that wasn't workable. The viewers wouldn't see the *same* vision unless it was a recording of someone's memory.

"And even if you managed to convince people it *was* faked, you'd still have to account for what you'd learned," Uncle Jalil said. "You might manage to explain away one very good guess. Maybe. But you've made too many good guesses for it to be believable."

He turned the orb over and over in his hand. "You have three choices, as I see it," he said. "You can refuse to play his games and dare him to do his worst. He *might* be reluctant to tell the world about these"—he peered at the orb—"*things*, but he won't have to show off his trick to convince people. They'll take a look at your record and suspect the truth. Or you can simply run."

I shook my head. I'd already decided that wasn't an option.

"And the third option?" I knew what it was, but...I hoped I was wrong. "What else can I do?"

"Surrender." Uncle Jalil held out the orb. "He's got you. You—and the entire family—are looking at total ruination if the truth gets out. You might betray him in turn, but how will you prove it? He'll say you have no proof and he'll be right."

"And he might have something on everyone else as well," I said. "What if he has something on...on *everyone*?"

"Then, as long as he doesn't get too greedy, he's got the entire world on its knees," Uncle Jalil said, curtly. "Lucy, the choice is yours. Fight, run, or surrender?"

I stared down at my hands. Malachi hadn't demanded money. He hadn't demanded anything, beyond a show of submission. That was going to change. He'd said as much. He wanted me for something and...and I had a feeling, when he told me, that I wasn't going to like it. Why me? He had to know I couldn't give him much of anything...I shook my head. It didn't matter. He could keep demanding more and more from me until I was a broken girl or I tried to fight back. I thought I had the measure of him. He wasn't interested in a single transaction. He wanted to make me dance and keep dancing...

He won't stop, I thought. *Even if I give him what he wants, he won't stop.*

My mind raced. If I dared him to do his worst, the family would be destroyed. If I tried to run, I'd be hunted down like a dog. If I surrendered... he'd never let me go. I needed a fourth option, but what? I needed a way to turn the tables—and quickly.

"We play along, for the moment," I said. "I need to know more about him. I need to find a way of stopping him."

"Dangerous," Uncle Jalil pointed out. "Are you gambling again?"

I winced. That hurt. Uncle Jalil was right. It *was* a gamble. But I'd taken Malachi's measure. He'd never let me go. He'd force me to compromise myself time and time again until I was broken beyond all hope of repair. Or redemption. I wanted—I needed—to destroy the evidence, then stop him. I'd have to play along until I isolated him and struck.

"There are ways to deal with a blackmailer," Uncle Jalil said. He sounded like a man clutching at straws. "If we put together a proper deal..."

"No." I shook my head. I could understand the logic—sure, we could offer a hefty one-time payment—but Malachi couldn't be trusted to keep his side of the agreement. And besides, what did we have to offer him? It made me sick just to consider the possibilities. "We need to find a way to stop him."

I stared at my hands, thinking hard. Malachi would have other victims, I was sure. I could find them...I shook my head. It was too risky. I was alone. I wasn't even sure I could trust my closest—and oldest—friends.

"I want you to dig up as much as you can," I told him. Uncle Jalil was a better researcher than I'd ever be. And he had contacts—fellow accountants—who might talk to him. "I want to know everything about him."

"I'll see what I can do." Uncle Jalil let out a heavy sigh. "I wish you'd listened to me.

"Me too," I said, quietly. "I wish I'd listened too."

CHAPTER
TWENTY-FOUR

The next four days were amongst the worst in my life.

I'd felt vulnerable before—you didn't go to boarding school without feeling vulnerable, particularly in your first few months—but this was worse. Far worse. I potted around the hall, unable to muster the determination to go out and do *something* as I waited for the message. I wanted to go riding or shopping or...or something, anything, but I didn't quite dare. I didn't even want to open the ever-growing pile of invitations, let alone attend the parties, soirées and everything else being organised by my peers. The doors were opening, yet I didn't want to walk through. My dreams were haunted by people staring at me with knowing eyes, my guilt on their lips...I woke up sweaty, my heart beating like a drum. I prayed to my ancestors, but they didn't answer. They probably thought I was a failure.

I studied the orb time and time again, trying to tell myself it could be faked. And yet, the more I looked at it, the more I came to believe there was simply no way to convince anyone it was anything but real. It *was*. I cursed myself as I paced the hall, barely able to make a list of patches in the walls that needed fixed or repainted or *something*. I'd compromised myself so badly that there was no hope of redemption. I tried to cling to the thought of finding a way to outwit Malachi, or maybe making myself so useful he'd treat me as an ally rather than a tool, but...it was hard to believe, as the days wore on, that either was possible. He'd use me, then throw me to the wolves.

My heart twisted as I walked down the stairs and onto the ballroom floor. The room was supposed to be cleaned, in preparation for Ayesha and Zeya McDonald's party…I knew, beyond a shadow of a doubt, that they'd turn on me in an instant if they knew what I'd done. They'd cross the road if they saw me coming, just to make sure that no one—absolutely no one—would believe they'd so much as give me the time of day. I'd be cut dead in the streets, shunned and abhorred by High Society. I cursed myself, again and again. I'd been sent to Coventry at school, but this would be worse. Far worse.

I stopped in front of a painting of some long-gone Lamplighter and stared up at her. She looked dignified, wearing expensive clothes that marked her wealth far more profoundly than the diamond necklace hanging around her neck. I wondered what she'd have thought of me, if she'd known what I'd done. The family tree was full of gamblers, of people who'd taken horrific risks to build the family fortune…people who'd won. The difference between a brilliant idea and something so stupid that no one would think it was a good idea was less than one might think. If it worked, it was brilliant; if it failed, it was stupid.

And you'd probably have been smart enough to set up a fallback position, I thought, studying the painting. There was no shortage of stories about paintings coming to life, about the ancients speaking though their images, but they were just stories. I'd never met a ghost who'd had anything useful to say. *You wouldn't have let yourself become so desperately exposed.*

I turned as I heard the sound of footsteps. Jadish was descending the marble stairs, a hint of aristocracy around her gait. I nearly laughed, catching myself just in time. She'd probably fantasised about having a Season, just like Kate and every other common-born girl I'd known. Walking down the stairs, into the empty ballroom, was the closest she'd ever come. I felt a stab of sympathy, mingled with envy. Jadish and Kate would never be put on display, like prize dogs and horses. They'd never be strongly urged to marry the highest bidder. And no one would care about their good names...

"My Lady." Jadish looked a little embarrassed. "I...Gary is here to see you."

I blinked, then cursed myself as I remembered. Gary had come once a week for the last month and...and I'd forgotten. With everything that had happened, I'd forgotten. I flushed as I looked down at myself. I'd barely remembered to shower and dress. My clothes were appropriate for indoor work, but not for meeting one's paramour. I cursed myself again as I realised Gary and his family would want to demand their money back, if they knew what had happened. Malachi could ruin me—without making waves—simply by tipping them off.

"Please show him to the kitchenette," I said. I ran my hand through my hair. I looked terrible, but...I couldn't simply tell him to go away. We'd planned the meeting. It couldn't be cancelled unless there was a *real* emergency. "I'll be along in a moment."

Jadish nodded and hurried away. I watched her scamper up the stairs, wondering if I could rent out the hall to wealthy commoners who wanted to introduce their daughters to High Society. The Grande Dames had been moaning about commoners putting on airs and graces—even holding Seasons—of their own...I smiled at the thought. There would be complaints, of course, but who cared? It wasn't as if we had many other options. I'd lost my taste for insider trading.

And we have to find a way to get out of the trap before we do anything else, I thought, as I followed Jadish at a more sedate pace. *There's no hope of doing anything until we're free.*

I felt a twinge of guilt as I stepped into the kitchenette. Gary was seated at the far end of the chamber, holding a mug of tea. He stood as I entered, bowing politely. I nodded in return, then motioned for him to sit. The chamber might be almost laughably small, compared to the family dining room, but it was comfortable. I would have felt relaxed, if I hadn't been all too aware Malachi had me over a barrel. Every time I forgot, the awareness snapped back into my mind with jarring force. It was simply impossible to relax for more than a few seconds.

"Lucy." Gary's smile was warm and welcoming. "It's good to see you again."

"And you." I tried not to feel guilty as I sat down, guilty and ashamed. "It's been a long week."

"You look as if you haven't slept at all," Gary said. I saw nothing but honest concern in his eyes. "Are you alright?"

"I'm having problems coming to terms with my father's death," I said. "I just realised, a few days ago, that he's really gone."

I tried not to feel too guilty. It wasn't entirely a lie. If my father had been alive, I wouldn't have set out to rebuild the family fortunes and compromised myself beyond redemption. And he could have disciplined me if I'd been caught, ensuring the consequences—such as they were—would have fallen on me and me alone. I would have felt better about facing the music if I'd been the only one in trouble.

"I'm sorry about that," Gary said. He reached out and touched my hand, lightly. "It never gets easier."

"I wish he'd lived longer," I said. "I didn't so much as lay eyes on him for six years, not until I saw his body."

I looked down at the floor. My father had died suddenly...too suddenly. I'd wondered, given the scale of his debts, if he'd committed suicide. The healers hadn't found any proof he'd killed himself—they'd blamed his death on a heart attack brought on by ill health—but that proved nothing. It would be fairly easy to brew a potion that would mimic a heart attack, then vanish into the bloodstream before the healers started the autopsy. And my father *had* had a small collection of books on dubious or outright dark magic. I hadn't been able to tell if he'd so much as read the books, but they could have been sold if he hadn't wanted to keep them.

Gary looked surprised. "You never saw him at all?"

"No." I had no idea how to explain it. "Girls at my school...we were discouraged from seeing our parents during term-time. It was rare for relatives to visit and, when they did, they were under strict rules. They were practically *chaperoned*."

"Chaperoned?" Gary made a show of looking around. *Our* chaperone had absented herself as soon as she'd shown him into the chamber. "Why?"

I shrugged. "It depends on who you believe," I said. "There were girls who thought the school simply wanted to discourage visitors. The headmistress didn't want to run the risk of the girls telling tales out of school. And there were girls who snickered that *someone* must have introduced her betrothed as her cousin as a ruse to sneak him into the school. But really...I don't know."

"Ouch," Gary said. "It wasn't *quite* that bad at Jude's."

"I'm glad to hear it," I said. "What happened?"

"Oh, we were allowed out as long as we managed to evade the groundskeeper," Gary said, wryly. "The walls were pretty high and topped with iron spikes and pieces of glass and all sorts of interesting spells. I think they thought that unravelling the spells and escaping would provide a challenge for the upperclassmen. Or something."

I shook my head, feeling a twinge of envy. If I'd gone to Jude's...I told myself, again, that there was no point in crying over spilt milk. There was certainly no way I could change the past. If I had a way to do that...I'd have gone back just far enough to tell my younger self not to risk breaking into Lord McDonald's office. And yet...I had a nasty feeling my younger self wouldn't have listened. I'd been too caught up in the thrill to care.

Gary finished his tea and put the mug to one side. "Lucy, do you want to go out?"

I blinked, surprised. "Go out? Go where?"

"You need a change," Gary said. "We could go...we could go *anywhere*. I can even take you shopping."

"You must like me," I said, lightly. He coloured, but he stood his ground. "I've never really been *into* shopping."

Gary pretended to be shocked. "Really?"

"Really." I smiled, but with little real humour. As a child, I'd never been allowed to shop; as a teenager, the only shops within walking distance had been dull and tedious. Now...I supposed I could visit some of the truly expensive shops, but I didn't have the money to buy anything. And I couldn't see Gary's father agreeing to let him pay a few hundred crowns for a dress. "It's just...boring."

"We could go somewhere else," Gary said. "There's a zoo. Or a park. Or...we could even visit the library."

"Nerd," I said, with a hint of affection. "I might have been interested, but we can't be seen together."

"Use a glamour," Gary said. "Pretend to be someone you're not."

I hesitated. Gary was right. I wanted to go out. I could feel the walls closing in already. And yet, I didn't quite dare. Malachi had me dangling on the end of a string. If he returned, or sent me a message, I needed to see it at once. I didn't dare go too far from the hall. It might mean the end of everything.

"We can walk in the gardens," I said, finally. I didn't want to turn him down completely. "And you can tell me about your apprenticeship."

"I thought you'd be bored of hearing about it by now," Gary said. He looked away—absurdly—as I stood and threw a cloak over my dress. "I'm trying to get certified before we get married."

My heart twisted, again. I liked him...I liked him too much. And I knew he'd turn against me in a heartbeat if he knew what I'd done. His father wouldn't give him a choice. I wouldn't blame him. I might doom his family as well as my own...if the truth came out. I ground my teeth, feeling a flash of pure rage. I deserved punishment—I conceded as much—but everyone else was innocent. Gary and his family didn't deserve to go down with me.

Gary looked doubtful as we headed down the stairs to the servant's entrance and out into the lawn. "Do you want to talk about it?"

I glanced at him. "About what?"

"About what's bothering you," Gary said. "Is it something to do with me?"

"No." I shook my head firmly, trying not to show my irritation. He had every right to wonder, but...I didn't think he had the right to ask questions. "I'm just a little out of sorts right now."

Gary said nothing as we strolled onto the lawn and around the hall. The potion gardens looked neater, now they'd been harvested of everything of worth. I'd convinced a pair of potioneers to tend the gardens, in exchange for half the produce. I wasn't sure who'd gotten the better half of *that* bargain, but it was better than leaving the plants to die. My father had made a serious mistake when he'd dismissed the gardeners. Some of the plants—given time—would give us a nice little income.

I glanced at Gary, wishing—suddenly—that he'd been raised as an aristocrat. An aristocrat would understand that we weren't marrying for love, but duty. He might be quite reasonable about such things. But a commoner would put love before reason, before his family...I remembered the stories Kate had loved and shuddered. I couldn't run away to be with my lover, even if it was more romantic than entire baskets of roses. My duty to the family came first.

I'm sorry, I thought. I didn't want to admit what I'd done, not to him. *I'm really sorry.*

"There's supposed to be a party the following week," Gary said, suddenly. "My sister is hosting...if she manages to talk my father into letting her. Would you like to come?"

"I might," I said. "What sort of party?"

"A terribly boring party men aren't allowed to attend," Gary said. "She asked me to invite you."

I hesitated. I'd never met my prospective sister-in-law, but...everything I'd heard about her indicated she'd be a welcome addition to the family. And a formidable opponent, if I got on her bad side. I'd heard all sorts of horror stories about wives—and sometimes husbands—who managed to alienate their in-laws. I supposed that wouldn't be a problem for Gary. My parents were dead. It was yet another reminder that I simply didn't fit. I was too high-ranked to hang with my age group and too young and isolated to work with my peers.

"I can't make any promises," I said. "But if she sends me a formal invitation, I might just be able to attend."

Gary smiled. "We don't do formal invitations," he said. "Just word of mouth."

I laughed. "Can I move into your house?"

"I wouldn't say no," Gary said. "My mother, on the other hand…"

"You make your life sound so easy," I said. "Can you imagine the sort of insult you'd deliver, over here, if you didn't send someone a written invitation?"

"No." Gary winked at me. "You make it sound so inviting."

My heart clenched. No one would be sending me any invitations, written or not, when the truth came out. I'd be shunned…I shook my head as my stomach started to churn. I was damned if I let that happen. I'd play along with Malachi until I got the drop on him and then put a knife in his back. And then…I smiled, rather wanly. If I wasn't the only one who'd been targeted for blackmail, I might *just* be able to get the others to speak up for me afterwards. Might.

"It's…just a way of life," I said. "We have strict rules about etiquette to keep us from actually fighting."

Rules I've snapped, my thoughts added. *Rules…*

"My Lady!" I looked up to see Jadish, hurrying towards me. "We just received a priority message for you!"

I took the charmed envelope and opened it, gingerly. A single note dropped out. A place, a time and a name. Malachi. I swore as I glanced at my watch. I'd have to hurry. I had a feeling he wouldn't tolerate lateness. And…

"I have to go," I said. "Jadish, get the carriage ready."

Jadish bobbled a curtsy and hurried off. I folded the note and stuck it in my pocket, then looked at Gary. He seemed irked, but understanding. I would almost have preferred him to be angry. It would be easier to break things off with him if he'd been outraged. We *had* arranged the meeting, hadn't we?

"I have to go," I repeated. "Will you be here next week?"

"You know I will," Gary said. "I enjoy your company."

I surprised myself by giving him a hug. It would be easy, very easy, to suggest that we ran off together. A charmsmith could find work anywhere. But he wouldn't want to abandon his family and run...I winced, inwardly, as he wrapped his arms around me and hugged me back. I'd been living in a fool's paradise. Now...now, all I could do was hope I got a clear shot at my tormentor.

"Thanks," I said. I wanted to hold him for hours, but I didn't have time. "I enjoy yours too."

CHAPTER TWENTY-FIVE

I breathed a sigh of relief as the carriage rattled to a halt outside an expensive and *very* exclusive restaurant on the very edge of North Shallot. I'd heard of it—of course—but I'd never actually visited. They said the food was fantastic, utterly perfect...I frowned as I scrambled down and ordered the driver to take the carriage back to the hall. I'd walk home, after...after whatever Malachi wanted from me. The waiter came forward as I stood outside, motioning for me to follow him. I did, frowning as I stepped out of the light. The restaurant struck me as an odd place for a private meeting, despite the formidable charms hanging in the air. We might be noticed.

The thought nagged at me as I was escorted through the dining chamber and down a long corridor to a private dining room. There were more charms on the door, each complex enough to require a couple of hours to dismantle. I could have done it quicker if I'd been prepared to set off the alarms. The waiter pushed the door open, then stepped aside to allow me to enter. Malachi sat at a table, wearing an ill-fitting suit that looked as if it had been tailored for someone quite a bit larger. I nodded to him as the waiter closed the door behind me. He wouldn't return until we were ready to order.

Malachi stood. "Kneel."

I groaned, inwardly, as I went down on my knees. I'd expected it, after everything he'd done last time we'd met, but it was still humiliating. He stared down at me, drinking in the sight. I'd picked my clothes carefully, trying to convey an impression of helplessness...I wondered, as his eyes wandered over me, if I'd gone too far. It was easy to pretend to be weak and powerless—I'd done it before—but he knew too much about me to be easily duped into lowering his guard. I'd just have to wait, biding my time. Uncle Jalil had yet to return with his report.

Malachi patted me on the forehead, then stepped back and sat down. I stayed where I was, all too aware he was just *waiting* for an opportunity to slap me down. He studied me for a moment, lips curved into a cruel smile, then shrugged and motioned for me to rise and take the seat facing him. I breathed a sigh of relief he hadn't ordered me to sit next to him. I suspected that would have been awful beyond words.

"Order whatever you like," Malachi said. His smile grew colder. "You'll be paying, of course."

I said nothing as I scanned the menu. There was a long list of fancy meals—half of them foreign—but no prices. I knew what that meant. If you had to ask the price, you couldn't afford it. I'd never been given the chance to develop expensive tastes—Marlene had said I was a plebe at heart, despite the family name—but I had a feeling Malachi would pick the most expensive thing on the menu because he could. I didn't have to look at him to know he was smirking. He was enjoying making me dance to his tune.

And he looks a slob because he wants people to think I'm meeting a slob, I thought, sourly. A man raised in High Society would know how to wear a suit. It would have been easy to have the outfit tailored properly. *It's all part of his game.*

Malachi rang a little bell. The waiter returned and bowed so deeply I thought his nose would brush against the floor. Malachi smiled and ordered a dish I'd never heard of, with a drink I knew all too well. I sighed inwardly, then ordered something simpler for myself with a glass of water. I knew better than to drink. My one experience with alcohol had been enough.

"This place is very private," Malachi said. His face twisted in a leer. "You could do anything here, anything at all, and the staff wouldn't say a word."

"I imagine that was why you picked it," I said. I reached out with my senses, as gingerly as I could. Malachi wasn't the strongest sorcerer I'd encountered, but he was far from inept. His protections were strong enough to keep me from weakening them without alerting him. "Do they even know who you are?"

"They like to consider themselves the most exclusive of exclusive places in the city," Malachi said, his words echoing my earlier thoughts. "But the blunt truth, my dear, is that they'll take anyone who can meet their prices."

I nodded, somehow unsurprised. "They have to make a living somehow."

"Of course." Malachi winked. "And so do you."

The waiter returned, followed by a waitress wearing a dress so low I wasn't sure what was keeping it in place. I was almost embarrassed to look at her. They both carried trays of food, which they placed in front of us. I was almost disappointed. The meal looked elegant, almost beautiful, but there was very little of it. I was going to be grossly overcharged. The waiter poured Malachi's wine, then bowed and retreated. Malachi's eyes followed the waitress as she left too.

"Please, eat," Malachi said. "You're paying."

Don't remind me, I thought, as I took a bite. I tasted pasta and fish and something I couldn't quite place. I'd never had the chance to follow food fashions either. Grayling's never served anything remotely fashionable—I was fairly sure we were overcharged, for the bland muck we were served—and there hadn't been any expensive restaurants nearby. *Whatever this is, it'll cost far too much.*

"You're quite an interesting person, you know," Malachi said. "Your father was just like you."

"So I'm told," I said. I wasn't sure if he was trying to make conversation, in mockery of social conventions, or if he was making a point. Had he known my father? It was possible. My father had never been very good at keeping records. There were enough gaps in his notebooks to hide an entire army of visitors. "Did you know him?"

Malachi ignored the question. "You've been quite brave and bold. I've only met a couple of people who were so determined to tear through everything in their path and they both had far less to lose."

"Thanks," I said. I tried not to sound sour, but I thought it was a losing battle. "I do whatever I have to do."

"Capital." Malachi clapped his hands. "An excellent attitude."

"I try." I took another bite of my dinner. It was good, but not worth more than a crown or two. "I have reports from school saying I keep trying until I win."

"And you have no qualms about cutting corners, according to your schoolmistress," Malachi said. "Of course, I knew that already."

I glanced up. "You talked to *her*?"

Malachi smiled, but didn't answer. I felt my heart sink. Malachi didn't *have* to talk to Mistress Grayling to get his hands on my reports. They'd be lodged in the records office, where anyone could see them. Or...he could simply have blackmailed someone at school to send them to him. Or...I told myself I was overthinking. It was summer, the season of love. He could easily have posed as a concerned relative, vetting me as a potential partner for his nephew. I didn't think Mistress Grayling would ask too many questions. She was always keen to brag about how her girls—her students, really—had made good matches.

"I didn't see that on my report card," I said. "What *else* did she say?"

"Enough to really interest me," Malachi said. "Your disciplinary record is quite remarkable."

I flushed. "And there I was, thinking it was burnt when I left school."

"Nothing is ever gone for good." Malachi smirked at me. "As I'm sure you're aware by now."

"Yes," I said. "You taught me that."

I thought about the memory orb and shivered. What *else* had he seen? Who else had he corrupted? Who else…I stared at him, wondering if he'd managed to subvert the servants without the servants being aware they *were* subverted. They'd pass loyalty checks because none of them would know they *were* disloyal. Truth spells could force someone to tell the truth, but only what they *thought* to be the truth. I studied his protections again, cursing under my breath. They were good enough to keep me from doing anything dangerous. The risk was simply too great.

"I suppose I did," Malachi said. "Does that make me the best teacher you've ever had?"

"Better than some," I said. My tutors had always been a hit-or-miss affair. Some had been very good, some very bad…I shook my head. I'd passed my exams and that was all that mattered. "You taught me something very useful."

"Glad to be of service." Malachi pushed his plate aside and peered at me. "And now, we get to business."

I swallowed a handful of sharp answers. Malachi was mocking me, aping the etiquette of High Society. I wasn't sure, but I was fairly certain he was common-born. He might well have married into an aristocratic family. I wondered why. He might not be inept, but he wasn't powerful or skilled enough to merit inclusion. Gary was far more capable and *Gary* was barely out of his teens. Malachi had to be in his forties, at the very least. He'd really let himself go.

"What do I want from you?" Malachi let the question hang in the air. "What *do* I want from you?"

"I imagine you're going to tell me," I said, stiffly. I didn't want to think about some of the possibilities. "What do you want from me?"

"We're quite alike," Malachi commented. "We're both prepared to do *anything* to advance ourselves."

I'm nothing like you, I thought, savagely. *I've never blackmailed anyone…*

It was all I could do to keep my face under tight control. I'd never blackmailed anyone because I'd never known anything—not much, anyway—that could be used for blackmail. Even if I had...I'd have been branded a sneak and ostracized for the rest of my schooling and beyond. My heart cringed at the thought. You could do a lot, as a schoolchild passing through her teens, but you could never tattle. No one would ever trust you again.

Malachi smiled. "You were willing to run a huge risk for money," he said. "You're *just* like me."

"I want to rebuild my family," I agreed, stiffly. There was no point in trying to hide it. He knew what I'd been doing and he probably understood why. "What do you want from me?"

"What an interesting question," Malachi said. "How many times have you asked it now?"

He reached into his pocket and removed a memory orb. Another memory orb. I'd left mine back at the hall, wrapped in so many wards even *I* would have trouble getting inside. I didn't dare run the risk of allowing anyone else to so much as touch it, for fear their magic would accidentally trigger it. I was in quite enough trouble already. I took the second orb and stared at it, suddenly fearful. What would I see when I looked into the magic?

"Go ahead," Malachi ordered. "Have a look inside."

I took a breath, then peered into the orb. The world seemed to spin around me. I was suddenly sitting in a study, sitting on a comfortable armchair...the scene looked odd, weirdly distorted. I puzzled over it for a long moment, then realised that whoever had recorded the memory had been significantly different from me. Bigger, perhaps. The study was quite large, by my standards, but small for a bigger man.

A young man—blond, blue eyes, strikingly handsome in a manner that proved he knew it—sat in front of me. He wore a Jude's uniform, carefully tailored to show off his muscles...I guessed he was around the same age as myself, maybe a year or two in either direction. And...he looked a little like Akin, but he had a cruel expression that reminded me of Malachi. A

Rubén? It was possible. He certainly had the looks.

"She turned Akin into a frog," the young man said. "She turned him into a frog with a kiss and dumped him in the girls' locker room."

I heard a chuckle. It took me a moment to realise it had come from my lips. Except they weren't my lips...I gritted my teeth, feeling more and more disorientated by the memory. It wasn't mine, but it *felt* like mine.

"Who?" My voice sounded masculine. Of course...it wasn't *my* voice. "And why?"

"Ayesha McDonald," the young man said. "He was very lucky to escape."

"She used the kissing curse on him," the masculine voice said. "That's interesting. That's very interesting indeed."

The memory came to an end. I fell back into my body, nearly dropping the orb. Akin...someone had hit Akin with the kissing curse? Ayesha McDonald had hit Akin with the kissing curse and tossed him into the girls' locker room? I swallowed hard as the implications dawned on me. There were almost too many to count. She'd threatened the alliance between House Rubén and House Aguirre, she'd threatened the relationship between Akin and Caitlyn and...she'd nearly disgraced Akin. If he'd been caught in the locker room...the girls would have hexed him bloody, then whatever was left would have been expelled. And he wouldn't have been able to defend himself without tattling on Ayesha. And...

Malachi chuckled. "Funny, isn't it?"

"Yeah," I managed. I suppose it would have been funny, to everyone watching from the sidelines. The damage would have been almost incalculable. "How did you...is it even true?"

"Francis was always quite boastful," Malachi said. I guessed Francis was the young blond man. "And I never had any trouble influencing him to tell the truth."

I stared down at the orb. I wasn't so sure. The story had too many holes in it. Ayesha was hardly stupid. She wouldn't do something that would risk her position. Akin might go down, but she'd go down too. Unless...

she might have gambled he'd keep his mouth shut. Men were strange creatures. The thought of being publicly humiliated, of being zapped by the kissing curse...I remembered what I'd done to Brantley and tasted bile. It didn't seem so funny now.

And a lot of people would think he'd deserved it, I thought, numbly. I knew the spell. The prefects had taught me, when I'd started to mature. It was the simplest way to stop a man in his tracks if he got a little too passionate. *The kissing curse needs a kiss to work.*

I didn't want to know the answer to the next question, but I had to ask. "What do you want me to do?"

"I expect you to have a word or two with Ayesha," Malachi said. "Tell her...tell her she can either go along with my demands or that recording will be released. And that will be the end for her."

My heart twisted. Ayesha—and her twin sister—were not exactly my friends, but...they didn't deserve to be blackmailed. Or did they...? Akin wouldn't find the recording very funny, nor would his family. Nor would Caitlyn. I'd seen them together. They genuinely *liked* each other. The recording would break them up and...Ayesha would find herself with a very powerful enemy, one with the skills to shatter House McDonald. Her family would disown her. They'd have no choice. And she'd be sent into exile...

I wondered, insanely, if Malachi was bluffing. His family would be affected...if, of course, he was a *real* Rubén. I wished I knew. He didn't need more enemies...I wondered, suddenly, if there'd be any proof of his involvement. It would be *me* who'd show the memory to Ayesha...Francis could have bragged to me or anyone or...my thoughts ran in mad circles. I was trapped. I wanted to beg, but I already knew it would be useless. Malachi would enjoy it, then order me to go ahead anyway.

"I'll want to see your memory afterwards," Malachi added, smoothly. He lowered his voice. "And if you cooperate, you'll be rewarded."

I ground my teeth. I hadn't even *considered* bluffing, perhaps trying to recruit Ayesha and Zeya to help me. They would have made powerful allies…I thought about trying anyway, but Malachi was one step ahead. There was no way I could recruit them without risking my entire family. I was caught in a trap of my own making.

"I don't want to see you disgraced," Malachi said. He sounded almost kind, but his face told a different story. "You're far more use to me in High Society than anywhere else."

"Thank you," I said, sourly. I wasn't fooled. He'd make use of me until I was no longer useful, then leave me hopelessly compromised. Ayesha and Zeya would hate me…everyone would. "I'll do my best for you."

Malachi reached out and patted my hand in an almost fatherly manner. "We'll do great things together, you and I."

My skin crawled.

Malachi stood. "Tell her I want a thousand crowns before the end of the week," he said, with a shrug. I had the feeling the money meant nothing to him. It was just a way to test his control. "Or else."

I watched him leave, then fled to the private washroom to throw up.

CHAPTER
TWENTY-SIX

I was in something of a daze for the rest of the day. If he'd asked me to blackmail Marlene, I might have done it without much hesitation. I simply didn't *like* Marlene. She'd been nothing but horrid to me for six years. She deserved everything she got, and then some. And yet...my thoughts churned as I trudged back to the hall, endlessly mocking me. I hadn't liked Ayesha McDonald *that* much—she had the arrogance of someone who'd never been sent away from the city, of someone who had no money worries at all—but...did she deserve to be blackmailed?

And what, I asked myself, *will happen if I go through with it?*

My imagination painted a grim picture. I'd turn Ayesha, not to mention her sister, into enemies for life. Maybe the threat of her secret being revealed would stay her hand, maybe it wouldn't. And if she lashed out at me...I shuddered as I contemplated the possibilities. There'd be no proof linking me to Malachi. I'd take the brunt of her vengeance...hell, if the truth came out, she'd have no reason to hold back. She'd have every right to take revenge in whatever manner she deemed fit.

And yet...what if I refused?

I shook my head. I knew the answer to *that*. Malachi had me over a barrel. If he revealed my secret, I'd go down and the family would go down with me. My thoughts ran in circles. Malachi could have demanded *anything* from me, anything at all. He could have ordered me to walk through North Shallot as naked as the day I was born and I'd have had to comply or risk losing everything. No, I *would* lose everything. I didn't have the wealth or power to survive my mistakes.

He won't push matters that far, I told myself. It felt like wishful thinking. *People would ask questions if they saw me walking naked.*

I snorted at the thought as I reached the hall and walked up the driveway. The Grande Dames would raise their eyebrows if I showed more than a hint of cleavage or raised my dress above the ankle. Even showing my *knees* would bring the most astringent remarks and brutal social exclusion. I was an adult now, a peer of the city. If I walked naked through the streets, people would ask *why*. Malachi knew better than to attract *that* sort of attention. Who knew what'd happen? The Grande Dames might take my side.

The driveway twisted, revealing the hall. A handful of wagons sat outside, a team of workmen carrying supplies for Ayesha and Zeya's parties into the hall. I felt my heart clench as I passed a pair of men unloading a smaller wagon, wondering if any of them could be trusted. They weren't family retainers. They'd been hired for the party. They might be spies…Malachi's spies. I didn't think it was a coincidence that Malachi had approached me shortly before I'd have the perfect opportunity to speak to Ayesha in private. He had someone in her hall, someone who'd spotted me…I swallowed, hard. Who could I trust? I didn't know.

Jadish met me as I stepped into the hall, clipboard in hand. "My Lady, we have nearly all of the supplies packed away now. We'll start decorating the hall later today."

"Good," I said. I felt another stab of paranoia. Could I trust Jadish? Could I trust *anyone*? She'd been a friend, once upon a time, but people changed. "Is there anything that requires my attention?"

"Merely the question of selecting a secondary host," Jadish said. "You may have to speak to Lady Dorcas personally."

I shook my head as it dawned on me that Auntie Dorcas was the *last* person I wanted anywhere near the party. She was far too perceptive...and old, really. I hadn't given the matter any thought, but I should have done. Ayesha and Zeya wouldn't want her anywhere near either. They'd see her as a spy, reporting back to the Grande Dames. I could believe it. Auntie Dorcas wanted to be *one* of them. My lips quirked, humourlessly. It was funny how far people would go to be one of the in-group. A particularly cunning and unpleasant social queen could keep someone dangling on a string through constantly moving the goalposts.

Welcome to High Society, I thought, with a flicker of insight. *It's just like school.*

Jadish cleared her throat. "My Lady?"

"Give me a moment," I said.

I thought, fast. I needed a co-host. I didn't have anyone from my own family who was suitable, yet...there weren't many others who fitted the bill who'd come through for me. Ayesha and Zeya were out. They needed plausible deniability, even though everyone would know what they'd done. I rolled my eyes at the sheer absurdity of it, then smiled as a thought struck me. I knew the perfect person.

"We have a messenger on call, don't we?" I didn't wait for her answer. "Send a note to Marlene of House Bouquet. Ask her if she wants to be co-host."

Jadish looked surprised, but clearly didn't want to question me. I wondered, not for the first time, just what'd happened while I'd been away. The Jadish I remembered had had few qualms about asking questions, when she'd wanted to *know*. But then, *that* Jadish had been a child. Her older self had been raised to serve the aristocracy. I felt a sense of...unease. I'd met commoners who'd been brilliant, who'd been given opportunities denied to the rest of their class. Did Jadish feel she could have made something of herself, if she'd been given the chance? Did she harbour the kind of resentment that might lead her to betray me?

I watched her hurry off, then walked slowly up to my office. My thoughts mocked me. I'd never questioned the aristocracy before. Why should I? My family—and the other Great Houses—had built the city, safeguarded it through the chaos after the empire fell and ensured we'd enjoy a degree of independence after the kingdom took shape and steadied itself. It was *right* that we continued to rule, absorbing the best and brightest of the commoners into our ranks. And yet, we couldn't absorb them all. Jadish was bright—we'd shared lessons—but my family hadn't turned her into a client or sent her to school. My heart twisted, painfully. My friend might have had a very different life from mine.

We're not the same any longer, I reflected. We couldn't *be* friends, not now. It would reflect badly on both of us. *We're not children.*

I passed through the office door, feeling discomfited. Jadish had been lucky. There'd been girls at school who bragged, openly, of tormenting the servants. I'd thought their stories funny...Kate hadn't. I understood, now. The servants had been powerless, helpless to resist hexes and curses from aristocratic brats. Or...I remembered Malachi forcing me to kneel, to kiss his boot, and felt sick. If I hadn't already emptied my stomach, I would have thrown up again. I knew what it was like, now. I knew all too well.

The pile of envelopes on my desk mocked me. I glared at them, feeling the insane urge to simply pick the letters up and throw them into the fireplace. The seals on the envelopes were worst me. I knew what they'd say. Notes of congratulations, offers of deals, party invitations...none of them would have been sent if the senders knew what I'd done. The stream would dry up, the moment the truth came out. Everyone would pretend they didn't know me, that they'd *never* known me. The newspaper accounts of the parties I'd held would be stricken from the record. Mistress Grayling would tell the world she'd never had a pupil like me. And everything I'd built would vanish...

I sat and stared down at my hands. Malachi had built a neat little trap. I couldn't enlist Ayesha in a plot to stop him, not if he wanted to review my memories afterwards. I wasn't even sure how he intended to do *that.*

Truth spells? I'd never heard of a truth spell that could bring out someone's *memories*. And yet…my eyes wandered to the sealed drawer where I'd hid the memory orb. He'd done it. I didn't know how, but he'd done it. I couldn't hope to trick him until I knew what he actually *did*.

The orb was hidden, but its mere presence tantalised and tormented me. Malachi had hinted I'd be working with him, that he could help me rebuild the family fortune. It would be a castle built on sand—or, rather, on swampland—but it was tempting. I might be part of High Society, yet I disliked it. The snooty older women, the sneering older men, the brats—male and female—who spent money recklessly in the certain knowledge their parents would pay the debts…I disliked them. The thought of making them suffer by revealing their secrets was thrilling. I was tempted. Yes, I was. The idea of making Marlene and her peers twist…

My stomach heaved. It was wrong, no better than an upperclassman hexing a firstie for giggles. It wouldn't be a solid victory, in a game where the rules were well-understood by everyone; it wouldn't even be a piece of cunning so astute that the entire world would be lost in admiration even as they hated me. It would be sordid, horrible beyond words. And I would be forever tainted by what I'd done. The house of cards would collapse, eventually. My family would collapse with it.

And it rested on Malachi. I shuddered, helplessly. I only knew one thing about him, one thing for sure, but it was a nightmare. He'd *enjoyed* exerting power over me, making me humiliate myself. There was no way I could rely on him to keep his word. He might promise me the world, but he'd snatch it back the moment I was no longer useful. Or when it would be funny. I had a sudden vision of me being framed for his crimes, of being branded the true blackmailer while Malachi absented himself. I had no doubt he was already preparing a fallback position. He could flee the city at any moment, assuming a new name and identity while I took the fall.

So I play along, for the moment, I thought. It wasn't much of a plan, but it was all I had. *I play along long enough to get the drop on him.*

There was a knock at the door. I brushed my hair out of my eyes and opened the door with a spell. Uncle Jalil stepped into the room, his eyes grim. I felt my heart sink. It wasn't good news. I was morbidly sure of it.

"I haven't found much, not yet," Uncle Jalil said. "I may have to go to an information broker."

I winced. "You don't have any accountants you can trust?"

"The accountants I know are all bound by oaths of perpetual secrecy," Uncle Jalil said, rather severely. "They may be able to discuss rumours with me, they may not. Furthermore"—his voice hardened—"asking questions may create waves. I don't think we want to be noticed."

"No." I looked down at the table. "But we're running out of time."

"Really?" Uncle Jalil frowned. "What happened?"

I braced myself, then told him about Malachi's instructions. He listened, his face growing pale as I explained what had happened. The memory orb felt impossibly heavy in my pocket. I held it out, letting him see the memory. His lips grew thinner as he watched it twice. I felt numb, as if I'd gone too far to care. Perhaps, just perhaps, it was time to fake my death and run.

"Interesting," Uncle Jalil said. "I notice there's no actual *proof*."

I frowned. "What do you mean?"

"The first orb, the one featuring *you*, shows you committing a criminal act," Uncle Jalil said, slowly. "*This* one is nothing more than a recitation of a story. It may not be true."

"It feels real," I said. "I think…"

"I have no doubt that the memory itself is real," Uncle Jalil said. "But all the memory really shows is a young man telling a tall tale to an elder man. It may not be true. I could tell you a lie about my schooldays, Lucy, and you wouldn't know I was lying."

"Perhaps," I said. I stared at the orb. If the memory was false…no, if Francis had been lying…I shook my head. It didn't matter. The memory of *me* was real. I had to assume the second memory was real too. And yet…Ayesha might just laugh in my face. She might know it was a lie.

Akin might know it was a lie too. "I..."

I forced myself to think. Malachi might be setting me up for public humiliation. But why? It made no sense. He'd gain nothing from destroying what little I had overnight. I simply wouldn't be useful to him, afterwards. And I'd have every reason to expose him in revenge. But...if he'd been lied to himself, he might have accidentally set me on a course towards destruction. If the story wasn't true...

It would be insanely stupid of her to risk a clash with the two most powerful families in the city, to say nothing of making personal enemies out of both Akin and Caitlyn, I told myself. *But how many stupid things did I do at school?*

I stared at the orb, then returned it to my pocket. I'd done a *lot* of stupid things at school. I'd done a lot of *cruel* things at school. And I'd been far from the worst. I knew girls who'd cursed each other, who'd betrayed each other, who'd subjected everyone they considered beneath them to humiliations abhorrent to a sane and decent mind. I could believe someone, mad at a boy, might just set him up for social destruction. Ayesha might have thought she could get away with it. The mere fact that nothing had happened to her suggested Akin had no interest in making the matter public either.

Because he'd look like a boob, I thought. Getting caught sneaking into the girls' locker room would be bad enough. Getting caught in the locker room because someone had trapped him there would be infinitely worse. And the way it had been done...I felt sick. I'd known boys who would sooner crawl across broken glass than admit they'd been hit with the kissing curse. *Caitlyn and her family would be utterly unamused when they found out.*

I swallowed. "I have to assume there's some truth to the story," I said. "And I have to go through with it."

"So it seems." Uncle Jalil took a step back. "With your permission, I'll approach an information broker. We may have to pay a steep price."

"It's worth it," I said. "See what else you can offer, as well as money. Something he wouldn't be able to get normally."

Uncle Jalil snorted. "We have very little to offer, and you know it."

There was another knock on the door before I could come up with a response. I opened it with a spell. Jadish stepped into the room, looking harassed. I frowned, remembering my earlier thoughts. When this was over, if it was ever over, I'd have to do something for her. I just didn't know what. I could ask her what she wanted, if it was something in my power, but I had no idea if she'd give me an honest answer. She might want something unreasonable.

"My Lady." Jadish dropped a quick curtsey when she saw Uncle Jalil. "Lady Marlene has arrived."

I blinked. "Arrived?"

"Yes, My Lady." Jadish's voice sounded emotionless, but I knew her well enough to hear the surprise. "She's waiting in the lower chambers."

"I see," I said. I puzzled over it for a long moment. The message had only been sent about thirty minutes ago. And Marlene had come at once? She should have sent back a polite note, then waited for the formal invitation. Very few people would have been able to come at once, unless it was an emergency. "I'll be down in a moment."

"I'll see to the matter we discussed," Uncle Jalil said. He bowed politely, then headed for the door. "And good luck."

"Thanks," I said. I valued his discretion. Could I—could we—trust *anyone?* "I'll see you later."

I tasted bile in my throat. I was caught in a trap. There was no way out that didn't involve *some* pain. I was going to pay for my crimes a thousand times over before someone figured out what I'd done. The only real question was who was going to figure it out first. Or when Malachi would reveal the truth. Or...I wondered, briefly, if I shouldn't simply make a full confession. It would land me in hot water, and probably destroy the family, but it would deprive Malachi of the pleasure of tormenting me. And yet, there was no way to tell where the pieces would fall. It might end with my destruction and Malachi finding someone else to torment.

And if I can't get the drop on him, I thought grimly, *I'll be his slave for the rest of my life.*

I stood, brushing down my skirt. "Have tea served," I said to Jadish. It was going to be hard enough talking to Marlene without tipping her off that something was wrong. I hated her, but...she was more perceptive than I cared to admit. "It's going to be a long day."

"Yes, My Lady," Jadish said.

CHAPTER
TWENTY-SEVEN

"Thank you for inviting me," Marlene said, as the first guests started to arrive. "I was getting bored."

I frowned, trying not to eye her suspiciously. Marlene was an aristocrat. She should have been making the rounds, being introduced to prospective matches so her parents could make the arrangements before they finally allowed her to wear her hair down. She should have been visiting salons, exchanging gossip with her army of friends and generally enjoying the last of her adolescence. Instead…bored? I puzzled over it for a long moment, wondering if she was trying to get under my skin. Marlene had never been *that* subtle, but I supposed even she had to grow up sometime.

My eyes wandered over her. She'd copied my style of wearing an older dress, rather than something more fashionable. It was a black dress, drawing the eye to her face and hair rather than her body…the lack of makeup and cosmetic spells only made her look more striking. I had to admit it looked good on her, although looser around the arms than I would have preferred. And yet, I was surprised she hadn't chosen something more recent. Perhaps she was trying to be nice. Or perhaps she was engaging in a subtle dig at me.

I put the thought out of my head as Ayesha and Zeya McDonald joined us. For once, the twins weren't dressed identically. Ayesha wore green, contrasting oddly with her brown hair, while Zeya wore blue. I supposed they didn't want their prospective matches to mix them up. I'd heard jokes about twins who'd married the wrong men, both declaring themselves perfectly happy with the results when the truth came out, but—in the aristocratic world—such jokes were rarely funny. It would make a mockery of family bloodlines. My heart twisted as I looked at Ayesha, remembering that I had to talk to her...that I had to *blackmail* her. I was tempted to run, to flee, to fake my death...I shook my head. Even if Malachi believed I was dead, he'd release the memory to ruin my family anyway. It would serve as a suitable lesson to anyone else who defied his will.

"Thank you for hosting," Zeya said. "We're very pleased."

"You're welcome," I said, automatically. "Try not to be *too* alone with the boys."

Ayesha smiled, an expression that faded as she looked down the drive. A new carriage was gliding towards us...I swallowed, my throat suddenly dry. Ayesha and Zeya looked nervous as they arranged themselves, hastily fiddling with their already perfect hair. They'd presumably met their prospective husbands before, but they would have been heavily chaperoned. This was the first time they'd meet the boys without someone from one family or the other watching them like a hawk. I felt a stab of envy, mingled with relief. I wasn't sure how I would have coped if my father had tried to arrange my marriage.

And he never even tried, I thought. I still had no idea why. *He could have betrothed me to Gary—or someone older and richer—if he'd wished...*

I put the thought out of my head as the carriage rattled to a halt. The driver scrambled out, bowed, then hurried to open the door. Two young men—a year or so older than me—climbed out and bowed. They both wore black suits and ties—men had it so *easy*—as well as wigs that marked them as young men of quality. Edmund and Harry Green were cousins, if I recalled correctly. I was mildly surprised Ayesha and Zeya's father had agreed to the match, when he could have placed one of his daughters elsewhere. I supposed the negotiations must have been complex. Even *I* knew House Green was a stickler for the old ways. They claimed to be the second-oldest family in the city and few challenged their claim.

They didn't look that alike, I decided as they walked up the stairs. Harry was handsome enough, but in a bland way that robbed his face of all character; Edmund was less attractive, yet I saw a sparkle of amusement in his eyes that suggested he was more mischievous than he let on. I hoped he wasn't going to play any pranks at my party. It would have earned him social death elsewhere, but I didn't have the clout to make it stick. I suspected Ayesha would make him pay, if he did. Formally, I was hosting the party. Practically, it was *her* day.

I watched the young men greet the young girls, unsure of my feelings. I'd been denied everything Ayesha and Zeya took for granted, from a formal introduction to society to an arranged match with a social equal. And yet, I knew the downside too. The couples would have been pushed together by their families, with a complete lack of sentiment. They might like each other, they might come to *love* each other…or they might not. I turned and followed them into the ballroom, feeling torn between envy and relief. How different would my life have been if I'd come back to my father, instead of inheriting what he'd left of the family?

It would be different, I told myself. *And there's no point in thinking about it.*

The band started to play. I was tempted to dance as well, but there was no time. I circled the room, lost in my thoughts. My eyes wandered over the guests, noting a handful of famous and powerful attendees, but I made no attempt to get closer. I'd lost my taste for eavesdropping. Besides, no one made any attempt to invite me. Interestingly, Marlene didn't seem any more popular than I did. It would have amused me more, I supposed, if my world hadn't turned into a twisted nightmare. Marlene had always bragged about her legions of friends in the city. I was starting to think she'd lied.

My stomach churned unpleasantly as the hours wore on. I wanted to chicken out, to run, or simply go back to Malachi and offer him anything—anything at all—for letting me off the hook. But it was useless. He didn't *need* me to land Ayesha in hot water. He had a spy in her house. All he had to do was pass the message to her in some other way, while revealing my secret to the world. I'd destroy the family for nothing. I wouldn't even save *her*.

My heart twisted as I walked past the buffet. We'd hired cooks to prepare the food and maids to distribute it. How many of them could be trusted? I saw a maid wearing a disgraceful dress, handing out treats to young men who weren't even *trying* not to stare. Was she trustworthy? Or was she silently listening to their chatter as they drooled? She could take her memories to Malachi and turn their world upside down. I shivered as another thought struck me. Ayesha and Zeya had brought two servants—a driver and a maid—with them. If either or both of them were reporting to Malachi, they would tell him—immediately—if I didn't do my job. And that would be utterly disastrous.

If I manage to get out of this, I promised myself, *I'll never do anything shady again.*

The thought hung in my mind as I turned and surveyed the room. Ayesha and Zeya were dancing openly with their partners, chatting in low voices as they swayed around the dance floor. I supposed they weren't going to go *too* far. They weren't married yet. Who knew how things would end up? The negotiations might still break down. And...I gritted my teeth as I signalled Jadish. House Green really *was* composed of sticklers. They'd abandon the negotiations in an instant if they suspected there was even the *slightest* hint of impropriety surrounding the girls.

"Tell Ayesha I need to speak to her in Room Seven," I ordered, curtly. "And make sure she's alone."

I felt sick—again—as I headed into the side corridor. A handful of rooms were already locked, although I had no way to tell if they were being used for covert discussions or illicit kissing. I'd taken the precaution of sealing off Room Seven during the last few hours of preparation, expecting I'd need to ensure I had ready access to the chamber. The wards were as strong as I could make them, with a handful of tiny additions. If things went *really* wrong, I might *just* be able to freeze Ayesha in her tracks and wipe her memory. If...

"Lucy?" Ayesha stepped into the room, alone. I breathed a sigh of relief. I had no idea if Zeya knew what had happened. If indeed it had happened at all. I'd have preferred more proof than hearsay. "What's up?"

"I hope you're enjoying the party," I said, more out of a need to say something than anything else. I felt wretched. It would be easy to run. I wished I'd had time to slip her a message, to suggest she played along... Malachi had timed things very well indeed. I simply didn't have the time to do anything but surrender or run. "We went to a lot of trouble to get you some privacy."

"Or the illusion of it," Ayesha agreed, as she took one of the chairs. "And who'll talk here?"

Your servants, I thought. Ayesha's maid might have access to her father's office. Might. I couldn't quite believe it, but...it was possible. Whoever had taken the memory hadn't stepped inside the office itself. They'd just peered inside. *You have a traitor in your house and I can't even tell you.*

"I have something to show you," I said. I took the memory orb from my pocket and held it out. "Look into the orb."

Ayesha looked at me, her blue eyes narrowing. She didn't recognise the orb. She had to assume it was...it was what? I'd never seen anything like it and, apparently, neither had she. It could have been anything. The Thousand Year Empire had used crystal balls to communicate, according to the stories, but there were no working models left. They'd all been broken long ago.

"Look into the orb," I said. "Please."

Her eyes went wide as the memory enveloped her. Her hand jerked, dropping the orb. It fell to the ground and bounced. I picked it up as she wilted, her face going dreadfully pale. She would have fallen, if she hadn't already been seated. I knew, beyond a shadow of a doubt, the story was true. I had hoped, despite everything, that Francis had made up a lie. Better to have Ayesha laugh in my face, or try to kill me, than...blackmail her.

"You..." Ayesha stumbled over her words. "How did you...how did you get that?"

"I'm just the messenger," I said. I knew it wouldn't make her feel any more well-disposed towards me. "I"—I met her eyes—"what were you thinking?"

Ayesha looked away. "I was mad at him."

"So I gather," I said. One couldn't use the kissing curse unless there was some genuine anger wrapped up in the spell. And yet...I found it hard to imagine *Akin*, of all people, doing something to warrant such anger. "What were you thinking?"

"I wasn't thinking." Ayesha stared down at the floor. "We...I just wanted to humiliate him."

I felt a sick thrill, mixed with guilt. This wasn't the thrill of breaking a pointless rule. This wasn't the glee of being out after Lights Out, or trying to evade the prefects, or seeing a boy outside the wards...this was sick. I was ashamed of myself for feeling the thrill, ashamed of myself for almost enjoying it. Ayesha...I saw tears in her eyes. Her entire body was starting to shake. She might be a brat—I knew she'd broken rules, just like me—but she didn't deserve to be blackmailed.

"I think you succeeded," I said. It was hard to talk. My voice kept threatening to break. "He must have been mad with rage."

Ayesha looked up. "What do you want?"

"It's really very simple," I said, feeling another rush of self-loathing. I was damned. I was damned and...I deserved to die. I wondered if she'd try to kill me in my own hall. It might work, if she put enough power into the curse. The wards weren't anything like as powerful or capable as *her* family's wards. "I want a thousand crowns, by the end of the week."

"Or you tell everyone." Ayesha was trying to sound strong, but I could hear the quaver in her voice. "Right?"

"Right." I tried to sound firm. "A thousand crowns, or else."

Ayesha said nothing. I waited, knowing she was considering her choices. The story might be hushed up, if it came out. Akin certainly had every reason to cooperate, if she went to him and asked for help. And his family might cooperate too. And...I remembered House Green and cursed under my breath. Ayesha had used the kissing curse. She'd kissed Akin. She would have *had* to have kissed Akin. And House Green would back off faster than a bully who'd just discovered her victim was powerful enough to make her *hurt*.

"You..." Ayesha glared. "A thousand crowns. And that's everything?"

"For the moment," I said. I wanted to reassure her, but we'd both know I'd be lying. There would be more demands. "Bring the money here, by the end of the week."

Ayesha looked faint. She was no fool. She knew it was merely the first demand. I wondered, idly, how she'd get the money. Her father might give it to her, if she asked, or he might ask some very hard questions. House McDonald was wealthy—a thousand crowns would be nothing to them—but there were limits. She probably wouldn't risk asking her father. If he forced her to tell him the truth, he'd never trust her judgement again. She *had* been a total idiot, after all.

Just like me, I thought. My heart twisted. I felt dirty. *She's just like me.*

"Very well." Ayesha stood, brushing down her dress. I heard her mutter a pair of cosmetic spells. She'd probably go straight to the washroom, just to ensure she was presentable before she went back on the dance floor. "Lucy..."

"Go," I said. I wanted to say I was sorry, I wanted to beg for her forgiveness, but...it was useless. There was nothing I could say that would make up for what I'd done. "I'll see you when you return with the money."

She left, closing the door behind her. I picked up the memory orb and pocketed it, feeling sick. Ayesha had been a fool, but she didn't deserve to be drained dry. Or have her life torn apart. She hadn't been anything like *me. She hadn't...* I swallowed hard, trying not to throw up. The thrill of bending someone to my will was both tantalising and horrific. I thought I understood Malachi now. He didn't want money so much as he wanted power. Direct, personal power. Making me submit to him was far more rewarding to his twisted mindset than anything else. He wouldn't have that pleasure if he paid or compelled someone to obey.

I forced myself to stand and headed for the door. I almost hoped Ayesha had told Zeya, that her sister had reassured her it wasn't the end of the world. Zeya seemed to *like* Ayesha, which was rare amongst the aristocracy. She might even talk Ayesha into confessing to their father, into trying to come to terms with Akin and his family. House Green might never know the truth. Or they might assume it was just a rumour and ignore it. They'd be throwing away their chance of a lifetime if they jumped too soon.

Particularly as there's no solid proof, I reflected. *Malachi didn't take a memory from someone who was actually there.*

"Lucy," Marlene said. She nodded to me as I walked back into the ballroom. "The guests are ready to depart."

"You wave them goodbye," I said. I was too wretched to do anything, but go upstairs and crawl into bed. It was probably a mistake—people would remember, I was sure. It didn't matter. I was in no state to do anything that involved talking to people. "I'll see you in the morning."

Marlene looked oddly pleased. Too late, I remembered she was meant to be going home after the party. There were no barriers to letting her stay the night—it wasn't as if she were a boy—but it would be far too revealing. Marlene was perceptive enough to notice the signs of hasty renovation, if we let her visit the other floors. And she might take advantage of the stay to search the entire hall. Why not? I'd done it myself.

"I would be quite happy to host another party," Marlene said, as if the whole thing had been her idea. Or a favour, one she intended to see repaid at a later date. "Let me know, please."

"Yeah." I let out a breath. I might need her. If nothing else, she might distract attention from me while I worked to outwit Malachi and get out from under his thumb. I was probably storing up trouble for the future… right now, I wasn't sure I had a future. I'd worry about her later. "I'll let you know."

And, feeling tired, defeated and *dirty*, I walked off to bed.

CHAPTER
TWENTY-EIGHT

I wondered, as I paced the street, if Malachi had set me up for... something.

The note had been very clear. I was to present myself on a certain street, at a certain time. There was no address, no hint of where I was supposed to go. It was not the most salubrious of areas, yet it was not the worst either. The houses were small and simple, belonging to the city's ever-growing professional class of lawyers, accountants and small businessmen. They weren't names, not yet, but they—or their children—might secure a place for themselves at the very highest levels. I was mildly surprised Gary's father didn't own an apartment here.

I frowned, looking up and down the street. The handful of pedestrians, their clothes marking them as middle-class professionals, ignored me. A trio of children ran past, looking free and innocent as they were followed by their elder sibling. I felt a pang of envy. Their lives were so *simple*, compared to mine. They didn't have to worry about saving their family, about rebuilding their fortune...I knew, intellectually, that I was being an idiot, but it was very hard to believe. They seemed so free, compared to me.

A carriage rattled along the road and stopped beside me. I jumped back, somehow unsurprised as the door banged open. Malachi sat inside, his hands resting on a cane that was probably a disguised spellcaster. I'd heard about the trick, although I'd never actually seen it. Girls weren't supposed to walk with canes. We concealed our surprises in our jewels instead.

"Get in," Malachi ordered. "We have a long way to go."

I sighed and clambered into the carriage. A network of spells enveloped me, pressing down on my magic. I couldn't sense anything outside the carriage itself. The door banged closed, the carriage rattling back to life seconds later. Malachi didn't believe in comfort, I realised dully. The vehicle was rattling so badly I was sure I was going to be aching for hours, after we reached our destination. I was careful not to say that aloud. He'd only take it as a sign of weakness.

We drove for what felt like hours before the carriage finally came to a halt. I'd read books where a genius detective, with a perfect knowledge of his city, could follow even the most winding course without needing to see outside, but I didn't know the city that well. Shallot had changed, time and time again, while I'd been away. The recent disruption had only made things worse. I was fairly sure we'd crossed at least two bridges, but that was meaningless. We could be in South Shallot, or Water Shallot, or simply doubled back into North Shallot. I just didn't know.

"Well," Malachi said. He opened the door with a flick of his finger. "Here we are."

I followed him out of the carriage. He didn't lift a finger to help as I scrambled down, even though I was wearing a dress. He wasn't a born gentleman...I snorted, inwardly, at the absurdity of the thought. He was *no* gentleman. The carriage had stopped inside a chamber, allowing us to get out without catching a glimpse of the outside world. I frowned. I'd never heard of anything like it, save perhaps for the post office...I had to admit it was neat. No one would know I was here. The wards around the carriage—and the house—were strong enough to hide me from all intrusion.

There was no sign of any servants, I noted, as Malachi led me through a door and up a weirdly-designed staircase. I couldn't imagine he had none, but he'd know—better than anyone—that servants could talk. The wards pressed down harder as I looked around, leaving me feeling naked and defenceless. The entire building felt weird, as if it had been jammed together willy-nilly. There were few lights, few hints of personality...the only jarring note was a large portrait of a blonde girl, hanging at the top of the stairs. She looked to be about twelve, her hair in braids. There was no name under the painting.

Malachi opened the door into an office. "Kneel."

I groaned, inwardly, as I went down on my knees. I'd had warmer welcomes. I'd practiced over the last two days, trying to get used to being in such an awkward position, but my legs still ached for hours afterwards. Malachi sat in an armchair, looking down at me. I had the feeling he wasn't as pleased with himself as I might have hoped. My submission was getting boring. The thought wasn't reassuring. Who knew what *else* he'd do?

"Stand." Malachi stood himself, motioning to an odd-looking chair. "Sit."

My legs ached as I stood and staggered into the chair. It felt hard, oddly metallic. Malachi walked behind me and fiddled with something. It was all I could do not to turn my head. I hated someone lurking behind me, even when I had no reason to expect trouble. Marlene had surprised me a few times, by sneaking up when my back was turned...I tried not to flinch as Malachi lowered a cap onto my head. His touch made my skin crawl.

He walked back into view. "I'd like you to think about what happened, when you spoke to our slave," he said. I didn't miss the 'our.' "And concentrate on *everything*."

I gritted my teeth as an unpleasant sensation ran through my body. It felt as if I was naked, utterly naked...as if every last molecule of my very *being* was being picked up and examined by cold, ruthless eyes before being placed back where it belonged. Marlene had hit me with a handful of compulsion spells over the years, but this was worse...far worse. My head started to ache—I felt stabbing pain in my eyes—before the sensation faded back to nothingness.

"Well done," Malachi said. "Let us see..."

I turned, just in time to see him wheeling a Device of Power back into a cabinet. It looked like...I found it hard to comprehend precisely *what*. A framework of metal strands, a handful of gemstones, a silver cap that looked like a weird coronet...my hair itched just from looking at it. He'd put that on my head and...and what? I winced, inwardly, as he removed a memory orb from the device and peered into it. His face cracked into a wry smile.

"Very good," he said. "You hit just the right notes."

"Thank you," I managed. "She gave us the money."

"Of course she did," Malachi said. He held out the orb. "Take a look at this."

I took the orb and stared into it. The memory—my memory—enfolded me. It felt as if I was slipping into a set of comfortable clothes. The earlier memories hadn't been *mine*, I remembered. They'd been someone else's... no wonder they hadn't felt quite right. I studied the entire conversation, noting details I hadn't spotted earlier. In the wrong—or rather the right—hands, the memory orbs could be very useful indeed.

But there have to be limits, I thought. The memory was nothing more than a memory. I couldn't say or do anything different. *I can't recall something I didn't see at the time.*

I fell back into my body. "Impressive," I said, trying not to hide my disgust. Malachi seemed blind to the true potential of his device. "Where did you get it?"

"Long story." Malachi winked at me. "And I may even tell you, when you take my place."

He took back the orb and strode to his armchair. "You did well, didn't you?"

"Yes, My Lord," I managed. "She gave us the money."

"And she's currently wondering what else you might know," Malachi said. He spoke with a certainty that convinced me that I was hardly his first victim. "She'll have secrets. More secrets. Right now, she has to be wondering how many more of them have been compromised."

I nodded, not trusting myself to speak. Everyone had secrets. Sometimes, they were tiny, almost pathetic. Sometimes, they were deadly dangerous. I'd spent most of my career at school ferreting out secrets. In hindsight, I should never have let myself get so used to the thrill. I really *was* like my father.

"We'll give her a week or two to think about her situation," Malachi added, after a moment. "And then we'll tighten the screws a little more. What do you want from her?"

Forgiveness, I thought. I knew I wasn't going to get it. *And what else can she give me?*

I hesitated. "Information, perhaps," I said. I'd played that game already and he knew it. "If we had inside information on her father's trades, we can take advantage of it..."

"Too small," Malachi said. "And too slow. I want something a little more interesting."

"Like what?" I stared at the table. "She's not the head of her family."

"Not yet." Malachi shrugged. "It will be quite some time before her father dies."

"Yes, My Lord," I said. There was no point in trying to disagree. "Unless there's another House War."

"Perhaps," Malachi said. "I think we'll see what she can find out about her father."

I felt my blood run cold. Ayesha would hesitate—I was sure she would hesitate—before betraying her father. It would utterly destroy her, if the truth ever came out. She might go to her father and confess everything, taking whatever punishment he meted out instead of betraying the entire family. Or...she might feel pushed into doing something desperate. I felt sick at the thought. She'd already shown a significant lack of judgement.

"I think she'd refuse," I said, carefully. "We can't push her too far..."

"That's my decision to make," Malachi said, curtly. "Kneel."

I sighed as I knelt, again. He had me at his beck and call...I groaned to myself as I stared at the floor, hoping and praying it wouldn't go any further. I had more enemies now, more people who would scream for my destruction if the truth came out. The thought mocked me, time and time again. He could escape. I could not.

"You'd be surprised at how many secrets there are, in High Society," Malachi said. I had the feeling he was talking more to himself than me. "How much happens, behind the wards, that the rest of the city knows nothing about."

And how much the servants see, I thought, darkly. *You might be the first aristocrat to realise just how insightful—and potentially disloyal—the servants can be.*

I felt sick, every time I thought about it. Servants saw *everything*. They brought the morning coffee, they helped their masters and mistresses wash and dress…they knew who visited, they knew who was in and out, they knew everything. Even the mere act of telling the servants not to watch something, or to pry, could be all too revealing. Why would anyone bother unless they had something to hide?

"And you, my dear, can profit, if you wish," Malachi said. "I have a reward for you."

I looked up and wished I hadn't. He was leering at me. The sight sent shivers down my spine as he stood and walked forward. I wanted to run, but…I couldn't. I knew what would happen if I ran. A dozen curses ran through my mind, curses I could use to stun him long enough to search his house, but…I knew it wasn't going to happen. His wards would stop me in my tracks, either killing me outright or freezing me in place until he recovered. My disappearance would become one of the world's great mysteries. I found it hard to believe anyone would care.

Malachi patted my head, as if I were a favoured dog. "You had a friend, didn't you?"

Kate, I thought. My heart clenched. Kate didn't deserve Malachi. *No one* deserved Malachi. I nearly stopped breathing. *Kate…*

"Marlene," Malachi said. "Would you like me to tell you something about her?"

I swayed, nearly fainting. It wasn't Kate! But Marlene...I swallowed, hard. A year ago, I would have been delighted for any dirt on Marlene. I'd certainly spent enough time looking for something I could use...I felt sick, once again. It no longer seemed such a funny idea. In hindsight...I wished I could go back in time and give my past self a good slap. She'd deserved worse. I deserved worse.

"I'm sorry, I didn't hear that," Malachi said. He cupped his ear, dramatically. "What did you say?"

I didn't say anything, I thought. *You just want me to surrender what's left of my integrity.*

It wasn't easy to calm my thoughts. I'd overheard hundreds of conversations. Most of them had been pointless—the tutors didn't seem to chat about their students in the staffroom, even if rumour argued otherwise—but some of them had been far too revealing. I would have been happier not knowing, I supposed, although I wouldn't have *known*. My tutors had always said it was better to know the worst at once, rather than being caught by surprise by something out of left field. I was starting to think they might be right.

"Yes," I said. "I'd like to know."

"Of course you would," Malachi said. He gave me a *very* superior smile. "How much do you know about Marlene, really?"

I frowned, carefully sorting through my memories. Marlene was the same age as me, but we'd never met—as far as I recalled—before we were sent to Grayling's. She was an aristocrat, the daughter of a powerful house... wealthy and powerful enough to become Head Girl. They said the appointments were on merit, but everyone knew that wasn't true. Bribes trumped merit any day. Akin and Alana would not have been Head Boy and Girl of Jude's if their parents hadn't shelled out a small fortune in bribes.

"She's a pain in the butt," I said, finally.

"Quite," Malachi said. "Why didn't she stay for graduation?"

"I don't know," I said. It was odd. Being Head Girl was an honour. Marlene should have stayed long enough to show off in front of her parents. And yet...her crony had been humiliated when she'd tried to give her speech. "She had enemies. They wouldn't have let her escape unscathed."

"Including you, no doubt," Malachi said. "What do you know about her family?"

I frowned. "Are they poor? I mean..."

Malachi laughed. "Not in the sense you mean," he said, cutting me off. "She's the daughter of a pair of servants."

"What?" I didn't believe him. "She's...she's a *commoner*?"

"Yes," Malachi said.

"Impossible." I just couldn't believe it. "How...?"

"Her parents work for Lord and Lady Bouquet," Malachi explained. "She was raised with their children. For some reason, they decided to fund her education at Grayling's. I imagine they allowed the headmistress to assume Marlene was a natural-born daughter, rather than a servant's child. They gave her enough money to support herself too."

"Impossible," I repeated. "It can't be possible."

"You're talking like an idiot." Malachi tapped my head, hard enough to sting. "Grayling's is *miles* from Shallot. The majority of the students are natural-born or disgraced children of aristocratic stock, with a handful of commoners mixed in. There weren't many people at the school who would have known, right from the start, that Marlene was lying. She probably kept everything as vague as possible, giving her plenty of room to evade pointed questions. And now...what is she going to do with herself?"

I stared at him, my head spinning. It was impossible. And yet...the signs had been there, if I'd had the wit to see them. Marlene had never brought her parents to school...she couldn't, not if they were commoners. No *wonder* she'd wanted to go home before the end of term. People would ask questions if her parents didn't come for the ceremony...I started to giggle, despite myself. Mistress Grayling hadn't known. She wouldn't have fawned on Marlene if she'd known the truth. She *certainly* wouldn't have made Marlene Head Girl.

No wonder she came so quickly, I thought. The pieces fell into place. *She has nothing to do.*

A year ago...a year ago, I would have been delighted to know the truth. I could have made her jump through hoops; I could have made her do anything...just like Malachi was doing to me. It was no longer funny. I felt numb, realising why he'd told me. He wasn't just rewarding me, if indeed he was rewarding me at all. He was offering me a chance to compromise myself still further, to twist the knife in Marlene and...in doing so, fall to him. He'd turn me into a willing ally, if I let him.

"Thank you," I said. "What...what do you want me to do with it?"

"Do whatever you want with it." Malachi patted my head again, then allowed his finger to trail down my cheek. "Use it, if you want. Or don't. The choice is yours."

I tried not to shrink away from his touch. The secret was largely meaningless. There might be some sniggering, if High Society realised Grayling's had been fooled by a servant's daughter, but little else. Marlene hadn't *quite* broken any laws. It wasn't as if she'd tried to marry someone while claiming to be an aristocrat's daughter. Sure, I could use it to make her life miserable, but...I'd lost my taste for playing games. No one else would care.

"I'll think about it," I said. "Thank you."

Malachi grinned. "I'll have you driven home now," he said. "I wouldn't want you getting hurt along the way."

CHAPTER TWENTY-NINE

Malachi's farewell statement haunted me for the rest of the day. *Don't get hurt on the way home?* It was odd, to say the least. I was an aristocrat. I had enough magic to protect myself against most threats, certainly the ones I might encounter on the streets. Anyone powerful enough to kidnap me would certainly know my family—and the aristocracy at large—could be expected to take a horrible revenge. The remnants of the last people to kidnap an aristocratic child were still screaming.

It—and what he'd told me—nagged at my mind. Marlene a commoner? It seemed absurd. She had the aristocratic arrogance down pat, up to and including complaints about the lack of maids at Grayling's. I'd believed she'd never brushed her hair with her own two hands. And yet…could it have been an act? Kate had picked up some of the aristocratic mannerisms, simply by sharing a dorm with me. So had Jadish. And Marlene really *had* come to the party—to help me with the party—on very short notice. It was odd. Even if she'd been enthusiastic about helping, she should have written back to haggle over the terms. She shouldn't have come right away.

I spent an hour, in my office, working through the genealogy books. *Marlene* was hardly an uncommon name. I could easily believe a pair of servants, trying to curry favour with their mistress, had named their daughter after her. There were few names that were exclusive to the aristocracy, if only because there was no effective way to police their use. I'd known a dozen girls at school who'd had the same name, though they weren't related. The tutors had resorted to calling them by number. I closed the books with a frown. There were quite a few girls called *Marlene* in the same age bracket, but none of them matched *my* Marlene. It didn't prove anything…I thought. Marlene could easily have gone by her middle name. And yet…

I couldn't decide, as I headed to bed, if I wanted to laugh or cry. I'd always been told there was something *special* about the aristocracy, that true might and magic came from blood. We were distinguished because our ancestors were distinguished, or so I'd been told. The thought of someone posing as an aristocrat, of fooling us all for years, was laughable. And yet, I could see how the deception might have been sustained. No one in Grayling's was surprised when parents failed to materialise, even when they were alive. They didn't send their kids so far away because they wanted to *see* them. I was hardly the only student whose parents never visited the school.

And if she did pose as an aristocrat, I asked myself, *what should I do?*

The thought mocked me. A year ago, I'd have been delighted. *Really* delighted. I could have blackmailed her into submission or torn down her house of cards, exposing her to the censure she so richly deserved. I could have made her my slave…I felt sick. Malachi had blackmailed me! How could I condemn Marlene when I'd done much worse myself? And how could I do something that I'd hated when it had been done to me?

I scowled as I closed my eyes and tried to sleep. Malachi hadn't told me about Marlene out of the goodness of his heart. I didn't think he had *any* goodness in his heart. No, he'd wanted to tempt me. He'd wanted to offer me the chance to blackmail Marlene, to twist the screws until she bent the knee to me…to become a player in his games, an ally in his bid to drain everything he could from people unlucky enough to fall into his power. I felt sick at the mere thought. I could become a monster if I used the knowledge he'd given me. I could…I told myself I wouldn't, as I drifted off to sleep, but I wasn't sure that was true. I was on the brink of falling into darkness.

The following morning brought no peace. I stumbled out of bed and staggered into the shower, feeling as if I hadn't slept. Malachi wanted to twist me until I became a monster, a monster just like him. If he failed... he might find another way to tempt me or...he might simply force me to do his bidding. And yet, Marlene couldn't have very much...could she? If she was a commoner, the daughter of a pair of servants, what could she possibly offer him? I cursed under my breath as warm water washed over my body, banishing the last remnants of sleep. Marlene didn't have much, apart from access to a Great House. He could turn her into a spy.

And yet, she doesn't have that much to lose, I thought. I had no idea how Marlene's master and mistress would react to her posing as an aristocrat, particularly if they'd hinted Marlene was a natural-born child. They might think it was funny. Marlene hadn't tried to court any aristocratic boys, as far as I knew. Her activities had never crossed the line. *She might get away with it.*

I washed my face, then dressed and headed to the kitchenette. Uncle Jalil was sitting at the table, reading a newspaper. The lead story contained lurid revelations about Prince Jacob of North Cairnbulg, who'd left the city after the infernal devices had started to explode. I couldn't say I cared very much, even though I understood precisely how he felt. In hindsight, I might have been smarter to leave my family instead of doing my duty. I might have felt a great deal better about myself if I'd simply left.

"We need to talk, after breakfast," Uncle Jalil said. He poured himself another mug of coffee. "Are you awake?"

"I...need...coffee," I said, as deadpan as I could. I took a mug for myself, then a pastry from the preservation cabinet. "What happened?"

"I suppose the *real* question is what happened yesterday," Uncle Jalil said. "I heard you were out for hours."

I felt a hot flash of anger, mingled with the grim awareness he had every right to be concerned. It took me several moments to calm myself. I was no longer the little girl who had to answer to her parents, her tutors and the school prefects. I could go wherever I wanted, see whoever I liked...I, not my elderly relatives, was in charge. And yet...I scowled as I sat down and drank my coffee. I'd made a bloody fool of myself. Even if I got out with my reputation intact, I'd still made a fool of myself. He knew it too.

"We'll talk about it later," I said. I hesitated, then leaned forward. "Uncle...have you ever heard of someone *posing* as an aristocrat?"

"It's happened, a couple of times." Uncle Jalil shot me a thin smile. "Why do you ask?"

"Long story," I said. "Why? Why did I never hear about it?"

"Because no one who got fooled wants to admit it," Uncle Jalil said. "Your father was never prepared to admit he'd made a mistake, that he'd let himself be conned until it was far too late to salvage something. High Society is just the same. The smarter ones learn from their mistakes, but they rarely admit them."

I shook my head. "How is that even possible?"

"For someone to pose as an aristocrat?" Uncle Jalil shrugged. "Every summer, legions of distant relatives invade the city, hoping to secure fame, fortune and a well-connected husband or wife. There's plenty of room for someone to slip inside, as long as they don't make any elaborate claims that can be easily disproven. Their marks might know everyone who lives here, but they don't know their distant cousins. And a couple of people have blended into High Society so perfectly that no one realised, for years, that they weren't actually aristocrats."

"Hah." It would have been amusing and outrageous, a year ago. "How did they get away with it?"

"Trickery." Uncle Jalil said. "Go to a fancy hotel. Wear fancy clothes. Make a show of having money—tip everyone, well over the odds. Talk up your connections whenever you have a chance, drop names and tell everyone you know everyone. As long as you appear wealthy, the sort of person who can buy and sell the hotel out of pocket change, they'll be hesitant to ask for actual *payment*. And make sure you don't give them any real details. You don't want someone poking holes in your story too quickly."

"I suppose not," I said. I'd seen Marlene at a couple of parties, but she'd been alone and seemingly isolated. The question echoed in my mind. "How do they get away with it?"

"People don't want to admit they've been fooled," Uncle Jalil said. "They'll go the long way around just to avoid having to admit, even to themselves, that they've been fooled."

He finished his coffee. "Shall we go upstairs?"

I nodded, refilling my cup and carrying it with me. The office was the most heavily warded room in the hall, although I knew that could be meaningless. Malachi's memory stripping technique would allow him to keep an eye on me, if he thought to use it. I could think of a hundred uses for such a device, ranging from the fun to the outright illegal. He could have made a dozen fortunes, simply by renting it out. He didn't *have* to resort to blackmail.

And what does it say about him, I thought, *that he does?*

"I did a great deal of research, after I spoke to the information broker," Uncle Jalil said, once the door was shut and sealed. "The information he gave me opened up several promising new lines of inquiry. I do intend to continue researching, although there are limits to how far we can go without making waves. I'd be surprised if he didn't have contacts keeping an eye on his records in the Genealogy Hall."

I nodded. The Genealogy Hall recorded bloodlines, from the oldest to the youngest. Everyone who was anyone was listed in the files, from birth to death; their children, legitimate or not, recorded for future matchmaking. I had a file, as did everyone in my family. The archivists were supposed to be neutral, but I was fairly certain they could be compromised. Everyone had his price.

"Malachi Rubén," Uncle Jalil said. "Born Malachi Pringle, forty-five years ago. Parents aren't listed in the records, suggesting he was born in Water Shallot. They may have kept him off the books deliberately, as the tax system of that era was designed to penalise poor people for breeding. The first real record of his existence I can find is his application to Jude's. His parents were clearly wealthy enough to pay the fees, as there's no suggestion he won a scholarship."

"Or he had the records removed, at some point," I said. "He's certainly got the influence."

"Yes." Uncle Jalil nodded, stiffly. "There are few records of his academic achievement. I haven't been able to get access to his actual school reports, but there are no mentions of him within the school newsletters. My guess is that he was neither at the top nor the bottom. He was, it seems, a close friend of Carioca and Davys Rubén. They were close enough that Malachi was permitted to court and marry Petal Rubén."

I frowned. "That would be Akin's father and uncle, right? Malachi is a Rubén by marriage?"

"In a manner of speaking," Uncle Jalil said. "Malachi and Petal had three daughters. The oldest—Penny—lives in Shallot. The other two live with their mother on her country estate. I believe, reading between the lines, that Malachi and Petal were on the outs well before...well, before *something* happened. There's no solid record, as far as I can tell, but Malachi was ordered to leave Rubén Hall. He may have been disowned completely."

"I can see why," I muttered. "Why? I mean...why was he invited into the family in the first place?"

"I don't know," Uncle Jalil said. "It's possible he's a powerful magician. It's also possible he's innovative enough to overcome his weaknesses. And...it's possible he really *was* a good friend to Carioca and Davys. They might have urged him to court their sister as a reward for his services."

"Yuck," I said. I didn't want to think about Malachi kissing anyone. "Didn't she have a choice?"

"I suspect not," Uncle Jalil said. "She certainly chose to leave the city as soon as she decently could, leaving her husband behind. There's no record of her attending any parties between her departure and now. The match might not have worked or"—he shrugged—"both parties might have assumed it would only last long enough to produce children, then they'd go their separate ways. There's no way to know. They might even have *liked* each other."

"Impossible," I said. "He's a creep."

"People change," Uncle Jalil said, reprovingly. "He might have been a quite agreeable character when he was a child."

"I doubt it," I said. "It's impossible."

Uncle Jalil shrugged. "There are a bunch of rumours, as always. I haven't been able to prove or disprove them. Malachi took part in the Challenge, during his last year at Jude's, when a student died. There's no suggestion, as far as I can tell, that whatever happened might have been his fault. *Francis* Rubén died four months ago, at roughly the same time Malachi was told to leave. It may be a coincidence, but Francis was doing the Challenge too."

I frowned. Francis Rubén? The one who'd told Malachi about Ayesha and Akin? It was certainly possible, but...he was dead? He'd died? That couldn't be a coincidence. And yet, what did it mean? What could I do with the information? What had happened when Francis died? I doubted anyone would tell me. Ayesha might...I winced. She hated me now. I was pretty sure she was already planning my death.

"There has to be a connection there," I said, slowly.

"There might not be," Uncle Jalil pointed out. "Correlation does not imply causation. Not *always*. People try to impose order on everything, building a narrative that links two or more events together without being sure there's actually a link. Malachi might have been kicked out for reasons that have nothing to do with Francis's death. We simply don't know."

"I'm sure there's a connection," I said. "I just don't know *what*."

My eyes narrowed. Malachi might have married into House Rubén, and sired three children of aristocratic blood, but…he wouldn't have been a true aristocrat. No wonder they'd been so quick to get rid of him, when…what had he done? I doubted he'd killed Francis personally, if only because Francis's parents would have demanded bloody revenge. An accident? Or something completely unconnected? It was hard to believe. The two events were so close together, practically on top of each other, that they had to be linked.

I stared down at my hands. "So he was kicked out," I said. "What's he been doing—openly—since then?"

"Nothing, as far as the records say," Uncle Jalil said. "You know better, of course."

"Yes." I let out a breath. "Are they funding him?"

"I think he'll get a stipend as long as he stays away from them," Uncle Jalil said. "He'd hardly be the first aristocrat to be paid to keep away from his family. There are entire communities composed of exiles in foreign parts."

"They get paid to stay away," I said. It was funny, in a sad kind of way. I would have felt sorrier for Malachi if he hadn't been a monster in human flesh. "What did they do?"

"They went too far, I guess." Uncle Jalil snorted. "They did something too repulsive for their families to tolerate, even though they had to cover it up. And so they got sent away, the whole affair buried under the carpet and…scrubbed from history. The records might have been incomplete, given Malachi's murky origins, or they might have been changed at some point. He's never been important enough to be listed anywhere, at least until he married into quality. I don't think he was ever truly welcome outside his family."

"I see," I said. I suppose it explained *something* about Malachi. The lack of concern for High Society's values was odd, for a born aristocrat, but if he *wasn't* a born aristocrat…he might even see himself as taking revenge on a society that had never really taken him seriously. No wonder he'd wanted to make me *crawl*. I was the personification of everyone who'd shunned him. "Where is he now?"

"I don't know," Uncle Jalil said. "I'm trying to work on it, but…it's not easy to look without making ripples. He could be living in the finest hotel in North Shallot or in a garret somewhere in Water Shallot. I just don't know."

I remembered Malachi's comment and smiled. "Look in Water Shallot," I said. If he'd been worried about me getting home, if *he'd* been worried, he had to be living somewhere dangerous. We'd certainly driven far enough to reach Water Shallot. "I think you'll find him there."

Uncle Jalil blinked. "How can you be sure?"

"I can't," I said. I had a feeling it wouldn't be that easy. "But they wouldn't have let him stay in North Shallot. Even South Shallot would have problems. And if…"

I scowled. "And if he was born in Water Shallot, he might have felt more comfortable there," I added. "There'd certainly be more places to hide."

CHAPTER
THIRTY

There was no name on the letter.

I glared, feeling my heart twist once again. There was no name, no seal, nothing to so much as *hint* at the sender. The letter was written in such vague terms that the writer could have been writing about anything, anything at all. And yet, I knew who'd sent it. I could read between the lines. Malachi wanted me to tighten the screws on Ayesha, to make her spy on her father...I swallowed, hard. If she went to her father and confessed everything, she'd destroy me. She'd be humiliated, but I'd be destroyed. Malachi—damn him—might just have time to make his escape before it was too late.

My thoughts ran in circles. I was supposed to be hosting another party in two days, one that would provide ample opportunity to speak to both Marlene and Ayesha. I wasn't sure what I wanted to say to Marlene, but Malachi would know if I failed to speak to Ayesha. Even if he didn't insist on reading my memories again, he had his spy in her hall. I wished I could give her a tip-off, perhaps a hint she should watch her back. She didn't know what had happened to me. She didn't know she needed to be careful. She might not even know precisely how her secret had fallen into enemy hands.

And if I do give her a warning, and her family sacks its maids, Malachi will know what I've done, I thought, grimly. He really *did* have me in a neat little box. I'd heard of servants being sacked before, for all kinds of misconduct, but never an entire household being sacked on the spot. Even a declining household wouldn't let all its servants go at once. The sacking would be the talk of the town. *There's no way he wouldn't hear of it.*

I cursed under my breath, my lips forming words I still didn't want to say out loud. Uncle Jalil had spent two days looking at records, but he'd been unable to determine where Malachi lived. The record-keeping in Water Shallot had never been very good, according to him; there was no way to be sure we weren't skipping over his home because it wasn't registered to him. And it might have been purchased—or rented—by his former family. I had a feeling they wouldn't have left him with much, if he'd betrayed them. They could—and should—have sent him a great deal further away.

It wasn't a pleasant thought. I could understand a blackmailer who was cold and professional enough not to back his victims into a corner, where they might go to the authorities themselves or simply try to kill the blackmailer. A secret became worthless when it became public, something I'd learnt at school. But...Malachi seemed determined to extract the maximum amount of public humiliation. He might have made noises about treating me as an ally, about eventually leaving his business to me, but I didn't trust him. He might let me compromise myself even more, then pull the rug out from under my feet.

He wants revenge, I thought. *And he'll destroy me to get it.*

I tried to imagine what it must have been like, to marry into a Great House. Malachi had grown up in *Water Shallot*. There were stories—none of them flattering—about people from Water Shallot. Criminals, whores, addicts...I scowled, remembering someone telling me how hard it was to get a job if one had an address in Water Shallot. It couldn't have been easy blending into the aristocracy. If I knew anything about the Grande Dames, it was that they loved to make themselves big by making everyone else look small. Malachi's origins would hardly be a secret. He could wash himself twice a day and wear the finest perfumes and people would still be making remarks about the smell. I would have felt sorry for him, if he hadn't been trying to blackmail me. No, he *had* blackmailed me. There was no way to escape the net he'd spun around me.

Jadish tapped on the door. "My Lady, you have a visitor."

I flinched. Malachi? I didn't think he'd come visiting, not now he had his hooks in me, but I could be wrong. He'd want me to come to him, to prove I was the servant and he the master, yet...what if I was wrong? Jadish's eyes narrowed as she looked at me. She was far more perceptive than most people realised and she *knew* me. She had to be wondering just what was going through my head.

"It's Gary Prestwick, My Lady," Jadish said. "Would you like me to send him away?"

"No." I cursed myself under my breath. I'd forgotten. Again. And yet...I was tempted to take her up on her offer. I wasn't sure I could face Gary—or anyone—right now. There were a hundred things I needed to do, none of which I wanted to do. "Send him up, then...go away."

Jadish smiled, but it didn't touch her eyes. I winced, trying not to show my dismay too openly. Jadish knew something was wrong. What would she do with the information? Ask my relatives? Talk to her father? Or keep it to herself? I wished, not for the first time, that we'd been able to stay in touch. We were different people now.

She dropped a curtsy, then withdrew. I stood, hastily checking my appearance in the mirror. I hadn't bothered to dress properly, let alone apply makeup or cast any cosmetic spells. Gary and I would be in real trouble, if I ruled a *proper* Great House. One of the old biddies would notice he'd visited me, without a chaperone, and draw entirely the wrong conclusions. I silently thanked my ancestors none of my relatives wanted to move back into the hall. It spoke volumes about their faith in me, but...it kept their prying eyes out. I didn't need more problems.

Gary entered, looking concerned. I wondered what, if anything, Jadish had said to him. They came from different walks of life, but they were both commoners. They had more in common with each other than I had with either of them. I winced as I held out a hand for him to shake, then kiss. Malachi had clearly had problems fitting into High Society. Gary would have the same problems, only worse. *He* wouldn't have any wealthy and powerful aristocrats smoothing the way.

"Lucy," Gary said. He kissed the air above my hand, then straightened and looked around the office. "Is this where all the decisions are made?"

"No." I tried to see the chamber through his eyes. "Most decisions are made in private rooms, each one close enough to the ballroom for everyone to come and go as they please."

"Oh." Gary walked to the window and looked over the city. "You have a nice view, if nothing else."

"I suppose," I said. A mansion was a sign of wealth and power...or so I'd been told. I'd never realised it could easily become a millstone around the owner's neck. "I've never really had time to look outside."

Gary glanced at me. "Not ever?"

"Not really." I stood beside him, wishing I could put my arm around him. "This was my father's office. I wasn't allowed in when I was a child. Now...I have too much work to do."

"I'm sorry to hear that," Gary said. "Come out with me."

I blinked. "What?"

"Come out with me," Gary repeated. "We can go somewhere...somewhere safe. You can wear a glamour or just change your clothes. No one will know you."

I snorted, torn between the urge to throw caution to the winds and the grim awareness I didn't dare. Too much rested on my reputation remaining unblemished...I sagged as I remembered, again, that I might lose everything. My life, my family...even Gary. I couldn't bear to look at him. He and *his* family might be dragged down too. I'd damned them all.

His eyes went wide as I choked back a sob. I'd been taught never to cry at school—it only made things worse—but I couldn't help it. I turned away, wanting to tell him to go and yet not daring to open my mouth. I'd never cried openly, not since I was a child. Marlene and the others would have made fun of me, just as they'd made fun of the homesick girls...I shuddered. No wonder Marlene had had so few problems adapting to school. She couldn't have pretended to be an aristocrat at Jude's!

Gary followed me. "Lucy? What's wrong?"

I stumbled to the sofa and sat down. I'd never broken down so completely before. It took every last ounce of willpower I had to keep from collapsing into his arms and sobbing my heart out. Tears ran down my face, despite everything. He put an arm around me, something no aristocrat would have done unless he knew me *very* well; I knew I should tell him to keep his hands to himself. Instead, I leaned into his embrace. He smelt nice. He hadn't gone in for the perfume so many aristocrats liked. I'd never liked it myself. They were so fake.

"I'm here for you," he said. "Do you want to talk?"

I wasn't sure that was true. Gary and I had been thrown together by circumstance...no, because I'd needed money and putting myself on the marriage market had seemed the quickest way to get it. He might turn away, the moment he knew what I'd done. He might refuse to have anything further to do with me; he might even go to his father and tell him to write off the debt and forget it. I wondered, bitterly, what his father would do. Demand I repay him anyway? Or insist I kept my side of the bargain?

"I don't know," I managed. I knew how to keep secrets. Anyone who told a secret couldn't be surprised if everyone knew, by the end of the day...it was no longer funny. Not now. In hindsight, it had never been funny. "I..."

"I'm here for you," he repeated. He held me, gently but firmly. "What happened?"

I allowed myself to relax into his hug, just a little. It was selfish—he might push me away, the moment I told him the truth—but I wanted to enjoy it. His touch was so *different* from Brantley's or Malachi's...I was tempted to kiss him, even though I knew it would have ended poorly. If someone found out...

"It's a long story," I mumbled. I'd been told confession was good for the soul, but I'd never truly believed it. Confession had always struck me as a way to get in more trouble. "I...I made a terrible mistake."

Gary looked down at me. "I'm sure it's not that bad."

"Yes, it is," I said. "And..."

I swallowed, hard. My thoughts mocked me. I'd damned him too. I'd damned him and his father and his family's chance to climb to the very top. I'd damned them all...he was going to hate me. I knew he was going to hate me. He was going to lash out at me...I almost wished he would. It would be the end I deserved. And yet, I couldn't let him. He'd be damned as a murderer.

"I..." I forced myself to stammer out the full story. "I let myself get into trouble."

Gary didn't let me go. I stared, unable to understand why. How could he not be repulsed? I'd known girls who were shunned, unable to attract any interest because the Grande Dames damned them for...nothing, compared to what I'd done. The poor girls had been doomed to become old maids, if they didn't move away. Shallot wasn't the world. It just felt like it. There were people who seemed to honestly believe the world ended just beyond the city limits. I guessed that meant they thought Grayling's didn't exist at all.

"And he's got you now," Gary said. I heard the anger in his voice, although it didn't seem directed at me. "Right?"

"Yeah." I couldn't meet his eyes. "I was a fool."

"Yes," Gary agreed. "You were."

I cringed. I'd been shouted at by prefects, scolded by tutors and even lectured by Uncle Jalil, but this was worse. Gary had every right to be mad. He had every right to let go of me and walk away. He had every right to end our relationship, such as it was, and demand the return of the dowry. I'd been an utter fool. He knew it, now. He had to be wondering what stupid things I'd do in the future.

"Why?" His voice was strikingly reasonable. "Why did you...spy on your peers?"

"They're not my peers," I said. Uncle Jalil had handled the marriage negotiations. I wondered, suddenly, just what he'd told Gary and his father about the family fortune. I'd told him to be a little vague, but really...why would we have asked for a dowry, a loan, if we hadn't needed it? "Gary, I don't have anything!"

Gary waved a hand at the wall. "Lucy, you have an entire house..."

"Which belongs to the family, not to me personally," I said. "It can't be sold. Everything we owned that could be sold was sold, by my father. What little we earn from our holdings has to be ploughed straight back into them, just to keep them alive. I have to spend money on maintaining this house or...or it starts to decay. Gary...I thought I had no choice."

"You could have told me," Gary said. "We could have done something..."

I snorted. "I wanted to rebuild the house myself," I said, crossly. Gary might have helped out of the goodness of his heart, but his father would have exacted a price. I was morbidly sure he would have demanded an immediate wedding, followed by the brutal sidelining of the old family conclave. It would have made sense—the conclave brought nothing to the table, even now—but it would have provoked a civil war. "I wanted to rebuild."

"And you managed to get into trouble," Gary pointed out. "What are you going to do about it?"

"I have to stop him," I said. "And do it in a manner that ensures the secret can't get out."

"Good thinking," Gary said. He didn't sound sarcastic, but I thought I detected a hint of it anyway. "What proof does he have?"

"He showed me a memory orb," I said, and explained. "He has a memory of me snooping."

"Dad was livid when he caught my sister reading his papers," Gary said. He frowned. "Let me see the orb."

"If you want." I retrieved the orb from its hiding place and held it out to him. "You have to peer into it to trigger the memory."

Gary smiled as he stared into the light. "It's pretty obviously a *male* servant."

I flushed. "And your point is?"

"Interesting set of charms," Gary said. He turned it over and over in his hand, muttering a pair of spells. "I wonder if the orb *can* be duplicated."

"He wouldn't have left it with me if it couldn't," I said. "Right?"

"You'd think." Gary sounded enthused by the puzzle. "But there's an astonishing amount of data wrapped up in the charms. I've never seen anything like it."

I scowled, feeling my heart sink again. "Could he have found an Object of Power from somewhere?"

"I doubt it," Gary said. "I've never heard of an Object of Power that did anything like this...nothing even close to it. I think the charms are understandable, just very complex. There's no...there's no lump of magic, no solid spellforms. I think he or someone else designed and built a very complex Device of Power."

"I hope you're right," I said. I'd lost track of the explanation. "If the memories can't be duplicated..."

Gary looked at me. "He took one of your memories, didn't he?"

"Yeah." I frowned. "I didn't...I didn't lose the memory. It was just copied."

"He might not need a copy," Gary mused. "He knows who gave it to him. He can make another orb, if he wants."

He smiled. "Can I take the orb to the workshop? I need to examine it properly."

I hesitated. It was proof I'd done something wrong. In the wrong hands, it could be utterly disastrous. Gary had a lot to lose, if the truth came out, but...I could see his father deciding to pull out of the agreement as fast as possible. The best I could hope for, if that happened, would be them keeping their mouths shut. They'd lose interest in marrying into my family if there was a very real chance we'd be blown out of the water within weeks or months.

And that they'd go down with us, I thought, grimly. *How far do I trust him?*

"Yes," I said. If I could trust Gary...I might just be able to get ahead of Malachi. "Just...just make sure you don't lose it. Or show it to anyone."

"Understood." Gary placed the orb in his pocket and concealed it with a spell. It was a neat piece of work. I knew the pocket was there and yet I couldn't *see* it. "And I'll try and track down the bastard too."

"Please do," I said. I hugged him, in relief and gratitude. "Just be careful."

"I will," Gary said. "I promise."

And he kissed me.

CHAPTER
THIRTY-ONE

"You're happy," Marlene observed, as we waited for the first guests. "What happened?"

I smiled. I'd spent most of the previous day in a daze. Gary and I had kissed for hours...or what felt like hours. It felt so much better than what I'd done with Brantley that I'd forgotten my problems, for a while. I hoped Gary could learn something useful from studying the orb, perhaps proving—to our satisfaction—that the memories couldn't be duplicated. Gary had seemed fairly certain it wouldn't be easy. It had honestly not crossed my mind just how much information went into the memories, even one as short as the one I'd used to blackmail Ayesha, until he'd pointed it out.

"I had a lesson in the limits of our education," I said. It was a remark that covered a multitude of sins. "Grayling's was more concerned with making proper young ladies out of us than giving us a good education."

Marlene shrugged and looked away. I studied her back, feeling more and more convinced that Malachi was right. Marlene was wearing an older dress, again. An aristocratic girl of her age would wear something *new*, unless her family was so short of money they couldn't even afford to keep up appearances. And there was an edge about the way she acted that suggested she had no room for mistakes. The Grande Dames were not remotely forgiving—as I was all too aware—but even they acknowledged that mistakes happened. They wouldn't be quite so tolerant of a servant girl pretending to be a noblewoman.

I wondered, idly, how Marlene intended to keep up *her* appearances. Sooner or later, *someone* would ask questions. Wouldn't they? They'd certainly wonder why Marlene was helping *me*. It might be seen as her helping a friend—I'd met my fair share of parents who appeared to believe that going to school together meant you were best friends—but that wouldn't last forever. I felt a twinge of pity, despite everything Marlene had done. The secret had to overshadow her mind, mocking her every waking moment. She knew she would be exposed, sooner or later. There was no fury like a Grande Dame who'd been fooled into accepting a commoner as an equal.

And I can do her at least one favour, I thought, as the guests started to trail into the hall. The party wasn't *that* important, according to the organisers. I recognised a number of famous faces, but most of the high-ranking aristocrats seemed to have stayed away. *I can warn her that someone knows.*

I kept the thought to myself as Ayesha and Zeya McDonald walked up the stairs and into the hall. Ayesha was wrapped in so many glamour spells I knew she hadn't been sleeping. Zeya, beside her, seemed cool and collected. Did she know the truth? Or had Ayesha decided not to tell her sister what had happened? I wasn't sure what I would have done, if I'd been in her place. Zeya was her sister, and they seemed to get on pretty well, but they couldn't *both* be Matriarch. Zeya might just betray her sister, just to ensure she won by default. I didn't know if Ayesha would take the chance.

"I need to talk to you later," I said to Marlene, as the dance band struck up a tune. Or something they claimed was a tune. It sounded more like a flurry of random notes held together by...by something. Angry cats fighting with dogs would sound better. "Can you come to Room Seven in an hour?"

"Of course." Marlene looked puzzled, but not alarmed. She had no reason to think I knew anything. "I'll be there."

I nodded and left her to welcome the guests, the ones who were on the verge of moving from being fashionably late to unbearably rude. The party was supposed to be a little lax, but still...there were limits. I smiled to myself as I moved from group to group, trying not to eavesdrop. The temptation was strong, but I resisted. I spotted Ayesha and Zeya dancing with their prospective husbands and shuddered. They didn't deserve to have their lives torn apart by Malachi. Maybe Ayesha deserved some punishment. She'd done something incredibly reckless. But she didn't deserve *that*.

You're one to talk, I thought, sourly. *You did something dangerously reckless, too.*

I wandered the room, exchanging a handful of greetings. The absence of the Grande Dames ensured the younger generation could speak freely. I wasn't surprised to see a handful of couples heading for the private rooms. Marlene was already heading towards one, alone...I felt another twinge of pity as I joined her. She'd never be able to keep the deception going indefinitely. The best she could hope for was an apprenticeship, if she didn't want to go into service. I didn't think her marks were good enough. Marlene was far from stupid, but Kate left her in the dust.

"Lucy." Marlene turned to face me as I closed the door. "We shouldn't be meeting like this. People will talk."

"Probably," I said. "But it doesn't really matter, does it?"

I hesitated, unsure how to proceed. "Marlene...are you really an aristocrat?"

Marlene wavered. For a moment, I thought she was going to fall down. "I...Lucy, whatever do you mean?"

"You heard me," I said. It no longer felt good to twist the knife. "Are you really an aristocrat?"

"I..." Marlene sat down, hard. "Does it matter?"

"Not to me," I said. I was surprised to discover it was actually true. "Who are you, really?"

"Marlene, daughter of Richard and Hyacinth," Marlene said. "I...how did you find out?"

"In a moment," I said. The names meant nothing to me. "How did you...?"

Marlene looked at the floor. "Lucy...my parents work for House Bouquet. Dad...my mother did the lady of the house a vast favour. She repaid it by funding my education and...and a few other things. I...I just ran with it. I couldn't bear to be a commoner amongst aristocrats."

"You already knew a bunch of aristocratic spells," I said. "How did you learn?"

"I took lessons with the other kids," Marlene said. "They taught me and...I learnt to be like them. How did you find out?"

I stared at her, the six years of hatred and disdain melting away. Marlene had lived a lie. She'd spent every one of those six years knowing she could be exposed at any moment. I supposed it explained why she'd declined to let us take her to her door. She was a servant's daughter. She'd be expected to use the servant's entrance. Her secret could have been revealed in a heartbeat.

"You were Head Girl," I said. "How did *that* happen?"

"Mistress Grayling believed I was a natural-born child," Marlene said. "And she wanted favours from my parents. How did you find out?"

I hesitated, unsure how to answer. I didn't want to tell her about Malachi. At the same time, I had to warn her that her secret might be exposed at any moment...I snorted to myself. Marlene already *knew* her secret might be exposed. She was no foreign visitor whose credentials could never be checked thoroughly, at least without more effort than most people would care to spend. It wouldn't be hard to check Marlene's background. I was pretty sure House Bouquet had never added her to their rolls. In hindsight, why had *Malachi* looked into it? Because of me?

"A couple of questions were asked," I said, finally. I didn't want to go into details. "In confidence."

"In confidence," Marlene repeated. "Are they...are they likely to tell anyone else?"

"I don't know," I said. "How...how long do you think you can keep this up?"

Marlene shook her head, slowly. When she spoke, her voice was so quiet I had to strain to hear her. "What else can I do?"

"You have reasonable marks." I felt another twinge of sympathy. Raised in a Great House, educated with the aristocracy...and yet, not an aristocrat herself? Marlene would be forever caught between two worlds, neither wholly one nor the other. "You could get an apprenticeship..."

Marlene snorted. "My marks aren't good enough and you know it."

"Yeah," I said. "Marlene, what are you going to do?"

She moved forward, kneeling before me. "Lucy...I'll do anything. Just... just don't tell anyone."

"Get up," I snapped. I wasn't going to feed the thrill. Not now. I'd learnt my lesson. "Now."

Marlene stumbled to her feet. I wondered, as she steadied herself, what she *could* do. She was right; she didn't have the marks for an apprenticeship. She probably didn't have the connections to set herself up somewhere fashionable...although, if her master and mistress had been willing to hint she might have a blood tie to their family, they might shell out the cash for her to buy and operate a shop. What else could she do? Go into service, and give up her dreams of being anything more than a servant? Or find a wealthy man and become a mistress? I didn't know and I didn't really care. I had worse problems now. The days I'd dreamed of bringing her to her knees, of winning a final crushing victory, were long gone.

"I don't want anything from you," I said. "And...I understand *precisely* how you felt. How you *feel*. I won't tell anyone. But others are starting to take an interest in you."

I let her draw her own conclusions as she fixed her face. She was a young girl of marriageable age, with a presumed blood tie to House Bouquet. The Grande Dames would be sniffing to determine her prospects soon, if they weren't already. Perhaps that was why Malachi had taken an interest in Marlene. He certainly had the connections to ferret out any embarrassing issues before they became a political nightmare. Perhaps it hadn't been my fault after all. She might never have known anyone was taking an interest, if they'd backed off before they could make anything more than polite inquires.

"You won't tell anyone?" Marlene met my eyes. "Really?"

"I won't," I said. It was just another secret. "Don't worry about it."

"I'll do something for you," Marlene insisted. "You only have to ask."

I nodded, gravely. "If I need anything, I will ask," I said. A thought crossed my mind. "You can help with the rest of the summer parties, if you like."

"I will." Marlene nodded, so quickly her hair spilled over her face. "Lucy...I'm sorry."

"We were stupid schoolgirls," I said. It would probably be a bad idea to ask precisely *what* she was sorry for. She'd played a lot of cruel pranks on me...I'd played a lot of cruel pranks on her. We'd probably deserved to spend a month on our hands and knees, scrubbing the floors after a prank had gone particularly bad. The books said it would make us friends. Reality said something different. "We're adults now."

Marlene snorted. "Have you ever thought that most of High Society is composed of overgrown schoolchildren, intent on continuing petty little feuds that started so long ago that no one really knows why they *really* started?"

"The thought has crossed my mind," I said, dryly. "You be careful, alright?"

I watched her brush her hair back over her shoulders, then turn and leave the room. She'd remain composed, I was sure. I'd seen her shrug off shocks...this one, at least, had been relatively contained. She had no reason to trust me to keep my word, but the mere fact I'd come to her—instead of landing her in the cesspit—spoke in my favour. I wondered what she'd do, when she went home. Where would she go? Who knew? There were supposed to be all sorts of opportunities in the minor cities and towns.

I felt flushed. I cooled myself with a spell, then returned to the ballroom to stroll for a few minutes before I sent for Jadish. Malachi might want to see my memories, again. I had no idea how his device worked, but I couldn't afford gaps in my memories or glitches that might suggest a fake. Gary had warned as much. His theory had included a lot of theoretical babble I hadn't been able to follow—he was far ahead of me in charms—but he'd made it clear that a fake memory would lack the impact of a *real* memory. It would be as bland and boring as reading a piece of text from a page.

Jadish took her orders with a nod—she'd been keeping more of an eye on me recently, hopefully out of concern—and hurried off to do my bidding. I returned to the room, feeling cold. There was no way to avoid doing *Malachi's* bidding, damn it. I'd have to tighten the screws on Ayesha and hope she didn't do something desperate before I got out from under his thumb. I sat down and waited, wondering if my luck was about to run out. The thought made me smile. My luck had run out weeks ago. If only I'd quit while I was ahead.

Ayesha entered, closing the door behind her. "What do you want?"

I winced. Her tone was so sullen it would have earned her a detention, or worse, at Grayling's. Jude's was supposed to be more progressive, probably because the majority of the parents lived in the same city and could be contacted at any moment. And the students didn't feel as though they'd been sent into exile. I put the thought aside, all too aware that *Malachi* would have humiliated Ayesha for being rude to him. I wasn't going to do that.

What does it matter? My thoughts mocked me, again and again. *You're already blackmailing her.*

"How are you?" I tried to keep my tone level. "It's been a week."

Ayesha glared at me, her eyes lingering on my throat. I held myself still, readying a spell. Ayesha was hardly a *weak* magician. She'd gotten lucky, when she'd hit Akin with the kissing curse, but...she wouldn't have made it through Jude's without being very good at magic. And her family probably had a few secrets it had never shared with the rest of the aristocracy. She might be a dangerously powerful—and unpredictable—opponent.

"Spare me the fancy words and small talk," she said, finally. She sounded as though she wanted to call me every name in the book. "What do you want?"

I controlled my temper with an effort. "I want you to find out what your father is planning to invest in," I said. I recalled the office I'd raided and shivered. Ayesha would have a far better chance than me of finding something useful. And...the spy, the spy in her house, might keep an eye on her. "And let me know in two weeks."

Ayesha wilted. "Lucy...please..."

"You can do it," I said. I wanted to reach out to her, to try to reassure her. I couldn't. Not yet. "I'm sure you can find something, even something small."

She glared at me, muttering a word I barely caught. It didn't sound pleasant. I wondered, once again, if she'd swallow her pride and go to her father. House McDonald could make atonement to House Rubén, then turn on me. Ayesha wouldn't have much to look forward to—she'd probably be sent into exile, just like Isabella Rubén—but she'd be better off than me. I'd be killed, or worse. I made a mental note to write a full account of what had happened, for delivery to the great and the good if I died. I might as well *try* to take Malachi down with me.

"I can give you money," Ayesha pleaded. She looked as if she was on the verge of dropping to her knees. "I have *bags* of money. I can give you a thousand. Two thousand!"

I shook my head. Malachi had left the money with me. He hadn't cared enough to count it, let alone take it. I wasn't sure if it was a bribe or a reward or...just another sickening incentive to throw myself in with him. I'd promised myself I'd give it back to Ayesha, when this was all over...if it ever was over. I had no idea how long it would be before I could get the drop on Malachi or I snapped and fled the city.

If that happens, I'll probably need the money, I thought. Returning the cash would be the last of my worries. *A thousand crowns would go a long way in a small town.*

"Fine." Ayesha stood and glared. Two red spots burned on her cheeks. "And that's the end. That's all I'll do for you. Understand?"

"Yes." I had my doubts. Malachi would want me to keep twisting the screws. Maybe he wouldn't take her seriously. Or maybe he'd want her to admit to her failings. I was sure, now, he got his kicks by watching aristocrats crawl. "I understand."

I watched her turn and storm out, banging the door behind her. My stomach was churning helplessly. I wanted to throw up, again. I wanted to...I wasn't sure what. I wanted—needed—to beat Malachi before it was too late. And yet, the more I compromised myself...

It doesn't matter, I told myself, as I stood and brushed down my dress. *I got myself into this mess. I have to get myself out of it.*

CHAPTER
THIRTY-TWO

"Welcome to *my* domain," Gary said, as he opened the door. "What do you make of it?"

I smiled, peering into the workshop. It was just as disorganised as any practical handwork classroom at Grayling's—desks and chairs were scattered everywhere, the former piled high with everything from scraps of wood to expensive gems and metallic strips—but there was a very definite *warmth* to the workshop my classrooms had lacked. I felt my smile grow wider as I stepped into the room, breathing in the magic-scented air. It was no office, no formal meeting room or clerical pool. The workshop was a place where people actually *did* things, *made* things.

Gary closed the door behind us. "What do you think?"

"It looks wonderful," I said, honestly. "What happened to your master?"

"He's gone on holiday for a couple of days," Gary said. "I think the stress of tutoring me is getting to him."

"You're a terrible apprentice?" I grinned, silently relieved we wouldn't be chaperoned. "You can't be that bad."

"He says he never wants another student like me," Gary said, all mock-innocence. "I don't have the slightest idea why."

I laughed as I circled the room. The walls were covered with paper charts, some diagramming out pieces of spellware, others listing the uses and abuses of certain spells, potions, metals and gems. They were admiringly comprehensive, completely up to date. The school's textbooks had always been two or more years out of date, something that had bothered Kate and her peers more than me. In hindsight, that had been a mistake. If I'd taken on an apprenticeship, I might never have tried to save my family from destruction.

"I work there, when I'm not studying with him," Gary said, pointing to a slightly isolated desk. It looked a little smaller than the others—and I had the impression it was cheaper, ensuring it could be easily replaced—but otherwise it was practically identical. Someone had carved a whole string of runes into the wood, ranging from basic protective charms that had long since been drained of power to rude sigils I was surprised hadn't been wiped away by the workshop's master. "I'm supposed to be graduating later this year."

I felt my heart twist. Gary couldn't get married, not properly, until his apprenticeship was over. We'd picked him for many different reasons, but one was that he simply *couldn't* get married—or even formally engaged—at once. It was hard not to feel guilty as he led me into a comfortable sitting room, so delightfully shabby that I *knew* there was nothing pretentious about it. The wards hummed, but made no objection to my presence. Gary's master either trusted him completely or...or simply didn't care *who* he brought to the workshop. It wasn't uncommon for apprentices to show off to their parents and families.

"Take a seat," Gary said. "Tea? Coffee?"

"Tea, please." I sat on an armchair that had seen better days, pieces of stuffing spilling out of the cushions. "Milk, no sugar."

"Sugar?" Gary winked at me, then put on a faux aristocratic accent. "We don't serve *sugar* here, My Lady. Our clientele considers it uncouth."

I giggled. "I'm sure I'll survive," I said. I'd never really liked drinking tea with sugar, even though it was fashionable to put so much sugar in one's tea that it couldn't really be called *tea* any longer. More like sugar with a little flavouring. "As long as it's brewed by you."

Gary passed me the mug, then sat next to me. I felt...I wasn't sure how. I wanted to reach for him and kiss him, I wanted to wait for him to kiss me, I wanted...I wanted to discuss why he'd invited me. He'd taken a risk, even though his master was miles away. It was lucky none of the Grande Dames knew I was here. Aunt Dorcas would have pitched a fit if she'd known I was travelling to Water Shallot alone. And then she'd have gleefully tattled to everyone she knew.

Probably, I thought, sourly. I hadn't seen anything of the elder woman for a while. I didn't care what she was doing, as long as it didn't come back to bite me. *She's not foolish enough to ruin me, is she?*

I sipped my tea, trying not to think about her and the others. It tasted good, although I wasn't familiar with the blend. Ellington had told me we could cut our household budget in half by purchasing food and drink in Water Shallot, insisting that none of the party guests would realise what we'd done, but I hadn't wanted to take the risk. Serving aristocrats plebeian food? They'd explode with rage.

"I was studying the orb," Gary said, suddenly. I was torn between gratitude that he'd gotten right to the point and regret that he hadn't thought to kiss me. "It's a fascinating piece of work. Whoever devised it was brilliant, truly brilliant. They could have made a fortune. I don't understand why they didn't take it mainstream."

Malachi probably blackmailed them into silence, I thought, morbidly. I didn't think Malachi had invented the Device of Power himself. He simply didn't have the mindset to invent anything. *Or there's something about it that can't be easily duplicated.*

I stared into my tea. An Object of Power? It was possible, I supposed. There were so many legends about the Thousand Year Empire's Objects of Power that it was hard to separate the truth from the lies. But...if that was the case, where would Malachi have *found* it? I couldn't see his family just letting it go, if it belonged to them. It was far more likely that it was a Device of Power.

"The charms are very complex," Gary added. "I think the memory is real."

"I know it's real," I said, more sharply than I meant. "I did it."

Gary didn't take offense. "My point is that there's just too much information wrapped up in the charms to allow for a fake, or a duplicate," he said. "I think there's no way to easily copy the memory."

"So there might be only one copy." I gave him a sharp look. "Are you sure?"

"No." Gary shrugged. "But the orb's impact comes from the sheer abundance of data woven into the memory. It isn't a recording of what someone *sees* or *hears*, it's *everything*. There's a sense of inhabiting their body, as well as everything else. It's compelling because it's so complete. And I think that if you copy the copy, the memories would start to... degrade. Glitch. It would simply start to lose the sheen. Sooner or later, they would stop being convincing."

"But too late for me," I muttered. It was the first piece of hopeful news I'd had in a while. "Is there no way to fake the memories?"

"I don't think so," Gary said. "Like I said, there's just too much detail."

He leaned back into his chair. "I may be able to work out how the charms view and copy a memory, given time," he said. "But they're an order of magnitude more advanced than anything I've ever seen."

I let out a breath. "But there's only one copy of each memory," I said. "That's useful to know."

Gary held up a warning hand. "There's nothing to stop him from taking and recording the memory time and time again," he said. "If I was in his place, that's what I'd do."

"Yeah." I shook my head. "But there have to be limits...right?"

"Perhaps," Gary said. "I just don't know."

I sagged, wishing he'd put his arm around me. Or something. I'd taken a risk in coming to the workshop and...I shook my head, again. I had too many other problems to worry about what High Society thought. Perhaps leaving the city and running was the best of a set of bad options. I could take ship to Hangchow, travelling right around the globe. There were dozens of lurid accounts of visits to the mysterious empire on the other side of the world. I could go in person and see how many of them were actually true.

"I do have one piece of good news, though," Gary said. "I found his home."

"What?" I stared. Uncle Jalil's quiet investigations hadn't located Malachi's home. I'd been starting to think he resided outside the city. "You found him?"

"Yes." Gary winked, again. "He lives in Water Shallot, surprisingly close to the docks."

My eyes narrowed. "And how did you find him?"

Gary laughed. "I had to call in a few favours," he said. "There were people I knew who'd had dealings with him, over the last few months. They were kind enough to locate him for me. I checked the records, once I had the address, and confirmed the entire block had been purchased by a blind trust. Whoever *really* owns it went to some trouble to ensure their names wouldn't be on the title deeds."

I smiled at him. I knew where he was. And that meant...I could get him.

"Thank you." I leaned forward and kissed him. "You're wonderful."

Gary laughed and kissed me back. I felt a thrill as he pulled me closer, our lips touching time and time again. His hands stroked my back...I wanted to relax into it, to let him go all the way. And yet, I couldn't. I pulled away as his hand started to inch under my dress. It would have been a step too far.

"Do you want to go there?" Gary stood, brushing down his shirt and trousers. His face looked flushed. "We can walk down and take a look at it."

I blinked, then nodded. "Let me use the washroom first," I said. "Am I properly dressed?"

"I'll find you a cloak," Gary said. He pointed me towards the washroom. "You might want to braid your hair too."

I hurried into the tiny room and inspected my face in the mirror. My lips were oddly puffy, too puffy. I muttered a charm to quell the swelling, feeling a pang of guilt for kissing him. It would be social death, if anyone found out…I laughed, humourlessly. The Grande Dames would have problems deciding what they were going to ostracise me *for*, if they ever found out *everything* I'd done. There were just so many good reasons…I put the thought out of my head as I braided my hair, feeling uncomfortably like I was pretending to be a child. Gary held out a drab grey cloak as I exited the washroom, looking away awkwardly as I pulled it over my dress. It was so drab, I had the feeling eyes would just slip over me as though I wasn't there.

"Ready?" Gary looked as if he were having second thoughts. "Shall we go?"

"Yes," I said. I'd survived boarding school. I could cope with Water Shallot. "Let's go."

The streets felt…cooler, somehow, as we hurried down the street and headed south. The gentrified parts of Water Shallot felt very much like South Shallot, with walls of shops, apartment blocks and everything else a city needed to function. The people on the streets looked poorer than their counterparts, but not that poor. And yet…the further we headed into Water Shallot, the darker the streets became. I splashed though muddy puddles as we passed through alleyways and crossed bridges, the air steadily growing fouler.

I looked around, silently grateful for the cloak. The buildings felt more and more oppressive, looming over us as if they were trying to trap me within their shadow. There were fewer people—almost all men—on the streets, their eyes following me as I walked. The shops looked tatty and old, a handful of ill-dressed women loitering on the corner…I recoiled as I realised they were whores. What *else* could they be? I felt sick as one of the women beckoned to us. She seemed to belong to a whole other world.

The stench—of rotten fish and hopelessness—seemed to grow stronger. I saw a man lying in an alleyway, a bottle clutched in one hand. A small boy ran past me, his hand brushing against my thigh. Gary snapped a hex at him, a spark of light the boy dodged with practiced ease before running into an alleyway and vanishing into the darkness. I recoiled, badly shaken. I'd never had anyone try to steal from me so blatantly. How could anyone *live* like this?

They don't have a choice, I thought. Kate and Gary and all the other commoners I'd met—even Marlene—hadn't grown up in the southern side of town. *What else are they going to do for a living?*

"We'll be turning the corner in a moment," Gary said, so quietly I could barely hear him. He was definitely having second thoughts. "Try not to look too interested in the house."

"I'll try," I muttered back. It wasn't the first time I'd paid close attention to something without letting on. "Just keep your senses open."

I did my best to look impassive as we walked around the corner. The street might have been a nice place to live, once. There were the remains of a good neighbourhood around it. The block was solidly built, probably older than its owners. And yet, it was clear the area had fallen into darkness. The shops were boarded up, the apartments looked drab...I shivered as I spotted a man escorting two teenage girls along the road. He looked armed and ready to fight. I wondered, morbidly, if he was their protector or their pimp. I'd heard the rumours about forbidden pleasures, things forbidden even to the aristocracy, but I'd never really believed them. I believed them now.

Malachi's house was surprisingly large. It looked, from the outside, to have been subdivided into smaller apartments a long time ago...I remembered what I'd seen of the inside and nodded. Malachi—or his family—had bought up the entire block, then taken out the walls to turn it into a house. I wondered if they'd accidentally destroyed the supporting walls. It would be funny if the house collapsed, burying him beneath a pile of rubble...I snorted as I allowed my senses to reach out and touch the wards. It wasn't likely to happen. Probably. It was easy to imagine his family plotting his death, going the extra mile to make it look like a terrible accident.

The wards were tough, surprisingly complex. They made the house stand out a mile...I wondered, absently, just what the locals made of them. Malachi had protected himself from everything he could, up to and including remote scrying. They were an order of magnitude more complex than the spells I'd used at home, or school; I thought I knew how to crack them, but if I got it wrong I'd probably be killed on the spot. Malachi had never struck me as the kind of person to forgive and forget. He'd have every reason to kill me and turn my body to dust.

My eyes wandered over the edge of the house and down the darkened alleyway. A trio of young men stood beside a large door, looking bored. They whistled at me, but didn't move. Guards? Malachi was certainly wealthy enough to hire guards. He'd want to keep the local thieves out without revealing too much of his defences too, I was sure. I felt their eyes burning into my back as we kept moving, trying not to run. I hadn't felt so unsafe since my first day at school, when I'd been told—in no uncertain terms—that I was no longer the little mistress of the house.

"I'm sorry," Gary muttered, as soon as we were clear of the street. He sounded embarrassed, as if the whole affair had been his fault. "That shouldn't have happened."

"It wasn't your fault," I told him. I knew enough magic to defend myself, if push came to shove. The boys could hoot and holler, if they liked, but I'd give them the fright of their lives if they did anything worse. "Thank you for bringing me."

"Really?" Gary looked doubtful. "This is not my idea of a fun holiday destination."

I nodded as we walked past another alley. A large poster proclaimed the virtues of electing someone for guild leadership. It had been defaced so savagely I was surprised it hadn't been replaced. Perhaps whoever had put it up had realised there was no point in putting up another one. It would just be defaced too. Another poster, a few metres on, was completely untouched. I frowned. It was an invitation to a socialist meeting, two days ago. I wondered, idly, how it had gone.

Gary said nothing until we reached the workshop, then took the cloak. "That's his home, isn't it?"

"Yeah." I had no doubt of it. It was impossible to be sure...I shook my head. I'd memorised the outer edge of the wards. I knew what they felt like now. It would be easy to confirm when he demanded I wait on him again. "It can't be anything else."

I relaxed into his hug, just for a moment. "I'll have to find a way to get inside," I said. "He knows how to defend his house, worse luck."

"If you need help, just ask," Gary said. He hugged me tightly, then gently kissed me. "Please."

I felt my eyes sting with tears. "Why? Why are you helping me?"

Gary blushed. "Because I like you," he said. "And because it's the right thing to do."

CHAPTER THIRTY-THREE

I was not surprised, the following day, to receive instructions to meet at the same time and place as before. I dressed carefully, concealing a handful of weapons and surprises around my person before heading out. I had no idea if Malachi knew I'd visited Water Shallot—it was unlikely that any of the aristocratic girls he'd known had ever willingly crossed the bridges—but it was possible. His wards might have sensed me as a prior visitor and reported me to their master. And if he wanted to kill me...

The carriage rattled into view, the door banging open as it slowed to a halt. Malachi motioned me into the carriage, then sat back and said nothing as the vehicle rocked back into motion. I also said nothing, reaching out as gingerly as I could to feel the wards. He'd woven a *lot* of protections into his carriage, enough to save him from direct and indirect attack. I hoped it was a sign of cowardice, instead of cold-blooded prudence. A coward was easier to scare.

I kept my face under tight control as the carriage's wards brushed against the house's wards. They felt familiar...very familiar. Gary *had* taken me to the right house. I tried not to look cheerful as Malachi scrambled out of the carriage and strode off, forcing me to jump down and practically sprint after him. It was rude—a gentleman should always help a lady to the ground—but I was almost relieved. I didn't want his hand touching me. I kept parsing out the wards as I followed him up the stairs, cursing silently as I realised the spells were all attuned to him. Malachi might or might not live alone—I knew he had at least one servant and I was fairly sure there were others—but he'd protected his house so thoroughly that he was the only person who could move within it safely. I glanced at the stained carpet and smiled. His servants couldn't navigate the house without him.

"Well," Malachi said. He sat down, motioning for me to stand in front of the desk. "What did your friend have to say for herself?"

"She said she'd try and find out what she could," I said. "I don't know how much she *can* find out."

Malachi gave me a sardonic look. "I meant your *other* friend. You *did* manage to chat to her, didn't you?"

Marlene, I thought. Someone had clearly noted we'd been spending time together...probably one of the hired servants. They had less to lose. *And there's no way to track down the blabbermouth either.*

I pasted a smile on my face. "She just let everyone believe she was an aristocrat," I said. I still couldn't believe it. Not really. "It's astonishing."

"Quite." Malachi eyed me for a long moment. "And you haven't tried to bend her to your will?"

I winced, inwardly. I hoped he couldn't see it. "No," I said. "She's got nothing to offer me."

"There's always something," Malachi pointed out. "She *does* have access to a Great House."

"She's a servant...the daughter of a pair of servants," I said. "She doesn't have *that* much access."

"There are ways." Malachi smiled, coldly. "I'm sure she can find *something* for you, if you tighten the screws."

I felt sick. Marlene...Marlene was no longer the figure of my nightmares, no longer the implacable and merciless enemy I had to destroy. She'd been a brat, as had I, but she wasn't a monster. The real monster sat facing me, a benevolent smile on his ugly face. I didn't want to twist the screws, I didn't want to bend her to my will...even if I did, I wasn't sure she could give me anything. She might have lived in a Great House, but she wasn't an aristocrat...nor, really, a trusted servant. She was more of a favoured pet.

My thoughts laughed at me. Marlene could run. Her parents could claim they knew nothing about her activities. It would even be true. Or... if their masters kicked them out...my heart twisted again. They'd wind up begging on the streets, pleading for mercy and charity that might never come. I hadn't understood how bad that could be, before Gary had taken me into Water Shallot. I knew now. I couldn't do that to them. I didn't even *know* them.

"You want to make her your slave, don't you?" Malachi's voice was light, but I could hear something dark and hungry in his tone. "You *want* to use her."

"Yes," I lied. It would have been true, once. "But there are limits to what she can do for us."

Malachi shrugged. "It is of no matter," he said. "Tighten the screws. Demand some money, then move on to secrets. She must know *something* her masters would prefer to remain secret."

I shrugged. "Really?"

"Oh, yes." Malachi rose, his beady eyes beaming. "You'd be surprised just how much happens within the Great Houses that never makes it into the papers."

"I believe you," I said. I *did*. Hell, it was easy to believe Marlene knew a dozen secrets her master and mistress would pay good money to conceal. I'd listened to the stories we'd swapped after Lights Out; I'd heard the rumours and whispered warnings about men—and women—who couldn't be trusted. "What if she runs?"

Malachi shrugged. "It is of no matter," he said. "There are always more where she came from."

He paced around the desk. I held myself still, keeping my eyes firmly fixed on the chair he'd vacated. "Why, only two months ago a pretty little serving girl was groped by her master and left in the family way. She came to me shortly afterwards, bearing a set of letters her master had written to his mistress…letters that, if they were exposed to the world, would destroy an entire Great House. They pay me now, just to ensure those letters go no further."

I swallowed. My throat was dry. "And what happened to the girl?"

"Oh, I paid her well," Malachi said. "I believe she left the city shortly afterwards."

He stepped up behind me. I could feel his breath on the back of my neck. It took everything I had not to recoil, not to show any sign of discomfort…I doubted he was fooled. Malachi was observant. He couldn't have worked his way into High Society, let alone become an accomplished blackmailer, if he wasn't. His touch—he rested his hand on my shoulder, just for a second—was creepy. I knew what he was doing—he wanted to make it clear that I was his, that he could do whatever he liked—but it didn't help. He enjoyed the thought of me sweating, for fear of what he might do, far more than actually *doing* it.

We fear the worst until it happens, I thought, as his hand trailed down my back. *And yet, when it does, we are no longer afraid.*

Malachi stepped back. I didn't dare turn to face him. "Your other friend will bring you something in due course," he said. "You can forward it to me when it arrives. Or use it yourself, if you can."

"Yes, My Lord," I said. "I don't know what she'll find. She might even go to her father."

"She'd be utterly ruined, if she did." Malachi stepped back into view. He was smirking. "Do you think a girl like *that*, on the cusp of reaching the very highest position society has to bestow, would throw it away?"

I said nothing. I wasn't sure what I'd do, if I was in Ayesha McDonald's position. Lord McDonald wasn't a monster and he wasn't abusive, but he'd find himself trapped when he found out. He couldn't allow Ayesha to remain as Heir Primus, even though she was sharing the role with her sister. Zeya would win by default. And Ayesha herself...she was too old to be sent to Grayling's. I wondered if she'd be given a lot of money and told never to return. It was the traditional fate for those who'd compromised themselves beyond repair.

"I don't know," I said, finally. If my father had been alive...would he have been understanding, if I'd confessed my sins to him, or would he have told me to get out of the city and run? "She may put the interests of her family ahead of herself."

Malachi snorted. "Do you really believe that? Really? The aristocracy tells everyone who will listen, and everyone *has* to listen, that they're the noblest people in all creation, the shining stars of the universe, the very souls of charity, the guiding lights of a whole new era...you know what it is? Bullshit, all bullshit. They tell those lies to conceal the truth, that they're in it for themselves and to hell with everyone else. They could give up half their wealth to fix the problems in this city"—he waved a hand at the wall—"but they won't. You know why? Because it would mean giving up half their wealth!"

He snorted, again. "They live a lie. They have always put their own interests first. And your little...*slattern* of an aristocratic brat will betray her family, rather than admit her failing and take whatever punishment her father decrees. And *he* will exile her rather than admit his failings as a father, in a bid to preserve his position and power. His self-interest comes first."

I swallowed. I hoped he was wrong, but...all of a sudden, I believed, really believed, that Malachi had been raised in Water Shallot. He'd have a very different view of the aristocracy than a pure-blooded aristocrat. And he was swearing like a trooper...

"You know it as well as I do," Malachi said. "Do you think your friend would hesitate, even for a second, if she had a chance to bend you to her will?"

You didn't, I thought, nastily.

I put that out of my mind. "I take your point," I said. "I'm sure Ayesha will bring us something useful."

"Take the time to twist the screws again, if she balks," Malachi said. "She's already given us the money. She'll give us more."

"Yes, My Lord," I said.

"And twist your other friend too," Malachi said. "She'll bring you something soon."

I nodded, not trusting myself to speak. It wasn't fair. It just wasn't fair. Marlene didn't have anything…we'd push her into committing crimes or running for her life. My thoughts mocked me, reminding me of all the times Marlene and I had clashed. Back then…I ground my teeth. I'd been a different person. And she'd been living a lie. She must have lain awake for hours, fearing what would happen when one of her cronies asked to spend the summer at her house…

Malachi cleared his throat. "But I didn't call you here just to talk," he said. "I have a job for you."

He walked around the table and pointed a finger at me. The world went black. I yelped, jumping back in shock. Blinding hexes were rare…I knew they were possible, but I didn't know the spell. There weren't many hexes that meant certain punishment at school, no matter who used them or why, but Mistress Grayling had made it clear that blinding hexes were very definitely on the list. I felt my cheeks burn as Malachi chuckled, enjoying my discomfort. I was blind, he could be anywhere…I heard a rustling sound from the far side of the room. I guessed he was opening a hidden safe…

Blinding light stabbed into my eyes. I covered my eyes hastily, then carefully lowered my hands. Malachi was standing in front of me, holding a memory orb in one hand. I wished I'd kept my eyes covered. He was staring at the orb as if it were the key to eternal life. I shuddered, feeling a pang of sympathy for whoever's memories were preserved within the orb. It couldn't be anything pleasant.

"Here," Malachi said. "What do you make of it?"

I took the orb and peered into the light. The memory rose up and enveloped me. I was peering into a kitchen, staring at a middle-aged woman as she dripped...something into a mug of liquid. The woman didn't seem to see me as she returned the dripper to her pocket, then contaminated a second mug. I—the person who'd seen the memory—inched back and down the corridor, then advanced forward, stamping so loudly that she sounded like a pair of charging elephants. The middle-aged woman looked annoyed as I walked into the kitchen, but didn't snap at me. She appeared to be raiding the cupboards for food.

No. I recognised the signs. *She's trying to conceal what she was actually doing.*

The memory went on. I passed the woman a book, then picked up the tray and headed upstairs. I felt my legs ache as I reached the top of the stairs and carried the tray into a study. A morbidly obese man sat there, reading a newspaper. His look, as I placed the tray beside him, was a blatant leer. His eyes left trails of slime on my breasts. My skin crawled as I curtseyed and backed out of the room. The memory came to an end...

"Lord Mathews," Malachi said. He sounded as if he'd known the man. "*Dear* Lord Mathews. Died thirty years ago, seemingly of a heart condition. Seemingly. There were no suggestions of foul play. He was strikingly overweight, with a habit of gorging himself from morning 'til night. It wasn't until recently that his wife's serving maid visited me. She told me her mistress poisoned her husband."

"Oh," I said. I'd never heard of Lord Mathews. If he'd died eleven years before my birth, it was unlikely anyone would have thought to mention him to me. "And no one noticed?"

"They would have had to perform an autopsy very quickly, if they wanted to find proof," Malachi said. "Lady Mathews used two separate potions to kill him. Separately, they're harmless. They don't set off alarms. Together, they're lethal. Lord Mathews drank both mugs and died. By the time anyone found the body, the traces of magic were long gone. No one was particularly surprised he'd died, either. He was on course for a *real* heart attack when he was murdered."

I remembered the obese man and shuddered. The girl who'd taken the memory had been terrified. I didn't blame her. "And…and what do you want me to do with the orb?"

"Lady Mathews has been living in North Shallot for the past thirty years," Malachi said. "She's had a pair of lovers in that time, but she's kept her husband's name and property. His will stipulated that it would be passed down to their children upon his death. However, as she murdered him, she could be legally stripped of his property at any moment. His family could reclaim it, without—perhaps—giving any to his children."

"And…" I shook my head. I'd heard no one could profit from their crimes—which was a joke, in the aristocracy—but the children were blameless. I assumed they didn't know their mother was a murderess. "There're not going to make any provision for the children?"

"I don't know." Malachi gave me a sharp look. "And you know what? I don't care. I want you to go to Lady Mathews, show her the orb, and explain she can either pay us or have her secret broadcast to the entire city. I'm sure she'll pay."

"You want me to go to her…"

"Yes." Malachi glared at me. "You can talk to her without arousing comment. You can handle the negotiations privately. You can even arrange for the money to be transferred without people noticing. And then you can give the money to me."

His eyes hardened. "Are you under the impression you have a choice?"

"No, My Lord," I said. Had I gone too far? I wanted to reach for one of the weapons and use it before it was too late. "I just…"

"Kneel," Malachi ordered. "Now."

I cringed, inwardly, as I went down on my knees. I didn't want to do as he ordered, I didn't want to blackmail someone who'd never done me any harm, but…I knew, all too well, that I was going to do it. I didn't have a choice. Malachi had brought me into his web, bent me to his will. I was going to do something that would compromise me still further…

Malachi looked down at me. "You will go to her," he said. "You will give her the message and make arrangements to receive the money. Do you understand me?"

"Yes, My Lord," I said. I tried not to sound sullen. Or to shudder when he ran his hands through my hair. "I understand perfectly."

"Excellent." Malachi tapped the orb. "When I see you again, I expect you to have good news. I want information from your friends and money from Lady Mathews."

"Yes, My Lord," I said. Sweat prickled at my back. Time was running out. "I'll see to it personally."

"See that you do," Malachi said. He patted my head, allowing his fingers to trail through my hair again. "The coachman will take you to the lady's house and drop you there. I wouldn't want you to get lost along the way."

"No, My Lord." I swallowed my pride as best as I could. "I'll do as you command."

CHAPTER
THIRTY-FOUR

Lady Mathews didn't live in one of the bigger mansions, somewhat to my relief. I didn't want witnesses. Instead, she lived in a relatively small house set within a neat little garden nicely isolated from the rest of the street. I jumped down from the carriage, hearing it rattle away as I studied the gate and the house beyond. It was small, with only two stories, but land was costly in North Shallot. Gary and his father would have to expend their entire fortune just to buy a tiny bungalow. There were a handful of wards drifting over the house, but nothing too elaborate. It didn't look as if Lady Mathews felt she had anything to fear.

I braced myself, trying not to feel too bad as I pressed my hand against the gate. The wards looked at me, decided I wasn't a hawker or a trader and opened to allow me to walk up to the door. The path was thinner than I'd expected, wrapped within bushes and trees that provided a natural barrier. It looked bucolic, but there was an edge to it that bothered me. I guessed Lady Mathews didn't want to entertain guests. Some of the plants within eyeshot were poisonous. A couple were even on the banned list.

Good thing Malachi never visited, I thought. The air was heavy with pollen, strong enough to make me dizzy. I hastily cast a filtering spell. *He'd have used that to blackmail her, too.*

The door was solid wood. I raised a hand and tapped smartly, wondering who'd open the door. A servant? Or Lady Mathews herself? She'd have servants...or would she? One of them had clearly betrayed her. I tensed as the door opened, revealing a young girl barely entering her teens. She wore a simple maid's outfit, so outdated I was sure it had been sewn long before she'd been born. I guessed she'd only recently gone into service. She lacked the flawless perfection of older, more experienced servants.

"I'm here to see Lady Mathews," I said. "I'm Lady Lamplighter."

It struck me, an instant too late, how *odd* it was for me to approach Lady Mathews without sending a message first. Lady Mathews would know something was wrong, the moment her maid announced me. I wondered if that was part of the point. Malachi had set out to unsettle me from the very first moment he'd entered my life. And he certainly hadn't given me time to do anything else. I felt dirty as the maid dropped a shabby curtsy and hurried back into the darkness, without so much as inviting me across the threshold. Poor girl. I knew mistresses who'd throw her onto the streets—*back* onto the streets, perhaps—for such a mistake.

The girl returned and bobbed another curtsey. "My Lady, My Lady will see you now."

My lips twitched as I tried to parse the sentence. Technically, it should have been...I smiled to myself as she led me into the house and up a flight of stairs. It didn't matter. The house was small, but comfortable. I guessed it was too small to have separate quarters, stairs and passageways for servants. Lady Mathews probably hadn't felt the need to isolate herself from her trusted retainers...I frowned. It wasn't the hall I'd seen in the memory. I wished I'd had time to do some research. It would have been useful to know just what the *public* thought of Lady Mathews.

I felt my frown grow deeper as we walked down the short corridor. The walls were lined with paintings, all showing landscapes and landmarks rather than ancestors. It was odd, for a person of aristocratic birth. We held our ancestors within our memories...I shivered, wondering precisely *why* Lady Mathews had murdered her husband. He might not have been a very nice man. His servant had clearly hated and feared him.

The little maid pushed a door open. "Your Ladyship, Lady Lamplighter."

I hid my amusement as I stepped into the room. It was clearly a reading room, rather than a study. There were no desks, no hard chairs...there weren't even any filing cabinets. The walls were lined with bookshelves, practically bursting with volumes on hundreds of subjects. Lady Mathews sat in an armchair, reading a book of magic. The giant window behind her provided all the light she needed.

"Lady Lamplighter," Lady Mathews said. She put the book to one side and studied me through calm blue eyes. "Welcome to my humble abode."

She glanced at the maid. "Thank you, Poppy. That will be all."

No tea, I thought. I would have been offended, if I'd come of my own free will. Refusing to so much as *offer* a drink was a very clear sign someone was unwelcome. *She doesn't want me here.*

I took a seat on the sofa and studied Lady Mathews thoughtfully. It was hard to believe she was the same woman I'd seen in the memory. Thirty years had left their mark. She was old, with fluffy white hair she'd made no attempt to straighten. Her clothes were older than the outfits I'd been trying to make fashionable again, in a bid to make a virtue out of necessity. She looked as if she'd stepped out of a period drama from the last century. I guessed she was old enough not to have to care about fashion.

"Lady Lamplighter." There was a hint of impatience in Lady Mathews's voice. "I assume you have a reason for visiting me?"

"Yes, My Lady," I said. I wanted to make small talk, even though I detested it. Anything, to put the moment off as much as I could. "I was asked to bring you this."

I took the orb from my pocket and held it out. Lady Mathews frowned, then took it out of my fingers and peered into the light. Her face went pale as the memory enveloped her...I felt a stab of pity, remembering the middle-aged women I'd seen. She was no longer a social beauty, but...she'd been beautiful in her way. Now...I looked around the reading room, realising just how isolated Lady Mathews truly was. She lived alone, save for a servant girl too young to do more than the basics. I wondered, morbidly, if she cooked for herself. The maid didn't look old enough to cook on the stove.

Maybe they send out for food, I thought. *She's certainly rich enough...*

The orb dropped from Lady Mathews's fingers and hit the floor. I snatched it up, half-afraid it was broken. I wasn't sure how much they could take—I'd certainly not risked trying to smash the orbs I'd been given—and I dreaded to think what Malachi would do if he realised I'd broken one. I was surprised he hadn't demanded them back. Or maybe not. He could simply copy the memory again if he needed it.

"You..." Lady Mathews stared at me, her face—already pale—going paler. "How could you...?"

"You have a choice," I said, as severely as I could. Malachi would want to see the memory, I was sure. I couldn't afford to appear *decent*. "You can meet our terms, or the secret will be exposed."

I hated myself at that moment, hated my weakness, hated the folly that had led me into Malachi's clutches. I would have given anything, anything at all, for the chance to redo my life, to leave the family well before it collapsed. But no magic ever devised could undo the past. I had to do as Malachi ordered; I had to twist the screws on a little old lady who'd never done me any harm, or watch everything I'd built fall into ruin.

"He was a horrible man." Lady Mathews sounded as if she were talking to herself, rather than me. "You don't understand...you're unmarried, aren't you? How can you possibly understand?"

"I'm sorry," I said, awkwardly.

"The marriage was arranged." Lady Mathews laughed, harshly. "*He* arranged it. Told my parents it would be good for both of us. Paid them enough money to make them go along with it. He promised them grandchildren with powerful magic and a name...a *real* name. And when we'd had the kids..."

Her hands shook. I thought I saw the air shimmer around her fingertips. "I was a prisoner. His prisoner. I couldn't leave the hall. Couldn't do anything. I banned him from my bed, and he went to the maids. He took delight in telling me he'd have the children raised elsewhere, so they'd look down on me. They went to school and didn't come back...I poisoned him. Ancients help me, I poisoned him. I should have known he'd find a way to blight me. I should have known."

She looked at me, her blue eyes seeming to peer into my soul. "You're just the messenger, aren't you?"

I nodded, knowing it wouldn't make me feel any better.

"Your master will demand more and more," Lady Mathews said. "I can give him everything and he won't ever be satisfied. I don't know who's enslaved you, girl, but I know the type. They take and take until you're a drained husk, then they betray you. I will not live like that."

Magic flared around her. I jumped up and stumbled back. Magic, powerful magic, was building up rapidly. My hair tried to stand on end. The door burst open. Poppy ran into the room, screaming something. I couldn't hear her. The magic was beating on the air, the entire building shaking so violently I thought it was going to fall to rubble. A form crashed into me, little fists pounding my back. Poppy...I paralysed her with a spell, her frozen body falling back and hitting the ground with a thud. Her mistress didn't seem to notice. Her armchair was smouldering. I realised, too late, what was about to happen.

Lady Mathews caught fire. The *wards* caught fire. The entire building shook as flames blasted in all directions, the walls and ceilings catching fire with terrifying—impossible—speed. A stench of burning flesh assaulted my nostrils as Lady Mathews died, her mouth locked in a silent scream as her body turned to ash. The floor cracked underneath my feet, threatening to collapse at any moment. I glanced at Poppy, seeing her eyes—the only things she could move—flickering back and forth in panic. Her mistress hadn't even thought to order the maid out of the house before she set fire to it.

I threw a hex at the cracking window, shattering it to splinters. I hoped no one was underneath as I levitated Poppy into the air, trying to ignore the heat under my feet. I might die saving her, but I owed it to my conscience to take some risks. Poppy flew out the window, propelled by my spell; I followed, dropping down to the ground and landing badly. The air stank of burning plants, some very dangerous. I muttered a charm to cover myself as I yanked the floating Poppy towards me, then blasted a hole in the gate. There was no one outside, but I knew that would change in a hurry. It was the sort of neighbourhood where everyone minded everyone else's business. I dropped Poppy to the ground, turned her into a statuette and shoved her into my pocket. There was no time to try to wipe her memory and drop her somewhere; no time to do anything. I wrapped a glamour around myself and ran. Behind me, the house burnt with a savagery that both awed and terrified. Lady Mathews had gone out in style.

A handful of people ran past me, heading towards what remained of the house. I evaded them as carefully as I could. The glamour should keep them from noticing me, but it wouldn't last if they actually ran into me. Guilt gnawed at my heart as I slowed, circumventing the outskirts of North Shallot. My family's hall was on the edges, peering over the waters. Once, I'd thought that a poor choice. Now, I was grateful. It made it harder for anyone to see me as I reached the back walls and levitated myself into the garden. The wards made no attempt to stop me. Why should they? They were *my* wards.

I sat on the garden bench and stared down at my hands. I'd killed. I'd killed Lady Mathews, as surely as she'd poisoned her oaf of a husband. I believed what she'd told me, I believed every word. And yet... she'd known, just as Malachi and I had known, that she would never be forgiven. My lips quirked into a cold smile. There'd be no question about the will now, I thought; there'd be no suggestion her husband's property should be returned to his family instead of being passed down to his children. Lady Mathews had made sure of that by killing herself. By the time the truth came out, if it ever did, it wouldn't matter. I felt a flicker of respect...which was driven away by the guilt. I'd killed her. I'd killed. My dress stank of smoke and ash and burning flesh, my hair...I didn't want to *think* about my hair. And it didn't matter, not compared to the simple fact I'd killed. Lady Mathews was dead. My thoughts sickened me. Who'd be next? Marlene? Ayesha? Brantley? I remembered the names and faces of my peers, back at school; I remembered the aristocrats who'd come to my parties and invited me to theirs...how many had secrets? It might not even be *aristocrats*. For all I knew, Kate and Gary—and their parents—had secrets of their own.

I can't go on like this, I thought. Who was next? Whose life would I ruin? *I just can't.*

I rested my head in my hands. Malachi was blackmailing me, but he was also offering me wealth and power...at the cost of my soul. He'd keep pushing me to compromise myself until it was too late...if it wasn't already. I learnt a harsh lesson, but not soon enough. But I was damned if I was going to risk getting someone else killed. He had to be stopped. I considered, briefly, heading to his house, weapon in hand...I shook my head. That wasn't going to work. His house was heavily defended. I'd need to sneak inside—somehow—and destroy the memories. And everything else he'd collected for blackmail. The more I thought about it, the more terrified I became. Servants knew *everything*.

And I ruined Poppy's life too, I thought. No one but Poppy herself knew I'd been in Lady Mathews's house when she died. Poppy, on the other hand...people would wonder if she'd died in the blaze or if she'd *set* the blaze. *They'll want to speak to her, even if they think she's innocent.*

I stood and walked to the hall. The rear door looked unwashed—we'd never allowed the partygoers into the back garden—but it opened at my touch. The hall felt cold and silent as I made my way up the servant passageways, cobwebs brushing against my bare skin. I'd experienced worse. The housemothers had forced me to stand outside, after Lights

Out...I rolled my eyes, seeing the system for the absurdity it was. They wanted to punish me for being out of bed by *keeping* me out of bed? Idiots.

A pile of letters greeted me as I entered my office. I glanced at them to make sure there was nothing I needed to check urgently, then closed the blinds and locked the doors. The wards were already strong, but I tested them before removing the statuette from my pocket and reversing the spell. Poppy staggered, convulsing so badly I was afraid I'd hurt her. I cursed myself under my breath. I was used to being hexed and cursed and all sorts of little indignities piled on me. Poppy had probably never been treated so badly in her life. Being frozen, then levitated and then transfigured had to have been terrifying if she hadn't been effectively kidnapped as well.

She forced herself to sit up and stare at me. "What..."

Her voice trailed off as she coughed. I understood. I'd scared her badly, really badly. She knew who I was—unless she assumed I'd given her a false name—but she didn't know anything else about me. I poured her a glass of water and watched as she drank it, half-expecting her to throw it in my face. She couldn't possibly know I had no intention of hurting her.

"You killed her," Poppy managed. "Why...?"

"She killed herself," I said. It was true, but I doubted Poppy would believe me. "I need your help."

Poppy glared at me, but I could see the fear in her eyes. I could do *anything* to her, anything at all. I wished, suddenly, that I'd thought to give a false name. Or something...I could wipe her memory and cut her loose... perhaps. It depended on just how much interest people took in the fire. If they thought Poppy was a suspect, they'd poke and prod at her memories until they realised someone had wiped her mind. I just didn't know.

"Help me and I'll give you money and a new name," I said. "It'll let you rebuild your life."

"I didn't have a life." Poppy looked down at the floor. "I'm an orphan."

"Then I can find a place for you," I said. It might be more than I could offer, but…the only alternative was keeping her prisoner until the affair was over. "Help me and I'll help you."

"Fine." Poppy said. I could hear the bitterness in her tone. "What do you want?"

"Right now, I want you to behave," I said. I couldn't think of anything else she could offer me, but…I owed her something. I'd torn her life apart quite by accident. "And I want you to tell me about yourself."

CHAPTER
THIRTY-FIVE

Poppy didn't have much to tell me, not entirely to my surprise, but her conversation bought me time to consider my next move. The evening newspapers had a brief note about the fire—it must have been a slow news day—but very little speculation about the cause. I hoped that meant there were no suspicions. The reporters would have turned a minor suspicion into a major scandal if they'd had a hint there was *something* criminal about the blaze. By the time I moved Poppy to a bedroom, with warnings about saying too much or trying to leave the hall, I had a rough outline of a plan. I wrote out a handful of notes for Jadish to take to my friends, then headed to the bathroom. I didn't feel clean even after an hour in the tub.

I didn't feel any better the following morning either, when I stumbled out of bed and lurched down to the kitchenette. Uncle Jalil was nowhere to be seen, somewhat to my relief. I was in no state to face him or anyone else. The morning newspapers seemed to believe Lady Mathew's death had been a terrible accident. There was no hint that anyone was looking for Poppy, or indeed that anyone had noticed her death. I shouldn't have been surprised. Poppy was an orphan, trading her service for accommodations. It was quite possible no one apart from her former mistress knew she even existed.

I can give her employment, if she wants, or arrange for her to go elsewhere, I thought, as I poured coffee down my throat. It tasted foul, but jarred me awake. *If I get out of this alive, I should be able to pay for her education and give her a good start in life.*

Jadish entered, just as I was finishing my fourth mug of coffee. "My Lady, your guests are starting to arrive," she said. "What should I do with your *other* guest?"

"Keep her in the bedroom, but make sure she has something to eat," I said. Poppy might be helpful—and she was too young to have witnessed the murder—but I didn't have time to make sure she could be trusted. "And then send the other guests down to the ironhold."

"Yes, My Lady." Jadish looked surprised. The ironhold was hardly a fit place for guests. "Should I serve coffee or tea?"

"Both, please." I put my mug in the sink and smoothed down my dress. "Tell them I'll be down in a moment."

I stared into the mirror, taking a moment to calm myself. My face looked as if I'd been in a fight, as if someone had blackened my eyes. I washed my face, then turned and headed for the stairs. I didn't *look* like someone who was about to receive guests, but it didn't matter. The people I'd summoned knew me, even if we weren't friends. And I was well past caring what anyone else thought. The Grande Dames no longer mattered.

The air grew cooler as I made my way down to the ironhold. It was empty, the stockpiles of potions and potion ingredients stripped bare long ago. My father had never been much of a brewer, even if he'd tried to harvest plants for sale. I shivered as I stepped through the iron door, hoping and praying the combination of wrought iron in the walls and the household wards would be enough to keep out prying eyes. I'd had no time to make the wards any stronger. My father didn't seem to have used the ironhold for anything.

My eyes scanned the chamber. Gary, Kate, Ayesha and Marlene sat on uncomfortable chairs, uneasily looking at each other uneasily. They were an oddly mismatched group. Marlene and Kate knew each other, knew enough to be *wary* of each other; Gary and Ayesha came from two different worlds. I was mildly surprised Ayesha hadn't brought her sister with her, even though I'd hinted she should come alone. Perhaps she was just being careful. Zeya was blameless. Ayesha would want to keep it that way.

Unless she did something dumb herself, I thought, sourly. I'd done something dumb. I wasn't the only one too. *We all have our secrets.*

I closed the door, then looked from face to face. "This chamber has been carefully warded," I said. "You'll find it impossible"—I hoped—"to share what you hear with anyone who isn't in our group. Whatever you decide, afterwards, please bear that in mind."

No one looked pleased. Gary had good reason to suspect I wasn't being entirely truthful. Marlene and Ayesha would fear what they were about to hear, even if they weren't annoyed at my presumption in setting up the wards in the first place. It was a pretty good rule of thumb that someone who didn't want you to talk wasn't your friend. Technically, even *hinting* at such wards was a breach of etiquette. I could get in real trouble if they believed me.

"We have a problem," I said. "Some of you already know parts of this. Others…I invited you because I thought you might help. I need"—I hesitated, suddenly unsure how to proceed—"I need your help. And so does everyone else."

I took a breath, then told them about Malachi. Kate's eyes widened as I glossed over some of the details—she knew me well enough to tell I was leaving parts of the story out—while the others just looked sick. Marlene and Ayesha knew *someone* was ferreting out secrets and blackmailing people, even if they didn't know who. Gary—of course—knew the whole story. I felt a moment of affection. I'd given him something he could use to ruin me, if he wished, and he'd done nothing. I loved him for it.

"Are you saying…?" Marlene swallowed and started again. "Are you saying we've all been blackmailed?"

"Not all of us," I said. My eyes lingered on Kate. I'd thought twice about inviting her. She'd never had any qualms about helping me at school, but this was the real world. She had a bright future ahead of her. I didn't think she'd want to risk throwing it away. "But yes, most of us have been blackmailed."

"He used *you* as the messenger," Ayesha said, tonelessly. "And now you want...what?"

"I had no choice," I said. "Just as *you* had no choice."

"Fine." Ayesha waved her hand in dismissal. "Why have you called this meeting?"

"He won't stop," I said. I gritted my teeth, then recounted how Malachi had treated me. The kneeling. The touching. How he'd made me kiss his boot. No one laughed. "He'll keep going until he's drained us dry, then expose us. And that will be the end."

"If he exposes us, we can expose him," Marlene pointed out. "He'll spend the rest of his life in prison."

"Yes, but our lives will be ruined," Ayesha countered. "What does it profit us to see him in prison, if we go into exile ourselves?"

"He may have enough influence to escape a blackmail charge, even if we *do* rat him out," I said. I'd given the matter a great deal of thought. Malachi might be banned from polite society, but so what? He was *already* banned. "How many *other* secrets does he know?"

Ayesha muttered a curse, just loudly enough for me to hear. "He could know *everything*."

"Yes." I looked from face to face. "He has to be stopped."

Kate looked uncomfortable. "What do you propose to do?"

"Stop him," I said. "We raid his house, we destroy the papers and memory orbs and everything else he uses for blackmail...and leave him powerless."

"He's still got his memory," Marlene pointed out. "He can spread stories from a distance..."

"He'd have no proof," Ayesha countered. "As long as everyone involved keeps their mouths shut, and refuses even to deny that it happened, they can pretend it never did. There are so many insane rumours floating around that a few more won't make any difference."

Particularly as Akin has his own reasons for keeping his mouth shut, I thought. *He won't want to admit he was hit with the kissing curse.*

"We have to capture or destroy the memory copying device, whatever it is," Gary said. "It'll make sure he can't do it again."

"Right." Marlene leaned forward. "Perhaps we should consider a more final solution."

I tried not to gasp. It wasn't easy.

"You mean kill him," Kate said. "Do you think that's a good idea?"

"If you don't think so, leave." Marlene scowled. "You say he'll have no proof, but…what if we're wrong?"

"Then we're wrong," I said. "But he wouldn't risk putting his proof outside his control."

"We can't be sure," Marlene insisted. "We're not the only people he's threatened. Someone else might easily have contemplated doing the same thing. He could safeguard himself by leaving the evidence with a trusted friend or two…"

"He has friends?" Ayesha rolled her eyes. "But you're right. We need to deal with him permanently."

I kept my face impassive, somehow. Malachi deserved to die. I was sure of it. I could never be safe, none of us could be safe, as long as he was alive. And yet, I didn't feel *right* about issuing a death sentence. It would be better if we could find a way to wipe his mind once and for all, but…

"I think you're forgetting something," Kate said. "Right now, we're the mice who voted to bell the cat. Sure, we need to bell the cat. But how are we actually going to do it?"

I had to smile. "You'll help us?"

"I owe you," Kate said. She leaned back in her chair. "But my father will be furious if this ends badly."

"A lot of our fathers will be furious," Ayesha said, dryly. "We have shared so much together. We might as well share exile too."

Marlene grinned, suddenly. "They'll be grateful, if we succeed. We might get a light sentence."

"Perhaps." I cleared my throat. "Does anyone want to leave?"

There was an awkward silence. No one moved to go. I breathed a sigh of relief. I didn't have any real faith in my wards. I thought everyone would keep their mouths shut, even if they refused to involve themselves further, but…I had no way to be sure. Too many people had too many secrets for them to be entirely trustworthy. Would Ayesha seek to make a private deal with Malachi? Would Marlene?

"Thank you," I said, quietly. "Like Kate says, we have to figure out how to bell the cat."

"I took a look at his wards, when we walked past his house," Gary said. He produced a charms notebook from his pocket and started to sketch out a diagram. "As you can see, they're fiendishly complex. No visible weak points. Worse"—he frowned as he diagrammed out the next section—"I think they're tied to him personally. The servants are probably confined to their chambers when their master isn't in the house."

"Does he *have* servants?" Kate studied the diagram thoughtfully. "He might not."

Ayesha made a rude sound. "Of *course* he has servants," she said. "He's spent the last umpteen years in a Great House. He'll have a small army of servants at his beck and call."

"He has a driver," I said. "I didn't see any other servants."

"He'll have them," Ayesha predicted. "They probably just stayed out of sight."

"We'll need to get a blood sample," Gary said. "It's the only way to attune ourselves to the wards."

I swore, feeling an icy hand clutching my heart. Malachi might not be as powerful a sorcerer as some of the others I'd met, but he was far from inept. His defences were tough, capable of handling almost anything we could throw at him. I dreaded what would happen if we tried to kidnap him and failed. He'd run, then reveal everything from a safe distance. My whole plan might be worse than useless. He would know what we'd tried to do.

"We can't catch him by surprise unless we get into his house and we can't get into his house without a blood sample," I said. My imagination produced a dozen schemes for obtaining a sample, each one crazier and somehow more impossible than the last. "We're doomed."

"We could set fire to the house," Gary said, doubtfully. "If we wove the right charms and potions into the blaze..."

Ayesha chuckled. "There's another way to get a blood sample," she said. "Malachi has a daughter."

"Three daughters," I corrected, absently.

"But only one who lives in the city," Ayesha said. "Penny. Penny Rubén. She's two years younger than me. There was some sort of scandal last spring in school that ended with her being stripped of her post as dorm monitor. She was actually booted down to lowerclassman."

"So?" It was meaningless to me. "What's the point?"

"Upperclassmen get the right to boss lowerclassmen around," Gary explained. "To be kicked down to lowerclassman is...well, it's pretty bad."

"Social death," Ayesha said. "Point is, Penny *isn't* living with the rest of the family. She's in a townhouse in South Shallot."

Kate eyed her suspiciously. "And you know this *how*?"

"She's a Rubén," Ayesha said, as though that explained everything. "Keeping track of them is what we do."

"Right." Kate shook her head in disbelief. "And can we use Penny's blood to get through the wards? Wards, as you have just finished explaining, are tuned to one person and one person alone. Can we make it work, if we got a sample of Penny's blood?"

"Yes," Gary said. "We'd have to strip the blood down to isolate her father's...contribution to her bloodline mix, but it's doable. Once we were through the wards, they should think we're authorised users and ignore us."

I nodded. "It should be workable."

"I hope you're right," Kate said. "What if you're wrong?"

"It makes sense," Gary insisted. "The inner wards know we wouldn't be inside the house unless the outer wards let us through, and the outer wards wouldn't let us through unless we had permission to be inside the house. They should overlook us on the grounds we couldn't have passed through the outer wards without permission."

"Fine." Ayesha stood and started to pace the room. "How do we get our hands on the little brat? She's been pretty much socially isolated since the end of term."

I blinked. "Her family isn't watching over her?"

"They bought her the townhouse." Ayesha shrugged. "My guess is that they're doing the bare minimum and nothing else. Whatever got her father kicked out probably impacted on her too. Akin never liked her...I think he played a role in getting her demoted."

"That couldn't have gone down well with his family," Marlene said. "I'm surprised they didn't tell him to *help* her."

"That's why people think she did something *really* bad," Ayesha said. "Perhaps she was involved with her father...well, with whatever her father did. Or something. We simply don't know."

"Perhaps we can ask her," I said. "Later."

I tapped the paper. "We invite her to a party. Get her here...get her nicely isolated, then take her blood. And then wipe her memory afterwards."

"Her father might have told her to stay away from you," Kate warned. "Perhaps we should invite her somewhere else."

"Anywhere else, she'd know there *wasn't* a party," Ayesha said. "She probably reads the society papers."

"So we kidnap her from her townhouse," Marlene said. "Can't we do that instead?"

"She'd have wards of her own, devised by her family," Gary said. "And possibly an Object of Power."

"I doubt it," Ayesha said. "But you're right. We need to act discreetly."

"So we invite her here," I said. "You invite her. Tell her to come here. We grab her the moment she arrives, then take her blood and hurry to Water Shallot."

"And then what?" Gary met my eyes, evenly. "If he's in the house, the wards might realise he's in two places at once and sound the alert."

I rubbed my forehead. "We have to get him out of the house," I said. "How do we do that?"

Kate laughed. "Invite *him* to a party?"

"No." Marlene grinned. "We send him a note, purporting to be from a servant with stuff to sell. Private letters, perhaps. Or something else, something that'll let her take revenge on her mistress. He goes to get the crap and we walk in and trash his house."

"And what if he doesn't leave?" Gary leaned forward. "He might not take the bait."

"Have Penny write the note," Ayesha suggested. "Invite her father to the townhouse."

"We don't know if Penny and her father are in contact," I said. "My father didn't contact me for six years."

Kate looked disturbed. "They're in the same city."

"But her family might have ordered her not to contact him," Ayesha said. "Or given her a flat choice between going with her father or remaining with the family."

"Better to keep it simple," I said. "We'll forge a note, telling him to meet the sender on the other side of the city. Poppy can deliver it. We'll watch from a distance...if he leaves his home, we move in and search the house. If he doesn't...we try again at a later date."

"Keeping Penny as a prisoner," Marlene pointed out.

"So what?" Ayesha looked dismissive. "It isn't as if anyone will miss her."

"If you say so." Kate didn't sound convinced. "How long do we have?"

"I don't know," I said, "which is why we have to move as quickly as possible. Tonight, if possible. Get it done before something else can go wrong."

"Then we'd better start planning," Gary said. He turned his notebook to a blank page. "Where shall we begin?"

CHAPTER
THIRTY-SIX

The planning session lasted for hours. We went through the whole plan, each of us bringing our individual skills to the table and blending them together into a single whole. I knew better than to expect everything to go according to plan—there were just too many variables—but we covered every contingency we could imagine. By the time we broke up to collect our gear and return for the final act, we thought we were ready. I felt as if some of the old thrill had returned.

This could still go horribly wrong, I reminded myself, as I paced my office. I'd sent a message to Penny, offering her a post as party coordinator. It had been Ayesha's idea, but I had to admit it was a good one. *If she's in touch with her father...*

I shook my head. Ayesha had told me everything she knew about Penny. It was hard to tell how much was reliable and how much was rumour and misinformation, but it was pretty clear Penny was socially isolated. She must have done something *really* bad to deserve such a harsh punishment. It wasn't the end of the world, but...to a teenage girl, it was probably worse. People would remember her demotion for years after she graduated and entered the real world. She'd be so isolated, I thought, that she'd jump at the chance to start crawling back into the limelight. And it was unlikely she was in contact with her father.

There was a tap on the door. I looked up. "Come."

Jadish opened the door. "My Lady, the afternoon newspapers have arrived," she said. She held a bundle out to me. "What should I do with them?"

"Put them on the desk," I said. I didn't want to read the papers. I'd been jumping every time a messenger arrived, fearful he carried a message from Malachi. "Can you...?"

I stopped myself and met her eyes. "Jadish...what do you want to do with your life?"

Jadish stiffened. "I'm sure I don't know what you mean, My Lady."

"Do you want to work here forever?" I held her eyes, wincing inside. It was hardly a fair question. The power disparity between us was too great. And yet, I needed to know the answer. "Or do you want to do something else with your life?"

Jadish said nothing for a long moment. "I'd like to open a shop," she said, finally. For a moment, she sounded like her old self. "Or become a seamstress. I've spent the last few years mending dresses and trousers and everything else.

"After this is over..." I swallowed and started again. "After this is over, I can try and get you lessons. Or help you buy a shop. Or *something*."

"That would be nice," Jadish said. Her tone was so flat I was sure she'd heard the same promise before. From whom? My father? "If it happens, it happens."

I dismissed her with a nod, my thoughts grim. I'd taken what precautions I could, in the event of everything going badly. The money Ayesha had given me had been earmarked for the servants, if I died or simply never came home. They'd have a decent chance to survive and make something of themselves, even if House Lamplighter vanished. Jadish and Ellington and the others would live...I brooded on the thought as the hours ticked by, wondering if I'd gone too far. I'd dragged Kate and Gary into the affair, too.

There was no choice, I told myself. *I needed their help.*

I put the thought out of my head as my friends returned, one by one. Malachi might suspect something, if he had people watching the hall…I told myself it was unlikely. Besides, he'd told me to turn the screws on Ayesha and Marlene himself. I could justify Kate and Gary visiting, if he asked. Penny was the joker in the deck. If she was spotted…would the observer even recognise her? I scowled as I realised Malachi could view the spotter's memories. He'd certainly recognise his own daughter.

Unless he hasn't seen her for years too, I thought. I'd been a scrawny brat when I'd been sent to Grayling's. I'd grown into a young adult by the time I'd returned. It was hard to believe my childhood portraits were of me. *What sort of father was he?*

"We're ready," Gary said, as we assembled in the hall. "Are you?"

"I think so," I said. My imagination helpfully provided a list of everything that could go horribly wrong. "She should be here at any moment."

The wards hummed a warning. I tensed as I walked to the door, the others slipping into the shadows to wait. I remembered lurking in ambush, back at school, and silently damned my former self for not…for not being older. In hindsight…I told myself not to be silly. I hadn't had the advantage of hindsight when I'd been a child. I opened the door, just in time to see a carriage rattle up the drive. It was fancy, but clearly rented. There was no family crest within view.

I clasped my hands behind my back as the vehicle rattled to a halt. The driver—he wore bland livery—clambered off the seat, dropped to the ground and opened the door. A young blonde girl, her hair in braids, stepped out of the cab. My blood ran cold as I met her blue eyes. They were hard and cold, her face set in a sour expression that had practically been carved from ice. She was prettier than her father—it would have been hard to be uglier—but there was something of him in her stance. I silently forgave Marlene everything as Penny walked up the steps. She held herself like a queen visiting a hovel.

And she doesn't have a future, I thought, as we eyed each other. I'd checked the books. Penny didn't have the blood or the accomplishments to reach for true power. *She'll be a pensioner for the rest of her days.*

"Lady Lamplighter," Penny said. Her voice was hard and cold. "Thank you for inviting me."

I reminded myself, sharply, that Penny was three years younger than me. "You're welcome," I said, gravely. Behind her, the carriage rattled down the driveway and onto the road. "If you'll come with me..."

Penny huffed as I turned and led her into the hall. I wondered, idly, what she'd expected. A formal parade? A row of footmen or armsmen, holding their spellcasters in salute? Or a formal welcome by the Grande Dames? It didn't matter. I braced myself as I walked through the field of charms, silently sending orders to the wards. They flared with power. Penny yelped and reached for her magic, too late. The wards froze her in place. Her eyes burned with anger as I turned to face her, my magic scanning for unpleasant surprises. She had nothing, apart from a purse and a pocket compact. I put them both to one side as my allies emerged from the shadows. The first part of the plan had gone well.

Too well, I thought.

Gary pointed a spellcaster at Penny, muttering a complex spell. Her eyes went blank. I felt a frisson of alarm as the wards released her, leaving her standing limply in front of us. We'd just crossed the line. We might get away with using minor compulsion spells, in or out of school, but here...? We were committed now. The spell was too powerful to be considered a practical joke. We'd practically turned her into a slave.

"She looks so much prettier like that," Ayesha said, quietly. "Do you not think?"

"No," Kate said, sharply.

I winced, inwardly, as Gary steered Penny down the stairs and into the ironhold. It was hard to tell how aware Penny truly was of her surroundings, how much she realised of what had happened to her. I hoped we'd shut down her mind completely. If a minor compulsion spell could be horrifying, how much more a *major* spell? She would be seeing her body moving under someone else's direction...

At least we're not trying to blackmail her, I told myself. It was no consolation. *And we'll try and make it up to her afterwards.*

"I'll take the blood," Gary said, once Penny was seated in an iron chair. "You ask the questions."

I glanced at Ayesha, then looked at Penny. "Who's your father?"

Penny's voice was dull, dead and dull. "Malachi Rubén."

"So we got the right person," Marlene muttered. "Ask her what she did to get demoted."

"Not yet," I muttered back. I cleared my throat as I looked at Penny. "What happened to your father?"

"They ordered him out of the hall," Penny said. "They told him to go."

I frowned as I fired question after question at her. Penny didn't seem to know much of anything. Her father had been kicked out...she seemed to believe it had something to do with *her*, although she wasn't clear on the details. I knew she was telling the truth—she didn't have the will to lie—but she couldn't tell us something she didn't know. Akin had caught her disciplining one of the younger girls, apparently; she didn't seem to think she'd done anything wrong. I shuddered. There was room for a great many sins in *disciplining*. I didn't think I wanted to know. I'd always thought Jude's was more progressive than that.

"So she's not in contact with him," Marlene said, when we were done. "That's good, isn't it?"

I nodded. Penny didn't seem to know anything about what her father did for a living, or what he'd done before he'd been kicked out of his home. I had the feeling Malachi had been an indifferent father... Penny didn't know it, but she'd been lucky. Very lucky. She was already a brat. I shuddered to think what she might have become if she'd been raised directly by her father. Her sisters probably had the better part of that deal.

Gary looked up from the table. "I've isolated the masculine aspects of the blood," he said. "It should be enough to fool the wards."

"Be very sure," I said. "We don't want it thinking we're in multiple places at once."

"It should be fine, as long as we stay close together when we pass the outer wards," Gary said. He poured half the blood into a vial and sealed it with a spell. The remainder was dumped into the disposal bin. "It should work. If it doesn't...we'll just have to back away and try something else."

If the wards let us, I thought, as I stared at Penny. *This could still go horribly wrong.*

"We could take her with us," Kate suggested. "Leaving her here..."

"Too great a risk," Gary said. "We couldn't trust her."

"And the wards might snap her out of her trance, if they mistake her for her father," Ayesha added. "We have to leave her here."

I nodded. "Make sure you collect everything," I ordered. "We don't want to leave anything here, just in case."

"Of course," Gary said. He passed me the blood. "Make sure you don't drop it."

Kate, Marlene and Ayesha headed up the stairs. I watched them go, then turned to look at Penny. Her face was blank, but I knew it was just a matter of time before she regained her free will. Probably. I'd thought about using a spellbinder, but they were too expensive to obtain quickly. Instead, I rested my hand on her head and muttered a spell. Her body turned to stone. She'd be aware of nothing, not even time passing, until the spell was lifted. I told myself it was the best possible choice. My conscience disagreed.

"We could just give her something to wipe her memory, then send her home," Gary offered, quietly. "We don't have to keep her prisoner."

I shook my head. There were too many variables. Besides, we might need her again. I keyed the spell into the wards, ensuring she'd stay stone long enough for us to go and come back, then headed for the stairs. If things went really wrong, she'd be discovered when the Kingsmen searched the hall. They'd take care of her.

"The charms on the door are pretty outdated," Gary said, as I closed the heavy iron door. "I could break them, with a little effort."

"I know." I shook my head. Penny might be a disagreeable sort who made Marlene look like a saint, but she didn't deserve to be entombed in the ironhold forever. "I'll worry about making them stronger when I have something to protect."

My heart sank as I looked at him. Guilt gnawed at my soul. I'd dragged Gary—and Kate—into a nightmare. Malachi would have us *all* if things went wrong. Malachi...or High Society. Ayesha might be sent into exile. Everyone else...we were looking at prison, or worse, if we were caught. I wanted to go back in time and kick myself, hard. I'd trapped myself. If I'd been a little more careful...no, if I'd never started at all. But that wasn't an option.

"I'm sorry," I said. The others should be out of earshot, but I wrapped a privacy ward around us anyway. "I should never have gotten you into this."

Gary said nothing for a long moment. I wished I knew what he was thinking. He was a practical man. My kisses couldn't be enough to make him stop thinking. He knew what would happen if we were caught. He'd be disgraced, his master would disown him, his *father* would disown him... he was legally an adult, old enough to face the consequences himself, but there was a very real chance his family would face them too. I cursed myself for even *thinking* of telling him. It would have been so much easier if I hadn't told him a thing.

No, I corrected myself. *I would just have felt better about it.*

"I made the decision to help you," Gary said. He glanced up the stairs, then leaned forward and kissed me. I felt my heart start to race. "You don't get rid of me so easily."

"I'm sorry," I said, again. "If it goes wrong...blame it on me."

Gary laughed. "What sort of gentleman would I be if I blamed it on you?"

"A practical one," I told him. I tried not to giggle. "I won't blame you for blaming me."

"*Impractical* is my middle name," Gary said. "I have it on my sister's good authority."

I smiled. "I'm sure she's a trustworthy source."

My heart sank as we turned and headed up the stairs. Gary might be chuckling at his joke, but…I knew he might come to regret it. I promised myself I'd make it up to him, even though I had no idea *how*. My family was poor. We might have a little income now, thanks to my…my heart clenched. I wouldn't be doing *that* again. I'd learnt my lesson. But that left me with the problem of figuring out what to do.

Marry Gary, my thoughts told me. *Use his money to rebuild the house.*

The others looked at us as we entered. "You took your time," Ayesha said. "Should we hold a quick wedding ceremony?"

I flushed. Was it that obvious? "No," I said. "We just needed to work on our wards."

"You'd better make sure you know the contraceptive wards," Ayesha said. "I have it on good authority they're not easy to cast when you're hot and bothered."

"I'll take your word for it," I said. It was on the tip of my tongue to point out that everyone knew the spells, even though no one would admit to teaching them. They weren't formally banned, of course, but the Great Houses wanted the next generation to arrive as quickly as possible. "I think…"

"Really?" Marlene smirked, without her old malice. "I'm surprised at you."

"Yeah." I rubbed my forehead. "If I'd thought, we might not be in this mess."

Kate cleared her throat, loudly. "Correct me if I'm wrong," she said, "but you're not to blame for everything. Are you? You didn't make Ayesha do whatever Ayesha did and you didn't make Marlene do whatever *Marlene* did. And you weren't even *born* when Lady Mathews murdered her husband.

You made a mistake, true, but you didn't make *every* mistake. You're not to blame for everything."

"She has a point," Marlene said. "I did...I did what I did without your help."

"True," Ayesha agreed. She shook her head. "I still can't believe Francis told Malachi, of all people. Why him?"

"I guess he seemed a good choice," I mumbled. Malachi could be charming, although I'd seen little of it. I could easily imagine him trying to work his way into Francis's good books. Hell, he might even be indirectly responsible for Francis's death. "I confided in my uncle when I was younger too."

"Francis had a dad," Ayesha said. "They even lived in the same house!"

Kate looked from Ayesha to me and back again. "Do you realise how uncommon it is for a child *not* to share a house with his father?"

"The rules are different here," Ayesha said. "Penny certainly lives alone."

"She probably hates it," Gary said, with excessive sarcasm. "A chance to live on her own, with all her bills paid...how *terrible*."

I shook my head. "Terrible indeed," I agreed, dryly. I glanced at my watch. It was nearly night. Poppy was probably already chafing at the bit. "Shall we go?"

"Yes," Kate said. "Let's get it over with."

CHAPTER
THIRTY-SEVEN

We said nothing as we piled into the carriage and drove to Water Shallot. Tension hung in the air, so thick I thought we could cut it with a knife. I tested my spells time and time again, wishing—not for the first time—that we'd had more time to practice. Gary and Kate had argued as much, pointing out that we couldn't afford to make a mistake. Marlene and Ayesha had disagreed, insisting we had to move at once. There was no time. Someone would notice Penny was missing and start looking for her, even if Malachi didn't find a new way to torment us. Who knew what other secrets were locked in his ugly head?

Water Shallot was wrapped in shadow as the evening turned to night. The streets were dark and cold. I saw a pair of pubs glowing with light, men staggering in and out in various stages of drunkenness, but otherwise the entire district appeared dead and cold. Gary had told me that the socialist riots had scared people, and convinced them to stay indoors...I hadn't really believed it until now. Water Shallot was nothing like North or South Shallot.

The carriage rattled to a halt. I braced myself as the door snapped open. Gary had taken the reins, insisting he could drive us to our destination without hiring a coachman. Outside, the air was dark and smelled of something I didn't want to think about. Gary had parked us in an alley, just down from Malachi's house. The buildings felt oppressive as we scrambled to the ground and looked around. There was no one in sight, not even a homeless man trying to catch some sleep. The entire district felt utterly lifeless. I shivered. It just didn't feel right.

I looked at Poppy. "You remember what you need to do?"

"Yes, My Lady," Poppy said. She spoke quietly, but her voice sounded loud in the eerie silence. "Now?"

I glanced at the others, then nodded. "Now," I said. "That house over there."

My heart started to thud in my chest as Poppy hurried down the street. I'd taken a serious risk in bringing her, not least because the district was far from safe. Malachi might not take the bait. It wasn't uncommon to give a kid a coin or two to deliver a message—I could easily see aristocrats sending children into Water Shallot without any thought of what could happen—but he might ask more questions than she could answer. I'd drilled her endlessly, going through everything I thought he could ask...

We've done all we can, I thought, as I wrapped a glamour around myself. *All we can do now is wait.*

Poppy knocked at the door. I waited, my eyes tingling as someone opened the door. A figure stood within the light, too tall and thin to be Malachi. A servant? Ayesha was probably right. Malachi would have more than one servant. It struck me, as Poppy passed the figure the note and held out her hand expectantly for the tip, that I might actually be *taller* than Malachi. He wasn't a dwarf, but he was quite short for a grown man. He'd probably hated being short when he'd been a kid. No wonder he'd made me kneel.

I braced myself as Poppy turned and headed back towards me. The door banged closed behind her. Poppy was smiling broadly as she stepped into the alley, clutching a golden crown in one hand. Malachi's servant had tipped her well. I blinked in surprise—as far as the girl knew, Poppy was a street urchin—and then nodded in understanding. Malachi stood to gain hugely from each and every piece of blackmail material. He could afford to tip handsomely.

"She took the letter," Poppy said. "What now?"

"You get back into the carriage and wait," I said. "Kate, you take the reins."

Kate nodded, her face half-hidden behind a glamour. She and Gary were the only ones who knew how to drive a carriage, although the rest of us knew how to ride. She'd get us out if all hell broke loose. I was silently relieved she was on the outside, able to run for her life if the rest of us were caught. Ayesha, Marlene and I had good reason to do everything in our power to stop Malachi. Kate...didn't have to put herself at risk. I wished that was true of Gary too.

It felt like hours before a carriage emerged from a distant alley and rattled down the street. I glanced at my watch, silently noting the time. Malachi would need at least thirty minutes to reach the meeting point, then another thirty to get back...assuming, of course, he realised he'd been lured away. He might hang around and wait for a few minutes before the realisation dawned. The note *had* promised dirt on Alana Aguirre, after all. It would be worth waiting for. I told myself not to count on it. We couldn't rely on anything.

"Now?" Gary inched forward. "Shall we go?"

"Yeah." I glanced at Marlene and Ayesha, motioning for them to bring up the rear. "Let's move."

Gary took the blood from me, opened the vial and started to use it to ink his face. I shuddered, feeling as if we were crossing the line...again. Blood magic was rarely *innocent*. Anything that involved blood taken from someone else without permission was dark by definition. But we had no choice. I felt my skin crawl as he drew out lines on my face with Penny's blood, then did the same to Marlene and Ayesha. They looked about as pleased as myself. I cast a glamour to ensure no one would see us clearly, then headed into the road. The clock had started to tick the moment Malachi had left the house.

The wards crackled around us as we made our way past the house and into the alleyway. A bigger door, easily large enough to take a carriage, blocked our way. Gary knelt in the gutter and started to go to work, pointing a spellcaster at the spellform and starting to key it open. I felt the magic growing stronger as I inched closer to him, hoping the blood was convincing enough to fool the wards. It might have Malachi's essence within it, but it was also unmistakably feminine. I told myself it was unlikely to matter. Malachi had allowed *me* to enter his house. He probably hadn't keyed the wards to keep women out.

As if anyone would, I thought.

The wards seemed to grow stronger again, then faded into the background as the door started to rise. I tensed, readying a spell. If there was someone waiting for us...there was no one. The door opened into a large chamber, the chamber I'd seen the first time he'd brought me to his house. I cast a spell to let me see in the dark, then inched forward. No powerful wards blocked my way. I breathed a sigh of relief as we moved into the darkness. The door at the far end of the chamber was shut and locked.

"Don't touch anything," Gary said. "And stay close to me."

I nodded, feeling my skin prickle as the wards drifted over us. They felt like cobwebs, cobwebs that could turn nasty in the blink of an eye. I sensed powerful and deadly spells hanging in the air like spiders in the web, just waiting for a chance to snap at us. Malachi clearly wasn't interested in taking prisoners. I supposed it made sense. The people who were most likely to burgle a house in Water Shallot had nothing worth the effort of ransoming or blackmailing them. My lips curved into a grim smile as we reached the far door. We were going to break Malachi, once and for all.

"There's a second set of spells here," Gary said. "Give me a moment."

"Hurry," Marlene advised. "I feel naked."

Gary shot her a sharp look, then turned his attention to the door. I understood. We were deep in enemy territory, too committed to back off and pretend we'd never been near the house. It wouldn't take a skilled wardsmith or charmsmith to realise what we'd done. Malachi might not know who'd kidnapped Penny, but he'd know *someone* had. He might even alert his former family, pushing them to search for her. The ironhold was designed to be impossible to locate, but...I shook my head. There was no point in wasting time worrying about it. We had to focus on what we were doing.

The door clicked open. I stepped into a dimly lit corridor. The wards seemed to draw back until they hung at the corner of my mind, a constant reminder that no one could see or hear anything within the house. I felt sick as I studied the spellforms, realising that Malachi could spy on anything in his domain. He could listen in to conversations, he could watch the maids as they undressed...I shuddered. It was a severe breach of etiquette to spy on one's guests, even one's servants...I wondered, sourly, why I was surprised. Malachi had shown no qualms about stripping memories and using them for blackmail. Why would he *not* spy on his guests?

My legs felt weak as I led the way up the stairs. It was no different—I told myself—than sneaking around school, but my thoughts kept reminding me the consequences would be worse. My heart pounded loudly as I reached the top, nearly stumbling over a poorly designed step. Penny's portrait hung in front of me. I wondered, as I eyed it, just how much the artist had been paid. She didn't look much younger—I guessed it had been painted towards the end of the previous summer, in line with tradition—but her face had been smoothed out until she looked pleasant. I was used to paintings being carefully drawn to remove imperfections—there were portraits of young boys that made them look like teenagers—but the painting in front of me was an extreme case. I really *hoped* the artist had been well paid.

"Come on," Marlene whispered. "Where now?"

"This way." I flushed as we headed down the corridor. "I think..."

A door opened. A young woman stepped out. Her eyes went wide as she saw us. I froze her at once, watching numbly as she fell over backwards and hit the ground with a thud. I stepped over her body and peered into the room. It was a large bedchamber, dominated by the biggest bed I'd ever seen. Another young woman, her face marred with an ugly bruise, clutched the blanket to her chest as she stared at us. I froze her too, feeling a twinge of sympathy. The bruise looked nasty.

Malachi probably forced them into his bed, I thought. I checked the rest of the room, then hurried back to the office. *Poor girls.*

Gary stopped in front of the office door and started to work. "He wasn't taking anything for granted," he said, as he fiddled with the charms. "There's enough spells here to stop an army."

I stared at his back. "Can you break them?"

"Trick them, yes." Gary's spellcaster twisted in his hand as he moved it up and down the wooden door. "Lucky we have the blood, or it would have been impossible without an Object of Power."

Perhaps we should have asked Caitlyn for one, I thought, sourly. *Akin might have spoken to her for us.*

I shook my head. Too many people already knew what had happened. And there'd be no guarantee Caitlyn would cooperate. Akin certainly wouldn't want to tell her what Ayesha had done to him. He'd be ashamed, even if she agreed it wasn't actually his fault. I knew how he'd felt. I'd dragged Gary into a nightmare...

The door creaked. "Hah," Gary said, using the spellcaster to push it open. "Let me go in first."

"You two check the rest of the house," I ordered the girls. I wasn't sure what we'd do with his servants. Take them home and...and what? "Then get back here."

I frowned as Gary stepped into the office, then motioned for me to follow. The air was heavy with spells. It felt like a gathering thunderstorm of magic, even though the charms seemed to slip over us as though we weren't there. A shiver ran down my spine as I looked at his desk, then at the bookshelves behind the chair. There had to be a secret compartment, probably behind the shelves. Gary walked around the room, waving his spellcaster in the air as he cast a string of detection spells. I sensed magic sparking around him, each charm deflected by the blood. My forehead itched, but I dared not wipe away the marks. They were all that stood between me and a very painful death.

"Interesting," Gary said, stopping in front of the bookcase. "There's something here, but I can't see any charms to unlock it."

I stared at the shelves. "He must have done something," I said. "How...?"

"Think about it," Gary said. "What happened? What did you hear?"

"I was blind," I protested. I forced myself to recall. I'd heard...something. And I hadn't sensed magic. I wasn't sure I would have sensed *anything* in such an environment. But ... I leaned forward, studying the bookcase. If it wasn't held shut with magic. "Ah..."

I tugged on the shelf. There was a feeling of resistance, then the entire bookshelf came free, revealing a hidden chamber beyond. My eyes widened as I saw a strange device sitting on a trolley, a combination of metallic strands and gemstones and a weird metal helmet...it had to be the memory reader. Gary advanced forward, studying the device with fascination. My eyes trailed over it, ruefully acknowledging I didn't have the slightest idea where to begin. Gary might be able to understand what I was seeing. I could not.

"Interesting," Gary mused. "The charms are so delicate that the slightest mishap could destroy them."

"Interesting," I echoed. I saw a row of memory orbs and scowled. They looked just like the others, but they felt empty. "Can you see how it works?"

"Yeah." Gary frowned as he poked at the device. "The charms are really quite fascinating."

"I'll take your word for it," I said. Up close, the device was very clearly a *Device*. Someone had forged it. Someone had designed it and forged it and given it to a blackmailer. I stared at the hodgepodge, wondering why the designer hadn't given it to someone legit. It wouldn't have been hard. There were a dozen Great Houses that would have paid through the nose for the design. "Make a note of it."

I stepped past him and peered into the chamber. The walls were lined with files and boxes, each marked with a name. I shivered as I spotted a handful of names I recognised, from Grande Dames to…to my father. I hesitated, unsure I wanted to know. My father had been a good man… hadn't he? And yet, look what *I'd* done to restore the family fortune. My hand shook as I reached for the file, opening it up to see a list of financial reports. They were hard to follow, and I thought there were chunks missing, but it looked as though my father had orchestrated a pyramid scheme. Hundreds of investors had trusted the nameless person behind the scheme with their money, unaware that my father…

My heart clenched. My father had defrauded them. Intentionally or not, my father had taken their money and lost it. My fingers swept through the papers, my mind pleading with the uncaring ancestors that it wasn't so. But it was…my father had taken their money and lost it and…and what? How had he escaped detection? I went through the papers, heedless of the growing danger. He'd placed the blame on someone who'd skipped town…as far as anyone knew, I reasoned, he'd looked like just another victim. I almost dropped the papers as I caught sight of another box, one marked with another familiar name. Auntie Dorcas.

I don't want to know, I thought. I'd always liked secrets, but there were limits. *I really don't want to know.*

"You can destroy the orbs with a spell," Gary said. He waved a hand at the device. "I think I'd like to take this thing with us."

"If you want." I was too stunned to argue. What had Auntie Dorcas done? And why hadn't Malachi ever contacted her? How…how did I know he *hadn't*? It wasn't as if she'd tell me, even if I pressed. "I think…"

I stared at the boxes. People I'd met, people I knew by reputation, people I'd never known…my throat was dry. They represented a huge temptation. I could take them, I could use them to rebuild the family,… no. I wasn't going to even try. I'd wind up just like him. And I'd learnt that lesson too late.

"Hurry," Gary said. He started to push the trolley out of the chamber. "I don't know .."

A surge of magic flashed into the chamber, brushing our defences aside with casual ease. I wanted to run, but there was nowhere to go. There was only one way in or out of the office and Malachi stood there, wearing a long dark coat. His face was lit with unholy glee.

"Well," he said. His eyes trailed over me, then Gary. "Come out where I can see you. Come into the light."

CHAPTER
THIRTY-EIGHT

"My, oh my," Malachi said. The naked anticipation in his voice made my stomach turn in disgust. "Who do we have here?"

My legs quivered, then moved of their own accord as the wards pushed me out of the chamber. Gary followed, stumbling along like a puppet hanging from tangled strings. I gritted my teeth, trying not to retch at the sensation of being controlled. Malachi's smile grew wider as we stumbled into the office, his eyes trailing over us with naked anticipation. I cursed myself savagely for not setting fire to the building and running, well before Malachi had realised he'd been duped and turned back. He was back early...

"Well, I suppose I shouldn't be surprised," Malachi said. He stepped up to me, invading my personal space. "I knew you had a habit of sneaking around."

He looked at Gary. "And who might *you* be?"

Gary glared. I could tell he was trying to cast a spell, to escape the wards. I doubted he could. Malachi had them under firm control, using them to control us. My magic was useless. I thought as fast as I could, considering my options. There were no spells I could cast that would reach him, even if they didn't backfire on me. The wards were just too strong. And yet...where were Marlene and Ayesha? Had they been trapped too? Or had they had the wit to escape? Or...

"Go fuck yourself," Gary managed. Sweat beaded on his face. "You're a monster."

"I'm a monster?" Malachi sounded shocked. "Do you know what *she's* done? Do you know what her *father* did?"

I gritted my teeth. I had to keep him talking. I had to keep him talking, even though every word grated on my nerves. He knew he had the edge. He knew he had us at his mercy. He knew...I knew he didn't *have* any mercy. I had to keep him talking until we found a way to escape or kill him or...I wondered, suddenly, what spell Lady Mathews had used to commit suicide. If I could cast it myself...

"You knew what my father did," I said. I doubted there was any point in pretending I hadn't read the files. "Were you blackmailing him too?"

Malachi said nothing, but I knew—from the way his smile widened—that I'd hit the nail on the head. My father *had* been blackmailed. My thoughts spun in circles as I put the pieces together. No wonder the family finances were in such bad shape. No wonder he'd taken such an outrageous loan from a criminal. My father had been desperately trying to meet Malachi's demands, all too aware he'd be betrayed when he ran out of money. I wondered, sourly, why he hadn't bothered to warn me. I...I swallowed hard as I realised my father might have committed suicide, taking his guilt to his ancestors. My heart twisted. They'd turn their backs on him.

Keep him talking, I thought, desperately. *Give Gary time to think.*

I forced myself to look at him. "Is that why you knew to keep an eye on me? You knew my father?"

"Not really." Malachi shrugged, dispassionately. "I never expected you to amount to anything. If you'd been a little more careful, a little more open, a little more honest...why, there would have been nothing to gain by blackmailing you. You couldn't be blamed for your father's sins. And then you went and committed sins of your own."

He gestured. I felt the wards pushing me to my knees. Beside me, Gary groaned in pain. I winced, cursing myself once again for getting him involved. I should have raided the house myself, using the blood...I should have simply tried to kill Malachi, the first time he'd entered my hall. Maybe my secrets would have come out, maybe they wouldn't. It would have saved everyone else from my stupidity. I stared up at him, knowing it was the end. He knew he couldn't trust me now.

"I did have hopes for you," Malachi said. He patted my head in mock affection. "I thought you'd make a willing ally. You were tempted, were you not? It's astonishing what people will do if you offer them wealth and power. They'll throw away their most cherished principles just for a little more..."

I forced myself to lift my head, despite the growing pressure. "Is that what you did to Francis?"

Malachi's face twisted. "The little fool just *had* to get himself killed!"

"What did you do to him?" I wasn't sure I wanted to know, but it would keep him talking long enough for Marlene and Ayesha to get out of the house. "Why did he die?"

"I spent years grooming him to listen to me." Malachi started to pace the room. "People like that, they resist if you block them. They resist if they think you're a threat. But if you act like a wise old counsellor, a man who wants only the best for you, they'll *listen*. I guided him for years, priming him to take Akin's place. He would have ruled the family, and I would have ruled through him. But he got himself killed instead."

I felt sick. I'd thought Malachi couldn't be any worse. But I was wrong.

"And they kicked you out," I said. "Right?"

"They'll pay." Malachi's eyes darkened. "They'll *all* pay."

He smiled, suddenly. "And now I have you. And your friend. And your other friends downstairs. I see you brought me some *real* prizes."

My heart sank. Ayesha and Marlene were trapped too. Kate and Poppy might get away, if they had the wit to realise something had gone wrong. I tried to think of a plan, of a way to alert them, but came up with nothing. A vapour message wouldn't get through the wards. I felt a tidal wave of guilt. I'd killed them all. No, I'd done worse. I'd delivered them to Malachi. They might be better off dead.

"Yeah." I forced myself to look submissive as a thought crossed my mind. "Let's make a deal."

Malachi cocked his head. "What makes you think you have anything to bargain with?"

It was a good point, I acknowledged sourly. I had very little. And yet, people *would* start asking questions if we never returned home. Ayesha's family would certainly want to know what had happened to her, where she'd gone; Gary and Kate and even Marlene had parents who'd be asking questions too. I wondered, idly, how Malachi intended to deal with it. He could wipe their memories, or force them to drink compulsion potions, or…it didn't matter. I had a window of opportunity. I needed to use it.

"You need an assistant," I said. I kept my eyes on the ground. "You need someone who can go places you can't. That's what you wanted me for, right? You wanted a servant."

"A slave." Malachi's voice dripped poison. "And your point is…?"

He knew it. I knew he knew it. But he wanted me to spell it out.

"I'll serve you," I said. "I'll do anything you want. I'll kiss your boot and your ass and everything else. I'll take your messages anywhere and everywhere. I will serve you."

Malachi said nothing for a long moment. "And in return?"

"You let them go," I said. I nodded towards Gary. "You let them all go. You take their oaths they won't breathe a word of what happened here, tonight, and let them go. I'll be your servant, your"—my voice broke—"your slave. And in return, you let them go."

I forced myself forward until I was prostrating myself. My heart clenched, again, as I heard Gary gasp. Girls of my class didn't kneel, let alone prostrate themselves. Ancients alone knew what he thought of me…I swallowed hard, silently praying Malachi would take the bait. I had his measure now.

A more practical man might take precautions, but he wanted to force me to submit. He wanted to watch an aristocratic girl crawl.

And I offered him a loophole he could use to break his word without actually breaking it, I thought, as I waited. *He'll see a chance to torment my friends without letting me break my oath.*

Malachi removed his boot, then put his bare foot forward. "Kiss it."

Gary gasped. I cringed inwardly as I inched forward, practically crawling on my belly. I hoped he'd forgive me, I hoped he'd forget, as I pressed my lips against his bare skin. Malachi started, too late, as I hit him with the kissing curse. It would have been more effective if I'd kissed his lips, but skin-to-skin contact was all that was really required. I shoved the spell at him with all the power I could muster, brushing aside his defences. He yelped in shock as his body melted into a slug, his eyes going wide with shock a moment before they were gone. I brought my head down on him as hard as I could, squashing him. The wards let me go a moment later and receded into the background.

"Fuck." Gary sounded stunned. "What did you...?"

"No time." I scrambled to my feet. Malachi was dead and I'd killed him and...I'd come to terms with it later. The wards were still humming, faint flickers of magic pressing against my mind. "Grab the device. We have to move."

Gary nodded and hurried to the cabinet. The memory device sat on the trolley. Gary yanked it forward, then cast a levitation spell to send the trolley gliding along the corridor and down the stairs. He scooped up a handful of notebooks—I guessed they were notes on how the device worked—and turned. I motioned for him to go, my eyes on the orbs and files. Temptation warred with common sense. The secrets of the Great Houses lay in front of me. I could take the files for myself: I could take the *house* for myself. I could use them...

My eyes lingered on Auntie Dorcas's file. What had she done? What had...I shook my head. I didn't want to know, even though part of me did.

I'd always loved secrets, but...I winced as I raised my hand and cast a spell. I'd learnt my lesson. It was time to let the secrets burn, unread and unwatched. The fire spread rapidly, the flames flickering strange colours as they consumed the charmed notebooks and memory orbs. I muttered another spell, sending the orbs crashing to the ground with as much force as I could muster. A whirlwind of images assailed me, the memories so badly jumbled that it was impossible to learn anything from them. I turned as the air grew hotter, waves of fire cascading out of the cabinet and into the office. The wards should have tried to suppress the fire, but did nothing. I guessed Malachi had wanted to make sure he could destroy the evidence in a hurry, if his enemies came to call. He couldn't have dirt on everyone.

"Come on!" Gary was standing at the top of the stairs. The frozen servants bobbled beside him, their eyes wide with fear. The spell wouldn't save them if the entire building came crashing down. We'd have to get them out. "Hurry!"

I turned and fled, chanting more and more fire spells. The office exploded into flames, the desk catching fire so quickly I *knew* it had been rigged to blow. I heard a bang behind me and forced myself to sprint. The entire house was starting to collapse. Flames licked along the walls and ceiling as I made it to the stairs, Penny's portrait starting to melt as the fires consumed it. I saw her face twist out of shape, an instant before the painting fell. I felt a stab of sympathy, despite everything. I knew what it was like to lose a father. Malachi hadn't been much of one—he'd clearly paid more attention to Francis than his daughter—but he'd been *hers*.

The painting hit the floor. Behind it, I saw a safe twisted by the sagging wall, with the door hanging open. I peered inside and saw a handful of bank books, each relating to a different bank. *Silent* banks, where everyone was sworn to keep their mouths firmly shut and no one—save for the account holder—knew who owned what. I hesitated, then grabbed the books and shoved them in my pouch. It was possible I might be able to claim the cash myself, on the grounds I held the account books, or simply pass them on to Penny. It might make up for what I'd done. I made a mental note to read them first, just in case. The accounts might be far too revealing if the books fell into unfriendly hands.

There'd be a list of who sent him money, I thought, although I wasn't sure that was true. Malachi hadn't seemed to care if his victims knew who he was or not—rubbing their nose in their servitude had been part of the thrill—but they had families. If the families traced the money, they'd want answers. And only a fool would rely completely on oaths of silence. *He's much more likely to have worked with untraceable cash.*

The smoke grew worse as we made it down the stairs. I muttered spells to protect myself, breathing a sigh of relief as I saw Ayesha and Marlene. Another pair of servants bobbled beside them. I muttered a silent prayer that we'd found them all as they hurried into the garage, leaving me behind. If we'd missed anyone, they were unlikely to survive.

And Malachi is dead, I thought, numbly.

I wanted to laugh—Malachi should have remembered what Ayesha did to Akin—but I could barely muster a smile. He'd deserved to die. I was sure of it. And yet, I'd done the deed. I'd turned him into a slug and killed him. He needed to die and yet…I swallowed, hard. It would be a long time, I was sure, before I came to terms with what I'd done.

He won't hurt anyone, ever again, I told myself. The ceiling started to collapse, burning debris falling to the ground. I felt the building shake and guessed the fires had reached the potions store. It was only a matter of time. Malachi's body would never be found. I wondered if anyone would care to look. He had plenty of enemies who'd be quite happy to be rid of him. No one would look too closely. *His secrets will die with him.*

A hand caught my arm. "Lucy!"

I turned. Gary stood there, his magic wrapped around him. He looked tired and sweaty and unkempt and *handsome*. I wondered how he could even bear to look at me. He'd seen me on my knees, promising Malachi the world…he knew how close we'd come to total disaster. I wouldn't blame him, not really, if he wanted nothing more to do with me. Ayesha and the others would probably hate me too. I'd come far too close to damning them forever.

"Come on," Gary said. He didn't let go. "The entire building is about to come down!"

He dragged me into the garage. Malachi's carriage sat in front of me, the horses missing...I hoped the driver had taken them to the stables. Or that Marlene had freed them. She'd always loved horses, even though she hadn't been a competent rider at first. In hindsight, that had been more than a little odd...I put the thought out of my head as I followed him into the street, casting the final spells as I ran. Behind me, the flames grew stronger. I heard a dull roar as the building collapsed. Malachi's collection of secrets was gone.

Ayesha and Marlene were waiting in the alley. "I put the servants in the carriage," Ayesha shouted, as we scrambled inside. "What do we do with them?"

"Take them with us," I shouted back. I had enough on my conscience already. I wasn't going to leave a handful of innocent girls to the mercies of the crowd. Besides, I was fairly sure they hadn't served Malachi willingly. I could wipe their memories if they refused to keep their mouths shut. "We'll deal with them later."

I stared out the window as Kate whipped the horses into life. The carriage rattled as it lurched forward, the horses pulling us onto the street. A handful of people watched the fires...I thought I saw others peeking from behind curtains, trying not to be seen as they watched the entire block burn. No one seemed to be trying to put out the blaze. I felt a twinge of guilt, then remembered that Malachi's family owned the whole block. No one else lived there. There'd be no risk to anyone else.

"We did it." Gary whooped as we raced down the street. "We won!"

I felt sick. Malachi was dead...I'd killed him. I knew I shouldn't feel guilt, but...I did. I'd killed him and...I'd done a lot of things. I wanted to curl up in a ball and cry. Nothing would ever be the same again. Ayesha would hate me, Gary and Kate would be wary of me, Marlene...even Marlene would have her doubts. She knew just how close I'd come to blackmailing her too.

And there's one thing left to do, I thought, as my eyes lingered on the memory catcher. I'd had an idea. A good one. *And then it will all be over.*

Ayesha cleared her throat. "Won't we be stopped before we can get away?"

"You only thought of that now?" Gary laughed. "This is Water Shallot. We'll be across the bridges before anyone thinks to stop us."

And he was right.

CHAPTER
THIRTY-NINE

Lord Carioca Rubén studied me thoughtfully. I studied him back. Akin's father was a tall, powerfully built man with an air of dignity and power I knew I couldn't match. His blond wig—I was sure it was a wig, if only because men rarely wasted their time doing their hair—was styled in a manner that dated all the way back to the Thousand-Year Empire. His family was the oldest in the city and never let anyone forget it. I wondered, as we waited to see who'd break the silence first, just how much they'd forgotten over the years.

And how much they chose to forget recently, I thought. I'd been very tempted to point out that we'd done House Rubén an immense service. They should have dealt with Malachi themselves, instead of merely kicking him out of North Shallot. *If they knew what we'd done for them...*

I sighed inwardly. Malachi's account books hadn't been as helpful as I'd hoped. Some were just too detailed, with names and accounts listed that were just too revealing. The money couldn't be claimed without raising too many questions. Others...I shook my head. Better to return the money to his victims, if possible. I didn't want to know what they'd done. It would be too dangerous.

"You requested this meeting," Carioca said, finally. "What can I do for you?"

I smoothed down my skirt, then opened my bag and produced a small collection of papers and a memory orb. "We have made a remarkable breakthrough," I said, carefully. The notes had named the designer—the newspapers claimed he'd died in an accident I was fairly sure was nothing of the sort—but I wasn't sure if they were telling the truth. Carioca's family might have devised the orbs and simply kept them secret. Approaching him was a calculated gamble. "We have devised a Device of Power that lets you copy memories for later viewing."

The orb glinted in my palm. Gary and I had worked out the designs, from the combination of notes and studying the stolen device, then Kate and her father had produced a working model of their own. I'd had to spend a great deal of money just to purchase the components, much to my family's horror. Uncle Jalil had been tight-lipped, when I'd told him what had happened, but he'd been the first to remind me that I was very short on funds. Thankfully, the rest of the family would have to wait before they could challenge me.

I held it out. "Take a look."

Carioca took the orb, his face expressionless. I watched as he peered into the light and became enveloped in the memory. *My* memory. I'd taken a walk through the park, bathing in sunlight as I'd watched people going about their business. The memory showed kids playing with boats and adults running around the lake, puffing and panting as they ran past. There was nothing incriminating in the memory, but it didn't matter. The memory orbs could be used for good as well as ill.

"Impressive," he said, finally. "I assume you have the patent?"

"Yes." I breathed a sigh of relief. We weren't about to be accused of stealing his family's work. "We filed it two days ago."

"I see." Carioca sat upright and returned the orb. "I assume you have a proposal?"

"Yes." I met his eyes, evenly. "I propose a split. You invest four thousand crowns in production and distribution. In exchange, you receive a third of the profits. I took the liberty of writing the figures down"—I held out the paperwork—"and running the calculations. It should make us all rich."

Carioca studied the figures for a long moment. "You intend to sell the devices as well as the orbs?"

"Yes," I said. We were going to have to come up with a better name. Neither the inventor nor Malachi had come up with a proper name for the device. "There is money to be made in copying memories, but everyone will want a copier as well as the copy."

"And some people will have memories they won't want to show to anyone else," Carioca said, dryly. "They'll prefer to own a copier themselves."

I nodded. My throat was dry. Carioca had a reputation for being cunning, cunning and ruthless. He might be more aware of what had happened to his brother-in-law—his former brother-in-law—than he was prepared to admit. It was quite possible Carioca had backed Malachi all along. Malachi had suggested otherwise, but he was the perfect example of an unreliable witness. Carioca might have something to gain if Malachi found dirt on Carioca's political enemies. And he could deny everything if caught.

"Four thousand crowns," Carioca said. "You price yourself low."

"I believe we can make that and more very quickly," I said. "Our rivals will, of course, try to find a way around our patent, but it will take time for them to come up with a working model. Until then, the market is ours. We should have an excellent chance to make a sizable profit."

And not have too close ties to you, I added, in the privacy of my own mind. *We're still the weakest of the Great Houses. We cannot afford to get too close to any of the more powerful houses.*

"I quite agree." Carioca put the paperwork to one side. "My people will speak to your people. You'll have a final contract by the end of the day."

I nodded. Uncle Stefano was already waiting outside. I'd given him some pretty clear instructions—and it looked as if Carioca wasn't going to haggle any longer than necessary—but it would be better if I stayed away. Uncle Stefano didn't have the final say in anything and everyone knew it, including him. If Carioca bullied him into producing a less favourable contract, I would be quite within my rights to reject it.

"And may I say how impressive it has been, watching you develop a name for yourself," Carioca said. "My son was quite impressed."

"Thank you," I said. Was that a hint Carioca knew the truth? Or should I just take it at face value? "I hope he'll host his next party at Lamplighter Hall."

Carioca looked pained. "It would be better not to speak of it," he said. "But we shall see."

I stood and curtsied. "It was nice doing business with you," I said. "And I hope to get the countersigned contract back to you tonight."

The butler met me as I left the office and escorted me down the stairs to the entrance hall. I stopped by a row of portraits, studying the line of blond boys and blonde girls. Penny's face leapt out at me...she looked younger, at least two years younger. I felt another pang of guilt as I turned away and followed the butler into the bright sunlight. Penny had taken one of the account books, when I'd freed her from the ironhold, and given her word to keep her mouth closed. I wasn't too worried about her talking. The only people who might take her seriously were Carioca and his family, and they had their own reasons to say and do nothing.

Which I pointed out to her, at great length, I mused. I hoped she'd listened. I didn't want to do anything more drastic, not after Malachi's death. *And offered to start reintroducing her to high society if she keeps her word.*

I walked down the driveway, not bothering to summon a carriage. It was a lovely day. I wanted to walk. My lips curved into a smile as I passed through the gate and stepped onto the road. The Grande Dames would be horrified if they saw me walking. After everything else that had happened, over the last few weeks, I found it hard to care. Let them foam at the mouth at the mere *thought* of a young girl walking a short distance. It was hardly something they could use to blackmail me.

My thoughts grew darker as I walked down the street, turning the corner and heading up the road towards the shore—and Lamplighter Hall. Malachi was dead, but he wasn't the only one. Lady Mathews was dead...I winced, inwardly. I hadn't been able to do anything for her children, although—thankfully—they'd inherited without challenge. Poppy had accepted my offer of employment, as had Malachi's former servants. Their lives had been turned upside down too. I breathed a sigh of relief he'd been such an awful master. It would have been harder to bury the story if they'd felt any loyalty to him.

And you really shouldn't be pleased about it, I told myself. I passed through the gate—we'd fixed the sign—and hurried up the driveway. *He could have gone on for years, bullying servants and blackmailing aristocrats, if he hadn't backed you into a corner.*

Jadish met me as I stepped into the hall. "My Lady, Lady Ayesha is waiting for you in the reception room."

I nodded. "Thank you," I said. I'd offered her the money for a downpayment on her shop, but she'd decided to wait until summer was over to look. "I'll see her there."

"Yes, My Lady," Jadish said. "Should I bring tea?"

"Please," I said. It was odd for anyone to visit without sending a messenger ahead, but...I supposed Ayesha counted as a friend now. We'd been through so much together. Marlene was a friend too now, of sorts. I would never have expected it. And Kate and Gary and...I winced. I'd have to talk to Gary soon. We hadn't sat down and talked properly since we'd fled the burning house. "Bring it when you have a moment."

I breathed a sigh of relief as I walked up the stairs and entered the chamber. Ayesha sat on a chair, reading a newspaper. I smiled at her as she stood, then gave her a hug. She returned it, before sitting down again. She looked as if she had something preying on her mind.

"Lucy." Her voice was very quiet, as if she feared someone was watching us. "What happened to the orbs?"

"Gone," I said. I'd smashed the two remaining orbs—the ones Malachi had left with me—after his death. "I destroyed them."

"Good." Ayesha relaxed, slightly. "Akin isn't the only person who knows what happened, but...everyone else has their own reasons to keep their mouths shut."

"Like me." I grinned at her. "What were you thinking?"

Ayesha shrugged. "I was mad at him," she said. "I guess I wasn't really thinking. There were plenty of ways I could have dealt with him without... without risking everything. I never thought he'd tell anyone."

"People have different reactions to different things," I said. "One person's nightmare is another person's dream."

"Yeah." Ayesha looked at her hands for a long moment, then looked up. "He has every right to be mad at me. Why didn't he care?"

"I don't know," I said. I didn't know Akin very well. "Maybe he figured he deserved it. Or maybe he thought it would make him look an utter prat."

"Perhaps." Ayesha laughed, humourlessly. "Not that it matters, I guess. My formal engagement will be announced at the end of the summer, with a planned wedding the following year. Long enough for my father to assess the boys and decide which of them would be more suitable for the role of consort. He promised he'd decide, then, which of us would be confirmed as his successor."

"Assuming the family conclave goes along with it," I said. "Did you tell Zeya what happened?"

"I told her about Akin," Ayesha said. "But not about...about everything else."

I said nothing. I didn't have siblings. I knew some siblings remained close, throughout their lives; I knew some became bitter enemies, so consumed with hatred that they would destroy their families just to slay their foes. Ayesha and Zeya seemed to have a good relationship, but that could change. Only *one* of them could take their father's place. And Zeya knew how to ruin her sister...

She'd damage the entire family, I thought. It was true, but...was it true *enough*? Would House McDonald punish *both* sisters? Ayesha for compromising herself, Zeya for compromising the entire family? *Who knows what she'll do?*

I dismissed the thought with a shrug. It wasn't my problem. Ayesha was a friend, and I'd help her if I could, but there was very little I could actually do. House McDonald wouldn't care about *my* opinion of *anything*. And if they knew what I'd done...thankfully, I hadn't been too clear when I'd explained that Malachi was blackmailing me. Without the orb, there was no proof of anything.

And the spy in their house has probably fled, I thought. *They'll have heard Malachi is dead now.*

"We'll be holding more parties, if you'll host them," Ayesha said, changing the subject completely. "We have to spend time getting to know the boys."

"And being careful, I hope," I said, dryly. "You don't want your father knowing *everything* you're doing."

"No," Ayesha agreed. "What about you?"

I felt another pang of guilt. "I don't know," I said. "Right now, I just want to make something of myself."

"I think you already have," Ayesha said. "How many people, right now, owe you favours?"

"Malachi's victims?" I shook my head. "I don't want to know. And I don't want them to know either."

"True." Ayesha stood. "We'll be in touch."

I watched her go, then leaned back into my chair. The world seemed a simpler place now, but...who knew? My eyes wandered up to the portrait of my father as a young man, barely older then than I was now. He looked as if he had the world at his feet. I wondered, once again, if he'd taken his life. He'd certainly had good reason to fear the worst. And...I told myself, firmly, that I'd avenged him as well as everything else. Malachi was dead. The secret would remain buried.

Someone cleared his throat. I looked up to see Uncle Jalil. He looked older, as if he'd aged a decade in the last two weeks. I winced, cursing under my breath as I stood. How much had Uncle Jalil known? He would hardly have approved a pyramid scheme that threatened to defraud thousands of innocent people, even if it was a poorly thought out plan instead of genuine malice. I doubted my father had asked him. He would not have approved.

"Lucy," Uncle Jalil said. He took a seat facing me. "How did the meeting go?"

"Very well," I said. "They'll be investing in the memory devices. We need a catchier name."

"Good, good." Uncle Jalil looked at me for a long moment, as if he was deciding what to say. "Lucy...I have to go."

I stared at him. "What?"

"I can't stay," Uncle Jalil said. "I watched your father make mistake after mistake, despite my advice, until he died. And then I watched you make *worse* mistakes. Yes"—he held up a hand—"I know you were desperate. You thought you didn't have a choice. And you managed to recover from your mistakes, even though you compromised yourself so badly you nearly lost everything."

"Things will get better," I said. "Uncle..."

"They might," Uncle Jalil said. "Lucy, your father was addicted to risk. He gambled everything, time and time again; he gambled even when he couldn't afford to lose. I watched him lose and lose and lose...even when he came out ahead, he doubled down until he lost. You have the same problem. You gambled and gambled until you lost."

"I know," I said. "I won't make that mistake again."

"Your father said the same thing," Uncle Jalil said. His voice hardened. "Every time I remonstrated with him, every time I pointed out that he was ruining the family, every time I told him he'd be leaving you with nothing...he looked me in the eye and promised he wouldn't do it again. Maybe he meant it, every time he promised. But he did it again and again until he died."

He shook his head. "You're just like him. You'll tell yourself you won't do it again and then you'll do it. Again. And I don't want to stay and watch you destroy yourself."

I felt my heart twist. "Uncle..."

"I can't stay," Uncle Jalil said. "Please. Respect my decision."

"I..." I swallowed hard, feeling torn between the sense I'd been abandoned and the grim awareness he might be right. The thrill had died, when Malachi had had me under his thumb, but it had returned when I'd raided his house. How long would it be until...until I got into trouble again? "Uncle...where will you go?"

Uncle Jalil shrugged. "I do have some savings. Not much, but some. And a house I can sell. I always wanted to travel and now...now I have the chance."

"That's not an answer," I said. "Uncle..."

"I don't know where I'll go," Uncle Jalil said. "But I can't stay."

"You'll always be welcome here," I said. I forced myself to stand. "And thank you for everything."

"I wish you the very best," Uncle Jalil said. He gave me a hug. "One other thing? Go speak to Gary. You owe it to him not to leave him dangling. Give him a clear answer and stick to it."

"Yes, Uncle," I said. I knew he was right. I'd put off the discussion I—and Gary—knew we had to have long enough. "I'll speak to him tomorrow."

CHAPTER
FORTY

If there was one advantage to forming and funding a partnership between three different parties, I decided as Jadish showed Gary into my office, it was that no one could reasonably question me inviting one of those parties to a private discussion. They might make snide remarks about chaperones, or hint that perhaps we were closer than we should be, but they couldn't object openly. It might end up rebounding on them.

I smiled as I stood and walked around the desk to greet him with a hug. He hugged me back, his touch suggesting he wanted to do a great deal more. I felt it too. Gary was special, in a way none of the other boys I'd known could hope to match. And yet…I wondered what he thought of me, even as I feared to ask. He'd seen me at my worst. He'd seen me offering to make a deal that would have destroyed me, even if it freed him and the others from a fate worse than death.

"Please, take a seat," I said. I wanted to sit next to him, but instead I sat facing him. "I have something to say."

"That's rarely a good sign." Gary's voice was light, but I could hear a hint of unease. "I'm ready to listen."

My lips quirked. "I guess that makes you the first boy who *ever* listened."

Gary snorted. "We say the same about girls."

I laughed, then sobered. My hands twisted in my lap. I'd tried to decide what to say, in the time between sending the message and his arrival, but none of the speeches I'd considered sounded remotely natural. Gary had every reason to shy away from me, to regard me as a dangerous menace...I winced, remembering Uncle Jalil's final words. He loved me—I was the closest thing he had to a daughter—but he couldn't bear to stay. I told myself that I'd learnt my lesson, that I wasn't going to destroy myself...it wasn't convincing. My father had said the same.

"I have a confession to make," I said. He deserved the truth, even if it reflected poorly on me. "I agreed to the engagement because your family planned to offer a sizable dowry up front. I hoped I could take the money and use it to earn enough to repay you and break the engagement. I think your father knew as much, when he agreed to the terms."

"He did," Gary said, tonelessly.

I winced and forced myself to continue. "I made mistakes, as you know. I let myself be compromised. I let myself be...be caught under a monster's thumb. I ran the risk of destroying myself and everyone else, including you. If you and the others hadn't helped, I might have lost everything. The family, the hall...everything. I owe you more than I can ever repay."

Gary said nothing. I wished I knew what he was thinking. Did he like me? Hate me? Trust me? Distrust me? He knew how stupid I'd been. He knew...

"I got the loan from House Rubén," I told him. "I can afford to repay the dowry now. You can break the engagement. You don't *have* to marry me. We can continue to forge and manufacture the memory devices, without any further commitments. You can"—I swallowed, again—"you can have nothing further to do with me."

I felt naked, naked and raw. I owed him the truth...I understood, now, why some people prayed for hours in the family crypts. Telling the truth to one's ancestors was cathartic, even if it was painful. No one would overhear, no one would tell...I felt as if I'd scrubbed myself clean. But Gary was alive, alive and well and perfectly capable of leaving me if he wished. I hated how the thought made me feel. I didn't want him to go, but I knew he might not want to stay.

"I like you," I admitted. It wasn't something I was supposed to say. High Society regarded marriage as a business arrangement, first and foremost. Feelings—everything from attraction and lust to affection and love—could come later, if they came at all. "I...I care for you. I...I don't know if I love you, but I could. And I..."

I broke off, finding it hard to continue. "If you want to have nothing more to do with me, I'll understand. Your father can handle the business side of the arrangement. You'll have the dowry back, with interest, so you won't lose anything. And...I won't blame you. I won't seek you out or..."

My voice trailed off. I didn't want to say *any* of it. I didn't want him to go.

"I like you," Gary said, quietly. "I...I *do* like you."

I stared at him. "But...don't you know what I *did*?"

"You told me," Gary reminded me. "Lucy...you made mistakes. Yes, you did. You got yourself into a world of trouble, a world"—his mouth twisted—"that could have destroyed you by turning you into a monster. You...yes, you made mistakes. But you also did what you could to set them right."

"I could have ruined you," I told him. "And everyone!"

"I could have walked away," Gary pointed out. "It was my choice to stay."

"I could have *ruined* you," I repeated. Didn't he understand how bad it could have been? We'd committed a whole string of crimes, from kidnapping Penny to setting fire to Malachi's house. "Doesn't that bother you?"

"I chose to stay." Gary snorted. "I could have left you to sort out your mess without help."

"Yes." I met his eyes. "I...thank you."

Gary nodded. "Lucy, I like you too. I do...I do want to spend time with you. I do...I don't think the idea of being married to you is *too* terrible."

I opened my mouth, then realised I was being teased. "Kate told me I snore," I said. "You'll have some very sleepless nights."

"I didn't have *sleeping* in mind," Gary said. "Really."

I let out a breath, more relieved than I could say. "I'll always feel guilty."

Gary met my eyes. "What do you want me to do? Hit you? Shout at you? Lock you in your room? Turn you into a frog? Or...or what?"

"That was tried, at school," I said. "I think they tried all of them, at one time or another. They didn't work."

"I guess not." Gary winked. "You kept going until you got *really* burnt."

I looked down at the floor. "How can you even bear to *look* at me?"

Gary leaned forward and hugged me. "You made mistakes, like I said. And you risked everything to put them right. And...you're not a bad person. I like you."

I felt tears in my eyes. "What...what now?"

"We spend the next year courting properly?" Gary leaned back, letting go of me. "You can give the money back or not, as you wish. If we still like each other next summer, we get married as planned. Or we go our separate ways, no hard feelings. How does that sound?"

Better than I have any right to expect, I thought. Gary might have a very different outlook on life than aristocrats, but...he knew, even if he didn't say it out loud, just how badly the affair could have ended. *He'd be quite within his rights to tell me to get lost.*

"It sounds ideal," I said. I leaned forward and kissed him. "What now?"

"Well, we *could* go to the zoo," Gary said. "I hear it's the place for young couples to go."

I laughed as I kissed him again. I had a *lot* of work to do. Lamplighter Hall was hosting a dozen parties and balls in the next two weeks, from formal coming-out dances to informal gatherings...I had the feeling, reading between the lines, that House Rubén and House Aguirre were planning to make a very special announcement next week. Caitlyn and her sisters would finally be raised to adulthood, starting the clock ticking towards Akin and Caitlyn's wedding. I felt a flicker of sympathy. It couldn't be easy knowing so much rested on their match.

And we have to push ahead with the memory catchers, I thought. *We can use them to make back our fortune...*

I put the thought out of my head. "Sure," I said. Our lips met, once again. Maybe it would work out, maybe it wouldn't...but at least I'd given him the chance to go. I promised myself, silently, that I'd never lie to him. He was...he made me want to be better. "I'd love to."

The End

The Zero Enigma Will Continue In:
The Family Name

COMING SOON!

AFTERWORD

I don't believe in perfect characters.

I'm not just talking about Mary Sue-type characters, although they are obnoxious enough to put me off whatever book (or film or whatever) they appear in. People are not perfect and a character who is just *awesomely* good at whatever s/he does, or gets away with everything because s/he's the star of the show, is just annoying. Rey Skywalker is, of course, the prime example of such a character. Compared to Mara Jade, who was both a very capable person and a deeply flawed character, Rey is very flat indeed. But she isn't the point here.

Mankind, as Heinlein put it, is not so much a *rational* animal as a *rationalising* animal. It is very easy to decide you want to do something, *then* come up with a rationalisation you can use to justify it to yourself. This rationalisation may seem utterly absurd, or worse, to someone else, but it's hard to see that when you're trapped inside your own head. You may be so lonely, so desperate for human contact, that you won't realise that you're crossing the line before it's too late. And once you cross the line, because you believe you have no choice, it will be easy to do it again and again. And that's how you get into real trouble.

Lucy has two major personality aspects that work against her. First, she believes herself committed to taking control of her family and rebuilding its fortunes. She is incapable of walking away and abandoning the once-great family. Second, she is a thrill-seeker in the truest possible sense. She isn't a bad person, not like Malachi, but she wants—she needs—the thrill of risking everything. The danger of getting caught, and possibly facing consequences that will destroy her, is part of the fun. One may argue that this is a very stupid, dangerous and immature attitude, but it's very common. And, of course, it makes her vulnerable to someone with darker intentions. On the other hand, of course, she's smart enough to realise she's messed up and do whatever she has to do to correct matters.

Malachi, on the other hand, is very different. He started his life as a contemptible social climber, befriending well-born students and oozing his way into their lives. He was a master at spotting how best to appeal to them, posing as a sycophant to Carioca Rubén and then pretending to be a wise old uncle to Akin, Isabella and Francis, all the while trying to gain influence. He was the one who slipped a dark book to Isabella; he was the one who primed Francis to challenge Akin, on the grounds that Francis would be easier to influence. And, when he was kicked out of the family, he started blackmailing his way through aristocratic society instead. He's so twisted, so wrapped up in himself, that he's beyond redemption. Even his *help* comes with a stab in the back.

This series continues to interest me, at least in part, because I can write a series of different viewpoint characters while inserting characters from other books into the mix. Malachi himself started life in *The Family Pride* and made an appearance in *The King's Man*, which is when the blackmail aspect of the plot came into focus. I intend to write one more Akin/Isabella story, provisionally entitled *The Family Name*, and then go on to write the next big trilogy. By then, there should be more than enough characters to pop up everywhere.

And now you've read this far, I have a request to make.

It's growing harder to make a living through self-published writing these days. If you liked this book, please leave a review where you found it, share the link, let your friends know (etc, etc). Every little helps (particularly reviews).

Thank you.
Christopher G. Nuttall
Edinburgh, 2020

Printed in Great Britain
by Amazon